OTHER BOOKS BY KAT

The Broken World S
Broken World
Shattered World
Mad World
Lost World
New World
Forgotten World
Silent World
Broken Stories

The Twisted Series:
Twisted World
Twisted Mind
Twisted Memories
Twisted Fate

The Oklahoma Wastelands:
The Loudest Silence
The Brightest Darkness
The Sweetest Torment

Zombie Apocalypse Love Story Novellas:
More than Survival
Fighting to Forget
Playing the Odds
Key to Survival
Surviving the Storm
The Things We Cannot Change
No Looking Back
Finding A Future

The Outliers Saga:
Outliers
Uprising
Retribution

Tribe of Daughters

The Blood Will Dry

Collision

The College of Charleston Series:
The List
No Regrets
Moving On
Letting Go

When We Were Human

Alone: A Zombie Novel

The Moonchild Series:
Moonchild
Liberation
Redemption

Anthologies:
Prep For Doom
Gone with the Dead
7 Sins of the Apocalypse
Dead Worlds 3

FAR from HOME

KATE L. MARY

FAR from HOME

FAR SERIES BOOK ONE

EAST
HISTORIC US 66

Published by Twisted Press, LLC, an independently owned company.

This book is a work of fiction. The names, characters, places, and incidents are fictitious or have been used fictitiously, and are not to be construed as real in any way. Any resemblance to person, living or dead, or organizations is entirely coincidental.

Copyright © 2020 by Kate L. Mary
Print ISBN-13: 9781674096711
Cover Art by Kate L. Mary
Edited by Lori Whitwam

All rights reserved. This book or any portion thereof may not be reproduced or used in any manner without the express permission of the author, except for the use of brief quotations in a book review.

Celebrating my 40th book,
on my 40th birthday.

Looking forward to 40 more.

1

There were at least seven Internet tabs open on my computer, one of which was set to the local news station in Dayton, Ohio, WHIO. Two reporters—one female and one male—whose names I didn't know were talking about the current crisis and how it was affecting not just the Miami Valley, but the rest of the country as well.

"...travelers are advised to display their papers at all times and to keep to approved routes. Anyone found traveling on closed highways or without papers will be arrested immediately and held until martial law has been lifted. The government and CDC are working together to do everything they can to stop the spread of this deadly virus, but they need your help. Stay inside as much as possible, and if you absolutely have to leave your home, take precautions. Wash your hands regularly and wear a mask. Avoid large crowds, especially if you're showing any symptoms."

Since that wasn't the page I was currently staring at, I couldn't see the reporters' expressions, but it didn't matter. Their grave tones told me everything I needed to know. It was serious.

"I want you to stay there, Rowan. Do you hear me?" Mom's voice rose an octave on the last word, and I cringed away from the phone pressed against my ear. "It's safer in Phoenix."

"How can you expect me to stay where I am with things as bad as they are?"

I scrolled through my Facebook feed with the hand not holding my phone, scanning each post before moving on to the next. Nearly every one of them had something to do with this virus. Either it was a news report, a post about someone who was sick, or a shared post that had gone viral, and each one had my gut twisting tighter until I thought I was going to hurl. One of my high school friends had moved to New York to try to make it on Broadway, and her post from three weeks ago was the one that made me finally pause. It was only one line, but it was enough to fill me with dread.

Deb Williams *Everyone here is sick.*

There hadn't been a single update to her page since that post, and it now had hundreds of comments from friends and family, all of them begging for information they had to know they'd never get. The reports coming out of New York were infrequent and sketchy at best, but what little I'd heard left no doubt in my mind. Deb was dead, and I couldn't be the only one who knew that. Odds were, everyone who'd commented on the post thought the same thing. They just weren't ready to accept it.

My gaze landed on one of the last comments, posted only a few hours ago. It was her mom.

Rachel Williams *Please respond and tell us you're OK.*

The words blurred together when tears filled my eyes, and I scrolled down before blinking them away, not wanting to see them again because it made all of this too real and much, much too personal.

I had to swallow before I said, "I want to come home, Mom."

On the other end of the line, my mom sighed, and it seemed as if something happened to the connection, making the noise sound far away. It didn't just emphasize the distance separating us, it made it feel bigger, as if someone had pulled on an imaginary

FAR from HOME

string and somehow stretched the miles out, making crossing them impossible.

"Rowan, I'm serious about this," she said, a small quiver in her voice. "Stay. There."

I clenched my free hand into a fist, digging my normally perfectly manicured nails into my palms. After days of gnawing on them, they were jagged. It was a bad habit from my childhood and one I'd thought I'd gotten over.

"You can't possibly expect me to stay," I argued. "They've canceled classes. Almost nothing is open. Everyone who lives even remotely close left weeks ago, and the dorms are nearly empty. I feel so trapped and alone here."

"I spoke with the university, and they've assured me the dorms will stay open for the students who can't go home. You are one of those students. It's too far for you to travel alone, and we are much too close to New York."

"Troy is almost ten hours from New York!" I nearly shouted into the phone.

Hysteria was creeping up on me, and I dug my nails deeper into my palm, trying to ground myself. It didn't help, because there was nothing to hold on to.

"Ohio is closer than Phoenix, which is where you'll be staying. I'm serious, Rowan. I won't talk about it anymore."

I squeezed my eyes shut when my head began to pound. Under my cheap, University of Phoenix dorm room desk, my legs were shaking, and even pressing my heels harder against the floor wasn't helping. When was the last time I'd felt like I needed my mom? I couldn't remember. Maybe after Doug had dumped me sophomore year of high school, but I'd been sixteen. I was twenty now and in my third year of college, I shouldn't need my mother to wrap me in her arms and tell me everything was okay. But I did. Desperately.

"Mom—" My voice trembled. "I've heard rumors about people in Phoenix coming down with it. I'm scared."

She sighed again, but this time it wasn't from frustration. Even hundreds of miles away, I could feel her fear. "I know you are. So am I. That's why I want you to stay there. Once they get this thing under control, you can come home. But until we know they've stopped it from spreading, you're staying in Phoenix. Do you understand?" When I said nothing, she said, "Rowan, no matter what else happens, I have to know you're okay. Please."

"Okay," I mumbled, my eyes still closed.

"Good," she said, letting out a deep sigh of relief. "Dad got called in to the hospital a few hours ago, but I'll tell him you called and you're okay."

"All right," I replied automatically.

"I've transferred more money into your account. Be sure to get the cash now just in case—" Mom's voice cracked, and the sound felt like it was stabbing me in the heart. I heard her swallow. "Get small bills if you can and stock up on supplies so you don't have to go out. Whatever you do, avoid big crowds. Got it?"

"I'll go to the bank today," I assured her, thinking about my dad and his job, and how avoiding crowds would be impossible. He was an ER doctor, for God's sake. I couldn't think of a worse job right now.

"Good," Mom said, the relief in her voice ringing through the air. "We love you, Rowan."

"I love you," I said.

"Talk to you tomorrow?"

"Yeah."

Mom let out a deep breath, and a second later, the call cut out.

I opened my eyes, and my gaze focused on the travel papers I'd gotten the day before. The travel papers my mom knew nothing about because she'd forbidden me to come home. But I was legally an adult, wasn't I? I was twenty. I could vote, and if I committed a crime, I'd be looked at as an adult, no questions asked. Sure, I couldn't legally buy alcohol yet or even rent a car, and I was still considered my parents' dependent since I was going to college full time, but those things were minor when it came to the big picture. I was twenty years old, and I should have been able to make my own decisions.

Yet I was listening to my mom when she told me to stay in

FAR from HOME

Phoenix.

I picked the papers up and unfolded them.

Approved For Travel

The words screamed from the paper as if taunting me, daring me to go against my mom's wishes, only I wasn't sure if I was brave enough. I'd always been a pleaser, and just the process of getting the physical so I could apply for travel papers had twisted my insides into knots. Forget the fact that it had cost me five hundred dollars and I'd had to get a cash advance on my credit card—something Mom was going to freak about when she finally found out. Which she would, because my parents paid the bill. They paid for everything I did, gave me everything I needed without batting an eye. My car, my insurance, money every month for gas and anything else I needed. Right now, though, what I needed was to be home, and for the first time, my parents were denying me. It felt...wrong.

But Mom was overreacting, wasn't she? The virus had started in New York, which was hundreds of miles from my hometown of Troy, Ohio, and six weeks had passed since martial law was declared and the government had locked down the area. Sure, a few people had gotten out, but as more cases had popped up, they'd locked down other cities as well. They were on top of this. They were determined to stop the spread. And the rumors I'd heard about people in Phoenix getting sick had to be just that. Rumors. The government and CDC were doing everything they could to stop this thing. Plus, based on what my mom had said, no one in the Dayton area was even sick at this point. We'd know if they were. Dad worked in the emergency room!

As if trying to justify my train of thought, I started scrolling through Facebook again, this time concentrating on the friends who were in or around the Dayton area. The first one I came to was Mandy Ditmar, a girl I'd graduated with who'd stayed in Dayton to attend Wright State. She'd shared the University's official post canceling classes more than three weeks ago, and when I clicked on her profile, an image popped up of her at a restaurant in the Oregon District with a group of friends only a week later. I recognized the place as the Dublin Pub—an Irish restaurant that had live music on weekends—and it seemed as crowded as usual.

Things must not have been too bad in Dayton if people were still willing to go out and party.

I returned to my Facebook feed and scrolled some more, this time stopping on a post from one of my high school teachers. Mr. Phillips had taught French and just so happened to be the father of the guy who'd dumped me sophomore year for a cheerleader with big boobs and an even bigger personality. As far as I knew, they were still together. Unlike Mandy, Mr. Phillips' page was full of warnings about staying inside and avoiding large crowds, but not a thing in his posts gave me any real pause. They were nothing but regurgitated warnings from local and national news stations. Then there were the official statements from the CDC. Nothing to really freak me out because I'd seen and heard the same things all the way out here in Phoenix, and I hadn't seen a single sick person.

I clicked the small Facebook icon in the top left-hand corner so I could go back to my feed, but didn't get far before being distracted by a YouTube video one of the girls in my hall had shared. It played automatically, but like always, there was no sound, and at first I couldn't figure out what I was looking at because it was too shaky. Then whoever was filming it steadied their phone, and a man came into focus. He was walking weird, dragging his feet, and his arms were up and grasping at air like he was trying grab something. Even crazier was the color of his skin. It looked grayish. Washed out. It had to be the lighting, though.

Without thinking, I clicked on the video, turning the sound on.

"What the fuck is wrong with him?" a guy in the background called.

"Don't know, man," another guy, maybe the one recording, responded. "He looks dead, though."

"Right." The first guy chuckled. "Hey, dude, you okay? You need me to call someone?"

FAR from HOME

The man walking toward them—no, it was more like he was stumbling toward them—let out a groan.

"Sounds like a fucking zombie," the guy recording muttered.

"Shut the fuck up. The dude's sick," the first guy said. "I'm out of here. I'm not catching that shit."

The video shifted, and suddenly only the street was visible, but the recording continued.

"Yeah. Let's get out of here before—"

There was a grunt, and the phone hit the ground, landing facedown. It didn't stop recording though, and a second later, screams and shouting rang through the air. One guy—the one in the background—was yelling, begging someone to stop, and scraping sounds followed, telling me there was some kind of struggle. Another shout sounded, only it was different than before. It was a painful cry, a scream of agony that made the hair on the back of my neck stand on end. Then there was a grunt, and the video ended.

I blinked and shook my head. Had the sick man attacked them? That was what it had sounded like, but it didn't make any sense. It had to be fake. Some assholes had staged the thing and put the recording on YouTube to gain followers. That was all. The world was full of people like that, and a national emergency didn't change things.

"Assholes," I muttered before going back to my feed.

Every profile I clicked on after that felt like a repeat of the first two. Shared posts full of warnings, but no real stories from anyone in the Dayton area that made it seem like there was anything serious happening. It confirmed what I'd already suspected. Mom was overreacting, being overly cautious. She had to be. What was more, it was just like her. I was, after all, her only child, and she'd always been overly protective. It made sense, too. She and dad had unsuccessfully tried to have a child for ten years. Even fertility drugs and in vitro hadn't worked, which was why they'd finally settled on adoption. My mom had been thirty-six by the time they finally brought me home, my dad forty-two. After all that time of waiting and trying, they'd finally had the family they'd always wanted, and Mom had been terrified something would swoop in and steal it.

Which was why she was being so cautious now.

I exhaled and sat back, thinking.

A good twenty-seven hours of driving separated me from home, and that was taking the normal route, which wasn't possible. With martial law in place, most major highways had been shut down, forcing the few people approved for travel to take very specific routes. I'd been given a map—a paper one, which I'd never used in my life—when I got my travel papers, so I knew most of my drive home would be on Route 66. I couldn't even imagine how much of it would be through the middle of nowhere or through old, rundown towns. Not exactly ideal, considering I was a twenty-year-old chick and would be traveling alone.

Which brought up another issue. I had my car since I'd insisted on driving out to Phoenix this year—much to my mother's dismay—but did I have enough money to get home? Mom said she sent more, but since martial law had been issued a few weeks ago and travel had been cut off, the price of nearly everything had gone up. Getting home would be expensive, and it wasn't like I could ask my parents to send more money when I wasn't supposed to be going anywhere, and I'd maxed out my one credit card so I could get the physical and papers required for travel.

I needed a travel companion.

Shoving my chair away from the desk, I got to my feet, pausing long enough to stretch before heading out.

The hall was quieter than a library and had an empty feeling to it. It was eerie, like something from a horror movie, and I couldn't stop from looking over my shoulder as I walked, half expecting some masked killer with a knife to be standing behind me. No one was there, of course. Not a murderer and not any students, either. Everyone on my hall had packed up and headed home except me and one other person, and I only knew she was around because I'd seen her coming out of her room yesterday. Until then, I'd thought I was alone. She was all the way at the other end, which was a different hall than the one I lived in, and we'd never spoken. I was pretty sure her name was Vanessa,

FAR from HOME

although I could have been wrong. I was notoriously bad with names.

The stairs and a small lobby sat at the center of the building, separating the two halls. Stiff, stained chairs and couches were positioned in front of the community television, and a handful of small tables sat off to the side as well. There was even a bookcase, which was stuffed with old, dog-eared paperbacks and board games someone had donated probably two decades ago—most of the games were missing pieces.

It was the bulletin board above the bookcase that I was interested in, though. Usually it was bursting with fliers for clubs or volunteer opportunities, the occasional job opening, and even postings for used textbooks—there was a website where you could buy or sell them, but some people still preferred to do it old school. Now, though, the bulletin board was covered with inquiries from students who were desperate to get home but had no means of transportation. Nearly all of them were from people who had already left, but I was willing to bet one or two were still hanging around, either because they hadn't decided to leave until more recently or because they hadn't located someone who lived close enough to their destination to find a ride.

The odds of locating someone who needed to get to Ohio were slim, but maybe there was someone who could ride with me part of the way—and help with gas money. Maybe they needed to get to St. Louis or somewhere else in Missouri. Hell, at this point, I'd be happy to have someone ride with me to Oklahoma. Anything was better than nothing.

I scanned the papers tacked to the bulletin board, pulling down the ones from people I knew had already left whenever I came across them. The crinkle of paper as I balled them up seemed loud in the quiet room, and like before, I found myself looking over my shoulder when my heart beat faster. I was being stupid. The virus sweeping the country was the only thing I should be really afraid of, and as far as I knew, it hadn't even made it this far west. It wasn't like something was going to sneak up and take a big bite of me or anything.

The image of that man in the YouTube video popped into

my head.

"Get a grip," I muttered to myself, trying to ignore the tightening in my gut.

When the postings on the bulletin board got me nowhere, I headed for the stairs, tossing the ball of paper into a trashcan on my way. One floor down, the halls and lobby mimicked the one I'd just left. Quiet and empty and totally devoid of any signs of life, making my already pounding heart beat faster as I scanned the bulletin board. Some of the postings were the same as the ones from upstairs, which I promptly removed, but there were new ones, too. The word Indiana leapt out at me, and I scanned the rest of the note scrawled across the small piece of blue paper.

Looking for a ride to Indiana.
Will pay for gas.
Room 223
- Kiaya Washington

K-i-a-y-a…

I studied the name, rolling the letters around in my head while I tried to figure out how it was pronounced. Key-a-ya? That couldn't be right. Kay-a? Maybe, but I wasn't positive. Oh, well. She was probably used to people butchering her name.

I pulled the paper off the bulletin board and headed down the hall. There was a phone number scrawled under the words, but since I was on the second floor anyway, I might as well check it out. If Kiaya was still around, odds were good that she'd be in her room. Everything on campus was closed, and even off campus not much was open. People were taking this shit seriously. Even all the way out here.

The door to room 223 had a couple pieces of blue paper just like the one I'd pulled off the bulletin board taped to it. One was a repeat of the post Kiaya had left in the lobby, but the other was older and had nothing to do with the virus.

Quiet! Studying!!!

She'd underlined the first word three times as if it would force

FAR from HOME

people to obey, and I couldn't help sighing. This girl sounded like a barrel of fun.

I rapped my knuckles against the door, and the sound echoed down the hall, and that spooky horror movie feeling returned full force. Even as I glanced around to make sure I was still alone, I rolled my eyes. Still, I couldn't help it. I blamed that damn YouTube video. It had me on edge even though I knew it was a fake. Zombies weren't real, and they never would be.

The door opened, and I let out a yelp and jumped back.

Laughing at my own stupidity, I put my hand to my heart. "Sorry. I guess I'm just jumpy."

The girl narrowed her big, brown eyes at me. "Can I help you?"

She was a tad taller than I was, and thin, and very delicate and innocent looking. There wasn't a stitch of makeup on her face, and her flawless, light brown skin gave off the impression that not a drop of the stuff had ever touched it. She was cute, even if she would have benefited from some eyeliner, and thankfully, nothing about her set off warning bells in my head.

When I said nothing, Kiaya lifted her eyebrows expectantly, and something about the way she pressed her full lips together gave off the impression she was deep in thought as she, in turn, studied me. It was the questions in her dark eyes that finally jolted me out of my stupor, and I shook my head, giving her an apologetic smile.

"Are you Kay-a?" I asked, taking a stab at the name.

"It's pronounced Ky-ya," she told me, but didn't seem all that bothered by my blunder.

"Sorry. I found your note." I shrugged apologetically as I held the paper up for her to see—as if I thought she might have forgotten she'd written it. "Indiana?"

"Oh." Kiaya blinked. "I thought I'd put it up too late and missed my chance."

"Nope," I said, the P popping out of my mouth and echoing down the hall. "There are a few of us still around."

"Not many." She looked past me toward the empty lobby.

"Yeah," I said, following her gaze.

11

For a second, we stood in silence, then I shook my head again and waved the note. "Anyway, I live in Ohio. I want to go home, and I have a car, but it's a long drive. I figured we could help each other out?"

Kiaya nodded, but eyed me like she was trying to make a decision. "I wasn't going to leave. I figured this whole thing would get sorted out pretty fast, and having the dorm to myself would give me a chance to get ahead in my classes, but now..." She swallowed and glanced past me again, and that feeling from before returned, raising the hair on my arms. "The news reports are getting scary."

"I know," I said around the lump of fear in my throat.

Once again, that damn YouTube video popped into my head. I had a feeling it would be playing on repeat in my dreams tonight, which was going to suck. Like I wasn't already freaked out enough, I had to dream about zombies. Great.

"You have papers?" I asked, wanting to get down to business.

Kiaya nodded, and her dark, wavy hair, which was pulled into a ponytail high on her head, bobbed. "Yeah."

"Me too." I mimicked the gesture, unsure of what else to do. She obviously wasn't much of a talker and really wasn't giving me much to work with. "I'd want to head out soon. Not tonight, but maybe tomorrow? I need to go to the bank and pack some things, and maybe stock up on snacks for the trip. What do you think?"

Again, Kiaya nodded even as she pressed her lips together, considering her options. "Yeah. Okay."

She didn't sound very sure.

"You do want to go, right?"

She gave a small, non-committal shrug. "It's not like there's much of a reason to stay here."

She looked down the empty hall again, but this time I avoided following her gaze. I was freaking myself out too much, and I needed to get a grip.

"Then tomorrow will be good?" I prompted.

"Yeah," was all she said. Again.

Holy shit. Over twenty hours in a car with her was going to

be annoying.

I blew out a long breath so I didn't sound irritated when I said, "Good. Meet me in the lobby tomorrow morning? Let's say seven. I want to get on the road early."

Kiaya only nodded in response.

This time, I didn't hold in my sigh.

"See you then," I said as I turned.

I'd only taken two steps when she called out, "Wait!"

The word echoed through the empty hall, and I had to suck in a deep breath to try to calm my pounding heart before turning. It didn't work, but I looked back at her anyway.

Kiaya was focused on me. "What's your name?"

"Oh." I laughed at my own forgetfulness and grabbed my braid, waving it at her to try and lighten the mood. "Sorry, blonde moment. I'm Rowan. Rowan Summers."

For the first time, Kiaya smiled. "Thanks, Rowan."

"No problem," I said, waving over my shoulder as I headed off.

I had a travel companion, which was good—as annoying as I suspected she was going to be. Not that it mattered. We'd drive to Indiana together, I'd drop her off, and that would be the end of it. It wasn't like we were going to be life-long friends or anything.

2

With class having been canceled weeks ago, it had been a while since I'd had to drag my ass out of bed early in the morning, and when my alarm went off at six o'clock, it took me a few minutes to clear my groggy brain enough to figure out exactly why I'd decided not to sleep in.

Oh, yeah. I was going home today.

The realization was enough to force me to move even if my body wasn't thrilled by the action. Like I'd thought, I'd spent the entire night tossing and turning as images of zombies floated through my head, and as a result, I didn't feel nearly as rested as I should have, considering a road trip was in my future.

Starbucks was going to be a necessity this morning.

I'd gone to the ATM yesterday like I'd promised Mom and had even stopped at one of the few stores still open to grab some snacks for the road, then packed everything I needed. It was all in my pink, hardcover suitcase and neatly organized. The only thing I still needed to pack were my toiletries once I was showered and dressed and I'd be ready to go.

The hot water helped my brain wake up, so by the time I was standing in front of the mirror with my long blonde hair dripping down my back, I felt more refreshed. I was excited, too. If everything went well, I'd be home by sometime tomorrow afternoon. I couldn't wait.

I thought about Kiaya as I applied a thin, black line to my eyelid—which really made my blue irises pop—wondering if I'd caught her during an off moment or if she never wore makeup. I honestly couldn't remember the last time I'd left the house without at least a little on—definitely not since coming to the University of Phoenix—and all my friends were pretty much the same. Even on those mornings when I rolled out of bed and dragged myself to class in my flannel pajama pants, my hair in a messy bun on top of my head, I made sure to put a little on so I looked good. You never knew when you were going to run into Mr. Perfect, after all.

Of course, even as I applied my makeup, I had to admit it wasn't exactly a necessity on a day like this. It wasn't like I was going to meet the man of my dreams. It was a cross-country road trip during a major viral epidemic, not *The Bachelor*.

Once I was ready and had loaded the rest of my things into my suitcase, I did one last quick inventory of my room. My cell phone charger was packed, as was the money I'd gotten yesterday. I was pretty sure I'd remembered everything else I would need, but I also knew I'd be able to replace anything I forgot once I was home. One quick trip to Meijer was all it would take.

"This is it," I said to myself even as guilt twisted my insides.

Mom was going to be pissed.

My suitcase wasn't an issue at first—it had wheels, after all—but I groaned when I reached the stairs. It was insanely heavy, and I was on the third floor. An elevator would have been nice. Since that wasn't an option, I headed down, dragging it behind me. It thumped against each step, the thuds echoing in the stairwell and through the silent building until I had the urge to run. My dreams from the night before returned, making my heart pound harder, but I told myself I was freaking out for nothing. The scariest thing facing me right now was the possibility of a boring road trip.

It was a little before seven in the morning when I made it to

FAR from HOME

the lobby. Kiaya was already waiting. She was sitting in the chair closest to the front door, a red duffle bag at her feet that couldn't hold more than two days' worth of clothes and a textbook in her lap. Yellow highlighter gripped in her hand, she studied the page intently, not even looking up when I plopped my suitcase down and huffed, and I found myself grinding my teeth. Already I was irritated with her, and we hadn't even gotten in the car. What would I do for twenty-plus hours if she refused to interact with me? Play the alphabet game by myself? No, thanks. Money and safety weren't the only reasons I'd wanted a travel companion. Having someone to talk to would make the drive go a hell of a lot faster.

I opened my mouth, ready to lay out my expectations for this trip, when something scraped against the floor at my back. My nightmares about flesh-eating monsters fresh in my mind, I spun around, automatically lifting my hands to ward off any attack I might face.

A guy, who was already a good six feet away from me, jumped back and lifted his hands. "Whoa."

Seeing that he wasn't about to eat my face off, I dropped my arms to my sides, chuckling at my own stupidity. "Sorry. You scared the shit out of me."

The thud of a book shutting drew my attention back to Kiaya, and I turned sideways so I could see both her and the guy who'd scared the shit out of me at the same time.

She stood, arms crossed and the textbook hugged tightly to her chest. "This is Kyle. He needs a ride, too."

Kiaya had all my attention now.

"I'm sorry? What do you mean, 'he needs a ride'?"

"Exactly what I said." She blinked like she wasn't sure what my problem was, and I noticed that like the night before, she wasn't wearing makeup. "He needs a ride to St. Louis."

"You offered him a ride? Without asking me?"

All Kiaya did was shrug. "I didn't know where your room was."

"And you couldn't have asked last night when we talked?"

"I didn't know him then," she replied, her voice emotionless and her expression giving nothing away.

Now I was really confused.

"Explain," I said, trying to keep my voice even.

Finally, Kiaya showed some emotion; too bad it was an impatient sigh. Seriously? Was she losing patience with me? I wasn't the one who'd sprung an extra person on her at barely seven o'clock in the morning.

"There were posts on the university's Facebook page from people who needed rides, so last night I went through them. I just wanted to make sure anyone who needed to get out of here could. I saw Kyle's post," she nodded to the guy, "and sent him a message to see if he was still around. He was, so I figured we could help."

Okay, that was kind of a considerate thing to do, but it still seemed a little strange, considering it wasn't her car.

I turned to face Kyle, studying him. He looked young, probably only a freshman, and was medium height and average looking. There wasn't much to the kid—he was all arms and legs even if he wasn't that tall—and he looked harmless enough with those big, brown eyes and sandy hair and forgettable face. Like the younger kid who lived down the street you waved to whenever you saw him even though you could never remember his name.

"St. Louis?" I asked, despite the fact that Kiaya had already told me.

Kyle's head bobbed once. "Yeah. Or really, just outside St. Louis."

Maybe he'd be able to keep me company on this trip since I didn't have high hopes for Kiaya. "You have papers?"

Kyle gave another head bob.

"Money to chip in?"

More bobbing.

Great. Looked like he was going to be a bust as well.

"Okay, then," I said with a sigh, already imagining the hours of silence stretching out in front of me. At least I'd be able to grab a nap when I wasn't driving. "Let's get this show on the road."

Kyle gave me a relieved smile that lit up his eyes, making

FAR from HOME

him less forgettable. "Thanks."

"No problem." I grabbed the handle of my suitcase, glad I could wheel it now that I was downstairs. "I'm Rowan, by the way."

"Nice to meet you, Rowan." The kid's smile grew. "I was starting to think I was going to get stuck here."

Kyle followed me to the door, jogging to catch up like he was afraid I'd leave him behind, but Kiaya seemed to be moving at a snail's pace. She tucked her textbook into her duffle bag before zipping it, and had just slung it over her shoulder and started following us when Kyle and I stepped outside.

Despite fall being on the way, the Arizona morning was warm and inviting. It was one thing I'd loved about going to school here, and while I was anxious to get home and see my parents, I was already dreading the cool, Ohio weather. I was a summer girl, which was why I planned to move somewhere warmer once I graduated. A bomb I hadn't yet dropped on my parents.

"Kiaya said you're from Ohio," Kyle said as we walked side by side, heading to the student parking lot.

"Yup. North of Dayton in Troy. It's a smaller town, but cute." It wasn't a lie even if I did hate the cold. I loved my hometown.

"Never been to Ohio," he said, sounding thoughtful.

"I'm sure it's not that different from Missouri," I replied.

Kyle cracked a smile as he nodded to the sandy ground. "Unlike here?"

"Exactly," I said.

Feet scraped against the ground behind us, and I looked back to find Kiaya following but keeping her distance. I wasn't sure if she was stuck up or just shy, but either way, I was suddenly very glad she'd invited Kyle. Despite my earlier trepidation, his warm smile made him seem like the perfect traveling companion.

Thank God.

My black Honda Civic came into view—my parents had bought it for me when I turned sixteen—and I clicked the button on my key fob, popping the trunk.

Kyle's smile grew. "It's lucky you have a car, but driving all the way from Ohio must have sucked."

"It was okay," I said, shrugging as I lugged my suitcase into the trunk. "My mom drove with me and flew home after I got settled in. This is the first year we did it, and it took a lot of convincing—she wanted me to fly again—but I'm glad. Especially now."

"It was good timing." Kyle dropped his own bag into the trunk next to mine—a small, black backpack.

These two were light travelers.

I waited for Kiaya to follow suit, but she kept her bag clutched close to her body like she thought I might speed off with her belongings. As if I wanted a cheap red duffle bag and a textbook for a class that might never meet again.

The thought made me swallow, and I pushed it away.

"Okay," I said almost to myself as I slammed the trunk.

Kiaya took the back, which I was grateful for, and I slid in behind the wheel while Kyle got cozy in the passenger seat. I'd filled the gas tank the night before—I'd visited three closed gas stations before finding one that was open—which meant the only thing standing between us and the open road was some caffeine.

"I'm going to make a Starbucks stop before we hit the road," I said as I started the car.

Kyle beamed at me. "Sounds good."

I already liked this kid.

"Kiaya?" I said when she didn't say anything. "You want some coffee?"

"I'm good," was her only reply.

I bit back a sigh.

Before the coffee heaven came into view, I was worried it might be closed like a lot of the other businesses in the area, but it wasn't. As if nothing had changed, a line of cars was already sitting in the drive-thru when I pulled in. It moved fast, though, and soon I had a steaming cup of energy in my hand. As I pulled away, a surge of gratitude that Americans thought coffee was a necessity shot through me, and the feeling doubled once I'd taken that first big sip of caramel deliciousness.

At my side, Kyle seemed just as thrilled with his drink, while

FAR from HOME

in the back Kiaya once again had her book out and was poring over the contents like she thought the words were the only thing that could save her from the virus. She was the most dedicated student I'd ever seen, and while I was sure she had her reasons, I just couldn't fathom why it mattered at this point in life. There were other things to focus on right now. Bigger things.

Kyle and I chatted while she studied. He probably wasn't anyone I normally would have hung out with, but I was thankful for the conversation. What was more, I liked the kid. He was open and friendly, and even a little funny—in a dry kind of way. Plus, he was super grateful for the ride.

"My parents have been going crazy," he said as I drove, following the signs for approved routes out of the city. "I'm the oldest of six, and they wanted me home a month ago, but of course by then air travel had been canceled. I thought I had a ride two weeks ago, but it fell through." He frowned at the memory.

"What happened?" I asked.

"The guy actually took a bunch of cash from me so he could fill the car up and get an oil change before we started out, then never showed to pick me up."

"Seriously?" I looked his way out of the corner of my eye while keeping most of my focus on the deserted road in front of me. People were really taking the government's warnings seriously and staying indoors. Which I was hoping would make the drive an easy one.

Kyle's head bobbed. "Yeah. My parents had to send more money, which wasn't easy. They're pretty strapped for cash right now since both their companies closed weeks ago and haven't reopened."

That was something that had never occurred to me before now, and Kyle's family couldn't have been the only ones in that situation. My mom was a retired teacher and had her pension, but my dad was a doctor. His job was a little bit of a necessity these days.

"What do they do?" I asked Kyle.

"My mom is a legal secretary for a big firm, and my dad works for an HVAC company in the area." He shrugged. "Neither one is exactly necessary with the way things are right now."

"Yeah," I said, thinking of my dad working at the hospital and what he might be exposed to. To try to distract myself I asked, "So, five brothers and sisters? I'm an only child, so I can't even imagine."

"It can be a lot," he said, laughing, "but fun, too. Sometimes."

"Brothers or sisters?" I prompted.

"Three brothers, two sisters," Kyle replied. "The girls are the youngest."

"Four older brothers?" I shook my head and grimaced. "Your poor sisters."

He laughed. "You have no idea. Tess turned ten over the summer, and this boy started calling her. But we don't have a home phone, so she had to give him someone's cell number. She gave him mine." He pounded his fist against his hand. "I gave him a nice talking to."

I snorted out a laugh. "Your poor sister. Did you scare him off?"

"You bet I did," Kyle said. "But if he isn't willing to fight for her, he isn't worth it. That's what I told her, anyway."

"I'm sure that made her feel better," I said, rolling my eyes.

Kyle just laughed again.

We reached Route 66 in what seemed like no time, and I had to slow the car as the first checkpoint came into view. I had all the proper documents—and the others had assured me they did as well—but the sight of the armed soldiers had my heart beating faster. I clenched the steering wheel, watching as one of them approached the SUV in front of me, and held my breath. He had an automatic weapon slung over his shoulder, but the three men blocking the road had their guns at the ready, and the knowledge that they would very soon be pointed at my car made me sweat.

"You guys have your papers?" I asked, and it suddenly occurred to me that I should have verified their stories before we left. What if they didn't actually have permission to travel? Would the soldiers think I was trying to smuggle them out of Arizona and detain me with them?

I held my breath, waiting for the others to produce their

FAR from HOME

papers. Kyle had his out first, passing me the slightly crumpled documents with a shaky hand, and a second later Kiaya had thrust hers out as well. Her hand was amazingly steady.

"Thanks," I said, taking them.

In front of us, the soldier handed the travel papers back to the driver of the SUV and waved to the men blocking the road. They stepped aside but didn't lower their weapons. Instead, they aimed them at us.

"Holy shit," Kyle muttered just under his breath.

I couldn't disagree.

The car in front of me drove off, and the soldiers moved back into position, once again blocking the road, while the man in charge of checking papers waved for me to drive forward.

I did as instructed, slowing to a stop beside him and rolling the window down. He did a quick survey of the car, his gaze sweeping first over me before moving to Kyle, then back to Kiaya.

Once he'd looked everyone over, he focused on me again, barking out, "Papers."

"Here you go." I held them out with a trembling hand.

The man looked them over, reading the details carefully before his gaze was once again on me. "Why are you traveling today?"

The papers should have told him everything he needed to know, but I answered anyway. "We're college students trying to get home."

"Three different places?" His eyebrows lifted, emphasizing the importance of my answer.

"I was the only one with a car, but I didn't want to drive alone. I'll drop them off on my way to Ohio."

He nodded as he refolded the papers. "You will stay on this route all the way to St. Louis. Do you understand?"

"Yes," I said.

He held the papers out, his gaze locked with mine, and I took them. "There will be no second warning. If you're found on a different route, you will be arrested immediately."

"I understand," I said.

"Good." He nodded and stepped back, not looking away from me as he waved to the men in the street. "Drive safely."

"Thanks," I said.

I took off the second the road was clear, probably driving a little faster than necessary, and didn't bother rolling my window up until the checkpoint was a good distance behind me. By then, some of my hair had broken out of the intricate braid I'd put it in before leaving the dorm, and the blonde tendrils tickled my face. I brushed them aside and shook my head, trying to shake off the fear that had settled over me at the sight of the armed soldiers.

"Man, that was intense," Kyle said, breaking the silence.

"I know." I let out a strained laugh. "I really hate guns."

"Yeah." He frowned and nodded. "Although I've never really been around them. We don't own any."

"Same here." My gaze moved to the rearview mirror as I tried to catch Kiaya's eye. "What about you, Kiaya?"

Her head snapped up. "What about me?"

I resisted the urge to roll my eyes. I seemed to have to do that a lot with her. "Does your family own any guns?"

"No." The response was quick and short, like she didn't want to have to answer and wanted to let me know I shouldn't ask anything else.

"Okay," I said under my breath.

She was the most closed-off person I'd ever met.

＃ 3

The turn lane for McDonald's was about ten cars long, and by the time I finally made it into the parking lot, I was afraid we wouldn't find a spot. If I didn't have to pee, I would have just gone through the drive-thru—even though it, too, was about ten cars long—but my bladder had reached the point of near bursting.

"I have to pee," I said as I circled the building in search of a parking place. "But other than that, I want to get in and out of here as fast as possible." I eyed Kiaya in the rearview mirror. "Okay?"

She shrugged and said nothing, but I took it as a yes.

"No problem," Kyle said, shooting me a grin. "I can take the next leg of driving if you want."

I hit the brakes a little too hard when a parked car's reverse lights lit up, and he lurched forward, but his smile didn't fade.

"Thanks, Kyle," I said and flipped my turn signal on.

Kiaya's company may have been a bust, but I liked this kid. He was easy to talk to, nice, and eager to show his appreciation for the ride. Unlike Kiaya, who hadn't uttered more than ten words since we left school.

"Sure thing." Kyle's grin stretched wider.

I tapped my chipped nail against the steering wheel as I waited for the car to back out of the spot and found myself wondering if the nail salons in Troy were still open. A manicure was a must. Mom and I could make a girls' day out of it, even. A visit to the salon to get a mani-pedi, followed by dinner at The Caroline—our favorite place.

I couldn't wait.

A honk sounded behind me, jolting me from my thoughts of home, and I glanced in the rearview mirror. The cars were lined up, and there were even more in the road waiting to turn into the parking lot. It was a madhouse, bringing to mind the warnings on the news and completely popping the little bubble of joy I'd created in my head. Mom and I wouldn't be able to go out. We were supposed to avoid crowds. I was supposed to avoid crowds. I'd promised her. But what could I do? I had to pee, and pretty much every place we could stop on this route was going to be crowded. We weren't the only ones trying to get somewhere, and in direct contrast to their explicit instructions, the government had corralled all travelers into the same area. Which was something I hadn't thought about before now. Why did they do that? It made no sense if they wanted to stop this thing from spreading...

The car I'd been waiting on pulled out of the spot, and I took its place. Even for my little Civic, it was a tight fit, but I wasn't thinking about that as I turned the car off and we all piled out. I was thinking about the people around me, about where they'd come from and what they might have been exposed to. What we might get exposed to by being here.

The sooner we got back on the road, the better.

Kiaya seemed to purposefully keep her distance as we headed for the restaurant, but Kyle walked alongside me, chatting about nothing in particular. Which was a good distraction. Inside, I wasn't surprised to find a line for the women's restroom, but it still made me groan. I felt like I was five again, practically dancing to keep my bladder from releasing.

"I can order while you wait," Kyle said, as eager to please as usual.

FAR from HOME

"Thanks." I shot him a smile even as I shifted my feet.

Kiaya was already in line. Figured.

Once I'd told him what I wanted, Kyle hurried off, and I watched him get at the back of the line—three people behind our other traveling companion. More people were stumbling into the already crowded restaurant by the second, looking worn and travel-weary, and several even looked like they hadn't slept in days. It was the woman who got in line behind Kyle that really drew my attention, though. She was hugging herself, a thick sweater wrapped around her body that looked way too warm for the hot, New Mexico day. Her red-rimmed eyes were bloodshot and appeared almost hazy, and there was a fine sheen of sweat on her face that shimmered under the bright fluorescent lights.

She was sick, I realized with a start. Not just a little sick either. It was obvious by the way she kept trying to pull the sweater tighter around her body, by the way she shivered despite the moisture beaded on her face. This woman had a raging fever.

She swayed and reached out, catching her balance by grabbing hold of Kyle. He turned to face her, and while less friendly people would have shied away from or even scowled at the unwanted contact, he didn't. Instead, he gave her a sympathetic smile and said something I couldn't make out but instinctively knew was nice. Probably he asked if she was okay, or even if he could do anything to help. Whatever he said, the only response the woman could give was a nod.

One head bob was all she got out before her eyes rolled back in her head and she collapsed.

The room exploded in panicked shouts and cries. Kyle knelt beside the woman and pressed two fingers to her neck, while a few other people also rushed to see if they could help. Even more people, however, ran *away* from the unconscious woman. Out the door, grabbing loved ones as they hurried off, their expressions filled with terror and worry. Kiaya hadn't moved, and she watched from her place in line—which now wasn't even a line—as Kyle and a few other people tried to get the woman to wake up. Like Kiaya, I was frozen, my full bladder forgotten as I watched Kyle press his ear against the woman's chest, his face turned toward hers as she let out a ragged breath.

I could almost see the virus jumping from her mouth to Kyle.

As if reading my mind, Kiaya turned her head in my direction, her eyes wide, and her gaze trapped mine. We might not have talked much and we didn't know one another at all, but in that moment it didn't matter. We were both thinking the same thing. Kyle had just exposed himself to this virus.

What the hell were we going to do now?

Without even knowing why I did it, I waved for her to come over to me. Her eyebrows jumped in surprise, but she ducked out of line without hesitating and hurried my way, darting a look toward Kyle as she passed him. The line for the bathroom, like the line for food, had vanished during the commotion, and when Kiaya reached me, I grabbed her arm and pulled her inside.

We nearly slammed into a woman who was drying her hands, and she let out a yelp of surprise before glaring at us. All I could do was look her over, silently praying she wasn't sick like the woman in the lobby because I didn't want to get exposed to the virus.

Then again, now that Kyle was exposed, I was pretty much screwed, wasn't I?

If he got back in the car. If he didn't, though, I might still be okay.

"What's wrong?" Kiaya asked, ignoring the woman we'd almost run into as she huffed and tossed her used paper towel into the trashcan.

"What do you mean?" I asked, totally confused by what she was asking. "You saw what happened, and you saw how close Kyle was to that woman. There's no way he isn't covered in germs."

I couldn't make myself voice what I was thinking, so I left it at that, hoping she'd get the point so I didn't have to say more.

Kiaya's eyes held mine, expressionless and blank.

When I realized she still didn't understand what I meant, I said, "We can't let him back in the car."

She blinked six times like she couldn't wrap her head around what I was saying. "You want to leave him behind?"

FAR from HOME

My insides twisted with guilt, but I couldn't take it back. It was self-preservation, not selfishness. Kiaya had to know that. Then again, this was the girl who'd offered a stranger a ride without a second thought, who'd searched Facebook to make sure there wasn't anyone else around who might need help. Maybe she couldn't understand.

"Yes." The word hissed from my mouth like a snake. I felt like a snake, too. Like a slimy, venomous snake, and it made me sick.

"We can't just abandon him in the middle of nowhere," Kiaya said. "Not only is it wrong, but we also don't even know if that woman has the same virus. She could be sick with anything."

I rolled my eyes. She had to be joking. "Do you seriously believe that?"

Either she did, or she just didn't want to admit the truth—even to herself—because she said nothing.

"Look," I told her, "there's a killer virus sweeping the country, and Kyle has been exposed. There's no other way to look at it. We can't just act like that didn't happen."

"So, your suggestion is to ditch him even though we know nothing?"

"Are you willing to chance it and risk your life?" I snapped.

I'd hoped putting it that way would make it almost impossible to argue with. *Almost* because deep down I knew how horribly wrong what I was suggesting was. I needed Kiaya to agree with me or I wouldn't be able to go through with it. Needed someone to justify the survival instinct that had made me say these things. I still had my humanity, and what was more, I liked Kyle. Leaving him at this shitty fast food restaurant in the middle of nowhere would haunt me forever either way, but if I could get someone to agree that this was the best option, at least I'd be able to tell myself I hadn't been alone in the decision.

"I won't leave him, so you'll have to leave us both," Kiaya said, lifting her chin and glaring down at me. "Besides, we've probably already been exposed just by being in the same building with that woman."

The blood drained from my face as the realization that she

was right sank in, and deep inside me, the dread that had been building for weeks grew and spread until it seemed like it had wormed its way through every inch of my body. If what she was saying were true, this could be it for me. I'd disobeyed my mom and gone on this stupid trip, and now I might pay with my life.

It also meant there was no point in leaving Kyle behind.

I turned my back on Kiaya, too ashamed and dejected and terrified to tell her I'd changed my mind. "I need to go to the bathroom so we can get back on the road. You should go, too. I don't want to have to stop in an hour."

"Yeah," she mumbled, but I'd already stepped into the stall, so I couldn't see her expression.

Back in the lobby, I found Kyle waiting for me, a bag in hand and a somber expression on his face. The woman was gone, but I didn't ask who'd taken her or where they'd taken her to, or even if she'd still been breathing. The truth was, I didn't want to know.

"The place cleared out pretty fast," Kyle said, nodding to the bag, "so we got record-breaking service."

"That's good." I held my hand out, and he passed me the bag. "Use the bathroom. I'll wait in the car."

He nodded and sighed, and I couldn't help noticing some of the light had left his eyes. Probably for good if, like Kiaya and me, he realized what this little pit stop meant. Which he probably did. Only a moron would've looked at that woman on the floor and not thought about the virus. Only a moron wouldn't be thinking about the virus every minute of every day now. Kyle was no moron.

Kiaya stepped out of the bathroom just as Kyle reached the little alcove where the two doors stood, and she didn't bother keeping her distance. As if something had suddenly occurred to him, he looked from her to me, his mouth pulling down into an exaggerated frown. The idea that he might suspect what I'd said to Kiaya, that he might know I'd briefly considered leaving him behind, twisted my insides into knots. How selfish was I? Very, apparently.

I waved the bag, forcing out a smile. "We'll be in the car."

Kyle nodded, but a glimmer of doubt flickered in his eyes.

FAR from HOME

He'd been ditched before, so it was understandable, and the thought made me feel ten times worse.

He turned without saying anything to Kiaya and continued to the bathroom.

She stopped in front of me, her big brown eyes filled with doubt and worry. It was more emotion than she usually showed, and despite the circumstances, I couldn't help thinking it made her look more attractive. "Will you be waiting in the car?"

"I will," I said, although there was still a small part of me that wanted to drive off and leave them both behind. Maybe I should have traveled alone. In some ways, it would have been a hell of a lot easier than this.

"Okay." She gave a firm nod, but a glimmer of doubt still flickered in her eyes. "I'll get my food and meet you at the car."

"Okay," I repeated.

Cars circled the parking lot looking for spaces like vultures searching for a carcass to pick apart, and I had to zigzag between them to get to my own car. Backing out was going to be a pain in the ass since no one wanted to leave even an inch of empty space just in case another car tried to worm its way by them, but at the moment, traffic seemed like the smallest of all my worries. The biggest was wondering if I'd make it home to see my parents. Something I was starting to seem less and less sure of.

I slipped into the passenger seat since Kyle said he'd drive and passed the time by nibbling on fries even though my appetite had gotten carried away with that woman's body. Honks sounded, filling the silence. Quite a few were probably aimed at me, but I ignored them. We'd be on our way soon enough, and then whoever was blaring their horn could take their turn in the fast food restaurant of death.

I sighed.

Only a few minutes passed before the driver's door opened, and Kyle smiled when he slid in. "I wasn't sure if I'd find you waiting."

"I wouldn't leave you," I said through a mouthful of fries, hoping they'd muffle my words and mask my shame.

"I don't know if I'd blame you." He pressed his lips together as he stared out the windshield, his hands gripping the steering wheel until his knuckles turned white. "If I don't make it, make sure to call my family. Please. I don't want them to wonder what happened to me."

"Kyle," I said, hesitantly reaching out to put my hand on his arm, "you're going to make it."

He blinked before turning to look at me, his eyes rimmed red, tears shimmering in them. "We don't know that."

"We don't know if any of us are going to make it."

It was the first time I'd voiced my deepest fear out loud, and just like I'd thought, it made things worse. Made the terror more real and present.

I closed my eyes and let out a deep breath, thinking about how my parents would feel if I died before getting to them. Worse still was the fact that they didn't even know I was on my way. I could get sick and die on the side of the road—left behind by Kyle, if karma was an actual thing—and they'd never know what happened to me. It was idiotic. I should have called them, should have let them know what I was doing. Even if my mom got mad, it was better than leaving them to wonder where I was. I should have called.

The back door clicked, and I opened my eyes as Kiaya slid in, paper bag in hand.

I turned back to face Kyle. "I'll make sure they know if it comes to that."

He gave me a weak and trembling smile. "Thanks."

All I could do was nod.

I was going to call my parents, but not now. Later. The next time we stopped. That way, I could have a private conversation with them. A private moment to say goodbye just in case this was the end.

FAR from HOME

The little bit of lightness we'd managed to conjure up when first leaving campus this morning had disappeared with the sick woman's body, and we'd been driving for what felt like hours in silence when Kiaya let out a gasp. I looked over my shoulder to find her not staring at her textbook for once. Instead, her eyes were glued to her phone and her mouth was hanging open.

"What is it?" I asked.

She lifted her gaze to meet mine, and the fear shimmering in her eyes filled me with dread. "The president died."

"Shit," Kyle muttered.

He lifted his gaze to the mirror so he could look back at Kiaya, but only for a second. Then he was once again focused on the road in front of us.

"What happened?" I asked, even if it was obvious.

"It says he got sick a couple days ago and died sometime yesterday." Her eyes flicked back and forth as she read. "The vice president is in charge and will be sworn in as soon as possible." She looked up. "That's all. They didn't comment when asked if it was the same virus going around, and they didn't tell anyone where he was when he died or if the vice president was exposed."

"Not surprising," I muttered. "They've been feeding us crap or as few facts as possible for weeks now. Why should this be any different? I mean, according to the news, the virus is contained, but we all know that's a load of shit."

I turned back around and slumped in my seat, thinking once again about the woman in McDonald's and wondering if that would be our fate and how soon we'd know if it was. That was the biggest problem with all the lies and government cover-up. The general public had no idea what to expect. I knew there was an incubation period for viruses, but without any information about this current bug, I had no idea if we had to wait two weeks or two hours to learn our fate, and it pissed me off. I hated waiting more than anything.

Luckily for me—or unluckily—I didn't have to wait long before learning the incubation period wasn't two weeks like I'd feared.

We'd just crossed into Texas, and the sun was moving toward

the horizon as dusk drew near, and the sky above us darkening to indigo while the horizon glowed pink and orange.

That was when I heard the first sniffle.

I sat up straight, my gaze snapping to Kyle. The approaching darkness created shadows in the car that made getting a really good look at him tough, but I couldn't miss the constant bobbing of his Adam's apple. Like he was swallowing over and over again.

"You feeling okay?" I asked, trying to sound casual.

In the back, Kiaya sat up straighter.

"Yeah." Kyle cleared his throat and purposefully didn't look my way. "My throat's itchy. That's all."

I looked behind me, my gaze meeting Kiaya's, and neither of us spoke for a second. My heart had started hammering harder with that first sniffle, doubling its pace at Kyle's response. When he let out a little cough, it nearly exploded.

This was it.

"Maybe we should find somewhere to stop for the night," Kiaya said slowly.

Kyle's hands tightened on the steering wheel, but he said nothing. He didn't look my way either, and I realized he was leaving it up to me. Whether he suspected that I'd suggested we leave him behind, I didn't know, but I did know he was going to give me the option now. Not that it mattered. It was too late. If we hadn't been exposed in the McDonald's, we were now. Which meant stopping was the best thing for all of us, because Kiaya or I—or both of us—could come down with symptoms at any second.

"Yeah," I said, the word coming out like a sigh. "Let's check out the next town."

The next town turned out to be Vega, Texas.

Maybe it had been something at one time, but it wasn't now. The main street looked like dozens of other small towns along Route 66. Old, empty businesses that probably hadn't been open since the 1960s lined both sides, their windows boarded up and their signs faded until they were nearly illegible. Deserted gas stations, their parking lots long overgrown with weeds, contrasted with the signs that declared Vega to be a historic town worth visiting. Here and there were older buildings that had clearly been preserved in an attempt to draw tourists, but they did little to erase the feeling of abandon hanging over the city. Even with the extra traffic martial law had filtered in, the place felt like a ghost town.

The first two motels we passed had the words NO VACANCY lit up on their signs, but the third one we came to didn't. It was an old Best Western motel that had seen better days, but I still said a silent prayer as Kyle pulled into the parking lot that they had a room available. With the luck we'd had so far, though, I'd probably go into the front office only to learn the NO on the sign had burned out years ago and the place was totally booked.

"I'll go in and see what we can get," I said, reaching for the door handle.

"You don't have to."

Kyle's words made me freeze.

I turned back to face him, but he was staring straight ahead, avoiding looking at me.

"What do you mean?"

"You know what I mean." His hands wrung the steering wheel, and despite the fact that he was only eighteen, he suddenly looked like an old man. So serious and mature. So certain he was facing his end. "You don't have to wait around with me. Not when I'm only going to die."

"We don't know that," I said, nearly choking on the words.

"We do." Kyle closed his eyes and swallowed then sucked in a deep breath before looking at me. "I'm sick. It's not just a tickle in my throat, and we all know it. I can feel it getting worse with each passing second. Actually *feel* it."

Tears had filled his eyes, and being the sympathetic crier that I was, I found myself blinking to stop my own from falling over.

"It doesn't matter," I said, having to swallow sobs. "I won't leave you to die alone."

The second the words were out, I knew they were true. Despite my instinct back in McDonald's, I couldn't have left him. It was too cold, too selfish, and that wasn't me.

"You don't even know me," Kyle said, his voice barely more

than a whisper.

"I don't need to." I pulled on the handle and shoved the door open. Before I got out, I said, "No one deserves to die alone."

I slammed the door seconds before my tears broke free. They slid down my cheeks, but I somehow managed to hold the sobs back. Kyle couldn't see me crying. Not when he was the one facing death.

I hurried toward the office, only able to find it through my tears thanks to the glowing arrow pointing around the corner. The second I was out of view, I pressed my back against the brick wall and set my sobs free. They broke out of me in a painful wail that shook my body. I was on the verge of breaking to pieces, and I wrapped my arms around my stomach in a desperate attempt to keep it together. It didn't feel like it was working, so I held myself tighter, but still I cried. I cried until my throat was raw, until my arms hurt from holding myself, until my legs shook and my eyes burned. This wasn't what I'd expected to happen when I decided to make this trip. I was twenty years old. I shouldn't have to hold someone's hand as they died in a shitty roadside motel in a slightly less shitty town.

"God," I gasped, barely able to get the words out. "What is happening?"

"End of the fucking world," a voice responded.

I jerked at the sound, not sure where it came from, and a second later a man stepped around the side of the Coke machine. Sharp, blue eyes swept over me, taking me in from head to toe before focusing on my face, and my scalp prickled under his scrutiny.

"Didn't mean to scare you." He gave me a tight smile that didn't reach his eyes. "I would have made myself known before, but you were a little preoccupied."

Swallowing the remaining sobs, I untangled my arms and swiped my hands down my face, wiping the tears away and probably smearing my mascara in the process. What the hell had I been thinking this morning when I put makeup on? Oh, yeah, I hadn't been. At least not about anything like this happening.

"It's okay," I managed to get out.

"Doesn't sound okay," he replied, lifting his brows. "You need anything? Help?" His lips twitched, and he lifted his right arm, flexing a very impressive bicep. "Muscle?"

I could tell he was trying to make a joke, to lighten the mood, but in the face of everything else, all it did was irritate me. Even if it hadn't, I wasn't in the flirting mood. It wasn't like he wasn't attractive, because he was. Very attractive, actually. Not too tall, but not short, he was built like someone who worked out on a daily basis and he had a square jaw and strong features, and the kind of eyes that made him look brooding even when all he was doing was standing there.

"I can't imagine a thing more worthless at a time like this," I muttered.

"Depends on what you're facing." He shrugged, unconcerned that I'd blown him off. "A flat tire might change your mind."

"If only life's challenges were as simple as a flat tire."

Exhaling, I worked at pulling myself together. I had a job to do. We needed a room, and then I had to give my parents a call. Just in case I was the next one to come down with symptoms. I swallowed and winced, but told myself the scratchiness in my throat was only from my crying. The runny nose was, too. That was all. I wasn't sick.

It wasn't easy to believe.

The guy was leaning against the Coke machine, clearly unconcerned that his attempts at talking to me had fallen flat, and I didn't bother telling him goodbye before heading into the office.

A bell jingled when I pulled the door open, alerting whoever worked in the office that there was a customer. The lobby was small with browning wallpaper that was peeling off in places and off-white tile in desperate need of a good mopping. A man of about sixty stood behind the desk, and he studied me with bloodshot eyes as I approached. He didn't offer a greeting or a smile, and even when I'd stopped in front of him, he didn't utter a word.

"I need a room," I said when he still hadn't spoken.

It crossed my mind to ask for two—the idea of sleeping in the same room with a dying person made me physically nauseated—but I'd promised Kyle I wouldn't leave him alone, and I couldn't go back on that promise now. No matter what.

"It's $69.95 a night," the man said in a gravelly voice. "Plus tax."

"I have cash."

I dug through my purse then slid the money across the counter once I'd found the right amount. The man took it, making change, and he didn't even ask for my travel papers or identification before sliding the key over the counter to me. Not that I'd expected it in a place like this. He probably didn't give a shit if the people checking in were legally allowed to travel. Until now, a place like this would have been lucky to have two rooms occupied at the same time. Now, though, they'd be full soon, if they weren't already.

"Thanks," I said.

He nodded in response.

The muscled man was gone when I stepped out, which I was more than thankful for. He was the only one who'd gotten to witness my breakdown, and I'd be more than happy to never see him again. Crying in public was not my thing.

Kyle had gotten worse during my short absence. He didn't tell me, but he didn't have to. I could hear his labored breathing when I opened the car door, could see the beads of sweat on his forehead when I slid inside. Could see his hands trembling.

I swallowed to keep my voice steady. "Room thirty-five."

"One room?" Kiaya asked.

I looked back at her, unblinking. "Yes."

She only nodded.

Kyle drove across the parking lot, pulling into a parking space in front of our room and turning the car off. We didn't talk as we gathered our bags and headed for the room. Kyle had his, a black backpack, slung over his shoulder, but I could tell just the exertion of walking from the car to the motel was wearing on him. Luckily, we didn't have far to go, and the second he made it inside he collapsed on the bed.

The room was dusty and musty, with an underlying smell of

cigarette smoke that had probably soaked into the carpet and walls two decades ago. The wallpaper was out of style and yellowed, the carpet stained, and the bedspreads scratchy. I refused to let myself wonder when they'd last been cleaned. On the whole, the place was a pit, but it was all we had, and in the face of everything else, it didn't seem very important. Which was crazy. I was a notorious hotel snob.

Kiaya and I stood at the foot of the bed, staring at Kyle in silence. I had no idea what to do next, and the expression on her face said she was as clueless as I was.

"What now?" she asked.

I thought about it for a moment, flipping through the times I'd been sick and the things Mom had done for me. I had to take a deep breath when a pang vibrated through my chest at the memories. Mom sitting up with me at night as I burned with fever, or me being curled up in her bed. Lying on the couch, my head resting in her lap.

"I should get him some medication, right?" I looked toward Kiaya for confirmation, but she only shrugged. "Tylenol or something?"

"If he has a fever, yeah," she said.

"Good point," I replied.

When she didn't make a move, I did. Everything in me wanted to run away, but I ignored it and lowered myself to the bed at Kyle's side.

"Hey," I whispered, putting my hand on his forehead. His skin burned against mine. "What can I do for you? Anything?"

Kyle cracked one eye and looked up at me. "I don't know. Everything hurts. Deep inside."

Tylenol was a must, but what else? He'd need to stay hydrated. Mom had always emphasized that when I was sick. *Drink more water, Rowan,* she'd always said, *Water and rest are the best medicine.* I wasn't sure either one could help Kyle, but they might make him more comfortable, and they were literally the only things I could do.

"You should drink something," I managed to get out. "I can get some ice chips. How does that sound?"

He nodded, but his eyelids had already slid shut.

I stood and turned to face Kiaya, who was now sitting on the other bed, her eyes wide and round and full of terror. "I'm going to drive to the pharmacy we passed and get him something for the fever. I don't know if it will help but…"

It's all I can do, I thought, but left the words unsaid.

"That's a good idea." She nodded and stood like my decision had motivated her. "I can get some ice chips while you're gone. Maybe a cold washcloth on his forehead?"

A memory of Mom wiping my forehead when I was little popped into my head, bringing with it the urge to cry. If only she were here to take on this burden. I was ill-equipped for this, wasn't strong enough. My whole life, she'd done everything for me, and now here I was in the middle of nowhere with all this responsibility. It was too much.

"A washcloth sounds good." I ran my hand down my face, feeling suddenly like I hadn't slept in days. "We can grab some dinner at the diner across the street after I get back. If you're hungry."

"That sounds good," Kiaya replied.

"Okay." I turned toward the door, saying over my shoulder, "I won't be long."

She said nothing.

Outside, I dragged myself back to the car and slid behind the wheel. My hands gripped it at ten and two, my fingers tightening until I felt like my bones would snap. Closing my eyes, I rested my forehead on the steering wheel between my clenched hands, breathing slowly, trying to stay calm. I'd thought my breakdown earlier had been enough, but now I felt on the verge of another one. I couldn't let it happen, though. I needed to get to the pharmacy and get some medicine, then maybe get a cup of broth or soup or something from the diner and force Kyle to eat some. Then I needed to call my parents and let them know what was going on. That was going to be the hardest part, the thing that would push me closest to the breaking point. Even then, I had to hold on. I didn't know if this was the end for me or not, but it was for Kyle. He was going to need someone to cling to over the next day or

FAR from HOME

however long it took him to die. I hoped it wasn't long. Not just for him, but for me as well. I wanted to get out of here, to keep driving so I could get home before things got too bad.

That was assuming I didn't get sick next.

I wanted my mom, and it made me feel like a child, but I couldn't help it.

Sucking in a deep breath, I forced myself to lift my head. A hotel door right in front of me opened just as my eyes did, and a man stepped out. He was in his mid-thirties with buzzed hair and a beer gut, and a bulge in his lower lip. He spit on the ground and looked around, his gaze stopping on me, and his mouth stretched into an animalistic looking grin. Even in the darkness, I could see the steely color of his eyes, and something about him made my skin crawl.

I looked away and started the car.

4

It was after eight o'clock by the time I found a few minutes to call my parents. I'd coaxed some Motrin into Kyle, gotten him to drink a little broth, fed him some ice chips, then ate the burger I'd gotten myself at the diner—which was cold by that point. Kiaya had surprised me by being stronger than I'd expected, considering how quiet and meek she'd been so far, and when I'd said I needed to step outside to make a call, she'd assured me she could stay with Kyle. Which I was grateful for.

The motel parking lot was packed and the NO was now lit up on the sign, telling me either someone had checked in after us or we'd gotten the last room. Either way, there weren't many places I could go to have a quiet conversation, so I opted to get in my car again before pulling up my mom's number. I took a deep breath, working to get my emotions under control so I didn't scare her to death, and hit send.

It rang twice before she picked up.

"Rowan?" Something in her voice immediately had me on alert, but I couldn't put my finger on what it was.

"It's me, Mom. Are you okay? You sound weird."

She swallowed, but didn't answer. Time stretched out while

I waited for her to say something, and with each passing second, I became more certain she was about to tell me Dad or someone else we knew as sick. This was it. This was the moment I'd known was coming for a while. The moment when I learned definitively that everything was going to change.

"It's here," she finally said.

I clung to the phone tighter. "What do you mean? Tell me what's going on."

"Your Dad didn't come home from the hospital last night, so I called him. He was too busy to talk for long. The ER has been overrun with patients, and he said there's no end in sight. There are so many sick people, all with the same symptoms." Her voice cracked. "I'm so glad you're in Phoenix."

Shit.

"I'm not in Phoenix, Mom." I had to force the words out.

There was a pause. "What do you mean?"

"I'm in Texas. I got my travel papers a couple days ago. I didn't want to stay there, so I found some people to travel with, and we left this morning. But—" The words stuck in my throat, either from more tears or from the guilt I felt at what I was doing to my mom. She'd wanted me to be safe. That was all she'd ever wanted.

"But what, Rowan?" Mom asked, sounding panicked. "What's going on?"

"The guy traveling with us, Kyle is his name, he got sick. We had to stop at a motel in Vega, Texas. I don't think he's going to make it."

"Oh, my God," she gasped. "I told you to stay there. I told you not to come here."

She had to know it wouldn't have mattered either way, had to know this virus wasn't contained and that I would have eventually been exposed whether I'd stayed in Phoenix or not.

"I'm sorry," I whispered, barely able to talk through the tears clogging my throat. "I just wanted to be home."

"I know. I know." Mom exhaled, the breath shaky and long. "I don't know what's happening, Rowan. Everything's so scary. Your dad's been gone for more than twenty-four hours now, and the last time I tried to call, there was no answer. I'm considering going over there to check on him."

I sat up straighter, thinking about the hospital and all the sick people, about my mom being there. Dad was exposed. I hated thinking it, but it was a fact and something I had to accept. But Mom was home. She didn't work, so odds were good she hadn't been exposed to this thing. If she went to the hospital, though, she would be.

"You can't do that," I said fiercely. "You know Dad wouldn't want you to."

"Rowan…" Mom sounded like she was on the verge of breaking. "What if I never hear from him again?"

I closed my eyes, picturing my dad. His gray hair, always falling over his eyes because he never made time to get it cut, the bushy mustache that had tickled my cheek when he kissed me, the laugh that had boomed through the house throughout my childhood. Thinking about never seeing him again was physically painful, but thinking about never knowing what had happened to him, that was like a knife in my heart. I understood, but I also knew I couldn't hang up this phone without making Mom understand what she'd be risking.

"If you go there," I said, emphasizing the words by drawing them out, "you will be exposed to this virus. Do you want me to get home only to realize I've lost both my parents?"

My voice broke, and tears streamed down my cheeks. I swallowed but couldn't find the strength to say anything else, because I'd just acknowledged something horrible and heartbreaking. My dad was going to die. I knew it deep in my bones, and I needed my mom to accept it so she would stay where she was and stay safe.

Somehow, despite the pain inside me, I managed to find my voice. "Promise me you'll stay away from the hospital."

"Rowan," she said again, but nothing else.

"Mom," my voice rose in a way it never had before when addressing my parents. "You have to promise me."

She swallowed, and I held my breath, waiting for her to respond. The silence seemed to stretch out forever, so that by the time she finally exhaled and said, "Okay," I felt as if I'd aged ten years.

I let out the breath I'd been holding. "Thank you."

"But you have to promise you'll get here. Understand? You won't take any risks, and you won't let anything stop you."

"I promise," I said.

"Good."

Mom sniffed, and I imagined her crying the way I'd only seen a couple times. At my grandma's funeral two years ago, and on the day I left for my freshman year of college. Those were the only times I'd ever witnessed her emotions get the better of her. She was so strong, had been through so much, and if anyone could get through this, it was her.

"I love you, Mom," I said through my sobs.

"I love you," she replied, her own voice shaking. "You and your dad are all I've ever wanted, Rowan. Please get home to me. Please don't leave me alone."

"I won't," I said, my shoulders shaking now. "I promise."

It took me a while to pull myself together after hanging up, but once I had, I still didn't move. It was a long shot and would probably just lead to me feeling more dejected, but I called Dad anyway. I had to try.

His voicemail picked up right away. I paused, the phone pressed to my ear, but said nothing. Should I leave a message? Would he be able to get it? Would it feel like a final goodbye?

It didn't matter, I realized, because I had to do it.

I cleared my throat. "Dad, it's me. I know you're busy or… Never mind." I shook my head. "I just wanted you to know that I love you." My voice caught and I had to swallow. "So does Mom. I'm on my way home now. That's all."

I sighed when I hit END.

I headed back to the room. Kiaya was stretched out on the bed farthest from the door, and she looked up when I walked in, her expressionless gaze taking in my red eyes and smeared makeup, but she said nothing. Her silence had annoyed me earlier, but not anymore. Now I was thankful for it because I wasn't sure if I would be able to talk even if I tried. My throat was too raw from crying.

In the other bed, Kyle lay. His eyes were closed, but he wasn't asleep. He was tossing and turning, moaning in pain, and probably delirious. The drugs had barely taken the edge off his fever, and despite constantly changing the washcloth on his forehead, nothing seemed to cool him down. It was torture just watching him, and I couldn't even begin to imagine what he was going through.

"Has he said anything?" I asked Kiaya, still looking at Kyle.

"Nothing that makes sense."

I moved to the bed without looking back at her, focusing on the sick boy I'd met just this morning. It was strange, thinking about watching him die when yesterday I hadn't even known he existed. Even stranger was the knowledge that it would hurt me. That I liked him, and the tears that welled up when I thought about his parents and five siblings never getting to say goodbye were real.

"I promised I'd call his family if he didn't make it home."

I finally looked toward Kiaya. She was staring at me, her eyes big and round. They still showed little emotion, but I now realized they weren't as blank as I'd first thought. It was something else, something I'd mistaken for apathy. Resignation. Maybe something even deeper.

"What about you?" I asked, unable to stop myself. "Do you want me to call your family if you don't make it?"

"No," she said, her voice flat.

"Don't you want them to know what happened to you?"

I was pushing it. I knew she didn't want me to ask, but I couldn't help it. I was stuck in this motel with her until Kyle died. I had no idea how long that was going to be, but however long it took, I knew the next few hours were going to be horrible. I wanted to talk about something, anything, that would distract me from the moaning boy in the bed at my side.

"No," she said again, and this time she looked away. "I don't have anyone for you to call."

"No parents? What about siblings?"

She flinched but didn't look away from the bedspread. "I

was a foster kid, and I aged out two years ago. I doubt my foster parents have thought about me since the day I left."

I waited to see if she would say more, but she didn't. Not that I was surprised at this point. At least now I understood her a little better. She hadn't had a support system like I had. No parents to dote on her, no mother who'd looked at her like she was a miracle. Kiaya was used to fending for herself, used to being on her own. I kind of envied her.

I exhaled. "Well, I have a mom. A dad, too, although..." My words died.

Kiaya lifted her gaze to mine. "He's sick?"

"I don't know, but he will be soon if he isn't now. If something happens to me, my mom will be alone. Can you call her for me? Tell her I went fast." I look toward Kyle. "Tell her I didn't suffer."

"Yeah," Kiaya said, her voice quiet and brimming with more emotion than she'd shown up to this point. "I can do that."

"Thanks," I said.

IT WAS A FITFUL NIGHT. KYLE MOANED IN HIS SLEEP, WHICH MADE MY zombie dreams twice as vivid as they'd been the night before. I tossed and turned, kicking Kiaya more than once. If she'd somehow managed to sleep through Kyle's delirious moans and rambling, I probably woke her every few minutes. By the time the sun had risen, poking through the cracks in the curtains, I felt like I was on the verge of turning into a zombie myself. I couldn't have gotten more than a few minutes of sleep. Since I was wide awake and Kyle's moaning had grown louder—his fever had probably risen—I dragged myself out of bed.

"It's okay," I whispered as I moved to his side.

His skin was as hot as an iron and clammy with sweat, and when he opened feverish eyes, they didn't seem to be able to focus on me. "Tess," he said, reaching out to grab my hand. "Skip got out. I've been looking for him all day, but I can't find him. I'm afraid he got hit by a car."

I didn't know for sure, but I was assuming Skip was a dog and Kyle was relieving some childhood trauma of having lost a beloved pet. He seemed frantic, so I did my best to soothe him.

"It's okay, Kyle," I said, trying to keep my tone gentle and calm. "We found Skip. He's sleeping now."

"You did?" Kyle started to sit up. "Where is he?"

"He's sleeping." I put my hands on his shoulders, urging him to stay down. "You've been up all night looking for him, but you need to rest now. You can see him later."

"We can play catch," Kyle said, giving in and lying down.

"That's right," I whispered.

Behind me, the bedsprings groaned, and I turned to find Kiaya getting up. "How is he?"

"Worse." I looked back at him. "His fever is up. We should try to get him to take something."

"I'll get it," she said, her voice soft.

I watched her head to the bathroom, a glass in her hand. After our little conversation the night before, something between us had shifted. I didn't know what, exactly, but I got the impression I'd broken through some barrier with Kiaya. That there'd been a wall between us—maybe between her and everyone she met—and something about our conversation had put a hole in it. Whatever the reason, I was relieved. Kyle was so much worse than he'd been the day before, and death couldn't be far off. When it happened, I would need someone to lean on just a little.

After making sure Kyle took some pills, I pulled my blonde hair back to get it out of my face and brushed my teeth, but that was all I bothered doing before putting my flip-flops on. I needed coffee, and while the stuff they had at the diner wasn't Starbucks, it was going to have to do.

It was barely seven when I stumbled out of the motel room, but I still had to pause when the bright light nearly blinded me.

Kiaya stepped out behind me, shooting a look toward the bed where Kyle thrashed before pulling the door shut.

"Where are you going?" she asked, keeping her voice low

even though we were outside now.

"Coffee." I nodded to the diner across the street. "Breakfast, too, if you want it."

She shook her head. "I don't need anything."

"Not even coffee?"

Kiaya shook her head again.

"I barely slept last night, and I know it couldn't have been much better for you. You sure you don't need a pick-me-up?"

"I can get through without it. Plus, I don't want to run out of money." She looked down. "This trip is going to take longer than I thought it would."

"Kiaya," I said, "it's coffee from a diner. How much can it be? Two bucks?"

When she looked up, her brown eyes were narrowed. "To some people, two dollars is a lot."

Two dollars? I couldn't remember a time when I didn't have two bucks to throw away. Even when I was little, my parents would stop at every quarter candy machine we passed so I could get my sugar fix. A side effect of being the long-awaited miracle child they'd been praying for.

I almost said this out loud, but something about the expression of pride and determination on Kiaya's face made me swallow the words. Instead, I said, "It's on me."

"You don't have to—"

I cut her off. "Consider it an apology for kicking you so much last night."

Kiaya hesitated, but after a second managed a small smile. "Yeah, okay, thanks."

"No problem." I waved my phone at her. "Text if you change your mind and decide you want something else."

I turned to leave but stopped when she said, "Rowan, I don't have your number."

Of course she didn't, because I'd never given it to her.

"I think I'm losing my mind," I said, turning back to face her.

"It's been a stressful few weeks," she replied.

"Yeah." I sighed.

FAR from HOME

Shaking my head, I rattled off my number, and she typed it in, her fingers flying across her phone's screen with expert speed. When she was done, she nodded and tucked it in her pocket.

Before I could turn away, the door to a nearby motel room opened, and the man I'd seen the night before stepped out. The early morning sunlight seemed to accentuate his gray eyes as he scanned the parking lot, making them look dangerous, and he wore a hardness about him that was impossible to miss.

He paused, the door behind him still open, and a second later two other people stepped out, a guy and a girl. They were a lot younger than he was, college age, and I couldn't think of a single place where the three of them would look at home together. While the older man was hard and rough, the other guy looked more like someone I'd see playing football with his friends on the weekend, and the girl was small with big, brown eyes that radiated innocence. Even stranger was the fact that she was Indian, and the college age guy was black, and the older man's body language made it seem like he wasn't too pleased with the company he was keeping. Although why they were sleeping in the same room was beyond me.

"Get the doc," the older man said, nodding to the motel room next to theirs without looking at the other two. "Axl won't be comin', but the doc's gotta be hungry."

As if sensing my gaze on him, the man turned his focus to me, and his lips twitched with the hint of a grin.

"Well, lookie what we got here," he said, eyeing me from head to toe. "We got ourselves another blondie. Just our luck, too. Looks like we're gonna have an openin' here real soon."

I crossed my arms, suddenly very sorry I hadn't put on a bra.

The younger guy rolled his eyes before jogging over to the other motel room but said nothing.

At my side, Kiaya shifted like she, too, was uncomfortable by the way the older man's gaze zeroed in on me.

As if noticing her for the first time, he turned his focus on her, his mouth turning down, and my spine stiffened. He didn't say anything, but he didn't need to. His thoughts were as clear as the blue sky above our heads. I wasn't totally sure if I even liked

Kiaya, but thinking this asshole was judging her because her skin was browner than his made me want to punch him in the nose.

I turned my back on him, grabbing Kiaya's arm. "Go back in and sit with Kyle. I'll be back soon."

She had to forcefully tear her gaze from the man with the steely gray eyes, and I was a little happy to see the fierce light in her eyes. Somewhere deep inside, Kiaya had spunk.

"Forget him," I said, keeping my voice low.

She glanced his way once and headed back to the room, saying nothing.

I didn't look at him again before heading across the parking lot.

5

The diner was brimming with activity just like it had been the night before, but something about it had changed. I couldn't put my finger on it at first, and when I paused just inside the door to look around, the feeling that something was off grew. The booths were just as full, the waitresses just as haggard, but there was less urgency in the air. More terrifying were the expressions most of the customers wore. Defeat and hopelessness were prevalent, but even worse were the people who looked like they could hardly hold their heads up. It wasn't loss or despondence, but illness. It was written in every line of their bodies. In their red eyes and noses, their shoulders, shaking from fever chills, their sniffling and constant swallowing as if trying to fight against the raging soreness in their throats. It reminded me of how Kyle had acted in the car when he first started showing symptoms, and it made me want to turn and run. Which was just dumb. I was already exposed, and there was nothing I could do about it.

Instead of running, I took a deep breath and forced myself to move farther into the diner.

There was a line at the counter since all the booths were occupied, so I took my place at the end of it, trying my best to ignore the coughs echoing through the air. It was impossible.

A few seconds later, the door opened behind me, bringing with it a burst of hot air and the ding of a bell, and I turned as the three people I'd seen outside the motel walked in. There was another man with them, but nothing about his presence made the group look any more at home together. The new guy was white, like the older man, but tall and gangly, almost awkward and somewhat alien in appearance. Even so, his big, brown eyes, although filled with exhaustion, were intelligent and alert as he took the place in, his frown telling me he had the same impression I'd had when first walking in.

The older of the four, the man who'd called me Blondie, spotted me and grinned. "There she is. Thought you'd gotten away from me."

Behind him, the others shifted and looked away, acting like they were afraid to be associated with him, but said nothing.

"Just getting breakfast," I said then turned my back on him, hoping he'd take the hint and realize I wasn't interested in talking.

Thankfully, he seemed to, but that didn't stop the group from talking amongst themselves, and in the absence of anything else to do, I couldn't help eavesdropping.

"How's Vivian this morning?" the girl asked.

"Same as last night," one of the men—the tall one, I was pretty sure—answered.

A grunt followed—the asshole. "Shoulda left her ass on the side of the road. Waste of time."

"You would have been leaving your brother behind, too," the tall man responded. "He hasn't left her side."

"He's always been too soft. It's gonna get him killed in this world."

"He's kind," a small, feminine voice responded.

The asshole only snorted.

"How long do you think it will be?" the fourth person asked.

"Not long," the tall man replied, sounding despondent. "The longest I've seen them last after showing symptoms is forty-eight hours, and that's pushing it. Usually, it's less than twenty-four."

The group lapsed into silence.

FAR from HOME

It was clear by their conversation that, like us, they'd stopped here because someone in their group was sick, but something about the tall man's words stuck out. He sounded like he'd seen people die before. And not a few, either. A lot.

Against my better judgment—I really didn't want to encourage the asshole—I turned to face them, focusing on the tall man. "Do you know something about this thing?"

Four sets of eyes turned on me.

The tall guy cleared his throat. "Um, yeah. A lot, actually." He paused, frowning as he thought something through, then said, "Are you sure you want to know?"

"I think I need to know. The guy I'm traveling with is sick."

He exhaled and his shoulders slumped as if weighed down. "How long?"

"He started showing symptoms yesterday evening. Maybe around six o'clock."

The guy nodded slowly, his gaze moving to the ground. "He'll go fast, and it's going to be bad."

"How do you know?" I asked, prompting him.

"I'm a doctor, and I was working in Baltimore."

My back straightened. Maryland. Holy shit. That was so close to New York, so close to where this all started. And he was a doctor? My thoughts went to my dad, and I had to dig my nails into my palms. I couldn't even imagine what this guy had seen, and my dad was facing the same thing right now.

"Tell me everything you know," I said even though all I really wanted to do was run back to the hotel room and cover my head with a pillow so I could block all of this out.

He gave three quick nods, breathing in a few times before blowing out a long breath as if gearing himself up for something horrible. Then he began to talk. "They locked Baltimore down about eight weeks ago, a lot earlier than they're saying on the news. When that happened, all nonessential businesses were shut down, hospitals were overrun, and they had to set up temporary clinics in the schools. People were literally dying in the streets. Then it just stopped." He paused and shrugged, then shook his head like he still couldn't believe it had happened. "It's not contained the way they're claiming. It's more like everyone who was going to die from it already did. The best guess is that eighty to eighty-five percent of the population is going to die. If you get it, you die. The end. If not, you're immune."

"Immune?" I looked from him to the rest of his group, so out of place with one another but wearing identical expressions of gravity. "So, you're all immune?"

"We are," the college guy said. "Parv and I were in New York, going to school at Cornell."

New York. Holy shit.

"And obviously, I am," the doctor added.

I turned my attention to the asshole, who didn't look as much like an asshole with the expression of defeat twisting his features. "You?"

"Gotta wait," he said. "Blondie's been sick for a day now, and we ain't come down with it yet." He shrugged like it didn't matter, but his gray eyes said differently. It mattered. A lot.

I let out a deep breath and shifted when the line moved forward, trying to absorb this new information. Kyle was sick, which meant it was only a matter of time for him. Kiaya and I had about an eighty-five percent chance of coming down with it, according to this doctor—who sounded like he would know—but we hadn't had any symptoms yet. Did that mean something?

"How long?" I asked, turning back to the doctor. "How long after exposure does a person know?"

He exhaled, his eyes darting to the older guy—almost like he hated to say anything in front of him—before once again focusing on me. "Honestly? There's a lot to take into consideration. Like hygiene, for example. I saw a few people go for a week or more caring for the sick and not come down with it because they were diligent about wearing masks and gloves and washing their hands, but even with all the precautions the medical staff at the hospital took, eventually the virus still won. For the average person, I think you're good if twenty-four hours have passed since exposure and you haven't gotten sick."

The older man's back stiffened. "You shittin' me? You've known that this whole goddamn time and never told me?"

FAR from HOME

"I told Axl." The doctor looked down. "You never asked."

The other guy gave him a nasty look. "Never thought I'd hafta ask somethin' like that. If a man's waitin' for death, you tell him when he's in the clear. It's the fuckin' considerate thing to do."

The doctor's cheeks were red, but the way he was staring at the floor told me he hadn't wanted this asshole to make it. Like he'd intentionally held the information back hoping it would make a difference.

Seemed like they had a bit of a stormy future in store for them if they planned on traveling together, but it didn't matter to me one way or the other. What mattered was that by this evening, Kiaya and I would know for sure if we were going to die. Ten hours from now we'd have our answer. It seemed both too soon and much too far away at the same time.

I turned back to face the line when it moved forward, and as if sensing that I needed to absorb the information, the group left me to my own thoughts. The news, I soon realized, wasn't all bad. Dad was at the hospital and he was exposed, and according to the doctor there was no real way to stop this thing from spreading. But Dad could be immune. He could be one of the lucky fifteen percent. If so, it didn't matter how many sick people he cared for, he wouldn't get the virus.

I had to pray that was the case. Not just for him, but for Mom as well. They had to make it.

My appetite had disappeared, so when I reached the counter, all I ordered were two cups of coffee. A few minutes later, steaming cups of energy in hand, I turned to leave but stopped beside the doctor.

"Thanks for telling me all that."

He exhaled. "I only wish I'd had better news."

"It isn't great," I admitted, "but I'd rather know."

"Yeah, I get that." He gave me a shaky smile. "Good luck."

"Thanks. You, too," I said, then gave the others a quick nod and headed off.

The bright day seemed at odds with the gloomy future facing me, and I found myself studying the people I passed as I made my way across the street and motel parking lot, headed for our room. Their expressions were nearly identical to the people inside the diner. Hopeless and weary, many of them looking like they were ready to keel over at any moment.

A guy in his mid-twenties drew my attention, but it took a second to remember why he looked familiar. It was the guy I'd seen the night before, the one who'd been leaning against the Coke machine. Now he was sitting in a chair outside one of the nearby motel rooms, a phone in his hand, and in the light of day I was able to better appreciate his broad, muscular shoulders. They were slumped in defeat, but powerful-looking nonetheless.

As if sensing me staring, the guy looked up, and his gaze captured mine. His eyes were pale blue and piercing in the early morning sunlight, but filled with sadness. Not sick, not defeated, just desolate.

I looked away when my scalp prickled and kept walking.

The parking lot was nearly full, and I saw people sleeping in more than one vehicle I passed. Probably, they'd gotten here only to discover every hotel in town was full and had chosen to spend the night in their cars rather than keep driving. It was even possible a lot of them had been unable to drive.

Thank God we'd gotten here when we did.

I passed a gray sedan with a man behind the wheel, his eyes sickly and sad as he stared out the windshield. He was trembling, probably raging with fever, and it only took one glance to know he was nearing the end.

Just like it did with Kyle when I slipped back into our motel room.

Kiaya was beside him, wiping his sweaty forehead with a washcloth as he writhed and moaned, and I found myself praying he'd go soon. Not just for us, although I had to admit I was anxious to get moving again, but for him as well. He was a nice kid and didn't deserve to suffer like this. I wasn't sure anyone did.

Kiaya looked up when I shut the door, her eyes looking twice as big, and swallowed. "He's worse."

"He's only going to get worse," I said.

FAR from HOME

Her eyebrows jumped, so I nodded to the other side of the room. It wasn't big—just a typical motel room—and I wasn't sure if Kyle would even be able to focus enough in his delirious state to understand me, but I still wanted to shield him from the worst of it if I could.

Kiaya got up, leaving the washcloth on his head, and followed me to where the bathroom sink sat. Like a lot of hotels, it was in the main room rather than with the toilet and tub, but even so, it was far enough away that we would be able to talk.

I passed her a cup, and she gave me a grateful nod, and for a moment we just stood in silence, each of us taking a couple sips as if wanting to avoid facing the truth.

But avoiding it was impossible, so after a few minutes I let out a deep sigh and said, "I met some people in the diner who came from out east, close to where this all started. They had some information."

Kiaya said nothing as I laid out everything the doctor had said, her expression barely changing. Maybe she was as relieved as I was to have a few more details and a better idea of what we were facing, or maybe she'd already accepted the truth. That this virus was the end of everything we'd ever known.

"So, Kyle will die today?" she said when I'd finished talking.

I nodded.

"And by the end of the day, we'll know if we're going to die?"

I nodded again.

Kiaya exhaled, and her expression grew dark, but she squared her shoulders as well. "At least we know."

"Yeah," I said and looked back toward Kyle. "At least we know."

"We can take turns sitting with him," Kiaya said, drawing my focus back to her. "That way we don't have to be stuck here all day."

Thinking about being able to occasionally escape the horror of Kyle's death made me feel a little lighter. As awful as I felt about it, I didn't want to have to stay at his side the whole day. I would, because no one deserved to die alone, but that didn't mean I had to like it. He seemed to be unable to rest, and the pain must have been awful, because even when he did drift off, he moaned and thrashed. It was torture to listen to.

"I can take the first watch," I said, although what I really wanted to do was run from the room and never look back.

Kiaya gave me a grateful smile. "Thank you."

All I could do was nod.

Kiaya showered and changed then disappeared from the room with her textbook while I spent the next few hours playing nurse, a role I wasn't the least bit used to or comfortable with. I forced ice chips into Kyle's mouth, even running the cubes over his dry, cracked lips in hopes of easing some of his discomfort. His skin burned like there was a fire raging inside him, so I wiped his face with a cold washcloth in a futile attempt to cool him down.

By the time Kiaya returned to relieve me, I was ready to scream. It made me feel horrible and selfish, but I couldn't help it. The room had gotten stuffy despite the air conditioning, and my hair clung to the back of my neck while every inch of my body was grimy with sweat. There was an undeniable sickness to the air, too, and I felt like I was breathing it in. It wouldn't matter—either I was immune or I wasn't—but filling my lungs with the tainted air had me jumpy and desperate for oxygen that wasn't teeming with germs, and the second the door opened and Kiaya stepped in, I was on my feet.

"You're back," I said, the words coming out sounding more like an accusation than the desperation I'd meant to convey.

As usual, Kiaya showed very little emotion when she nodded. "Sorry, I got busy reading and lost track of time."

She tossed her textbook on the nearby bed—I couldn't figure out why she'd bothered with it—and I was able to see the cover for the first time. Physics. It sounded like the most unlikely reading material to get lost in.

"It's okay." I glanced toward Kyle, who was having a rare moment of silent agony. "I'm just going stir crazy."

"I get it," she said then nodded to the door. "Take a break. I'll be here."

FAR from HOME

My gaze moved to the bathroom, and I cringed when I thought about how filthy I was, but I just couldn't handle the thought of staying in the room a minute longer. Not even to shower. It wasn't like me, I was always made up and clean and put together, and stepping toward the door and away from the shower wasn't exactly easy, but I told myself it didn't matter. The world was falling down around me, and I didn't have anyone to impress.

"I'll be back in a couple hours," I said, pausing at the door. "I'll bring dinner."

Kiaya nodded, but her focus was already on Kyle. "Okay."

Stepping out of the dark motel room and into the bright, Texas day was shocking to my system. It was like I'd stepped into another dimension, because the bright, sunny day greeting me shouldn't exist in the same world as the death and suffering I'd just left behind.

I squinted and lifted my hand to my forehead, trying to block out the light as I looked around. The parking lot was just as full as it had been earlier, but there seemed to be fewer people out and about. There was an ambulance parked to my right, its lights off but its back doors open. One of the rooms also had its door open as well, and the muscled guy I'd seen earlier was sitting beside it, in the same chair as before. He wore an identical expression on his face as three exhausted looking EMTs carried a stretcher out of the room. A black body bag was strapped to it.

Without thinking about it, I found myself moving in that direction, my heart beating faster until it pounded in my ears. I'd only taken a few steps when the inside of the ambulance came into view, and the sight made me freeze. There were other bags inside. A lot of them. They were piled up, one on top of the other like a pyramid of death.

My stomach convulsed, and I turned away from the sight only to find my gaze focused on a gray sedan. I'd seen it earlier, had noticed the man behind the wheel who was clearly sick and suffering. Not anymore. Now he was unmoving, his head back and his eyes closed, all the life drained out of him. His body nothing but a shell.

It was heartbreaking, devastating. Seeing this stranger alone in his car, probably far away from everyone who loved him. Did they know where he was? Would they survive this virus only to spend the rest of their lives wondering if he was okay?

Was that Mom's fate? Dad's? Mine?

I pulled my phone out of my back pocket and hit the button, lighting up the screen and revealing a picture from last spring break. I was standing on the beach with a group of friends, all of us in tiny bikinis. We were smiling, our arms around one another as the ocean shimmered at our backs. It seemed like another lifetime.

According to my phone, it was a little after three o'clock. I still felt fine. My head pounded, but it probably had more to do with stress, because I had no other symptoms. No sore throat, no aching bones, no runny nose. I'd felt worse after a night of partying.

Did that mean I was okay?

"God," I mumbled, still staring at the time, "let me be okay. Let me get home to find my parents okay."

I clicked the button, and my phone went black. Three more hours, and I could feel more confident in my fate. Then I would call my mom.

6

As much as I dreaded it, I headed back to our room around seven-thirty, two burgers in hand. The sun was getting low, moving toward the horizon and painting the sky bright colors that contrasted with the dark mood hanging over me. I was so focused on it that I'd made it halfway across the parking lot before I noticed Kiaya. She was sitting on the ground beside our door, her knees pulled up and her arms wrapped around them, hugging them to her chest. She was watching me, her eyes for once not empty, and the expression in them told me everything I needed to know.

"He's gone," I said when I was still five feet away.

She nodded as she pulled herself to her feet. "About twenty minutes ago. I was going to come looking for you, but I just—" Her voice broke.

"I get it." I exhaled, not sure what else to say about Kyle, but knowing there was a question I needed to ask her. "How do you feel?"

"Fine," she said with a shrug. "At least physically. You?"

"Same," I replied flatly.

The burgers were hot, and the greasy scent strong enough

to make my stomach growl, but it felt so wrong. Being hungry when Kyle would never eat again. Plus, where would we eat? I couldn't even imagine going into the room, let alone eating in there. It was too sick and twisted.

Kiaya's gaze was focused on the bag of food, and I could tell she was also struggling with what to do next. Maybe it was wrong or maybe it was just human nature, but I couldn't let the food go to waste. Especially not with the way things were. Who knew when we'd be able to get a hot meal again? Who knew what we'd face once we got on the road?

I scanned the area, my gaze landing on the fenced-in pool in the center of the parking lot. I'd barely given it a thought before now, too focused on death and illness, but suddenly the crystal blue water with the shimmering pinks and oranges of the sunset reflecting off it looked inviting. Even better, there were a couple tables beside it where we could sit and eat, then discuss our next move.

"This way," I said, nodding toward the pool.

Kiaya followed me without comment, and I found my gaze moving to where the ambulance had been earlier, thinking about the body bags I'd seen and also about the guy. Our deadline for getting sick had come and gone, which was more than a relief, but with it had come a new and equally terrifying question. Were we alone? I didn't think so. The people in the diner, the group who'd told me about the virus, had been immune, and the muscled guy had looked healthy. That was something, at least. Although what, I didn't yet know. I just liked knowing Kiaya and I wouldn't be the only two people to survive this thing.

We settled around a table beside the pool and ate our burgers in silence. I felt like it should have been one of those moments I'd read about where a person ate on autopilot, barely tasting their food because the heaviness of the situation they found themselves in was too great, but it wasn't. The burger was thick and greasy and utterly delicious, and I savored every bite. Kiaya, too, seemed to be enjoying it, and for a few minutes, we were able to focus on the act of eating and push everything else aside.

I finished first, balling the wrapper up when I had, the

FAR from HOME

crinkling of the paper seeming loud in the silence surrounding us. A few minutes later, Kiaya took her last bite and did the same, and when she looked up and our eyes met, the uncertainty and tension came screaming back.

"What now?" she asked, her voice quiet.

"We need to call someone to get the body. Let them worry about how to get him home." I winced because even to my ears it sounded callous, but to be honest, I was just ready to be done with the responsibility of taking care of Kyle.

Kiaya nodded, and her hair, once again pulled into a ponytail, bobbed. "Yeah, okay. Who, though?"

"There was an ambulance here earlier," I told her. "Removing bodies."

She shuddered and wrapped her arms around herself. "Bodies?"

"Yeah," was all I could say.

I stood, pushing my chair back harder than I needed to, and the metal legs scraped against the cement. The sounded echoed through the air, making me look around the way I had in my dorm room. It also had my scalp prickling as I remembered the feeling from that day. The fear that someone was sneaking up on me, the terror of being all alone and stalked. Like Kiaya, I shivered.

"The guy in the office can probably tell us who to call," I said, working to hide my unease.

"Good idea," she replied

She stood as I headed for the gate, following me away from the pool and across the parking lot to the motel's office. We passed the Coke machine where only last night I'd had my little breakdown, and once again I thought about the guy, wondering who he'd been traveling with. Who he'd lost.

The same man who'd been behind the desk the night before looked up when we walked into the office, but now his eyes were bloodshot and sickly. As always, it made me want to shy away, and I had to remind myself we were in the clear. Kiaya and I were going to be okay. At least in regard to the virus.

"We need a body removed," I said, wanting to get right to the point.

The man turned his head and let out a hacking cough before saying, "No dice. They stopped answering calls an hour ago. Recording says they're all sick."

"All sick?" Kiaya repeated.

"In case you haven't noticed, there's a bug going around," the man said bitterly.

Kiaya's back stiffened, and the same light I'd seen earlier when the asshole looked her up and down flashed in her eyes.

I stepped in front of her before she could say anything. "What are we supposed to do?"

"Get in your car and pray this thing don't catch up with you," he growled.

He had to turn his head away again, but this time the coughing went on longer. A lot longer.

Kiaya shifted when it didn't stop, looking uncomfortable, and I found myself stepping back despite the pep talk I'd given myself.

When the man finally stopped coughing, he focused feverish eyes on us but said nothing.

"We need to get a night of rest before we go," I said, focusing on Kiaya. "Right?"

"Yeah…"

She let the word hang, and I knew why. We couldn't sleep in that room with Kyle's body. It was too creepy.

I focused on the man. "Do you have another room we can have? Just for the night?"

"Got a couple recently vacated rooms." He lifted his eyebrows, letting me know why they were recently vacated, and I shuddered. "They ain't been cleaned, and I got nobody to do it, but I can give you fresh sheets if you're willing to change the beds yourself."

It sounded awful, but a lot less awful than sleeping in the room with Kyle's body.

I looked toward Kiaya. "What do you think?"

"I can't drive tonight," she said. "I'm exhausted."

"Me too," I replied then turned back to the man. "We'll take it."

FAR from HOME

He nodded, and when I reached into my purse, waved me off. "Look at me. What am I gonna do with your money? I'll be dead in a day. Keep it. I hope it gets you where you need to go."

My hands dropped to my sides. "Thank you."

I hadn't thought this gruff, unfriendly man could have made me cry, but I'd been wrong. Tears pooled in my eyes as he headed to the back room, refusing to be held at bay, and I swiped them away. It was touching, finding kindness in the least probable place when you least expected it.

We left the office, fresh sheets in hand, and headed to room eighteen. It was right next to the one I'd seen the muscled guy sitting outside of only a couple hours earlier, and I couldn't help wondering if it had been his friends who'd died here.

The room was stuffy and stank of sweat and sickness, so we propped the door open using a chair. We got to work stripping one of the beds, then worked together to remake it, not saying a word. We were still going to have to go to our old room to get our things, and I was mentally preparing myself for it. Kiaya probably was, too. Having to see Kyle, no longer suffering but motionless and drained of life, was going to suck.

The sun had set completely by then, lowering the temperature significantly. It cooled my sweaty skin, causing goose bumps to pop up on my bare arms and legs, but was actually refreshing after the long, hot day. We left the door propped open since no one was around and we had nothing in the room for anyone to steal, then headed across the parking lot. Kiaya was as quiet and thoughtful as usual, something I had almost gotten used to. It wasn't like I was in a talkative mood, anyway.

We'd just reached our motel room when the door next to us burst open and someone rushed out. I recognized the doctor from the diner and stopped walking.

"Doctor!"

He skidded to a stop almost reluctantly, his eyes wide and frantic as he looked around. When he saw me, it seemed to take a few seconds for him to register who I was. Once he had, he blinked and said, "You're okay."

"Fine." I shrugged. "No symptoms."

"That's good," he said. "Good."

He seemed oddly distracted, and I could only assume it had to do with his sick friend.

"Your friend, is she dead?"

"No." He let out a slightly manic, slightly exhausted laugh. "In fact, I think she has something else. Strep throat, maybe? I'm not positive, but I'm going to get her some antibiotics just in case."

"That's great," I said, but my voice fell flat. I couldn't help thinking of Kyle, dead in our motel room, his body growing colder by the second.

"Your friend?" the doctor asked. "Is he..."

He acted like he couldn't finish the sentence.

"Died," I said. "A couple hours ago."

The doctor's shoulders slumped. "I'm sorry."

"Me, too."

He let out a breath and took a step away from us. "I need to go."

"I know. Good luck."

"Thank you," he said before turning away and dashing toward a big, dark blue Nissan Armada.

I turned back to find Kiaya watching him.

"That was the doctor you met?" she asked.

"Yeah."

All she did was nod before heading for our old room.

We paused outside the closed door to gather our courage, sharing a look of support but saying nothing. Kiaya had the key out, and she took a deep breath as she slid it into the lock. She turned it, and the door clicked, and I braced myself, not sure what to expect. The stink of death, maybe? It had only been a few hours, but I had no clue how long it took for a body to start to smell. I'd never needed to know. Why would I? Now, I found myself wishing I had some knowledge of the decomposition process. It wasn't like Kyle's was the last body I was going to run into. With eighty-five percent of the population dropping from this thing, there were bound to be more than a few dead bodies in my future. As much as I hated to admit it.

FAR from HOME

"You ready?" Kiaya asked.

I nodded as I sucked in a deep breath, giving myself a silent pep talk as well.

She pushed the door open and stepped inside, and I forced myself to follow. The room looked exactly the same as it had when I left a few hours ago. My suitcase was on the floor, flipped open and the once neat contents ransacked. Kiaya's small duffle bag sat beside the old tube television, none of the contents visible, and her textbook was right where she'd tossed it. Kyle's book bag sat on the floor beside the bed, untouched since he'd been too sick to do anything but sleep and moan. He, too, hadn't moved. Not that I would have expected him to. His body lay in the bed, the thin sheet pulled up to cover his head. I could only assume Kiaya had done that after he'd taken his last breath, and I was both touched by her thoughtfulness and thankful I didn't have to see him.

"Let's get our stuff and get the hell out of here," I said, hurrying to my suitcase.

Thankfully, I hadn't taken much out of it, and after grabbing my toiletry items off the sink and tossing them in, I was able to zip my suitcase and right it. Kiaya, having very little to begin with, was already waiting by the door, and I headed her way. On instinct, though, I paused to give Kyle one last look.

"He was a nice guy," I said, suddenly feeling like he deserved a few words even if I didn't really know what to say.

"He was," Kiaya agreed.

"I promised I'd call his family." I sighed at the memory. "I don't want to. I don't want to have to tell them he's dead."

"I know," she whispered.

I tore my gaze from Kyle's body so I could focus on her. "Do you think it matters?"

"I think," she said slowly, as if trying to decide what to say, "they might not even be alive, but a promise is a promise."

"Yeah," I replied, letting out a deep sigh. "You're right."

"I can do it for you. If you want." She shrugged when I gave her a questioning look. "I know you need to call your parents, and it's not like I have anyone to check in with."

69

"Are you sure? It's going to suck."

"I'm sure," she said.

"Thanks," I mumbled as I knelt beside his book bag and dug through the small pockets until I located his cell phone.

I hit the button, but having gone nearly two days without being charged, it was, of course, dead, so I slipped it in my back pocket as I stood. Before turning to leave, I paused to look at Kyle one final time. Through the sheet, only the outline of his body was visible, which I was more than grateful for. It was creepy enough without actually having to see him. Like something from a movie.

A shiver ran down my spine, and I turned away from him.

"Let's get out of here," I said, grabbing my suitcase.

Wordlessly, Kiaya followed me out, and the door shut behind her, the click bouncing off the walls of the motel and echoing through the night.

The only sound as we made our way back across the parking lot was the pounding of our footsteps and the scrape of my suitcase's wheels against the pavement. It wasn't until that moment that I realized just how quiet it had gotten. There was no distant hum of cars, no voices or music, or drone of an airplane flying over. Even the animals had fallen silent as if awed into muteness by the sudden decimation of the human race. It was eerie and disturbing.

"It's so quiet," I whispered, keeping my voice low as if afraid the sound would wake the dead or something equally ridiculous.

"I know," Kiaya said, her response as quiet as my statement had been.

We hadn't been gone long, but it had been enough time to air the room out a little, making me immediately feel better about sleeping where someone—or more than one person—had died.

The first thing I did was plug Kyle's phone in so Kiaya could make the dreaded call to his family. Part of me prayed they didn't answer, but I immediately felt selfish because I knew that was wishing they were dead. With eighty-five percent of the population on the way out, it wasn't even a long shot, but I still silently chastised myself for the thought.

FAR from HOME

"I'm going to call my mom," I said, waving the phone like Kiaya needed proof as I headed for the door.

"I'll be here," she replied.

I didn't bother going to the car before pulling Mom's number up. There was no one around to hear me anyway.

My grip on the phone tightened a little more with each ring while my heart pounded harder and faster. Thankfully, it cut off after the fifth one and Mom's voice, breathless and ringing with hope, followed.

"Rowan."

"It's me," I said, thinking about Kiaya calling Kyle's family and the hope his parents would feel at seeing his name light up the screen. I had to swallow before I could talk again. "I'm okay. How are you?"

"Scared. I haven't left the house, but it's so…dead outside. There's nothing happening, and it's terrifying."

"I know," I said, fighting to keep my emotions in check so I didn't scare her even more. "It's the same here."

"Tell me you're on the road." Mom's voice shook. "Tell me you're on your way home."

"Not yet. Soon." I swallowed. "Kyle died, so we can leave tomorrow. Thankfully, Kiaya and I are healthy."

"Thank God," she said, the words sounding a little bit like a prayer. "I'm sorry for his family, but I'm so grateful you're still okay."

"We are. Both of us. We just need to get a good night's sleep before heading out, but I plan to get moving early."

"Good." She exhaled, and I could tell she was struggling to stay calm. "I've been so worried, Rowan."

The echo of a door shutting drew my attention, and I turned to find the asshole from the diner standing outside his motel room holding a Coke can.

His gaze was on me, when I said, "I know, Mom, but I'll be there soon. I promise I'll get home to you."

"I know you will," she said, but she sounded more like she was trying to convince herself.

We talked for a few more minutes, and I did my best to avoid

71

the gaze of the creep from the diner, but he seemed intent on listening to my conversation. He wasn't doing anything, really, just leaning against the wall outside his room like he couldn't stand being in there anymore. Maybe it was the company, or maybe he just wanted to be on the road.

By the time Mom and I said our goodbyes, after I assured her over and over again that I'd be careful, I was more than ready to get back to my own room. Instead of going right away, though, I pulled up Dad's contact info and hit send, crossing my fingers despite how childish it was. Just like the last time I'd tried, the phone didn't even ring, but instead went right to voicemail. Shit.

I hit end without leaving a message and headed for our room. The asshole hadn't looked away from me once, and it was starting to give me the creeps. I did everything I could to avoid looking at him as I hurried off.

Inside, Kiaya was stretched out on the one bed we'd bothered remaking, and she looked up when I walked in. "Everything okay?"

"Yeah. She's healthy, and thankfully, she took my advice and stayed inside." I set my phone on the table. "Now I just need a shower. I feel disgusting."

I'd only taken one step when she said, "I called them."

I froze. "Kyle's family?"

Kiaya nodded. "They didn't answer, so I left a message."

"You left a message telling them he was dead?"

"No. I told them to call me. If they haven't called by the time we leave, I'll just take the phone with me. It isn't like he needs it."

"True," I said, nodding. "Thanks."

"I don't know if we'll hear anything, but at least we gave it a shot."

"Yeah." I let out a long sigh, suddenly feeling exhausted, then continued my trek to the bathroom. "I'll be out in a minute."

I showered, taking extra time to allow the sweat to rinse off my skin despite the lukewarm water. The towels were thin and scratchy and too small to wrap completely around my body, but I was too exhausted to really care. I ended up pulling my pajamas

FAR from HOME

on even though my skin was still damp and my hair was dripping.

When I dropped onto the bed beside Kiaya, I felt certain I wouldn't be able to get up for a week.

"I'm exhausted," I mumbled into the lumpy pillow.

"Me, too." Kiaya scooted down and pulled the covers up to her chin. "Let's just go to bed. The sooner we get to sleep, the sooner we can get out of here."

"Agreed," I said, shifting so I could crawl under the covers.

A second later, the light clicked off.

"Goodnight, Rowan," Kiaya said.

"Goodnight," I mumbled.

I was asleep in what felt like seconds.

7

I woke before Kiaya, and despite my experience the previous morning, once again stumbled from the room without getting a bra. There seemed to be fewer and fewer people each time I left the room, and in the light of everything else going on, it just didn't seem important—or worth it—to bother with putting one on.

Like I'd expected, the motel parking lot was deserted of people even though not a single parking spot was empty. After seeing the man in the gray sedan, I did my best to avoid looking into the cars I passed. There were bodies in more than one of them—of that, I was positive—but knowing and seeing were two different things. I was determined to get away from this motel without actually seeing any more.

The diner felt deserted compared to the other times I'd been here. The booths were mostly empty, and there was no line at the counter, and even the number of waitresses had been reduced. Where before I'd spotted at least five, now there were only two, and one of them didn't look healthy.

"Two coffees," I said to the woman at the counter.

Her red eyes seemed to have trouble focusing, and she

blinked three times before finally nodding. On the other side of the room, the other waitress paused to stare at her co-worker, her expression filled with fear and worry. Unlike the woman in front of me, she looked healthy, although exhausted. She'd probably been running ragged over the last few weeks, had possibly even been wishing for a break in the crowds. This probably wasn't what she'd wanted.

I looked around, studying the other people in the room, and was unsurprised to discover that of the dozen or so customers sitting at booths, not a single one of them looked well. People were slumped in corners, some coughing, some feverish, all of them looking like they should be tucked into bed, not sitting in a diner.

They probably had nowhere to go.

The waitress came back with two cups and set them on the counter. "Five dollars."

I nodded as I dug the money out, and I only felt a little guilty when I didn't give her a tip. I needed the money, but in a few hours, she wouldn't.

Outside, I hurried back across the street to our room, a cup in each hand, but had only made it halfway when I veered right instead, heading for my car. I wanted to get out of here as fast as possible, but it hadn't occurred to me until now to check the gas gauge. Kyle had been driving when we got here, and I wasn't sure how much gas we had left.

I set the cups on the roof so I could unlock the door then slid inside. The needle was on E, but I knew I needed to start the car to get a proper reading. Too bad once I had, the needle only lifted a tiny bit. The tank was almost empty.

"Shit," I said, turning the car off and yanking the key free.

I'd need to drive down the street and find a gas station. Hopefully, there was one close. We got damn lucky we hadn't run out on the way here.

I slammed the door and relocked the car before grabbing the cups off the roof, but froze when I turned and came face to face with the asshole. He seemed to be everywhere these days.

"Mornin'," he said, and I couldn't help noticing that some of his earlier hardness seemed to have disappeared.

Still, I kept my greeting stiff so he didn't see my response as an invitation. "Morning."

He looked me up and down, puckering his lips in thought before saying, "You ain't sick."

"No," I replied. "I'm not."

"Lucky." His gaze moved past me to my car, and my body stiffened. "You headed out soon?"

"That's the plan," I said against my better judgment. I wasn't really interested in this man knowing anything more about me, but it seemed stupid to lie when he'd just seen me in the car.

His gray eyes focused on me again. "Your friend die?"

"He did," I said, quieter than before.

"So it's just you and this other girl? All alone?"

I stiffened even more, but something in his expression made me answer. "It is."

The man puckered his lips again and a second later spit. A glob of brownish saliva landed on the ground between us, making my stomach contort. The pain only got worse when he took a step closer to me. I wanted to back away, but there was nowhere to go. Quickly, my mind played through what I'd do if he decided to attack me. I'd throw the coffee at him. It was hot and might give me a chance to get away. If I screamed loud enough, maybe someone would come to my rescue. It was my only shot.

The man's gaze darted around, almost like he was checking to see if anyone was paying attention, then he focused on me again, and the way his gray eyes flashed reminded me of clouds before a particularly violent storm. "I know I can be a hard ass, but what I got to say is important. Hear me?"

Part of me wanted to tell him to go to hell, but another part tingled from the urgency in his voice, so I whispered, "Okay."

He nodded once in approval. "The first thing you gotta do is get you some supplies. Survival stuff and campin' gear. And weapons."

"Weapons?" I repeated, dumbfounded.

"Yeah," he snapped, but more out of urgency than impatience. "Don't be as dumb as that blonde hair makes you look. Got it?

The first thing to go when shit hits the fan is law, and you're goin' east, which means you're headed for a world of trouble. There's a lot of nasty folks out there, and with nothin' to stop 'em, they're gonna be on the prowl. You and that girl is gonna be travelin' alone, which ain't a good place to be. You gotta be prepared. You gotta be ready to defend yourself when the time comes."

The man standing in front of me radiated violence, which made his warning ten times more ominous. If he was worried, if he was telling me to watch my back, then things were really bad.

I had to swallow before I could say, "I've never shot a gun."

"Ain't much to it." He paused so he could turn his head and spit again. "Aim and shoot and pray the asshole in front of ya thinks you ain't worth the trouble." His gray eyes moved over me, and he frowned. "It'll be a long shot, but it's the best I can do for you. If you was headin' west…" He sighed and shook his head then muttered, "Two girls travelin' alone. You're gonna be a walkin' target."

"Why are you helping me?" I asked, unable to keep the question in. The little bit I'd seen of this guy didn't mesh with any of this. He didn't seem like the type who would put his neck on the line for others, or who would even give them more than a passing thought. Yet here he was, giving me advice.

"Let's just say I'm feelin' a tad generous at the moment." He sniffed and his lips puckered again. "Or maybe you remind me of somebody I used to know."

"A girlfriend?" I was still trying to understand this man.

"Naw. I'm old 'nough to be your daddy." He let out a gravelly laugh and shook his head. "Thank God I ain't never done that to the world." He blew out a long breath as he looked back toward the motel, not focusing on me when he said, "Had me a girlfriend for a bit, long time ago, and she had two girls. Cutest things I ever saw." His gaze moved back, studying me, but there was nothing in the look that made me uncomfortable this time. "One of 'em was blonde like you. She's probably 'bout your age, too."

"What happened to her?" I asked. "The girlfriend, I mean."

"Same thing that always happens." His upper lip curled. "She got to know me. Decided I wasn't worth the effort." He let out a snort that was half bitter, half ironic. "Don't matter no more. She's probably dead or will be soon."

"True," I mumbled, my thoughts on his warning more than on what he was saying now.

He had a point. I wasn't really big into zombie fiction, but even I'd paid enough attention to my friends' Facebook posts about *The Walking Dead* to know one thing. The zombies hadn't been the only bad guys on that show. Yes, it had been fiction, but it was based on reality, and what this guy was saying rang true. People were nasty, and there were a lot who spent their lives masquerading as normal people when deep down they were anything but. A twist of fate, and society disappeared, and now their darker selves were free to come out. It made sense, even if I hadn't thought about it before now.

"Thank you," I said after a few seconds of silence.

The man's eyebrows jumped in surprise, and his expression softened, giving me a glimpse of the person he'd probably been with those two little girls.

"You watch your back out there, ya hear?" he said.

"I will."

He nodded twice. "Good."

He turned away without another word and headed toward the diner, but had only gone a short distance before I called out, "What's your name?"

He didn't stop and didn't look back, but he did answer me. "Angus. Angus James."

People could surprise you, I knew that, but I hadn't expected him to be one of them. Not in a million years.

He'd just passed the pool when I turned my back on him, heading for our motel room. I'd only taken two steps when the door next to ours opened and the muscled man stepped out. His eyes were red, and every inch of him looked exhausted, but he seemed to be healthy still.

He saw me and stopped, watching me head his way like he thought I was coming to see him. His expression was so thoughtful and full of scrutiny it made my scalp prickle, and I tried to force myself to look away but couldn't.

"You're still here," he said when I was only six feet away.

"Not for long." I jerked my head behind me toward my car. "Heading out this morning. Just have to get gas."

I was just passing him when he said, "No gas."

I froze, turning his way, telling myself I'd heard him wrong because that couldn't possibly be true. Not when I wanted to get home so badly. "What did you say?"

"The gas stations in town are all out," he replied in a flat tone, as if he was talking about the weather and not the possible destruction of my plans.

My stomach dropped when I thought about what that might mean for us. He couldn't be right. He had to be lying.

"They can't be."

He gave me a thoughtful look. "They are, though."

For a moment, I could think of nothing to say, because what I needed had always mattered in my world. I needed new shoes? We had them that night. A new book bag? It was mine. Even things I hadn't needed had been mine for the asking, which made it inconceivable that this huge thing, which I needed so badly, was out of my reach.

"But I have to get home," I managed to say.

"And yet the world doesn't seem to care," he said, his tone dry.

I jerked away from his words. "You don't have to be an ass."

"I'm just being honest." He looked past me, blowing out a long breath. "Trust me, there's nothing in this godforsaken town. Nothing but bodies and more people waiting to die." His blue eyes snapped my way. "And people like us. Stranded and fucked."

For a moment, all I could do was stare at the guy with my mouth hanging open.

"There has to be a way," I finally got out.

"If you come up with any ideas, let me know." He exhaled and shook his head, his gaze moving over me as he did.

I nodded but barely registered what I was doing because I was too busy thinking about what the asshole had said and what this guy was saying and all the bodies in this motel and how we were in the middle of nowhere. We needed things, supplies and weapons, but could we get them here? This was a small town, and it wasn't like there was a Wal-Mart. In fact, I'd only seen a few businesses, nothing that would really help us.

I couldn't think, especially with this guy staring at me, so I headed for my room, waving one of the cups of coffee at him as I started walking. "I'll see you later."

"Yeah," he mumbled, but I didn't look back.

Inside, Kiaya was awake and dressed and sitting in a chair, her bag packed and resting at her feet. Seeing it made my stomach drop. I hated being the bearer of bad news more than anything.

She smiled when I handed her a cup. "Thanks. I'll pay you back, I promise."

I wasn't sure that it mattered anymore, but I nodded.

I needed to tell her we weren't going to be leaving, at least not yet, but I took a few minutes so we could both drink our coffee. My brain was groggy and muddled, and I needed to wake up a little before we tackled the next challenge.

A few minutes passed in silence, but it didn't take long before Kiaya had narrowed her eyes on me. I was caught. She could tell something was up. Knew I had news that was going to change our plans yet again.

"What is it?" she finally said.

I exhaled and slumped onto the bed. "The car is on empty, and apparently all the gas stations are as well."

Her back stiffened. "How do you know?"

"A guy I ran into mentioned it." I shook my head. "What's more, even if we were able to leave, I think we're totally unprepared for what we're about to face. I bought some road trip snacks, but not a lot. We need supplies, things that will help us if we get stranded in the middle of nowhere. Assuming we can find gas."

"What kind of supplies?" Kiaya asked.

I gnawed on my lip, trying to figure out what to say, then decided to just go for it. Repeating everything the asshole had said to me, I laid it all out for Kiaya. The more I talked, the more her expression darkened, but I couldn't tell what she was thinking. Up to now, she'd been so closed off most of the time, making it tough to get a read on her.

When I'd finished talking, I sat back and waited for her to respond.

She blew out a long breath like she'd been holding it, and genuine worry flashed in her eyes. "You're right. I should have thought about it. God knows I've seen the worst kind of people in my life."

For a moment, I said nothing, not sure if I should ask or let it go. Kiaya definitely wasn't one for sharing, something that had really irked me at first. Now I realized it was because I couldn't possibly understand the things she'd probably been through. My family had been the ideal. The kind featured on television. Kiaya, however, had never had that.

"Weapons…" She shook her head, her frown growing deeper. "We've already established that neither of us has ever been around guns, so even if we managed to get our hands on one—which seems like a long shot in this tiny town—we have no clue what we're doing."

"I know," I said. "I feel like I'd be more likely to shoot myself in the foot than anything."

Kiaya's eyebrows jumped. "You have amazing confidence in yourself."

Despite the dire circumstances we found ourselves in, her lips twitched. She was being sarcastic, I realized, poking fun to try to lighten the mood, and I appreciated it. Things were getting heavier by the hour, and it was making me tense.

A small laugh popped out of my mouth. "In most things, I'd say I'm pretty confident in my abilities, but being able to figure out a gun probably isn't one of them."

"Yeah," she said, the serious light returning to her eyes. "Weapons aside, we need to think about what we might face and plan for it. Things have gotten pretty quiet in this town, and odds are it's not going to get any better."

I started gnawing on my nails as I gave it some thought, barely aware that I was doing it. Just a few weeks ago, right before martial law, I'd gotten a manicure. What a waste of money.

I spit out a tiny sliver of fingernail before saying, "We should

FAR from HOME

try to stock up on food." I thought about how many hours of driving through the middle of nowhere it had taken to get us here, and how many more we'd face. A lot. "Water, too. Just in case."

"In case of what?" Kiaya asked.

"In case we get stranded," I replied.

She sat back, saying nothing.

"If only I'd watched more end of the world movies," I mumbled to myself, trying to think about what we might need.

"We're smart," Kiaya said. "We don't need fiction to figure this out. Right? We just have to think about what we might face."

"I guess," I replied, shrugging.

Was it even possible to really prepare for most of the population dying?

I WALKED TO THE END OF THE PARKING LOT AND STOPPED, LOOKING UP and down the road. The diner was across the street, but other than that, there were few businesses in sight. And not just in sight, either. I'd thumbed through the yellow pages in the motel room hoping to find a listing for a Wal-Mart or a similar store but had come up with nothing. The best shot we had at getting any of the supplies we needed was going to be one of the several gas stations in town, and that was assuming they were open, which was a long shot at best.

"What are you thinking?" Kiaya asked.

"That we're going to have to take a hike."

"A hike?"

I tore my gaze from the empty road in front of me and focused on Kiaya. "I don't want to drive the car anywhere, not with as low on gas as it is, which means walking. I could take some stranger's word for it that every gas station was out, but that would be stupid. I don't know him, and I have no reason to trust him."

83

"Why would he lie?" she asked.

I shrugged. "Why does anyone lie?"

"Different reasons."

"Exactly. There are a million reasons to lie, which means we can't know them all. The smartest thing to do is to check things out for ourselves."

"Okay." Kiaya nodded and turned to study the road the way I had a moment ago. "So, we walk to the gas stations and verify they're out. Then what?"

"If we happen to find some gas, we can walk back and get the car. If not… Well, I don't know. We'll have to cross that bridge when we come to it."

Kiaya gnawed on her bottom lip, worry flashing in her eyes.

"It's going to be okay," I said, feeling like I needed to reassure her. "I don't know how, but I do know I won't rest until we find a way out of this. If we have to walk or ride bikes or even horses, we will."

"Horses?" Kiaya asked doubtfully.

"I saw a listing in the phone book for a horse ranch. It was just a thought."

"I've never been on a horse."

"I haven't since I was a kid, and even then it was a guided ride." I exhaled. "But if it comes down to trying to figure it out or being stuck in this shithole, I'm willing to try."

"Me, too."

"According to the phone book, there are seven gas stations in Vega, so we better get moving," I said as I started walking.

Kiaya jogged to catch up.

The sun pounded down on us as we walked, neither of us talking. I could see the sign for the first gas station in the distance, probably only a few blocks down. It was a long shot, but I found myself whispering a silent prayer that the guy at the motel had been a compulsive liar.

Not a single moving car was in sight, and just like yesterday, the day was deathly silent. The emptiness that had fallen over the world felt like it belonged in a movie, not in reality, and I found myself suddenly wanting to scream just so there was noise.

FAR from HOME

Since I was pretty sure that would only freak me out even more, I decided instead to try to fill the silence with conversation.

"Tell me something about yourself," I said.

Despite how quiet she'd been since we met, Kiaya didn't hesitate to say, "What do you want to know?"

"Anything. I just need some noise to distract me."

"I get it." She blew out a long breath as if thinking then said, "I got a full ride to the University of Phoenix. I chose it because it was far away from Indiana and seemed like a totally different world. I never wanted to go back, haven't been back in two years." She paused before adding, "I'm not even sure why I'm going now."

"So, you really have no family?"

She shrugged. "I'm sure my mom is around somewhere, although I haven't seen her in years. My dad hasn't been in the picture since I was little, and I don't remember a thing about him. Not that it matters. I have no desire to see either of them."

"I'm sorry," I said, not sure what else to say.

"I'm not. Foster care wasn't always great, but it wasn't that bad for me. Or at least it could have been worse. I know it would have been worse if I'd stayed with my parents, so if nothing else, I'm thankful they decided I wasn't worth their time."

"I can't imagine that," I said, thinking about how different our experiences with parents had been. "I mean, my parents tried for years to have me. They wanted me more than anything, and once they brought me home, I became their everything. Their lives have literally revolved around me for the past twenty years."

Kiaya looked at me out of the side of her eye. "What's that like?"

"Depends on the day," I said, shrugging the way she had a few minutes ago. "Sometimes it's great because I basically get whatever I want. Other times it's suffocating because my mom's focus is always on me."

"And your dad?"

"He had his job," I said, barely noticing that I'd used the past tense. "Plus, it's different with a dad. It's not as all-consuming. I guess that's the best way to describe it."

We reached the gas station and paused next to one of the pumps. I couldn't tell just by looking at them whether there was gas, but the dark interior of the station didn't make me very hopeful.

"They look closed," Kiaya said as if reading my mind.

"Yeah."

I exhaled and closed my eyes, the urge to scream coming over me again. The midday sun was hot, and my skin was moist with sweat, my hair clinging to my neck and my shirt sticking to my back. By the time we returned to the motel I'd be a sweaty, burned mess. It would have been nice if I'd packed sunblock, but I hadn't thought about it. This wasn't how my trip was supposed to go. I should have been home by now, or at the very least getting close. Instead, I was stuck in the middle of nowhere with very little hope of getting out of here.

I was going to have to call my mom and let her know what was going on.

"We should keep moving," Kiaya said, jolting me from my thoughts.

"Yeah," I replied, sighing.

The next closest gas station was a few streets over and more than a mile away, so we headed off, following the directions on my phone. Once again, we were silent, but this time my brain was too full of thoughts and questions to really notice. I was too busy thinking about what we would find at the next gas station and the one after that, about the supplies we might need and how we were going to get hold of them, and about what was happening at home. I'd purposefully avoided asking Mom about Dad the night before, both because I hadn't wanted to upset her and because I'd wanted to shield myself, but the way my calls went right to voicemail was something I couldn't ignore. If he were alive, he would keep his phone charged. He would call Mom even if he didn't want to go home and risk exposing her. He hadn't done either of those things, which meant he had to be dead.

Movement caught my eye, and I turned, squinting as I peered through the large picture window of a nearby house. The glare made it tough to see at first, but after a moment, I saw it again. A figure just inside the house, standing at the window as if watching us.

"Someone is in there," I said, nodding to the house.

Kiaya followed my gaze and had just opened her mouth to reply when something banged against the window. We were fifteen feet or more away, but the sudden thud still made me jump.

"Shit." My hand went to my heart. "That scared me."

"I know." She shook her head, squinting like she was trying to make out the person better. "You think that was the point? That he was trying to scare us away?"

"I guess so. Why else would someone throw themselves against a window?"

"Well," Kiaya said, grabbing my arm and pulling me with her as she started walking again. "It worked."

"No shit," I muttered under my breath.

The next gas station was a repeat of the first, dark and empty with no one in sight, so I typed the address for the third one into Google maps. By then, I was past the point of hot. My mouth was dry, my head pounding from the combination of the heat and the sun, and I couldn't stop thinking about the pool back at the hotel. Diving into the water sounded amazing right about now.

A Coke machine at the side of the building caught my eye, so I dug my wallet out of my purse, nodding to it. "I need a drink. You?"

"Yeah," Kiaya said, her voice scratchy like she was feeling as parched as I was.

I found a couple dollar bills and tried to insert them into the machine, but nothing happened. Of course, the damn bill acceptor would be busted. I wasn't sure if I had enough change to get two drinks, but I dug through my purse anyway. Until this whole virus thing, I hadn't carried cash very often—everywhere took cards these days—and usually when I did, I ended up just tossing the change in that bottom of my purse, so it took a few minutes to locate enough coins for one drink.

"That's all I have," I said, holding my hand out for Kiaya to see. "You?"

She avoided looking at me, instead focusing on the machine.

"I only have bills."

"We can share?" I said.

"Yeah." Kiaya's head bobbed. "We can share."

"Cool." I turned back to the machine.

I slipped the first quarter in, and a second later it clanged into the change return at the bottom. I knew what that most likely meant—that the whole thing was out of order—but I put a second one in anyway. A clang followed.

"Shit," I muttered, scooping the quarters up.

Kiaya's eyes were narrowed on the building when I turned to look at her.

"What is it?" I asked.

She took a step closer to the gas station. "I think the power's out."

Following her gaze, I studied the building. The interior was dark, which I'd taken to mean the place was closed, but I now realized it was abnormally dark. The signs hanging in the window that should have been lit up weren't, and the refrigerators in the back of the store weren't illuminated the way they usually were either.

"You're right."

I turned so I could study the surrounding area, curious if the electricity was out in the whole town or just here. It was the middle of the day, though, and the sun was bright, so the streetlights weren't on, and at first I couldn't see anything else that would tell me one way or the other. Then I spotted the stoplights hanging over the intersection at the end of the street. They were dark.

"I think it's out everywhere," I said, pointing down the road.

"It must have just happened," Kiaya replied. "It was on at the motel."

I hadn't even thought about the motel, and the realization that we were going to get back to no power made me groan. "Shit. I guess there's no real point in checking out the other places on my list. I mean, even if they had gas, we wouldn't be able to get it without electricity. Which means we're stuck, and not just in the middle of nowhere anymore. We're stuck in a town full of rotting bodies with no chance of getting away and no power. Do you know how hot and smelly it's going to get?"

I was starting to think nothing was ever going to go my way again, and the thought brought on a wave of panic. I was used to having everything my way, and I didn't know how I would cope in a world where that wasn't the case. How would I survive? Could I adapt to this new reality? Suddenly, I was more unsure of the future than I'd ever been.

"It will be fine," Kiaya said, sounding so sure that I tried to grab hold of her certainty.

It didn't work.

"I don't see how," I said. "Unless you have an idea of how we can get some gas, we're either stuck or we walk."

"We can siphon it from other cars," she said, her voice quiet and uncertain even though her expression wasn't. "I've been thinking about it since you brought the whole gas thing up. I mean, there are dozens of abandoned vehicles in the parking lot and more all over the city. It might take a while, but it could work."

I stared at her while I thought it over, but no matter how I looked at it, I couldn't imagine a scenario where I would be able to siphon gas from a car. The first—and most important—reason was that the only real experience I had with something like siphoning gas was what I'd seen in movies and on television, and I had no clue if the way it was depicted was actually how it worked. It wasn't like you could trust movies to be totally realistic.

"I see a few problems with that," I said. "The main one being that I have no idea how to siphon gas. Do you?"

"Honestly," she said, her expression thoughtful, "I don't think it would be that hard. It's basic physics, really. It's all about gravity, liquid cohesion, and air pressure. Simple."

"Simple?" I blinked. "Not to me."

"Oh." She frowned. "To me, it is. I mean, it's really just a matter of the air pressure in the gas tank forcing the liquid out. Although, I think I remember reading something about the manufacture of newer vehicles that prevents siphoning the simple way. If that's the case, we'd just have to look for older cars."

I thought about our trek through town and the cars at the motel. There had been some newer ones, but there had been plenty of older ones, too. "That shouldn't be a problem. There are a lot of older cars around."

"Then we could do it." Kiaya gave an unconcerned shrug, which for some reason made me feel more confident even if the idea of siphoning gas was still foreign to me. "We just need to find a hose and a gas can."

"How do you know this?" I asked her.

"I told you. Physics."

"Like, the class?"

"Yeah," she said, sounding almost irritated.

I thought about the textbook she'd thrown on the bed in our first motel room and how much time she'd spent reading it. It had seemed like such a waste at the time. Who knew there'd be something useful in there?

"Okay," I said, thinking it through. "So, we need a couple gas cans and a hose. Where can we get those?"

Kiaya looked back toward the closed gas station. "In there, probably."

I frowned. "Too bad it's closed."

"Does it matter?"

My gaze snapped to her. "What do you mean?"

"Look, we're facing a pretty dire situation if we don't decide to take some risks and bend some rules. What did that doctor tell you? Eighty-five percent of the population is going to die, right?"

"Yeah," I said, knowing what she was getting at but letting her go on.

"So, basically, everything is going to be closed from here on out. I mean, who's going to bother opening the local grocery store when everyone they know and love is gone? Nobody. So, the way I see it, this is all fair game now."

She had a point, but being the consummate rule-follower I was, I had a hard time swallowing the reality of it all.

"So, you think we should break in?" I asked just to clarify.

"I think we'd be stupid not to," Kiaya said.

She was right again. Damn, this was going to be a tough

FAR from HOME

world to get used to. Even tougher than I'd originally thought.

"Okay," I said despite my uneasy insides.

Kiaya gave me a smile that said she knew I was having a difficult time with it but was grateful I was willing to step out of my comfort zone. Yet another thing that wasn't easy for me. I was used to being comfortable, used to things being simple. Hardships were new to me, but I had a feeling I was going to have to get used to them. Thankfully, Kiaya seemed well-versed in the world of hardships.

"Let's do this," she said, sounding more chipper than I felt.

We headed for the building, Kiaya in the lead and me only a couple steps behind. She was eyeing the area as she went, and I knew she was looking for something to break the window with. The idea of smashing the glass and having it rain down on the ground, of someone hearing us and coming to see what we were doing, made the tension in me double. But it wasn't just the thought of doing something that would have been considered vandalism only a few days ago. It was the warning Angus James has given me. I didn't want to draw attention our way if we could avoid it. We weren't prepared to defend ourselves, and while most of the people in this town were dead at this point, there were bound to be a few still around. If we could avoid them, it would be better.

Kiaya was still looking around when I headed for the door. It was a long shot, but before we did something that might get us in a situation we couldn't control, we needed to explore every available option. Including checking to see if the front door was unlocked.

I didn't expect anything to happen when I pulled on the handle, so when the door opened easily I nearly let out a shout of joy. Still holding onto it, I looked back at Kiaya, grinning from ear to ear.

"Holy shit," she said. "I never in a million years would have expected the door to be unlocked."

"I didn't either, not really, but I figured it was worth a shot."

"Wow," was all she said as she headed my way.

The smell hit me before I'd taken a step inside. I coughed,

turning my head as my stomach rolled. It was the stink of rot, of death and decay, and it was strong enough to make my eyes water.

"Oh, my God," Kiaya said, pausing at my side.

She covered her nose but looked a hell of a lot more in control of her body than I was. My stomach was convulsing, my mouth had filled with saliva, and I could feel my throat beginning to spasm. I was dangerously close to puking, but since it wouldn't do a damn thing to improve the smell in the building, I did my best to swallow it down.

"You okay?" Kiaya asked.

I nodded, three quick bobs of my head that only made the nausea intensify.

"Take a moment," she said. "If you can't do it, you can wait outside while I look around."

"Okay," I managed to get out but didn't attempt another word.

Kiaya kept her hand over her nose as she headed inside, her gaze moving around as she went, while I stayed at the door, trying to get my stomach to obey me and hold on to its contents. I watched her progress from my position as the nausea slowly eased. She headed first to the back before moving up a nearby aisle, stopping in the middle to look at something on the shelves. By then I was more in control of myself and a hell of a lot more certain that I wasn't going to barf all over the place. Turning my head away from the store, I sucked in a couple deep breaths of clean air before biting the bullet and heading inside after Kiaya.

Hearing my footsteps, she looked my way. "You okay?"

"Just okay," I said, careful not to breathe through my nose. Not that it helped that much. I could practically taste the rot.

Kiaya nodded to the refrigerators at the back of the store. "They're still cold. We must have been right, and the power just went out."

Which meant we were definitely going to get back to the motel to find it without electricity. Damn.

"At least we can have cold drinks for a little longer," I said, trying to grab on to the positive despite how bleak everything looked.

"Yeah," she muttered as she turned back to focus on what she was doing.

There were two five-gallon gas cans at her feet, and she had a reusable bag slung over her shoulder. Already it was bulging with items she'd tossed inside. I followed her example and grabbed a couple bags off a nearby display, then started moving up and down the aisles so I could fill them. Each item I dropped into the bags made us a little more prepared for the future, but that didn't mean knowing I was going to walk out of here without paying didn't bother me. I'd never shoplifted a thing in my life. I'd had friends who'd gone through phases, and I supposed a lot of other kids did as well, but not me. I'd been too afraid I'd get caught, too scared to disappoint my parents to risk it. This wasn't even close to the same thing, but I still found myself looking over my shoulder as if expecting the store's employees or even the cops to swoop in and stop me.

No one did, of course, and I went about my task uninterrupted. The place was stocked with pretty much any junk food you could want, but I stuck mostly to the things that had more substance. Nuts, beef jerky, protein bars, and even peanut butter crackers. After filling one entire bag with food, I set it by the front door and went to the back with another one, this time grabbing bottled water and Gatorade. I paused after filling the bag and grabbed a huge bottle of SmartWater off the shelf, untwisting the cap and gulping it down. Just like Kiaya had said, it was still cold and incredibly refreshing after being out in the hot sun for hours, and I was half tempted to pour it over my head. Since I didn't want to waste it, I resisted the urge.

I was still drinking when my gaze landed on a pair of feet. They were just visible behind the counter, and from their position, it was obvious the owner was on the ground, lying on his or her back. The knowledge that this was the source of the smell had my stomach convulsing all over again, and I had to turn away.

Kiaya saw me. "What is it?"

"Behind the counter," I said, nodding in that direction. "A body."

She sighed, but it wasn't irritation. More like resignation. "We're going to have to get used to seeing them, I think."

"I know," I said, wanting to defend my weak stomach and squeamishness. "But it's going to take some time."

"I know," she repeated.

Knowing the body was there gave me a renewed sense of purpose, so I carried the now full bag to the door and set it next to the other one before grabbing a third. This one I filled with all the first aid items the store had, which wasn't much, but more than we'd had before. Then I grabbed some medicine, mainly pain relievers like Tylenol, some sunblock—just in case I found myself in this position again—and finally some hygiene products. My gaze landed on a package of baby wipes, and with a sigh, I tossed them in. No electricity eventually meant no water, which would result in no showers. Like it or not, we were going to have to find other ways to stay clean.

With the third bag full, I turned to Kiaya. "You good?"

"Yeah." She had two full bags slung over her shoulders and a gas can in each hand when she headed my way. The sight of all the supplies made some of my unease melt away. We'd managed to get a few things, at least. That was something.

I'd just stopped in front of my own bags and was getting ready to scoop them up when something scraped against the floor in the back of the store. Frowning, I looked around but didn't see anything.

Kiaya stopped next to me. "What's wrong?"

"I thought I heard something," I said.

She followed my gaze, but when nothing moved, shook her head. "There's nothing here that can move but us."

"Yeah," I said, but the hair on the back of my neck stood up, and for a reason I couldn't explain, that horror movie feeling returned.

Wanting to get the hell out of there, I scooped up my bags and headed for the door.

The second I set foot outside, I sucked in a deep breath, filling my lungs until I thought they would burst before letting it out. Behind me, Kiaya did the same, although less dramatically than I had, and I turned to face her. Our eyes met, and for a reason I couldn't comprehend, we both burst out laughing.

"That was the grossest thing ever," I said through uncontrollable giggles.

Her smile widened. "I can't disagree. Hopefully, it's a while before we come face to face with another dead body."

"Seriously," I muttered.

I looked down the street, already calculating how long it was going to take to get back to the motel. Just thinking about the walk made my body hurt. The sun was getting low in the sky, but I was guessing we had a good hour and a half of daylight left. Enough to get us back, but literally just enough. It would be dark soon after.

"We should get going," I said. "It's getting late, and I want to be back before the sun sets."

"Yeah," Kiaya replied, sighing like she was dreading the walk as much as I was. After we'd started walking, she said, "I can't wait to take a shower."

I snorted. "Forget taking a shower. I'm just going to strip down and jump in the pool."

A swimsuit hadn't been one of the many things I'd packed before leaving campus, but with as deserted as the world now felt and as hot as I was, I didn't give a shit if I had to jump in naked. I needed a good swim.

"You can't be serious," she said with a laugh.

"It's not like anyone is around to see me."

"True," she said, and looked away as she shook her head. "I think I'll stick to the shower."

"Suit yourself," I replied with an unconcerned shrug.

By the time the motel came into view, my calves were aching, and I'd been transformed into a giant ball of sweat. Even worse was the way the straps dug into my shoulders. The bag with the bottled water and Gatorade felt like it contained a boulder. We would need it, but I was seriously regretting getting so much.

The shimmering water of the pool came into view, and I wanted to take off running, but instead I headed toward the room with Kiaya. She had to set a gas can down to get the door unlocked, but once she had, I practically threw my bags into the room.

"You're serious about the pool?" she asked, lifting an eyebrow.

"Dead serious," I said then cringed when I thought about the bodies currently surrounding me.

Kiaya stepped into the dark room, pulling out her phone and hitting the button to turn the flashlight on. "Well, enjoy yourself. I'm going to rinse off in an actual shower."

I only waved over my shoulder before heading off.

Every inch of my exposed skin was tender from hours in the

sun, and my clothes were clinging to my body. In the distance, the horizon was pink. The air would soon cool off, but at the moment, the heat of the day was hanging on, and all I could think about was diving into the pool.

I pushed the gate open, and it clanged through the silence when it slammed shut behind me. My gaze was focused on the water, registering nothing else as I stopped beside the pool. I only thought about it for a second before kicking my shoes off. My shorts were next. They dropped to the ground, and I kicked them aside as I peeled my tank top off and dropped it as well. Standing in nothing but my bra and underwear, I let out a deep sigh. Already, I was cooler, but I'd feel even better when I jumped in.

I was just about to take the plunge when a male voice said, "I'm guessing you came up empty-handed."

Yelping, I threw myself into the pool.

The cool water that engulfed me was more refreshing than I could have imagined, and I pulled myself deeper, wanting to avoid resurfacing. I knew who I'd find sitting there once I did, and while I didn't care that I'd stripped down in front of him—my underwear wasn't much different from my swimsuit—I wasn't looking forward to seeing that a smug *I-told-you-so* expression on his face.

I stayed under until my lungs burned then kicked my legs, resurfacing with a gasp.

"I thought I was going to have to dive in and save you." He stood at the side of the pool now, watching me with a slightly amused expression on his face.

"Believe me, there will never be a time when I need your help," I snapped.

What was it with muscle-bound men that made them think all women were damsels in distress who needed saving?

"You never know what's going to happen," he said, lowering himself to the side of the pool so his bare feet were hanging in the water. "You could find yourself in need of a big, strong man yet."

Ugh.

"I know exactly what's going to happen," I said, treading water as I glared up at him. "I'm going to find a way to get out of

FAR from HOME

here, and then I'll never see you again."

He grinned, which lit up his blue eyes and deepened the dimple in his right cheek. "An optimist. I like it."

"A realist," I snapped. "And the reality of the situation is that I have to get home, so I'm going to do whatever it takes to make that happen."

His smile faded, and genuine sympathy flashed in his eyes. "I'm sorry you're stuck."

"I'm not the only one," I muttered, unwilling to accept his apology.

"True." He blew out a long breath, his focus moving from me to the distant horizon, darker now than it had been just a few minutes ago when I'd dragged myself to the pool.

He still wasn't looking at me when he said, "Where's home for you?"

"Ohio," I said with a sigh. "Dayton area."

"Really?" His gaze snapped back to me, and he shook his head. "Small world."

"Why?" I kicked my legs harder, working to keep my head above water. "Where are you from?"

"West Chester."

It wasn't far from me, an hour south on Interstate 75. That was all.

"It is a small world," I agreed.

The guy watched me as I treaded water, his expression slightly amused but curious as well. There was something about him that bugged me, although I couldn't quite put my finger on it, and the look he was giving me had the hair on my scalp prickling.

Wanting to focus on anything but him, I leaned back, allowing my body to float on the surface of the pool with my arms out at my sides so I could stare up. The horizon may have still had some light, but the sky above me was black and the stars had begun to appear, twinkling down as if winking at me.

"What's your name?" he asked as I floated.

"Rowan," I said, for some reason not even hesitating.

"I'm Devon," he replied, and I glanced his way to find his eyes still on me. "What has you stuck so far from home during

99

the apocalypse?"

The word *apocalypse* slammed into me, almost like a punch, and I flailed from the shock of it. I hadn't thought about it in those terms before, but he was right. This was the apocalypse, wasn't it? A virus sweeping the country and killing most of the population was the very definition of apocalyptic.

"What's wrong?" he asked, the small smile that had been on his lips disappearing completely.

I righted myself, once again treading water, and swallowed. "I hadn't thought about it that way until now. About this being the apocalypse, I mean. I guess I was still too focused on getting home to look at the big picture."

"Sorry," Devon said, and he sounded sincere.

"Forget it." I shook my head, more to shake the tears and desperation away than anything else. "To answer your question, I was away at college. The University of Phoenix."

"And you got stuck," he said.

"And I got stuck," I repeated. "My parents wanted me to stay where I was because they thought it was safer. I listened to them, like I always do, but only at first. Eventually, I decided I had to make my own decision, so I got a physical and the papers I needed, then found people to travel with. Which was how I ended up here."

"Let me guess," Devon said, "you were on the road and someone got sick, so you had to stop."

"How'd you know?" I asked even though I'd already guessed.

I'd seen the ambulance removing the bodies. Had seen Devon sitting outside the room with an expression of devastation on his face.

"The same thing happened to me," he said. "Hell, the same thing probably happened to everyone who stopped here."

"True," I whispered.

He let out a deep breath, and it sounded like he was trying to keep himself calm. Silence followed, and I wasn't sure if he was going to say anything else. I didn't have anything else to say. It wasn't like I was going to share any personal details—or at least any more than I already had—with this stranger.

FAR from HOME

Then, out of nowhere, Devon started talking.

"I was on a trip with some buddies from high school. A bachelor party getaway." He shook his head like he couldn't believe it was all gone. "A group of us went rock climbing and camping in New Mexico, the Sandia Mountains. We were there when this thing started and travel got cut off. A few of the guys got permission to travel and left right away. They had families to get back to, but the rest of us weren't really worried about it. We figured getting stuck on vacation was just good luck. So we camped, we climbed, did some white water rafting. We waited for it to blow over."

"And it didn't."

"It didn't." He smiled down at me, but it was tinged with sadness. "A week ago, we finally went into Albuquerque and applied for travel papers. We only made it this far before the first one of us came down with symptoms. So we stopped. Then someone else got sick, then another person. Soon they were all sick but me, then they were dead, and I was alone."

"I'm sorry," I said, genuine remorse for his situation tightening my insides. "How many of your friends died?"

"Seven of us left New Mexico together. I'm the only one who made it."

He exhaled and without warning lay back, stretching out on the cement so he was staring up at the sky with his feet still in the water. I stayed where I was for a moment before taking the opportunity to swim to the side of the pool, pausing when I reached the ladder so I could look back at him. I'd told myself stripping down wasn't a big deal, but I was grateful he was still focused on the sky.

Water dripped off me as I pulled myself up, splashing against the pool and onto the cement. Once I was out, I paused so I could wring out my hair, focusing on the puddle at my feet so I didn't have to think about the guy at my back who now had an excellent view of my ass. Even so, my scalp prickled as I thought about how skimpy my underwear was and the way the wet fabric clung to my skin.

The sound of a door opening drew my attention, and I looked

up to find Kiaya heading our way, one of the scratchy motel towels in her hand.

"I thought you might need this," she said when she reached the gate.

She moved to open it but paused when she spotted Devon sprawled out on the ground, her eyebrows lifting.

He shifted so he could see her and gave a little wave. "I'm Devon."

"Kiaya," she said, opening the door.

He watched her for a moment as she headed my way, then his gaze shifted to me. It was dark now that the sun had disappeared, and in the absence of electricity to illuminate the area, making out his expression wasn't easy. Still, I knew he was checking me out, and a flush moved up my neck to my cheeks, eventually spreading throughout my body when he didn't look away. I did, though, choosing to focus on Kiaya when she stopped in front of me.

She shot me a questioning look but didn't utter a word.

"Thanks," I said, taking the towel.

I avoided looking at either of them as I wrapped the tiny towel around my body. It didn't do a very good job of covering me, but it was better than nothing.

Devon pushed himself to a sitting position with a grunt. "What's the plan now?"

"Sleep," Kiaya said. "Then tomorrow we can go back to figuring out how we're going to get out of here."

"Any ideas?" Devon asked.

I worked to keep my expression blank even as my back stiffened. I wanted to look at Kiaya, to give her some sign that she shouldn't tell this guy anything, but I was too afraid it would give us away. We didn't know him, had no idea if we could trust him, and the last thing I wanted to do was tell him about our plan for siphoning gas and have him go behind our backs and empty every gas tank he could find before we had a chance to.

"Not at the moment," Kiaya said, her voice even and her expression unchanging.

She was a hell of a liar.

"Me neither," he said with a dejected sigh. "Maybe if we put our heads together tomorrow we can come up with something?"

"Maybe," I said, working to sound as cool as Kiaya.

I must not have pulled it off, because Devon's eyes narrowed on my face.

"I'm beat," Kiaya said before anyone else could speak.

She lifted her arms and stretched, letting out a loud yawn. As usual, the gesture was catching, and only a moment passed before I yawned as well. Devon followed suit, turning his head and covering his mouth.

"I could use some rest," he said once the yawn had ended. "See you in the morning?"

He looked right at me.

"Sure," I said, sounding more enthusiastic than necessary.

I wasn't a good liar.

Devon shook his head but didn't call me out. "Okay, then."

He headed off while I started gathering my clothes, taking my time about it so we didn't have to walk back with him.

Once he was out of earshot, Kiaya whispered, "A friend of yours?"

"Hardly," I said. "We've bumped into one another a couple times, that's all. I didn't see him sitting here when I walked up. He must have been in the shadows."

"Can we trust him?" she asked as I pushed the gate open, holding it for her.

"I don't know him, so I can't say one way or the other. I do know I'm not willing to risk it."

"Good," she said, "then we're on the same page."

Devon had reached his motel room—which was right beside ours—and paused outside the door to look back at us. I gave him a smile that wouldn't convince anyone, but since it was dark, I was counting on him not being able to get a really good look at it. He gave a little wave before going into his room, and the door shut with a click.

"We need to get moving early," Kiaya said. "Get the car loaded and gather any other supplies we might need, then siphon as much gas as we can."

"Yeah," I said, nodding. "I need to check how much cash I have left. I don't know if it will be worth anything on the road. Who knows what we're going to come across, but it will make me feel better to have it." I glanced toward Kiaya. "How much do you have left?"

She looked away. "Not much."

"What's not much?" I asked, suddenly remembering all the times she'd declined things like coffee and how she hadn't even had change when we stopped at the Coke machine. I grabbed her arm, forcing her to turn and face me. "Kiaya, how much money do you have?"

She still wouldn't meet my gaze. "I'm not sure, exactly."

"Kiaya," I said more firmly this time.

She only hesitated for a few more seconds, before sighing and saying, "I have less than five dollars."

Less than five dollars? She couldn't be serious.

"I asked if you had money before I agreed to let you travel with me, and you said yes. Were you lying?"

"I thought I had enough to pitch in, but I wasn't sure," she said, her gaze still on the ground. "I spent most of my money just getting permission to travel. You know how much that cost. I thought I had enough, but since I wasn't positive, I found someone else to go with us."

"That's why you invited Kyle."

"Partly, yes. Plus, he needed to get home too, and I figured between the three of us we could pool our resources and make it." She finally looked up, and even though it was dark, her expression was apologetic. "It was my only shot. I had no idea how expensive things had gotten."

I let out a deep sigh. "I get it. It's okay."

"It is?" She blinked, looking uncertain.

"Yeah," I said, "It's not great since I have no idea what we're going to face and how much money we'll need to get through it, but we can make it work. It's not like there aren't businesses we can break into if necessary."

I grimaced even as I said it. It wasn't easy adjusting to the mindset that we weren't stealing when we took something, but I needed to because I had to make it home. Mom was counting on me.

"Kyle had money," Kiaya said suddenly. "It's in his book bag."

"In the other motel room," I reminded her.

We both turned so we were facing the first motel room we were given. The one that contained our traveling companion's body.

I shuddered. "We'll worry about that tomorrow. When it's light."

"Good idea," she said.

We continued walking in silence, and it hit me that sometime over the last two days this had become almost normal for me. It was strange considering how much it had annoyed me when I'd first met Kiaya, but so much had changed since then, and I found I was glad she didn't have to fill every moment with chatter. It wouldn't feel right in this new world. It would be irreverent and wrong, and unnerving to have noise when surrounded by so much death.

Thinking about it made me shudder again, and I grabbed Kiaya's arm, moving faster so we could get to the safety of our room.

9

I'd set my alarm for six o'clock, wanting to get the jump on Devon, but getting up early had become a habit with me over the past few days—probably because I was so focused on getting out of here—and I was awake before it went off. Without power, I had to use the flashlight feature on my phone so I could see what I was doing, but even that wasn't going to last for long. I was at twenty percent on low power mode, and I hadn't been able to charge it the night before thanks to the lack of electricity. Unless we got some gas soon, I was going to be screwed. Charging it in the car was the only option left at this point.

I took a quick shower—both because I smelled like chlorine from my swim the night before and because the days of being able to do it were numbered. Without power, the water wasn't even lukewarm, and I was out in record time. When I came out of the bathroom, dressed but my hair still dripping, I found the curtains open and the room filled with early morning light, Kiaya ready for the day and waiting for me.

"I'll only be a minute," I said as I towel dried my hair.

"I've been thinking," she said, watching me from where she sat on the foot of the bed. "Maybe we should try to get to know

Devon a little. If he's a nice guy, he could help us. Plus, it seems shitty to leave someone in the middle of nowhere when you can help them."

The warning Angus James had given me came back, and I paused in the middle of trying to soak the water from my hair. Kiaya had a point. Even if Devon hadn't been a man, there was safety in numbers. But I wasn't sure if we had the time necessary to get to know him, and I wasn't willing to risk inviting him along without being a hundred percent sure.

"We'll see," I said instead of committing to anything. "Let's follow through with the plans we made and see what happens after that." Accepting that my hair was as dry as it was going to get for the moment, I tossed the wet towel aside and tucked my blonde locks behind my ears. "Ready?"

Kiaya got up, nodding. "Where to?"

"Let's go to Kyle's room first and get that out of the way." I blew out a long breath.

I was dreading it but trying not to let my nerves over seeing another dead body get the best of me. It was time to get used to things like that. Time to toughen up.

You can do this, I told myself.

I repeated the pep talk over and over again as we headed across the parking lot, but it didn't really help. My stomach was a ball of nerves.

We paused outside the motel room again, longer this time than we had before. Almost two days had passed since Kyle succumbed to the virus, and although I didn't know much about decomposition, even I knew he'd be ripe by now—especially with no power—and my stomach was churning just thinking about it.

This was going to suck.

"I wish we'd thought of this last time we were here," I muttered, taking a deep breath.

"We'll make it fast," Kiaya said. "You can hold the door open, and I'll run in. I'll grab his bag and run out. Less than a minute. That's all."

"Yeah," I said, but I sounded as unhappy about it as I felt.

FAR from HOME

"Let's do it," Kiaya said, a little more impatient this time.

"Yeah, yeah, okay," I grumbled.

I turned the key, sucking in a deep breath and holding it before shoving the door open. The blinds were pulled shut and the room was pitch black, and now that the power was out there was no opportunity to even flip on the lights. If only we'd been able to find a couple flashlights at the gas station. With the battery on my phone as low as it was, I didn't want to risk using it unless absolutely necessary, so I didn't bother pulling it out. As soon as we had our gas and got out of this damn town, I was going to take Angus's advice and load up on supplies. This was Texas. There had to be a gun or camping store around here somewhere, right?

Thankfully, having the door open allowed enough light into the room to illuminate everything we needed to see. Kiaya darted in the second I had the door open, and I stayed where I was, leaning against it with my breath held and fighting the urge to exhale as I waited for her to come back. She knelt to grab Kyle's bag, and a zip followed, then she was standing. She started to turn, and I was ready and waiting for her to make it back outside so I could shut the door and breathe again, but instead of heading my way, she froze beside the bed. Staring at it.

I shifted, trying to figure out what she was looking at, but only the foot of the bed was visible.

I let all the air out of my lungs in a burst and sucked in more, nearly gagging at the putrid scent, and said, "Come on! What are you doing?"

"Kyle?" Kiaya said, not looking at me.

I took a step farther into the room, leaving one hand on the door. "What's wrong?"

"Kyle—" Kiaya looked back at me. "I thought he was dead."

The hair on my neck stood up as a feeling I couldn't describe came over me. It was familiar, but at the same time so foreign I couldn't put a name to it. When had I felt like this? When had I ever been in a situation when dread had pooled in my stomach? When my heart had beat in such an erratic rhythm? I didn't know.

Kiaya was back to looking at the bed, and she dropped the book bag as she took a step closer, her hand out as if reaching for something. "Let me help you, Kyle. I'm so sorry we abandoned you. We thought you'd died."

A moan sounded, and all at once I remembered when I'd felt this way. In the dorm after watching that stupid YouTube video. I'd walked to the lobby and hadn't been able to stop looking over my shoulder. It had freaked me out so much.

Sounds like a fucking zombie.

The guy's statement came screaming back, filling me with dread. It hadn't been real. It couldn't have been. Zombies were fake.

Weren't they?

Kiaya stepped closer to the bed.

"Stop," I called, reaching for her with my free hand while holding the door open with the other. "Don't go any closer."

She looked my way. "I don't know how he's alive, but he is. He's sitting up. The sheet is still over his head, but he's moving. I can see him moving, Rowan."

"Kiaya," I warned, "don't go any closer. That isn't Kyle."

"Of course it is." She looked away from me, her focus on the bed as she took another step toward the thing that used to be Kyle. "I'm going to help you."

I wanted to run to her, but letting go of the door would plunge us into darkness. Then what? How would we fight Kyle off if he was a zombie?

The thought struck me as so absurd that I let out a hysterical-sounding laugh, earning me another look from Kiaya. She was at the very end of the bed now, her gaze focused on me, so when he made his move, she didn't see it.

But I did.

I saw the blankets shift, saw the bed dip and shake, saw the hand reach from the darkness. Inches from Kiaya.

"No!" I screamed and dove without thinking.

My body crashed into Kiaya's a second before the door slammed shut, and we went down in a painful thud of arms and legs, hitting the ground as we were plunged into total darkness. A growl echoed through the room somewhere to my left, while beneath me Kiaya swore and groaned.

FAR from HOME

"Rowan, what the hell are you doing?"

"He's a zombie," I said as I rolled off her.

I was already reaching for my phone, tucked in my back pocket, but when cold fingers brushed my arm, a scream ripped its way out of me. It caught me off guard, and I dropped my phone as I scrambled away from the cold hand of death, losing it in the darkness. Kiaya's heavy breathing sounded to my right, while somewhere in front of me were other noises. Inhuman noises. Moans. A snarl. The bed squeaking as zombie Kyle tried to find us. A growl, followed by a shriek from Kiaya.

"What's happening?" I screamed, still scrambling to find my phone.

A second later, a snarl sounded inches from my face, and cool, moist breath hit my arm. My body was trembling as I ran my fingers over the carpet, searching for my phone. It was all I could think to do. The room was too dark to make a run for it—for all I knew, zombie Kyle was between me and the door—and I couldn't find anything to fight him off with if I couldn't see. Plus, I had no idea where Kiaya was, and I couldn't leave her. Wouldn't leave her.

She let out a yelp, and my mind conjured up images of decaying teeth sinking into human flesh, blood going everywhere in the process. A sob shook my body, but I didn't stop searching the darkness for my phone.

Seconds later, Kiaya said, "Rowan? Where are you?"

"I dropped my phone." I moved a little to the right, and my fingers brushed something cool and soft, sending me scrambling back again. "We need light."

"Hold on," Kiaya said.

My hand was still sweeping the floor when the light from her phone flicked on, illuminating the room and lighting up the distorted and decayed face of Kyle only a foot from me. He lunged, snarling as he slammed into me, sending me back. I hit the floor, my head slamming into it and him on top of me. He was stronger than I thought a zombie would be, stronger than he probably would have been in life, and desperate to get at me. I did my best to hold him back, my hands on his chest as he snapped his teeth in my direction, trying to take a bite out of me. To my right, Kiaya was shouting, and I yelled in response, barely registering what either of us was saying. I was probably yelling for help, telling her to hit him. I didn't know. I just knew my arms ached, and he wasn't going to let up any time soon.

I registered movement seconds before something slammed into Kyle's head and he went flying. The phone was on the floor, the beam of light pointing up toward Kiaya, who stood over me with a ceramic lamp in her hand and her shoulders heaving.

I sucked in a breath, trying to collect my thoughts and figure out what to do next. There wasn't enough time, though. Kyle was up in seconds, on his hands and knees and pulling himself toward me, growling.

"Hit him again!" I screamed.

Kiaya obeyed, swinging the lamp around and down and slamming it into his head while I pulled myself to my feet. I was trembling from head to toe but unsure if I was actually hurt. I couldn't register anything other than the lamp as it made contact with Kyle's skull a third time. It shattered, sending shards of turquoise ceramic raining down and destroying the only weapon we had.

I spun in a circle, trying to find something else we could use to defend ourselves, but there was nothing. Kiaya had grabbed the only lamp, and the chairs in the room were on the other side of Kyle. The television was bolted to the wall, and everything else was too big or too useless.

Kyle lunged again just as something banged against the door. I shoved Kiaya back on instinct, falling to the ground a second time when the zombie that had been Kyle slammed into me. A sharp pain in my lower back made me scream, but I couldn't focus on it because I was too busy trying to hold Kyle off.

"Kiaya!" I screamed just as the door opened in a burst of splintering wood.

Someone rushed in, grabbing Kyle and pulling him off me and throwing him to the floor, and it only took a second to recognize Devon. He still had hold of Kyle and was slamming him down, his skull banging against the floor over and over again. A sickening crack sounded the third time he did it, but he didn't let up, not until Kyle had stopped moving and a puddle of gray matter and blood that looked black in the limited light had collected under his head.

Devon stepped back, gasping for breath as he stared down at the thing he'd just killed, then he turned to us. "Are you okay?"

"I—" I swallowed. "I think so."

I started to stand, but gasped when a sharp pain stabbed me in the back. I reached behind me, brushing my fingers against my lower back, and winced. They were stained red when I pulled my hand away.

"Let me see," Kiaya said, urging me to turn.

She lifted my shirt as Devon knelt in front of me, waiting.

"Looks like a shard from the lamp," Kiaya said. "There's a lot of blood."

Devon held out his hand. "Let's go outside. I can look at it there."

I took his outstretched hand, allowing him to help me up, and together we stepped over Kyle's body.

Outside, Devon led me to the pool where he urged me to sit on one of the lounge chairs before kneeling behind me. Kiaya sat at my side, her expression shaken and worried, and put a gentle hand on my knee as she waited for Devon to speak.

"Looks like it's still in there," he said from behind me. "I'll have to clean it and try to patch you up as best as I can."

"Are you qualified to do that?" Kiaya asked.

"Not really," he said. "I'm a cop, so I've taken basic first aid courses. That's it. It's not like I'm a doctor or anything."

"It's more than I can do," Kiaya said.

"You can siphon gas." I winced when Devon dabbed at the cut.

Kiaya gave me a shaky smile. "In theory."

"Well, it's more than I can do," I muttered, feeling suddenly useless.

Devon stood. "We'll get back to this gas siphoning thing in a minute. First, I'm going to run to the main office and look for a first aid kit."

I half stood but stopped myself when pain throbbed through me. "You think that's a good idea? I mean, what if there are more of them?"

"More of who?" Devon asked. "More crazy assholes? I think I can take them. Muscle, remember?" He lifted his arm and flexed his impressive bicep, shooting me a halfhearted wink. "Plus, I'm a cop. I'm trained to take care of assholes."

"No," Kiaya said. "More zombies."

Devon's smile disappeared, but he didn't lower his arm. "What?"

"That wasn't just a guy you killed," I said. "It was a zombie."

"Shut up." He let out a nervous laugh, his eyes flicking between Kiaya and me. "You can't be serious."

"He was dead," Kiaya said, her voice barely above a whisper. "I watched him die two days ago."

When Devon looked at me again, I nodded. "It's true."

He finally dropped his arm as he shifted his gaze, focusing on the motel room we'd just fled, his expression still doubtful. "That doesn't make any sense."

"Don't you think I know that?" I snapped. "Why would we lie about something so ridiculous at a time like this?"

I blew out a breath, both from frustration and because my back was throbbing. It seemed like every interaction I had with this guy irritated me more than the last one, and this was no exception. Sure, I got why he was having a difficult time accepting that he'd just killed a zombie, but had he not smelled the rot in the room? It had been pretty pungent.

Devon swallowed, his focus still on the motel, but not just the one room. He was studying everything. The parking lot, the closed doors to other rooms, the cars surrounding us. All the places where people had died. Where their bodies still sat because there was no one to collect them.

"We're surrounded," I whispered as realization dawned on me.

Kiaya's back straightened as she, too, began looking around. I thought of all the people I'd seen the first day we got here and how there had been fewer and fewer each day even though the

FAR from HOME

parking lot hadn't emptied out. Like Kyle, they'd come here and died, and like Kyle, they would probably come back. When? Almost two days had passed between his last breath and when he attacked us, but was that how long it took for everyone to turn? Would they all turn? It was impossible to know because this whole scenario was ridiculous and crazy. Bodies couldn't reanimate. They just couldn't.

"We need weapons," Devon said, finally turning his gaze back to us. "Guns. Hell, even knives would be better."

"You said you were a cop," Kiaya pointed out. "Aren't you armed?"

"I'm from Ohio. I was on vacation. I didn't bring my fucking gun with me."

Devon spun around, sweeping one of the metal chairs up and slamming it against the ground a second later. The bang echoed through the air, making my heart beat harder. I scanned the motel, expecting to see a horde bearing down on us, but there was nothing. Why?

"They're trapped," I said, looking from Devon—who was once again slamming the chair down—to Kiaya. "Most people died inside. In motel rooms, in their cars, or in houses. They're trapped just like Kyle would have been if we hadn't gone back to the room."

Devon slammed the chair down a third time, and it broke apart, metal pieces raining down on the cement with multiple clangs that echoed through the motel courtyard. Despite what I'd just said, I found myself looking around, waiting for undead creatures to come running. The parking lot was still empty.

Devon scooped up one of the legs and held it like a club, turning to face us.

"That's a good point," Kiaya said.

"Which means we just have to avoid letting any of them out," Devon added.

"Right," I said.

I stood, wincing from the throbbing pain in my back.

Kiaya was up a second later, her hand pressed against my still bleeding back. "You need to take it easy."

"I need to get the hell out of here," I muttered.

"She's right." Devon was at my side now. "I need to get the glass out and patch you up. You're bleeding like crazy."

"It hurts like crazy," I said, tears suddenly stinging at the back of my eyes.

It wasn't from the pain. It was the stress and uncertainty, the feeling of being trapped, and the overwhelming urge to get home and see my mom.

"We'll get you something for that, too," he said.

Devon pulled his shirt over his head, revealing a sculpted chest and abs that would make Channing Tatum envious—assuming he was alive, which was doubtful. A hiss of pain broke out of me when he pressed it against my back, but he didn't apologize. He wasn't even paying attention to me because he was too busy surveying the area.

"I think the office is our best bet." His focus turned to Kiaya. "Hold this against the cut and follow me. I'll go in first and make sure there's nothing dangerous. Once it's clear, you can come in. Hopefully, there's a first aid kit, and we can do something about this. If not, I'm going to have to make a run to the pharmacy down to the street."

"We got some things yesterday," Kiaya said, looking at me for confirmation.

"Not much. All they had at the gas station was rubbing alcohol and Band-Aids."

Devon shook his head. "The rubbing alcohol will come in handy, but I'm going to need some tweezers so I can get the glass out."

Just thinking about it made my back throb.

Devon grabbed the chair leg and headed for the gate, motioning for us to follow. I did, with Kiaya glued to my side, pressing Devon's shirt against my throbbing back every step of the way. It was strange that the shirtless god in front of me didn't serve as a distraction from the pain, but I couldn't keep my eyes on him for more than two seconds because I was too busy scanning the parking lot for any sign of movement. It was as empty and quiet as it had been the day before, but I still found

FAR from HOME

it impossible to stay calm. They were out there, and I knew it.

"You think that person from yesterday was one?" Kiaya asked, breaking the silence when we were halfway across the parking lot. "The guy who threw himself against the window, I mean."

I thought about the barely visible figure that had banged against the window when we passed and shuddered. "Probably."

"I'm glad he couldn't get out."

"Me, too." My gaze focused on the interior of a car as we passed it, or more accurately, on the person in the back seat. Dead and unmoving, and probably getting ready to turn into a zombie. "I'm glad none of them can get out."

Devon paused when he reached the office, his hand poised above the doorknob as he peered in through the window. I couldn't see much from my position behind him, but what I could see was more of the same. Darkness and nothing moving.

"Looks clear," he said, his voice low. "I'll go in and make sure. Stay here until I come back."

He started to pull the door open, but I stopped him by reaching out, putting my hand on his arm. "What if you need help?"

His lips twitched when he looked back at me. "Believe me, there will never be a time when I need your help," he said, throwing my words from the night before back in my face.

My cheeks got hot, but before I could respond, his smile had disappeared, and he was once again focused on the motel office.

"I'll be right back." Then he shoved the door open and darted inside.

"What was that all about?" Kiaya asked.

"He has a knight in shining armor complex," I said, not looking her way, too focused on watching Devon tiptoe through the lobby. "I set him straight last night. Told him I didn't need a big, strong man to save me. Unfortunately, today proved the opposite."

"You did a good job holding your own," Kiaya said. "It's not your fault we weren't exactly prepared for a zombie attack."

She had a point, but I still felt like a moron for throwing those words in Devon's face only twelve hours before he ended up saving my ass.

Only a few minutes passed before he returned, and he was more relaxed when he shoved the door open. "It's clear."

I stepped inside when he motioned us forward, Kiaya following me, and inhaled. "I could have told you that after one whiff."

"I wasn't willing to take any chances." He waved to the small lobby where a couple stiff couches were set up. "Sit down and I'll grab the first aid kit."

"He sure is bossy," Kiaya said, just loud enough that I could hear.

"And a major pain in the ass," I added.

Every move made my back throb, but lowering myself to the couch was the worst. It was like the glass was cutting me over and over again, and now that the adrenaline from my fight with Kyle had totally worn off and we were safe for the moment, I was having a difficult time thinking about anything else.

Devon came back holding a black metal box with a big red cross on the front and took a seat on the coffee table in front of me. He didn't look at me when he opened the lid, saying, "Turn around so I can get a look at it."

I obeyed despite how much his tone irked me. He needed to learn to ask, not order.

"Kiaya, I'm going to need you to hold a light up so I can see what I'm doing."

"Got it," she said.

I looked over my shoulder to find him wiping a small pair of tweezers with an alcohol pad, and my stomach flipped. Seeing the cut was impossible thanks to its location, but I could see Devon's shirt. It was on the floor at his feet, balled up and covered in enough blood to make my head spin.

I looked away.

"This is going to hurt," Devon said only a few minutes later. His hand touched my back, urging me to bend forward a little. "Ready?"

I sank my teeth into my lower lip and nodded.

A sharp pain stabbed me in the back, and I jerked, barely

biting back a yelp of pain.

"Try to hold still," he said. "Kiaya, move the light a little higher. Right there. Perfect."

More pain followed, throbbing through me, and this time I couldn't hold back my wail. It took everything in me to force myself to stay still as he dug in the cut, trying to find the shard. I had to dig my nails into my palms, had to tense every muscle in my body. It seemed to go on and on, and soon drops of sweat had beaded on my forehead.

"Almost got it," Devon said.

I squeezed my eyes shut, biting back whimpers.

"There." A second later, he pulled it free.

I dropped forward, allowing all the tension to leave my body, and sucked in a deep breath.

"It's okay," Kiaya said, her words gentle and soothing.

"You did a good job," Devon told me. "I'm almost done. I just need to clean it and bandage it. I wish I could stitch it up, but it doesn't look like that's an option right now."

I let out a slightly hysterical laugh. "Thank God, because I don't know if I would be able to stay conscious."

"You did good." This time his voice was lower, his face just behind mine so his warm breath brushed the back of my neck, raising the hair and making my face heat up.

I looked over my shoulder, but he was already focused on cleaning my cut. The alcohol stung, but it was nothing compared to having Devon dig the shard from my body, so I barely reacted. Plus, I was focused on him, studying his intent expression as he patched me up and trying to understand who he was. The cocky guy who'd flexed for me when we first met was gone, pushed away by someone serious and resourceful. Someone capable.

Once he'd cleaned it, Devon tossed the alcohol wipe aside and pulled a piece of gauze and some medical tape from the first aid kit. When he was finished, he looked up, his gaze meeting mine.

"Good as new." He gave me a reassuring smile. "Well, not really. I'm sure you'll have a nasty scar since we couldn't get you to an emergency room, but there are worse things in this world."

"Like being the walking dead," I replied.

"Yeah," he said, his smile disappearing. "Like that."

For a moment, we stared at each other in silence. I didn't know what he was thinking, but I was still mulling him over, trying to decide what to do next. Sneaking out of here under his nose was no longer an option, but I wasn't quite ready to give in and trust him. Even if he had come to our rescue, killed a zombie, put himself between us and possible danger to search for a first aid kit, and patched me up.

Okay, all those things made him pretty badass and most likely trustworthy, but still…

Kiaya cleared her throat, and I blinked, tearing my gaze from Devon. She lifted her eyebrows but said nothing. Neither did I, because I still didn't know what to do about this.

"You mentioned siphoning gas," Devon said as he started cleaning up the first aid supplies.

"Yeah." Kiaya shrugged, and when I still said nothing, cleared her throat. "I haven't tried it yet, but it's basic physics, so assuming we can find some older cars with gas still in them, it shouldn't be too hard. We got a couple gas cans and a hose at the gas station yesterday, so now all we have to do is try it out."

Devon studied her for a moment before his lips twitched and pulled up into a smile. "Basic physics, huh?"

"Yeah…"

She looked at me, but I shrugged.

"I don't know any criminals who would have described it that way, so I'm assuming you're applying hard-earned knowledge to survival and not speaking from experience."

"Do I look like a criminal?" Kiaya shot back, some of her fire breaking free.

"No." Devon looked her up and down, his grin widening. "Not at all."

She relaxed. "Good."

He stood, the first aid kit in one hand, and motioned toward the door with the other. "The sooner we give it a shot, the sooner we'll know if it really is basic physics."

"We?" I asked, unable to stay quiet.

FAR from HOME

Devon's smile faded. "Yeah. We. You have to be thinking the same thing I am. We could team up. Watch each other's backs. It would be safer and easier. We'd get you home sooner."

I eyed him, considering it, as well as the warning Angus James had given me, and I couldn't help thinking that traveling with a man—especially one so capable—would be to our benefit. As much as I didn't believe I needed a knight in shining armor. I wasn't totally sold on Devon, but the truth was I didn't have to like him, I only had to trust him. So far, he hadn't done anything that made him seem untrustworthy. The opposite, really. He'd saved our asses and patched me up.

Before answering, I turned my focus to Kiaya, who was still sitting next to me on the couch. She shrugged, telling me she was thinking all the same things, and I let out a sigh.

"So, I guess we're a trio again," I said, moving to stand.

Devon grabbed my arm like he was going to help me, but I brushed him off. "I told you I don't need your help."

"I seem to remember a moment when you very much needed my help."

"Not because you're a man," I snapped. "Because there was an undead creature on top of me."

"But I still helped." He flashed me a smile that crawled under my skin, and not in a good way.

I rolled my eyes. "Is this is how it's going to be the whole drive back to Ohio?"

"I guess we'll just have to wait and see," Devon replied.

It was Kiaya's turn to sigh.

He let out a small chuckle as he turned away, first aid kit in one hand and the metal chair leg in the other. "Stay behind me just in case. Hopefully, we'll come across something more useful than this soon, but for the time being, it will have to do."

Kiaya and I exchanged a look once his back was turned. She rolled her eyes, and I mimicked her, then we followed Devon outside.

10

Kiaya jogged back to our motel room to get the gas cans and hose while Devon and I headed for the car closest to the office. It was a light blue Buick, probably a good fifteen years old, and seemed promising. Even better, there were no bodies inside. I wasn't looking forward to opening some of these cars knowing people had died in them and been trapped in the hot sun for a few days. Even if they hadn't turned into zombies yet, they were going to reek.

Devon stopped beside the driver's side door and lifted the metal chair leg, ready to slam it into the window, but I grabbed his arm to stop him.

He looked back at me, a slightly irritated expression on his face. "What?"

"Don't you think we should try the doors first? It could be unlocked."

"Who leaves their car unlocked in a motel parking lot?" he asked, his frustration growing.

This guy had a serious issue listening to other people.

"Someone who's sick and delirious and only wants to lie down," I said, allowing my own annoyance out.

He exhaled, but since he lowered the leg, I took it as a sign that my logic made sense to him.

He tried the driver's door, which wasn't unlocked, while I moved around the car to check the other side. Keeping one hand pressed against the still throbbing cut, I tried the handle first in the back and then the front. When neither door budged, I looked over the car's roof to where Devon stood.

He shook his head, looking somewhat smug. "Locked."

It was the expression on his face, combined with the muscles, that got to me, and yet I still couldn't figure out why. Of course, it didn't help that he acted so superior all the time.

"Fine." I blew out a long breath, resisting the urge to grind my teeth. "You were right, but it didn't hurt to check. We need to remember there are zombies out there. Making noise could draw them our way."

His smug expression faded as he looked around. "That's actually a good point."

I lifted my eyebrows, mimicking his self-righteousness.

He only shook his head in response.

It was going to be a long few days of travel.

"I'm going to break the window. You keep a lookout for any movement, okay?" he said, once again lifting the metal rod.

"Okay."

Hand still pressed to my wound, I turned in a slow circle and scanned the area. Kiaya was headed our way, gas cans and hose in hand, and my back was to Devon when a crash sounded. I'd known it was coming, but I still jumped and barely bit back a yelp. The sound bounced off the surrounding buildings and came back to us more than once before finally fading, and by the time it had, my heart was pounding violently in my chest.

Still, nothing moved.

Kiaya jogged over, and she, too, looked like she'd almost jumped out of her skin. "There has to be a quieter way."

"Unless you want to go through the rooms and search belongings then take the time to match keys with cars, there isn't," Devon said.

Kiaya and I exchanged a look but said nothing.

No, we did not want to do that.

Devon reached through the now missing window and unlocked the car, then yanked the door open. The tinkle of glass hitting the pavement followed as he brushed the seat off then slid in.

"Looks like a quarter of a tank," he called. Louder than necessary.

My already swiftly beating heart pounded faster, and I looked around again. Nothing. We were surrounded by nothing. Still, I couldn't settle down because it was an illusion. More zombies were out there. Somewhere.

A second later, there was a pop and the gas tank was open.

Kiaya moved to it, scanning the parking lot just like I was as she did.

"I'm watching," I assured her.

She nodded twice then focused on the task of unscrewing the cap so she could feed the hose into the tank.

I didn't watch her work since I was on lookout duty, but I did hear the trickle of liquid only a few minutes later, and the sound was sweeter than the whispers of a lover.

"It's working!" she called excitedly.

"Basic physics," I said, risking a look her way so I could shoot her a grin.

"I told you," Kiaya said, a little laugh popping out with the words.

My smile widened, and she looked up at me, returning it. It was one of the few moments since we'd met when I saw genuine emotion on her face, and it lit up her brown eyes, making them sparkle, and for the first time I didn't think she'd benefit from a little eyeliner. She didn't need it, not when she smiled like that.

"Good job, Kiaya," I said.

"Thanks."

We looked at each other for a moment longer before I tore my gaze from her, turning my focus back to the parking lot and coming face to face with the zombie.

It was a woman, her skin gray and loose, her eyes milky and her hands reaching for me as she lunged. I screamed and stumbled back, slamming into the car. Pain radiated through me, nearly blinding in its intensity, and for a moment I couldn't focus. Then my vision cleared, and the rotten creature in front of me came into view once again. It snapped its teeth, and I jerked away, but I was backed up against the car with nowhere to go.

Like I'd done with Kyle, my only option was to do everything I could to hold the thing back.

"Rowan!" Kiaya screamed from my right while from behind me Devon yelled, "Shit! I'm coming!"

The car shook, and the creature growled and tried harder to get at me. She didn't make any progress, though, because only a few seconds later she was ripped away. I slumped to the ground, holding my throbbing back, blood seeping through the bandage and covering my hand while Devon shoved the zombie to the ground. She growled and tried to get up, but he stopped her by slamming his foot against her throat, keeping her down. Then he jammed the metal chair leg through her skull and into her brain, and she stopped moving.

He ripped it free with a sickening squish and spun to face me, gasping. "Are you okay?"

I nodded, then shook my head to let him know the thing hadn't gotten me but I still wasn't okay.

"Let me see," he said, kneeling next to me.

I shifted, allowing him to get a look at my injury.

He swore under his breath. "It's bleeding like crazy."

"I know." I swallowed when my head spun.

Kiaya knelt on my other side, filling my nostrils with the scent of gasoline. She must have gotten some on her clothes because it was even stronger than the stink of death radiating off the body only two feet away from me.

Devon focused on Kiaya. "She really needs stitches."

"What can we do?" she asked.

"Get some gas, get out of here, and get to a hospital," he said.

At the mention of a hospital, I couldn't help thinking about my dad. About how busy he'd been, about all the infected people who'd come in even though there was no hope. How they'd all died and had probably turned...

"Too dangerous," I somehow managed to get out.

"What?" Devon asked.

"Think about how many people died in a hospital. It would be overrun."

He let out a long sigh but didn't argue, then focused on Kiaya. "How's the gas coming?"

"The first can is a little more than half full," she said. "A couple more cars, and hopefully we'll have them both filled up. Then we can get out of here."

"Okay." Devon stood, and this time when he grabbed my arm to help me up, I didn't protest. "I want you to rest while we do this. Understand?"

His blue eyes were deadly serious, and even if I hadn't felt like crap, I wouldn't have been able to argue with him.

"Yeah, okay," I said.

"I'm going to open the gate to the pool, and you're going to lie down on one of the lounge chairs. You'll be fenced in there and safe, and Kiaya and I will be able to focus on getting gas." He looked from me to Kiaya. "Sound like a plan?"

"Yeah," we said in unison.

"Good," Devon replied.

Despite the fact that he irritated the crap out of me most of the time, there was something about the authoritative way he took over that almost would have made me smile if things weren't so tense.

We were headed across the parking lot to the pool when something banged to our left. Devon moved, stepping in front of me while raising the chair leg, his entire body stiff and tense, and for a moment, none of us spoke. My hand was pressed against my still bleeding back, and it felt like my heart was lodged in my throat as I scanned the parking lot. Nothing was in sight, but after being jumped by yet another undead person, I couldn't relax. We all knew we were eventually going to run into more.

"I don't see anything," Kiaya whispered.

Devon's head bobbed, but he didn't speak.

Another thud cut through the silence.

Something caught my eye, and I lifted my free hand to my forehead, trying to shield my eyes from the bright sun. That was when I spotted it. The gray sedan I'd passed the day before with the dead guy behind the wheel. He was moving now, crawling around the inside of the car and banging against the window as he tried to get out.

"There," I said, pointing to the car. "There's a zombie inside."

Devon let out a breath that sounded relieved, but his shoulders didn't relax. "He's not going to be the only one. Hopefully, they can't open doors."

"Is that even possible?" Kiaya asked. "I mean, they're dead. How could they open doors?"

Devon turned to face us. "How can they be walking around?" He shrugged. "At this point, I'm going to assume anything is possible."

Kiaya and I traded a look, but neither of us responded.

Another thud sounded, this time from the other side of the parking lot, and Devon pressed his lips together. He didn't look toward the noise, but instead focused on the metal rod in his hand.

"We have to find some better weapons," he said, almost to himself.

With the way he was holding the chair leg, his expression serious and his stance defensive, he looked like a cop, and I found myself suddenly able to picture him in uniform. He fit the part, and not just because he was so muscular. He was brooding and severe looking when he didn't smile. I bet he was intimidating, and I knew just from the little bit we'd interacted how capable he was.

Maybe running into him had been a stroke of luck after all.

"What about the police station?" I suggested, the image of Devon apprehending bad guys fresh in my mind. "There has to be one here, right?"

Devon nodded, his expression thoughtful. "It's a small town, but it's possible. They wouldn't have a lot, but even one gun would be better than this." He shook his head at the chair leg like it had disappointed him.

"We need three," I pointed out, giving him a challenging

FAR from HOME

look.

His already exaggerated frown deepened. "Can you shoot?"

"I don't know how, no, but I can actually be taught to do things," I shot back. "Of course *you* would think a woman couldn't do something like that."

Devon's eyebrows lifted. "A woman, yes. You? No."

"What's that supposed to mean?" I snapped, glaring up at him.

His lips twitched like he was trying to hold in a grin, and it made me want to claw his eyes out—too bad I'd practically gnawed my nails down to nothing.

Kiaya stepped between us. "Enough." She turned to face me. "Go sit down." She focused on Devon. "Next car."

I scowled but did as I was told. Mainly because my back was throbbing and the bandage was now damp, telling me I was bleeding all over the place. As much as I hated thinking about it, we were going to have to find a way to get me stitched up.

Maybe a craft store?

Even a mini sewing kit might work. It was something I hadn't thought about when we were at the gas station yesterday, but as I headed to the fenced in area in the center of the parking lot, I found myself mentally retracing my steps through the store as I tried to remember if I'd seen something like that. No matter how hard I tried, I couldn't remember, but that didn't stop me from thinking about it as I took a seat on one of the chairs.

My gaze followed Kiaya and Devon's progress as they made their way from car to car while I mentally compiled a list of items I hadn't even considered needing before now. A sewing kit was only one of the dozens of little things that could come in handy while we were on the road, and I was sure I was overlooking other major items.

Across the parking lot, Devon stood guard above Kiaya as she worked with the cars. Inserting the tube into the gas tank then the can, then waiting for the fuel to trickle out. They seemed to be picky when it came to which cars they chose, and I could only assume it had to do with what was inside. In a few of the ones they skipped, I caught sight of movement, but in most I couldn't see anything from where I sat. Still, I knew there were either bodies inside or the undead.

An involuntary shudder shook my body at the thought.

After the fourth car, Kiaya stood and said something to Devon, who nodded. He looked around before responding, and a second later she was lugging the cans off the ground while he took off, headed my way.

I stood, my hand pressed against my throbbing back, and headed for the gate.

"What is it?" I asked when he was close enough I didn't have to yell.

"Keys," he huffed. "Both cans are full, and we want to fill your car up so we can try to get some more."

"Good idea," I said, shoving my hand in my pocket.

I passed him the car keys, and he gave me a tight smile that didn't reach his eyes, which were hard with concern. "How you doing?"

"I think you were right. I need stitches." I looked past him to my car where Kiaya stood waiting. "I was thinking maybe we could find a small travel sewing kit or something? That way we won't have to go anywhere near a hospital."

When I looked back, Devon was nodding appreciatively. "Good idea."

"I guess I'm useful for something," I said, his earlier comment still fresh in my mind.

He'd started to turn away but stopped at my words and frowned. "That's not what I meant, you know."

As if I believed that. He'd seen me break down the other night, saw me sobbing, and because of it, he automatically assumed I was fragile and worthless, and it pissed me off. No, I wasn't prepared for this, and I hadn't needed to work hard for much of anything in my life up to this point, but that didn't mean I couldn't learn. Hadn't I proven myself capable and resourceful so far? He hadn't walked through town gathering supplies, Kiaya and I had. Yes, he'd had to save me from zombies, but Kiaya had been right, I'd held my own. It wasn't fair of him to assume I was worthless without taking the time to get to know me.

"Whatever." I waved toward my car instead of saying any of that out loud. "Let's finish this so we can get on the road."

Devon frowned like he wanted to say more, but instead nodded and headed off.

I didn't go back to sitting, but stood by the gate and watched as they poured the gas into my car before heading for the next.

They skipped the one parked beside mine—the gray sedan—but stopped at the next one. Kiaya went around the car while Devon moved to the driver's side, and he'd just pulled a door open when movement at his back grabbed my attention.

I blinked and shook my head. My eyes had to be playing tricks on me, because there was no way one of the sedan's doors had just swung open. I blinked again, but nothing changed, and I watched in dumbfounded horror as the dead man pulled himself from the car.

Had he opened the door? How? Did that mean all zombies could open doors?

Questions thundered through my head as my gaze darted around, doing a quick scan of the motel rooms and cars just to reassure myself none of the other dead had gotten free. Once I was sure nothing else was about to bear down on Kiaya and Devon, I refocused my attention. By then the zombie was on the move, heading around the car to where Devon stood with his back to the creature. He was distracted, focused on the car's contents and totally unaware of what was going on around him.

"Devon!" I screamed.

He spun around as my voice bounced off the walls, echoing around us. Distracted from his current target by my shout, the zombie changed course and headed my way. Devon had spotted him by then, but he seemed too shocked by the creature's sudden appearance to move at first. He looked around, either trying to figure out where the thing had come from or checking to make sure there weren't any others, and I could tell when he noticed the sedan's open door, because his eyes widened.

He was already on the move when his gaze snapped to me a few seconds later, and he'd only taken two steps when he lifted his hand. This time it wasn't the metal chair leg he was holding, but a gun.

That was why he'd been so distracted.

Gun up, he charged after the dead man staggering toward me. I was safe behind my fence of concrete and metal, but my heart still beat faster, and I still took a step back. Staying totally calm was impossible because the scenario was just too terrifying, and the thing too grotesque. Having been trapped in a hot car for days, he was now bloated and swollen, and his skin was a shade of gray that would have made it impossible to mistake him for a living, breathing person. His was definitely more decayed than Kyle had been, and seeing him lumbering toward me made my stomach convulse.

Thankfully, he wasn't very fast, and Devon caught up in no time. I expected him to shoot the dead man, but instead he grabbed the creature by his shirt and shoved him to the ground. Like he'd done with the woman a little bit ago, he put his foot on the dead man's chest to hold him down, then pulled a knife.

Where'd he get a knife?

A second later, the blade entered the dead man's skull, and the thing stopped moving.

Devon pulled the blade free, pausing to wipe it on the man's shirt, then looked my way. "Did he come out of that car?"

"He opened the door," I said.

"Shit." Devon looked around again, frowning.

He had the knife in one hand and the gun in the other. I wasn't the least bit familiar with guns and never thought I'd be thrilled to see one, but the sight of the weapon made the future seem a little less bleak than it had a few minutes ago.

"Where'd you find the gun?" I called to him.

"Car." Devon reached behind him and shoved it in the waistband of his pants, then lifted his other hand, showing me the knife. "There was a hunting knife, too."

The sun glinted off the long, pointed blade, reminding me of the way jewels in television shows sparkled. At this moment in time, the knife was about a million times more precious than any gemstone, and I couldn't possibly be happier to see it than I was.

"I was thinking," Devon said, looking back to where Kiaya

FAR from HOME

stood, her wide eyes focused on us, "we might want to go through all the cars. Just to see what we come up with." He looked back at me. "The person who owned this car couldn't have been the only one who planned ahead."

"Good idea," I said.

It hadn't occurred to me that we might find weapons in any of the cars, but like Devon, now all I could think about was what else we might find. Most people traveling across the country had probably been like us—totally unprepared—but there were bound to be others. Again, I thought of Angus James and the things he'd said to me. Asshole or not, I couldn't decide. Either way, I was willing to bet he'd been prepared for this and so much more.

"What about your stuff?" I asked Devon, thinking about the list of things Angus James had told me to get. "You said you were camping. Don't you have gear?"

He let out a deep sigh. "A little, but not a lot. I flew out here, so I rented all the big gear I used. What I didn't rent, my buddy brought down from Nevada. Obviously, he wasn't traveling with us."

"Damn," I said, under my breath.

Devon only nodded.

My hand was still pressed to my back, and there was fresh blood on my fingertips when I pulled it away. Every move hurt and probably made me bleed more, but doing nothing was driving me crazy.

"I want to help," I said, focusing on Devon.

He shook his head as he took a step back. "Stay there. You can be our lookout."

"That's stupid," I called as he turned and started jogging back.

He ignored me.

That guy was too irritating for words.

Being the ever-obedient person I was, I didn't leave the safety of the fence. I didn't sit down either, though. Staying where I was, I watched Devon and Kiaya work. She siphoned gas while he went through the vehicles, and soon they'd returned to my car and not only added more gas to the tank, but carried supplies over as well.

Instead of putting them in the trunk, Devon started a pile on the ground next to the car, and from where I stood, I could see bottled water and snacks, and even some canned goods. I was praying we'd make it back to Ohio with no issues, but since we had no idea what we were going to face once we got on the road, we needed anything and everything we could get our hands on.

Even after they'd filled my car and both the gas cans—which they added to the ever-growing pile of supplies—they didn't stop going through cars. It was when they were searching what was probably the fifteenth vehicle—a big, yellow truck—that Devon passed Kiaya something. At first, I couldn't see what it as, but she held it up as he talked and pointed to it, and the thing came into view. A second gun.

Now I was the only one not armed.

I ground my teeth together as I looked around, double-checking that nothing was moving. The occasional thud echoed, telling me there were zombies trapped in rooms and cars still trying to figure out how to get free, but none of them had figured it out like the others had. At least not yet. If they did, we were at least a little more prepared. Well, Kiaya and Devon were. I was still trapped in the fence like a toddler in a playpen. It was infuriating.

Probably fifteen more minutes passed before Devon and Kiaya headed my way, talking as they went. They paused when they passed my car so they could add a few more things to the pile, but Devon was still carrying something when they started walking again. It was small, fitting in the palm of his hand, but I couldn't see what it was from this far away.

"You found another gun," I said when they reached the gate.

"A 9mm," Devon said—as if that meant anything to me. "Also, this."

He raised his hand, waving the item he'd carried over. A sewing kit. What were the odds?

Relief swept over me at the sight of it even as my stomach dropped. I wasn't an idiot. I needed stitches, but with nothing to numb the area, it was going to hurt like hell.

I swallowed, trying to control my voice, and said, "Good."
The word still trembled.

"I'm sorry," Devon said as he opened the gate.

He waved for Kiaya to go first, which she did, then he stepped inside and pulled the gate shut. The clang of metal against metal echoed through the courtyard.

"I'll be okay," I said. "I'm tough. Plus, don't they say women have a higher tolerance for pain?"

I wouldn't know for sure since the most pain I'd ever been through at this point in my life was when I got a bikini wax before spring break last year.

Not that I was about to tell Devon that.

"So I've heard," he said, shooting me a grin that was almost disarming in its warmth. "If you want, I have some vodka in my room."

I snorted. "I don't think getting drunk at a time like this is the best idea."

"Probably not," Devon said, nodding to the nearby table. "So, we should just get it over with?"

I exhaled. "Yeah."

11

I leaned forward, holding on to the table in hopes it would keep me grounded. Behind me, Devon was cleaning the wound while in front of me Kiaya was sanitizing the needle and thread. I watched alcohol drip to the tabletop as she poured it, collecting in a little pool that reflected the sunlight. My legs were already trembling, and Devon hadn't even started. Maybe a couple shots of vodka would have done me good. I'd seen people in movies do it, after all.

"Ready?" Devon asked, and the sound of his voice made me start.

"Just a sec," Kiaya replied.

Devon put his hand on my shoulder, his touch gentle, and leaned forward. "You need to relax. I know it's going to be tough, and I'm sorry, but I promise I'll make it as fast as possible."

All I could do was nod, and when my head barely moved, it occurred to me how tense my muscles were.

I exhaled, working to ease the tension in my body. "I'll try."

Devon gave my shoulder a little pat before moving his hand.

Something behind me rustled, and I looked back to find him pulling gloves on. Once he had, Kiaya passed him the needle, which now had black thread dangling from it. Then she moved so she was standing next to me. When she slipped her hand into mine, I looked up. Her smile was tight and didn't reach her eyes, but she was doing her best to reassure me, so I returned it with a tense one of my own.

A hand touched my back, and I stiffened. "I'm going to start. Try your best to hold still."

I nodded but said nothing.

The first poke made me jerk, but Devon's firm hand on my back reminded me to hold still. I squeezed my eyes shut and focused on my breathing as the string pulled tight, tugging at the throbbing cut. Another prick came a second later, and I had to bite back a scream. My grip tightened on Kiaya's hand until her bones were grinding together, but I couldn't relax because every inch of me was preparing for the next jab of pain. It came fast, and even my closed eyes couldn't hold the tears in. They rolled down my cheeks, hot against my skin, and more forced their way out with the next poke of the needle.

"One more," Devon said, his voice low, "you're doing great, Rowan. Just hang on."

I nodded, bobbing my head faster than necessary, and ground my teeth. One last poke, and I let out a deep breath, my body slumping against the tabletop while Devon tied the stitch off. A second later, he grabbed the scissors and a snip followed, then he let out a breath as well.

"Finished."

I opened my eyes but didn't move. Kiaya's hand was crushed in mine, and I had to force my grasp to relax so she could pull it free. She flexed her fingers, wincing.

"Sorry," I said.

"It's okay," Kiaya assured me.

She wiggled her fingers again.

"I'm just going to clean it up and put a bandage over it," Devon said from behind me.

"Okay," I mumbled.

After the pain of the last few minutes, the cool alcohol almost felt soothing against my cut when Devon wiped it down,

FAR from HOME

then Kiaya passed him some gauze and the medical tape, and a few seconds later, he was done.

I finally sat up.

"You okay?" Devon asked when I turned to face him.

His expression was softer than usual and filled with sympathy and concern, which was a relief. I'd really been afraid he'd tell me to stop being a baby.

"I'll be fine," I said and forced out a smile. "Thank you."

"Sorry I couldn't do anything about the pain."

"It's not your fault." I let out a deep sigh and looked around.

It had to be midday by now, and in the midst of everything else going on, I hadn't thought about food. Now, though, my stomach growled, reminding me that I needed to eat.

"We should grab some lunch before we load the car," I said, looking back and forth between my two traveling companions.

Devon's gaze moved past me, focusing on the diner. "We could see what they have that hasn't gone bad. The electricity hasn't been out that long, and they could have a gas stove."

Again, my stomach rumbled. "That sounds amazing."

Devon got to his feet and held his hand out to me, and I took it without thinking. A throb radiated across my back when I stood and the stitches pulled tight, but at least I wouldn't start bleeding again.

We gathered the few things we had sitting around before heading across the street.

I walked between Devon and Kiaya, who both held guns, all three of us keeping our eyes open as we went. The silence that had fallen over the world was still foreign, but even worse were the sounds breaking through the quiet. A clatter in the distance that was impossible to identify or a thud that sounded like a door. Hell, even the distant bark of a dog made me jump.

"The world has turned into a horror movie," I muttered.

We slowed as we approached the diner, and Devon let out a snort. I shot him a look, thinking he was making fun of me, but he was nodding when he looked my way.

"I couldn't have said it better."

"I've always hated scary movies," Kiaya said.

"I used to like them," I replied. "Not anymore."

Since I was the only one not armed, I hung back while Devon pushed the door open a couple inches. My heart was already pounding, and when a bell chimed, it beat faster. I'd forgotten all about the bell above the door.

"Shit," Devon muttered, looking first behind us and then into the restaurant.

Kiaya had her gun out but not up, and I found myself suddenly mesmerized by it. The thing looked so out of place in her hand. So out of place in the world I was used to. But this wasn't that world, was it? This was something new and scary, and in this reality, weapons were a necessity.

Too bad I didn't have one.

Devon had stepped inside, but stopped as if waiting for something. Kiaya was behind him, one hand holding the door open while the other gripped her gun. I moved so I could take her place as the door holder, and she gave me a tense smile. None of us spoke, and no one stepped farther into the diner. It was dark and as silent as it had been outside, and while there was an underlying scent of rot in the air, it wasn't very strong, and it didn't make me think of death. It was more like spoiled food.

"I think it's clear," I hissed, keeping my voice low just in case.

Devon's back stiffened at the sound of my voice, but he nodded to indicate he thought the same thing. He didn't look back when he said, "I'm going to do a quick sweep. Stay here."

He took off, and I stepped in but didn't shut the door. The bell was mounted above it, and I didn't want it to ring again if I could avoid it, only I wasn't sure if we'd be able to get it down.

"Kiaya," I hissed, drawing her attention. "Grab a chair and pull it over. See if you can get that bell down."

Her nod was stiff, but she didn't hesitate. I kept my focus on the open door while I waited, just in case something had heard the bell and decided to check it out. The coast stayed clear, though. Nothing moved as Kiaya set the chair in front of me and climbed up then messed with the bell. I couldn't see what she was doing, I was too focused on keeping watch, but in a matter of minutes she'd climbed down.

"You're good," she said as she moved the chair.

Despite her reassurances, I glanced up. The bell still hung above me, but the little piece inside had been removed. Smart. I released the door, and it swung shut with only a small clang that didn't even make my heart beat faster. I threw the deadbolt.

I smiled when I turned to face Kiaya. "Nice."

"It was bolted in pretty good, so I figured this was the next best thing." She waved the little metal piece.

Footsteps banged against the floor, heading our way, and we both turned.

"Clear," Devon said, looking a hell of a lot more relaxed than a few minutes ago. "You hungry? It looks like they have gas."

"Thank God," Kiaya said while I answered, "Yes."

We found meat in the freezer, barely thawed out, and plenty of buns. Kiaya and I munched on dinner rolls while slicing tomatoes and chopping lettuce, and Devon warmed up the cooktop. I tried not to think about how this might be our last hot meal for a while. It was too depressing, and too terrifying.

"So, what's next?" he asked as he pried the frozen hamburger patties apart. "Do we head out tonight or get some more rest before taking off?"

"Leave," I said. "There are too many zombies trapped in rooms, and after seeing one open a door, I don't want to risk it."

"I agree," Kiaya said.

"Sounds good to me," Devon said, his gaze focused on his task. "If all goes well, we'll be in Ohio tomorrow."

"We have to stop in Indiana first," Kiaya said.

I froze in the middle of sliding a knife across a tomato. "What do you mean? You said you didn't have anyone there. You said you weren't even sure why you were going back."

"I lied." She didn't look up.

I set the knife down and turned, grabbing her arm so she was forced to face me. "Talk. Now."

"I have a sister," she said, still not looking at me. "I haven't seen her for a few years—she's in foster care, too—and we haven't been on great terms for a while. It's why I hesitated to head back, but I decided I needed to find her."

"Why didn't you tell me that to begin with?" I couldn't keep the hurt out of my voice. I'd thought Kiaya had opened up to me, but it turned out she hadn't, and it stung.

She ventured a look up, and even the guilt swimming in her eyes couldn't ease my pain. "It's nothing personal, okay? I don't share anything about my life with other people. In my experience, other people will only hurt you, so it's just easier to keep your distance."

I released her, dropping my arm to my side. "And you think I'm going to hurt you?"

"Rowan," she said, "it isn't like that."

"I don't know what else it could be like," I replied before turning back to my tomatoes.

This time when I started slicing, the action was violent, the blade slamming into the cutting board and the thud ringing through the silent room. Kiaya returned to what she'd been doing as well, not trying to comfort me or defend herself, and I brought my knife down harder.

"I take back everything I thought about you," Devon said, breaking the silence. "Based on the way you're butchering those tomatoes, I have a feeling you could handle yourself pretty well."

I shot him a warning look, and when he responded with a wink, it occurred to me that he was only trying to break the tension. Or at least redirect some of my anger so it wasn't aimed at Kiaya. It was kind of a sweet thing to do, but I only rolled my eyes before going back to my tomatoes.

My annoyance was short-lived, because deep down I knew I had nothing to be upset about. Kiaya didn't know me, and she didn't owe me anything. Especially not the darkest details of her life. I was being unfair.

That didn't mean it didn't sting.

The sizzle of cooking meat filled the room, and the greasy scent had my stomach begging for food. Beside me, Kiaya was going through some of the containers we'd found in the fridge, smelling the contents to decide what was still good. The potato salad was apparently a no-go, but she put a big serving spoon in

FAR from HOME

the giant container of coleslaw and another in the macaroni salad.

"So where in Indiana are we stopping?" I asked as I piled the slices of tomato onto a plate.

She didn't turn my way, but I could tell she was watching me out of the corner of her eye. "Indianapolis. Or just outside it, really."

"You have an address for your sister?"

"I do," she said.

"Okay." I let out a deep breath, nodding. "Indy is on the way to Troy, so it should be an easy detour."

Almost hesitantly, Kiaya turned to look at me. Her smile was shaky, but it felt like a peace offering. I nodded twice to let her know I was good, and her shoulders relaxed.

Devon cleared his throat. "Not to interrupt, but I think these are done."

We made our burgers and piled generous helpings of macaroni and coleslaw on our plates before heading to a table. It was strange seeing the diner empty after how busy it had been when we first arrived. I hadn't even been able to find a place to sit that day, and now it was deserted and would most likely remain that way indefinitely. Just like nearly every other place in the world.

The thought was almost depressing enough to make me lose my appetite. Almost.

We ate in silence for a few minutes, our chewing the only sounds in the diner. My mind was mentally tracing the path we would take. From Texas to Oklahoma, then up to Missouri before heading over to Indiana. Then finally, after weeks of wanting to be there, I'd be home in Ohio.

What would the world be like?

If this empty town were any indication, it would be like another world. Home would be familiar, but different at the same time, and I couldn't even imagine it. Would I be alone? I didn't know for sure if Mom would be there—I prayed she would be, though—but what about the others? Would Kiaya and her sister come with me? Would Devon stay in Troy, or head to West Chester?

Realizing I was open to Kiaya coming with me, and possibly even Devon staying, seemed odd, but I couldn't deny it was true.

I swallowed my food and focused on Kiaya, saying, "What happens after we stop in Indianapolis?"

She shrugged, chewing slowly as she thought about it, then swallowed. "I don't know. I guess my sister and I will have to talk about it."

"You could come with me," I said. "I mean, I don't know what I'm going to find at home, and I don't want to be alone. Safety in numbers, right?"

She nodded, but it was slow and noncommittal. I knew why; she'd made it clear dozens of times by now. Kiaya didn't trust other people, and that included me.

"We'll see."

"We have time," I replied. "Just think about it."

"Does that go for me, too?" Devon asked, drawing my attention.

"You don't want to go home to West Chester?" I asked him.

"No point." He shrugged. "I don't have any family there. I don't have any family anywhere, really."

"What happened to them?" I found myself asking.

"My parents died when I was ten." He frowned like the memory still hurt. Thanks to this virus, I didn't even have to work that hard to imagine how awful it had been. "Car accident. After that, my grandma raised me, but she died the year after I graduated from high school. I'm not married, and my girlfriend and I broke up about six months ago. There's nothing for me in West Chester but things, and let's face it, most of that stuff is worthless now."

I snorted, thinking about the items I left in my dorm room, things I'd never see again but would also never miss. Books, clothes, shoes. Some of the pictures would have been nice to have, but I could live without them. In fact, I had a feeling most of the things I used to think were so important I'd soon discover had been pointless. Like Devon said.

"I hear you," I said before taking another big bite of my burger.

FAR from HOME

Devon grinned and his dimple deepened. "Does that mean I get an invite to the apocalypse sleepover, too?"

Something about his expression, about the grin and the playful glint in his eyes, combined with the bulging biceps, brought my ex-boyfriend to mind. That was when it hit me why he got under my skin so easily. He reminded me of Doug, the guy who'd dumped me for the cheerleader.

God, I'd liked him so much. All freshman year we'd flirted, then finally he'd asked me out the second week of sophomore year. I'd been ecstatic. Over the moon. We'd gone out once, twice, three times. Months passed, and we went to homecoming, then prom in the spring. That was when we'd slept together, at a hotel room he'd booked for the night. He'd been my first, and when he'd whispered that he loved me, I'd believed it. More than a year we dated, and when he'd dumped me for Jessie Simpkins a few weeks into my junior year, I'd been utterly heartbroken. I never thought I'd get over him, had barely dated since.

Of course, as time moved on, those feelings of loss and pain had morphed into others. Bitterness and eventually hatred. Which was why Devon had irritated me the moment he opened his mouth. He had that same cocky self-assurance about him. At least on first impression. Now, though, I was starting to see something else. Something better and stronger.

Still, I had a tough time shaking the image of Doug.

His smile faded when I didn't answer. "What is it?"

"Nothing." I shook my head as I picked at my macaroni salad, avoiding his gaze. "I just realized you remind me of someone. That's all."

"Someone you like, I hope," he responded.

I only snorted in response.

"Oh."

I wasn't being fair, but I couldn't push away the similarities between the guy who'd broken my heart and the man across from me. Hopefully, as we got to know one another, it would get better. Otherwise, this was going to be an awkward trip.

Kiaya took a bite of her burger, looking thoughtful as she chewed. Even before she'd swallowed, I knew she had something on her mind, and while I didn't know why, I braced myself when she opened her mouth to say something.

"We should talk about this whole zombie thing."

Devon froze in the middle of scooping up some macaroni salad. "What about it?"

"Well, about what we know so far, which isn't a whole lot. We know this virus, whatever it is, kills people and they come back. But Kyle died almost two days ago, so it looks like people don't come back right away."

"True," I said, trying not to think about the terror I'd felt in that room when I'd had to fight him off.

"We know we're immune to the virus, too, but what we don't know," Kiaya continued, "is what happens if we get bitten."

Devon set his fork down, and it clanged against the plate, the sudden noise making me jump in the otherwise quiet diner. "In the movies, people always turn from a bite."

"Exactly," Kiaya punctuated the word. "But this is real life."

We lapsed into silence.

I'd fought two zombies off at this point, both times trying to avoid letting them get their teeth in me on instinct alone. Maybe in the back of my head I'd been terrified what a bite might mean, but not at the time. Then I'd only been focused on survival. But Kiaya was right, and zombie fan or not, I knew what could possibly happen if bitten.

"Well," Devon said thoughtfully, "I'm sure we'll eventually find out one way or the other. In the meantime, let's just try to avoid getting bitten altogether. It's the only way to be sure."

"Seriously," Kiaya muttered.

Devon went back to eating his macaroni while Kiaya picked at her coleslaw, but my appetite had disappeared. We were probably all thinking the same thing. About watching our friends die from the virus and how horrible it had been and how we'd been sure we were safe, only now that certainty was gone. No one was safe.

I thought about Mom, home by herself and possibly clueless about what was happening. There were so many houses around her, so many dead neighbors who would come back. Was she staying inside like she promised? God, I hoped so.

I jumped to my feet, my hand already moving to my back pocket. "I'm going to try to give my mom a call."

When I hit the button and the screen lit up, the little bar in the top right hand corner made me frown. Fourteen percent. I'd need to charge it in the car.

"Stay close," Devon said, his tone serious.

I nodded to the back of the restaurant. "I'll just step into the kitchen."

The others nodded, and I headed off, already pulling up my recent calls so I could click on Mom's name. The phone was pressed to my ear when I stepped into the kitchen, and the cloying scent of rotten food made my nose wrinkle. It wasn't death, though, so I had that much to be grateful for, at least.

I thought of what I would say to my mom as the phone rang. If she didn't already know about the zombies, I had to warn her. I could only imagine a neighbor, now undead, stumbling down the street. Mom was a kindhearted person, like Kiaya, and if she saw someone she thought might need help, I wouldn't put it past her to go outside. She had to know how imperative it was that she stay indoors.

I was so focused on my thoughts that I barely registered when the ringing stopped and her voicemail picked up.

That was odd.

I disconnected the call without leaving a message, ignoring the way my stomach tightened, and tried again. Like before, all it did was ring, but this time when her usual chipper recording asking the caller to leave a message greeted me, I didn't hang up.

"Mom, it's me. We're heading out soon and I wanted to let you know." I paused, wondering if I should tell her about the zombies. I didn't want to freak her out, or make her think I was insane. Instead I said, "Stay inside and call me back when you get this. My phone is almost dead, but once we get on the road, I'll be sure to charge it. I love you."

I hung up but didn't move right away, instead staring down at the phone. Why hadn't she answered?

The possibilities were too scary to even consider.

12

We didn't bother cleaning up our mess before leaving the diner, which of course left me with a bad feeling.

Outside, things were exactly how we'd left them. Hot and sunny and empty, with only distant sounds breaking the quiet. They got louder as we crossed the street, heading back to the motel, and I knew what they were before I even saw the movement in the nearest car. Still, I found myself stepping closer to Devon without thinking.

He eyed me but didn't smile, almost like he was afraid to be playful. "You're not stepping closer to me because you need protection, are you?"

Okay, not afraid.

"No." I rolled my eyes. "It's because you have a gun and Kiaya has a gun, but I have nothing."

I lifted my hands to show they were empty.

Why hadn't I taken a knife from the diner? That would have been smart.

"Shit." Devon pulled a knife from the newly acquired sheath strapped to his waist and held it out to me. "Sorry. I'm an idiot."

"Thanks," I said, forcing out a smile.

He returned it but said nothing, and I knew why. I'd made things awkward—or more awkward—and still hadn't answered his question about whether he could stay. It was a shitty thing to do and not like me. I wasn't a selfish person.

"You know you can stay at my house if you need to," I told him, then playfully elbowed him in hopes of easing the tension. "I mean, I think I kind of owe you for saving my ass and stitching me up."

"I don't want you to feel like you have to do something you don't want to," he said.

"No," I assured him and almost sighed with relief when the word came out firm. "It really is okay."

"Thanks," he said, a genuine smile pulling up his lips.

No one said anything else until we'd reached our room.

"I know we want to get on the road, but I'd like to take a shower while the water is still working," Kiaya said when we stopped outside the closed door, looking between us. "You think that's okay?"

The bangs as zombies tried to free themselves from cars were almost constant now, and as much as I wanted to get out of here, I had to admit the idea of taking a quick shower was appealing. Between the lack of AC in the diner and how sweaty we'd gotten loading the car, I felt like a ball of dirt.

"What do you think?" I asked Devon, not trusting myself to make the decision with the lure of a shower calling to me.

"As long as we make it fast, I don't see how fifteen extra minutes will make that much of a difference." He shot me a grin. "Which means no skinny dipping today, I'm sorry to say."

"I wasn't skinny dipping."

I rolled my eyes as Kiaya shoved the door to our room open and followed her inside. She'd flipped on one of the flashlights we'd scavenged from the cars and set it on the dresser. The beam was pointing up, illuminating the area surrounding it but not the corners, but it was better than nothing.

"I know," Devon said. "Which is another thing I'm sorry about."

My glare was met with his smile growing wider.

FAR from HOME

"You two are going to be a load of fun to travel with." Kiaya grabbed some clothes from her bag and headed for the bathroom. "I'll make it quick."

The door clicked shut a second later, leaving Devon and me alone.

He was still smiling, so I turned my back on him and got busy digging through my suitcase. It took a minute to find the leggings I was looking for, but thankfully the shirt and bra I'd wanted were right under them.

I was still searching my bag, looking for underwear, when Devon said, "That's a lot of stuff."

"What do you mean?" I looked over my shoulder at him.

He nodded to the bag. "The suitcase. It's a lot of stuff to pack."

"I was going home, and I didn't know when I'd be back at school, so I took as much as I could. What's it matter, anyway?"

"Doesn't matter," he said, "I'm just making an observation. That's all."

That I was high maintenance. I could read between the lines. Figured. Just when I was beginning to thaw toward him, he had to be an ass.

"Well, you can just keep your observations to yourself, thank you. The fact that I packed heavy for a trip home doesn't say a thing about who I am in any other scenario, so don't get any ideas."

He chuckled. "You're awfully defensive."

"With you?" I lifted my eyebrows as I looked over my shoulder at him. "I think I have a good reason."

"You don't."

"Right," I said just as the shower cut off.

He shoved himself off the dresser and headed my way. "I want to take a look at that cut before you take a shower."

Before I could respond, he'd grabbed my hips and turned me so my back was facing him, then ran his hands up each side of my waist, moving my shirt aside. His skin was warm against mine, and his hands calloused and strong, and something about the firm way he grabbed me made my knees suddenly weak. My body

151

responding to him this way was ridiculous, because I wasn't even sure I liked him. Yes, he was reliable and capable, but he was also irritating and judgmental, and he teased me about stupid things at inappropriate times.

"Relax," he said, his breath brushing my cheek.

I shivered, and he let out a low chuckle that seemed to wrap around me. It was more irritating than his teasing.

"Hold still," he said as he removed the gauze.

I looked back as he knelt, his hands still on my hips but his focus on the cut. My heart had sped up and it was thumping through my head loudly enough to drown out every other sound, but I could feel every move he made. Could feel his breath caressing my back when he exhaled, could feel his fingers as they flexed on my hips, could feel his pulse thumping.

"It stopped bleeding, so that's good." His gaze moved up to meet mine and he smiled. "You'll be ready for regular physical exertion in no time."

I flushed and his smile widened.

He stood but didn't move his hands, and when his gaze moved down, he wasn't looking at the cut anymore. He was looking at me, caressing my backside with his gaze, memorizing my curves.

The bathroom door clicked, and he released me, stepping back.

The second his hands were off me, I was finally able to breathe.

"It's cold, but it's better than nothing," Kiaya said when she stepped out.

"Good." My voice came out higher than usual, and I cursed myself for being so affected by Devon.

Kiaya froze and looked between us, but I refused to meet her gaze as I scooped my clothes up and hurried into the bathroom. I shut the door and leaned against it, letting out a sigh. Right now, I was more than grateful the shower was cold, because that was what I needed. That and a lobotomy. How the hell was I attracted to Devon? Not only did he remind me of my asshole ex-boyfriend, but he was also irritating as hell.

FAR from HOME

When Devon slid behind the wheel and held his hand out, I wanted to scowl, but the truth was, I was happy not to have to drive.

I slapped the keys into his hand and rolled my eyes when his sparkled.

"Someone has their panties in a bunch," he commented with a smirk.

"Don't look so smug," I said, "you have no effect on my panties."

"Not yet." He slid the keys into the ignition. "Just wait until things settle down, and we'll see."

I rolled my eyes again before turning away.

Kiaya had already slid into the back seat. Shit.

I walked around to the other side of the car and stuck my head in through the open passenger door. "You sure you don't want to sit up front?"

"It's your car," she said.

"I'm really okay with the back."

"So am I." She lifted her eyebrows and jerked her head toward Devon, who saw it in the rearview mirror.

He chuckled and grabbed my hand, pulling me inside. "Let's go before more of the dead figure out how to open doors."

Grudgingly, I pulled the door shut.

The first thing I did was plug my phone in, and the little lightning bolt telling me it was charging was a welcome relief. Mom would call. She had to.

We were silent as Devon pulled out of the parking lot. Finally being on the road was a relief, but it wasn't totally stress free. We had no idea what was next. What dangers we would face or what would greet us when we reached our destination. The fact that I hadn't been able to get through to my mom weighed on me, and no matter how much I told myself it was downed cell towers or something like that, there were no guarantees. I could get home to find her dead from the virus. Or worse, from the zombies.

The town of Vega, Texas flew by, ghostly in its silence. We passed dark houses, and I didn't miss that more than a few had doors hanging open. Each time I saw one, I searched the surrounding area, expecting to see one of the dead, but there was nothing. In fact, we'd almost reached the edge of town before I saw one. The zombie was small—a kid, maybe—and far away, ambling down the road with its arms raised. Possibly it was headed toward us, drawn by the sound of the car, but it wouldn't reach us. It was too slow and too far off. Still, dread built in my stomach as it stumbled down the road, moving faster at the sight of the car. In seconds, it was out of sight, but the unease inside me didn't disappear.

When Devon continued on Route 66, I turned to face him. "We can probably take a different route now. I mean, I doubt anyone is out patrolling anymore."

"I think sticking to Route 66 would be the smartest thing to do." He took his eyes off the road long enough to glance my way. "The other roads will take us through major cities, but Route 66 is more scenic. We'd be driving through small towns, most of which were probably sparsely populated. It will mean a lower chance of running into trouble."

He had a point.

"Okay," I said, nodding as I thought about it. "That sounds smart."

Unfortunately for us, Route 66 and Interstate 40 happened to be the same thing, which meant driving right through Amarillo.

We came upon it less than thirty minutes after leaving Vega, but I didn't see it coming since my eyes were closed, and I was only alerted to the possibility of trouble when Devon started swearing.

I sat up, my eyes flying open, and looked around. "What is it?"

"Amarillo." His hands were wringing the steering wheel and his gaze was focused on the road in front of us. "Shit. This could be bad."

FAR from HOME

I followed his gaze, and my stomach flipped when I caught sight of the city in the distance.

"We're going to drive right through it?" Kiaya asked from the back.

"Looks that way." Devon glanced at the rearview mirror, and since the road was totally deserted, I knew he was looking at her. "It could be fine. Most people probably died inside, and just because that one zombie was able to open doors doesn't mean they all can."

I thought about the houses we'd passed on our way out of Vega and all the front doors that had been hanging open.

"There were others," I told him.

Devon shot me a look. "What do you mean?"

"As we were leaving Vega, I saw a lot of front doors open. I think other zombies figured out how to get out."

"We didn't see any," Kiaya said.

"I saw one." I looked between them. "It was far away, but it was walking around. There were probably others, too. We only went down that one street, and we were gone so fast. It makes sense why we didn't see more."

"Shit," Devon said again.

"We'll just drive," Kiaya said. "I mean, we're in a car and they're just people, after all."

"Undead people," I reminded her.

"But they're still flesh and bone. They're no match for a car."

"That's true." Devon nodded a few times, and I got the feeling he was trying to convince himself. "Okay. We'll drive through and not stop, and it will be okay."

"Yeah," I said, but like him I was trying to make myself believe it.

One or two zombies weren't a match for a car, but hundreds? Thousands? I had no idea how many people had lived in Amarillo, but if all of them had figured out how to open doors and had crowded the streets looking for a meal, getting through would be tough. If not impossible.

Not that I said this to Kiaya and Devon. Part of me didn't want them to be as scared as I was, but another part of me felt like voicing the words might give them more validity. That was the last thing I wanted to do.

We reached the city, and I leaned forward, scanning the street in front of us as well as the areas surrounding it. Stores were dark, and many had broken front windows like they'd been looted. Glass littered the ground, shimmering in the sunlight, and for the first time the chaos of what had happened became real. Cars were half on sidewalks, their doors hanging open like the occupants had fled in a hurry. We passed a body lying on the side of the road outside a Mexican restaurant. It was bloated from the sun, but even worse were the bites on the arms and legs and the bloody mess that had once been its face.

I turned away when my stomach convulsed, but the next thing I saw was no less grotesque. A zombie stumbled toward us, practically dragging one of its legs behind him. The ankle was bent almost at a ninety-degree angle, but that didn't stop the creature from trying to use it. Except every time he tried, the ankle bent even more.

"Oh, my God," Kiaya said, covering her mouth with her hands when she saw the creature.

I swallowed the bile that rose in my throat and looked away. "Keep driving."

It didn't matter how fast Devon drove or where I looked, though. The farther into the city we got, the more zombies came crawling from the woodwork. Our car was like a dinner bell in the silent city, and they must have been able to hear us from really far away, because more and more converged on the street in front and behind us the farther we drove, so that soon we were on the verge of being surrounded.

"Shit, shit, shit, shit," Devon muttered.

"What do we do?" Kiaya cried.

I inhaled slowly then blew the breath out, concentrating as I repeated the process over and over, trying to maintain control. But even the simple act of breathing wasn't easy at the moment. Not with what we were facing. This was what I'd been afraid of. The worst case scenario at the top of a long list of bad scenarios.

Devon's gaze flicked to the rearview mirror, but this time he

FAR from HOME

wasn't looking at Kiaya. He was looking at the road behind us.

His hands, firmly positioned at ten and two, tightened on the steering wheel. "I have to keep going. It's our only option."

Kiaya's head bobbed in silent agreement, but her wide eyes didn't stray from the road in front of us.

So that was what we did. We powered through even as the throng of rotten bodies grew thicker, but like I'd feared, it wasn't long before Devon was forced to slow. A little at first and then more and more as the horde grew thicker. It was too dense to maintain our speed, and only getting worse by the moment.

A creature slammed itself against the side of the car, right outside my window, and I let out a yelp of surprise. When a chorus of moans followed my scream, more zombies followed the first one's lead and banged against the car. I clamped my hands over my mouth to stop any other sounds from coming out, but it did nothing to keep the tears at bay.

Until that moment, the zombies had been satisfied to simply surround us. It was like they hadn't known what to do, only that the sound of the car was too alluring to resist. But with that first bang, followed by my scream, more of them seemed to wake up. Thud after thud sounded as the undead hurled themselves against us, and Devon had to slow more. We were only going fifteen miles an hour now, and there was no end in sight. It was like we were driving through a sea of rotting bodies, and deep inside, I knew we were going to drown.

A constant stream of curse words flowed from Devon's mouth, but behind me, Kiaya was silent. My hands were still over my mouth when I twisted to look at her, and like me, tears were streaming down her face. Her already huge eyes looked bigger than ever when she turned them on me, but she still said nothing. Really, there wasn't anything to say. Goodbye? Goodbyes were for the living, something they could cling to after the person they cared about was gone. Soon, we'd both be dead, so there was no point. No reason to make this any worse than it already was by acknowledging the truth to one another.

The car rocked as the zombies became more desperate. Something banged against the hood, and I turned back to the front.

A rotting man in striped pajamas had climbed on the hood and was clawing at the window, his mouth open and pressed against the glass, his black, rotting tongue jutting out. My stomach convulsed, and I looked away, but no matter where I turned, I was greeted by the decaying faces and hands of the zombies.

I chose to focus on Devon.

He hadn't stopped trying, hadn't stopped the car completely even though we were barely making progress at this point, and his hands were still gripping the wheel. His jaw was tight, exaggerating his already square jawline, and his Adam's apple bobbed over and over again, giving off the impression that he was trying to swallow his fear. As if sensing me staring at him, he tore his gaze from the horde in front of us and focused on me, and when our eyes met, something in me tightened.

"Thank you," I said, having to talk louder than normal so he could hear me over the pounding.

"For what?" He shook his head. "I drove us straight to our deaths."

Hearing the words acknowledged out loud brought a fresh wave of tears, and I had to swallow so I could say, "For saving me earlier. I don't remember if I thanked you."

"You saved me, too," he said. "When you warned me about the zombie sneaking up on me."

"You would have been able to take care of yourself." I managed a smile through the tears. "You know, since you're such a big, strong man."

He returned my smile with a shaky one of his own.

When his gaze moved from me, it was only so he could turn and focus on Kiaya. "I'm sorry you won't make it to your sister."

She swiped her hand across her right cheek then her left. "Me, too."

I let out a deep breath, trying to gather all the strength inside me. With the constant banging of the dead against the car, it wasn't easy to think, but I had to. We were barely moving now, not even two miles an hour, and Devon would soon be forced to stop completely. After that it wouldn't be long before the dead managed to break the windows. Then they'd have us.

FAR from HOME

The thought of being eaten alive made me shudder.

I couldn't think of a worse way to die.

"How many bullets do you have?" I asked Devon, having to talk even louder this time.

His eyebrows lifted in surprise, but I could tell he knew what I was getting at. "Enough."

I nodded.

Plenty of bullets, but only two guns.

We could each kill ourselves, but one of us would be left alive after the other two were gone. It was horrible to even think about, having to wait for a gun so you could end your own life, but it was our only option. And it was still better than being ripped apart by the dead.

I looked from Devon to Kiaya. "Who goes last?"

Devon swallowed before finally stopping the car and putting it in park. "I will."

The pounding increased tenfold, and I had the urge to cover my ears again, but when Devon pulled his gun, I found I couldn't move.

"You know how to use it?" he asked me.

"Point and shoot," I said, the last word distorted by a sob.

He held it out to me. "That's pretty much all there is to it."

My hands were shaking when I took it, and with as small as the thing was, I was surprised by how heavy it felt. Not that I should have been. Something that could do so much damage should be heavy. You should be able to feel the responsibility of holding a weapon the second you picked it up.

Kiaya had the other gun out, and she held it in her hands, staring down at it wordlessly. When she looked up and her gaze met mine, I lifted my eyebrows, silently asking if she was on board with this because I couldn't bring myself to say the words out loud.

She swallowed but nodded.

This was it. We were choosing our own end, which was horrible and scary, but at least it was ours.

Between the banging and the moans, loud enough now to penetrate the glass and metal encasing us, it had gotten too noisy to even try to talk. Not that it mattered. I couldn't think of a single thing to say.

I swallowed twice before I managed to raise the gun. The barrel pressed against my temple, the metal cold and biting, and I turned to face Kiaya. I didn't want to look at her as she died, but I wanted to know we were on the same page, and since we were no longer able to talk, this was my only option. She nodded again and copied me. Watching her lift the gun brought on a fresh round of tears, but this time I didn't try to blink them away. I wanted them to blur her face, wanted them to block out everything around me, if I was being honest, but since that wouldn't happen, I was happy to settle for not being able to see Kiaya as she died.

I moved my finger to the trigger as I silently began to count down, starting at twenty. It was cowardly, but I needed time to prepare myself. To gather the courage. To convince myself this was the only way.

Although I wasn't sure twenty seconds would be enough.

Twenty, nineteen, eighteen…

I sucked in a deep breath.

Seventeen, sixteen, fifteen…

I squeezed my eyes shut and focused on my finger as I forced it to move, positioning it over the trigger.

Fourteen, thirteen, twelve…

You can do this, Rowan. You know you have to.

Eleven, ten, nine…

My brain was focused on counting, but a part of me registered that something had changed even before Devon grabbed my hand and pulled the gun away from my head.

The pounding had lessened.

My eyes flew open and met his, then I spun to face Kiaya, letting out a sigh of relief when I saw she no longer had the gun pointed at her head. Her eyes were wide and full of questions, and she seemed to be listening. With each passing second, the thuds grew fewer and fewer, and before long, another noise became audible. It was distant and hard to distinguish at first, but eventually I registered what it was.

A car alarm.

FAR from HOME

It had to be several streets over, because even now that the pounding had stopped completely, the siren was faint. Still, it was loud enough to draw the dead. I didn't know if it had gone off by accident—it was possible a zombie had bumped a car and set it off—or a person could have done it, but either way, I would be eternally thankful. Even if I died later today, at least I got a little more time to try to get home.

We sat in silence as the road began to clear. Devon had turned the car off at some point—when, I wasn't sure—and with the engine no longer running, there was nothing to keep the zombies interested in us. The windows were smeared with black, reminding me of Kyle's smashed skull. The blood had looked so dark, but I'd assumed it was the lighting. Now I could tell I'd been wrong; it made total sense when I really thought about it. When a person died, their heart stopped pumping blood, and it stood to reason that the blood trapped inside the body would rot just like the rest of the corpse.

After maybe ten minutes of waiting, Devon finally moved. Wordlessly, he pressed a button, and streams of fluid shot up, hitting the windshield and cutting through the layers of black gunk. He kept it going as he flipped on the wipers. At first, all they seemed to do was smear the stuff around, making it more difficult to see out, but Devon kept it up, and things soon got clearer as the layers of black gunk were wiped away.

Once he was able to see, he shut the wipers off and turned the key. When the engine roared to life, I let out a sigh and slumped back, feeling suddenly more exhausted than I ever had.

"Let's get the fuck out of here," Devon said before throwing the car into drive.

Kiaya and I said nothing, but I did look back. When our eyes met, she gave me a shaky and relieved smile, and I returned it.

Devon drove faster than he had coming into town, and I watched as the speedometer ticked higher and higher, soon reaching sixty. Occasionally, something in the road made him swerve. An abandoned car with its doors hanging open, a sixty-inch television still in the box like it had been looted and cast aside when the thieves were forced to run, a bicycle. A body.

Despite how fast he was driving, Devon maneuvered around them effortlessly, not even having to slow. But he was so intent on what he was doing, so focused on getting us away from Amarillo, that when the person ran out into the road maybe a hundred yards in front of us, Devon didn't react at first.

The guy waved his arms, signaling to us, and almost on instinct Devon veered the car to the left like he was planning on going around him.

"Stop," Kiaya called out, and I shouted, "Devon!"

As if our words had snapped him out of it, he slammed his foot on the brake. Kiaya, who wasn't wearing a seatbelt, lurched forward, and the tires squealed against the pavement as we skidded and slowed. I had buckled up, but my body was still thrown forward from the sudden change in momentum. In front of us, the guy who'd rushed into the road dove out of the way even though we weren't headed for him, and the way he rolled toward the sidewalk made my body throb with sympathy pains.

I'd thrown my hands out to brace myself on the dashboard, and my hands were still there, palms down and fingers splayed, when we came to a complete stop. Devon was gripping the wheel, and behind me Kiaya had her hand on her head, which must have slammed into the back of Devon's seat.

In the road, the guy pulled himself up and dusted himself off, his eyes on us.

"What now?" Devon muttered.

He threw the car in park and swept up the gun, which I'd set in the console after my abandoned suicide attempt. A second later, he had his door thrown open and was standing half out, the gun up and pointed at the guy.

"Hands up." Devon's voice boomed through the silent city.

The guy's hands shot up, and his eyes widened. "I'm not dangerous."

It was difficult to get a good look at him thanks to the black smeared all over my window, so I rolled it down, and he came into view. He was young, only a teenager, and the red undertones of his brown skin told me he was probably of Native American descent. His shoulder-length black hair was unkempt like it hadn't been washed in days, and the dirt smeared across his face only emphasized the impression. His plump body contrasted with the agility he'd shown when diving out of the way, and his round face and big, brown eyes appeared innocent and youthful. Trustworthy.

His eyes darted from Devon to me, then to the back where Kiaya was peering out her own window. "I swear. I'm nobody. I'm just trying to find other people."

"Who are you?" Devon asked. I couldn't see him, but since the kid hadn't relaxed, I figured he still had the gun raised.

"Hank Begay. That's all."

"Why did you jump out in front of us?" I asked.

"Let me handle this, Rowan," Devon snapped.

He couldn't see me, but I still rolled my eyes.

FAR from HOME

Hank turned his gaze on me. "Same reason I set off the car alarm. Because you're the first people I've seen in days."

"You set off the car alarm?" I looked him up and down. "So, you saved us?"

"Yeah." Hank's head bobbed. "I was hiding in a store and heard the car drive past. By the time I got out, the zombies were surrounding it. I knew you'd never make it out of there if I didn't do something, so I went a few streets over and started banging into cars until I found one with an alarm. I had to draw them away."

He still had his hands raised, meaning Devon hadn't lowered his gun, so I shoved the door open and climbed out. I turned so I could see Devon on the other side of the car and found the gun aimed right at me.

He lifted it, finally, pointing it toward the sky. "Dammit, Rowan. Don't step in front of a gun. Ever."

"Put it down and stop scaring the poor kid. He saved us."

"You don't know that," Devon snapped. "He says he saved us, but we know nothing about him."

"Why would I lie?" Hank said.

Devon's gaze snapped his way, and I turned so I was once again facing him.

Hank shrugged. "If I wanted you dead, I would have just let the zombies get you."

"He has a point," Kiaya called from inside.

A faint moan rang through the air, and I spun around, searching for its source. Nothing was in sight, but it wouldn't stay that way for long. We needed to get out of the city.

I focused on Devon. "We have to go."

He swore even as he nodded, looking past me at Hank. "What's your plan?"

"To get out of here," the kid said. "That's it."

"We're going to Ohio," Devon replied.

"As long as there are other living, breathing people, I don't care where I go."

One last sigh, and Devon nodded. "Fine. Get in so we can leave."

165

A smile spread across Hank's face, and his hands dropped to his sides. A second later, he was jogging toward the car.

I climbed back in just as a zombie stumbled from a side street, and Devon was two seconds behind me. The second the back door slammed shut, he had the car in drive and was accelerating once again, leaving the undead creature in our dust.

"Thanks for saving us," I said, turning to face Hank.

He gave me a smile that was relieved and grateful at the same time, and the way it lit up his face made him seem even younger. "Thanks for letting me come with you."

"Have you been alone for long?" Kiaya asked him.

He shrugged, and his smile faded until it was nothing but a memory. "Three days. My family all got sick and died, so I was with a friend for a while." He looked down. "The zombies got him."

I swallowed, thinking about having to watch the dead rip apart someone I cared about. I couldn't even imagine it.

"I'm sorry," Kiaya said, her voice gentle and brimming with empathy.

Hank nodded but said nothing, and he didn't look up.

After a moment of silence, I cleared my throat. "Well, I'm glad you found us. I'm Rowan, by the way, and this is Devon and Kiaya."

Hank lifted his head, forcing out a smile despite the sadness brimming in his eyes. "Nice to meet you."

Kiaya gave his arm a gentle pat and said, "You, too."

Hank looked down to where her hand had touched his arm. Pink spread across his cheeks, and when he'd once again lifted his head to look at her, a little bit of life sparked in his eyes.

Oh, Lord.

Devon, unaware of the teenage crush blooming in the back seat, lifted his gaze to the rearview mirror. "How long have you known about this zombie thing?"

"Um..." Hank's voice came out squeaky the way only a teenage boy's could, and he cleared his throat. "Only three days. My friend, Justin, and I were trying to blow off some steam and thought we'd recreate that scene from *Zombieworld*." His gaze darted between us. "You've seen that movie, right? The one with Hadley Lucas?"

Devon nodded, and Kiaya said, "Yeah."

"Sorry." I gave him an apologetic smile and shrugged. "Scary movies aren't really my thing."

"It's more of a comedy," Hank said, returning my shrug. "But I get it. Zombies are an acquired taste." He frowned. "Or were, anyway. Now I guess we're the acquired taste."

Devon snorted out a laugh.

"Anyway," Hank shook his head, "there's this scene in the movie where the characters try to blow off some steam by destroying a store. It's stupid, but funny, and Justin and I wanted to recreate it. It was really more about distracting ourselves from what was really happening than anything else, but it was fun, too. At least at first.

"We were in this touristy gift shop in the historic Route 66 district, just smashing things up with baseball bats, when this guy stumbled in. He looked weird, and he smelled like shit, but we just thought he was sick. Since we didn't want to catch anything from him, we told him to go away, but he wouldn't listen. Then Justin tried to scare him by swinging the bat. He wasn't trying to hit him, although it might have been better if he had." Hank paused and frowned. "The guy grabbed his arm and took a bite out of him."

Kiaya put her hand on Hank's arm again, this time leaving it there, and the kid's gaze moved down. Despite his sorrow over his lost friend, a smile tugged at his lips, and I had to bite back one of my own. Only a teenage boy could manage to swoon over a cute girl at a time like this.

"I'm so sorry that happened to you," she said.

"I fought the guy off." Hank sat up straighter, squaring his shoulders. "I hit him until he let go of Justin, and we took off. He was bleeding everywhere, but probably would have been okay if we hadn't run into more of them. We did, though. We turned a corner, and there was this huge group. There had to be sixty of them. Justin was already bleeding, and they must have been able to smell it, because they were on him in no time." Hanks's shoulders slumped. "I couldn't do anything. I tried, but all I managed to do was get bitten myself."

He lifted his left arm, the one Kiaya's hand wasn't resting on, revealing a bite just below his elbow.

I gasped, and Kiaya scooted away from him, her eyes widening in fear.

"Shit." The car swerved, and Devon righted it before looking over his shoulder at the kid. "How long ago was this?"

"I told you. Three days." Hank looked between us, confused and uncertain. Then understanding dawned, and he shook his head. "I know what you're thinking, believe me. Even though I managed to get away, I thought I was dead because I'd been bitten. I mean, I watched zombie movies. I know how it's supposed to work. But nothing happened. It hurts like a bitch, but I'm still alive."

Kiaya, who was as close to the door as she could get, relaxed a little but didn't move back—much to Hank's disappointment. "So, the bites don't turn you?"

"We were wondering about that," I explained to Hank. "We only found out about the zombie thing this morning, so we don't know much. That was one of our biggest concerns."

Hank shrugged and waved his arm. "I was bitten, and I'm good."

"I guess whatever made us immune to the virus makes us immune to the bites as well," Devon said, his expression thoughtful.

"I guess so," I agreed. "I mean, it sure seems that way."

"Thank God," Kiaya said. "That's one less thing to worry about."

She was right. Not that I had any intention of letting a zombie get close enough to sink its teeth into me, but it was nice knowing if it did happen, I wasn't doomed to turn into a flesh-eating monster.

"We still need to be careful," Devon said, as if echoing my thoughts. "The human mouth is riddled with germs, and just because a bite won't turn us into a zombie, that doesn't mean it can't kill us. There are no more hospitals, no more doctors we can run off to if we get hurt. An infection could mean death, and we can't take that lightly."

"Agreed," I said.

"That's a good point." Kiaya turned to face Hank. "Maybe I should check out that bite? Make sure it looks okay?"

The kid shrugged like he didn't care, but he didn't stop her from taking his arm. He did, however, gaze up at her like a lovesick puppy, and I had to stifle a laugh.

I leaned back so I could get a good look at it as well, and the red, angry bite came into view when Kiaya twisted Hank's arm in her direction. It was swollen, and the skin around it shiny. If it wasn't infected already, it was getting close.

"That doesn't look good," I said.

"It hurts, but it's not awful," Hank tried to assure me.

I could tell he was lying when Kiaya probed it and he grimaced like he was biting back a hiss of pain. His gaze darted to her face as if trying to make sure she didn't see it, though. Luckily for him, she was focused on the bite. Not that it would matter. He was a maybe fifteen or sixteen at the most. Too young for Kiaya.

"We need to find some antibiotics," I said as I turned to face Devon.

"Not sure what we're going to come across from here on out." He nodded to the paper map stuck in the console—the same one I'd been given when I got my travel papers. "Want to take a look?"

"Sure."

I pulled out the now familiar piece of paper so I could scan the route. Not many towns were marked since the map was more or less just an indicator of which way the government had expected me to travel, but there were a few.

"Shamrock, Texas isn't too far," I said, looking up like I would be able to see the town looming in the distance. "We could give it a shot."

"Okay." Devon blew out a long breath and rolled his shoulders like he was trying to ease the tightness in them. "But only if it's a small town. I don't want to run into the same problem we had in Amarillo."

"Agreed," I said, refolding the map and stuffing it into the console.

In the back, Kiaya mumbled her own agreement, but Hank said nothing. When I snuck a peek at them, I found the kid still staring at her. I wasn't even sure if she noticed, but if she did, she was doing a great job of acting like she didn't.

We drove for a while in silence, each of us lost in our own thoughts. I'd still been tense when we left Amarillo behind, and I took the opportunity to convince myself that—at least for the time being—everything was okay. It was a difficult thing to wrap my head around, considering the world was now overrun with the dead and I'd been seconds from shooting myself, but I still tried.

The world whirled by as Devon sped down the deserted road. After about a half hour of driving, we came upon a group of old VW Bugs that had been buried nose down and spray-painted in bright colors. I turned in my seat as we passed, watching them disappear in the distance and trying to reconcile that old world—the one where people had spent free time creating odd attractions to amuse strangers—with the one I now found myself living in. It seemed unreal.

A little after that, a giant cross came into view, looming in the distance. The thing looked huge at first sight, but the closer we got, the more I realized exactly how big it actually was. Hundreds of feet tall, probably.

"Look at that," Devon muttered, breaking the silence that had followed us out of Amarillo.

"Weird," Kiaya said.

"Seems like a waste of money." I shifted so I was looking at Devon. "Like that huge Jesus statue off Interstate 75. Remember?"

His lips twitched. "The one that got struck by lightning and burned down?"

"Yeah. We called him 'Touchdown Jesus' because of the way his hands were lifted toward the sky." I raised my own hands in imitation of the statue, shaking my head as I did. "I never got why a church would spend money on something like that. Imagine all the people they could have helped."

FAR from HOME

"They didn't learn their lesson either," Devon said. "They built a new one when all this started."

"I know. 'Five-dollar footlong' Jesus," I said, letting out a laugh as I once again imitated the monstrosity of a statue, this time holding my arms out as if trying to illustrate how big a footlong sub was. After dropping my hands, I said, "Maybe God was the one who sent this virus. I mean, He did use the flood to wipe out humans when they got too corrupt. Who's to say this wasn't His doing as well? It's not like the world is a beautiful, happy place anymore."

"No," Devon replied, nodding thoughtfully like he agreed but was also thinking it through, "but this isn't likely to make it any better. Let's face it, with the collapse of society, the assholes are going to rise up and try to take power. Just wait. You'll see."

"I don't need to see," I muttered. "I've never been under any delusion that people are basically good. I'm a realist, remember?"

The corner of his mouth turned up and he looked my way. "I remember."

We passed the cross and the town of Groom, which was little more than a blip on our map. Just outside the city limits, we were greeted by yet another Route 66 historic spectacle. This time it was an old water tower with the words *Britten USA* painted on it, only it wasn't like any water tower I'd ever seen because it was leaning dangerously to one side. It looked like it might fall over at any minute.

"You think that was done on purpose?" I asked to no one in particular as we sped past it.

"Naw," Devon said. "It's just old, I bet."

"Actually," Hank leaned forward, putting his head between the seats, "some old guy a long time ago put it up as a way to attract people. He had a restaurant and thought it might help business."

"Did it?" Kiaya asked.

"Yup." Hank beamed at her as he sat back. "People call it the leaning tower of Texas."

"Weird," I said again.

After that, we passed a whole lot of nothing. Brown, flat

landscape stretched as far as the eye could see only broken up by the occasional sign or building, many of which looked like they'd been abandoned long before the virus hit. We didn't talk, and I felt a little bad about not trying to get to know Hank, but to be honest, I wasn't sure what to say to the kid. I could ask him questions, but everything that popped into my head was bound to lead to pain, considering what he'd just been through, which put me at a total loss for words. It wasn't like me. Although not many of the things I'd done over the last few days were like the me I was used to.

Devon slowed when we approached a checkpoint, and I started to reach for my travel papers but stopped when nothing moved. A makeshift shelter was set up beside the road that reminded me of something you'd see deployed soldiers in a movie sleeping in, and one vehicle. It was a big military Humvee, Army green from top to bottom. But not a single person was in sight.

Devon slowed even more before finally stopping only six feet from the Humvee, but he didn't turn the car off.

"What are we doing?" Kiaya asked.

He gnawed on his bottom lip for a second before replying. "I want to take a look around." He twisted so he could see the rest of us. "If whoever was here got sick and died, they might have left some guns behind."

I thought about the other checkpoints we'd gone through and the large automatic weapons the soldiers had carried. Having one—or more—of those would come in handy if we ran into another horde.

"Yeah," I mumbled as I scanned the area surrounding the checkpoint. "Good idea."

Nothing was moving, but my heart was still pounding like crazy. There was literally no way to go into an unknown situation anymore without worrying, because dead bodies were walking the Earth trying to eat the few of us who were left. It was a strange reality to face, but there it was.

Devon let out a deep breath before grabbing the gun from the console once again. "Here goes nothing." He shoved his door open and started to get out but froze when I reached for the door handle. "What are you doing?"

"I'm coming," I said. "I stayed behind earlier because I was bleeding, but I'm not bleeding anymore, so there's no reason to stay here."

"How about the fact that you're not armed?" Devon snapped.

"I may not have a gun," I said, pulling out the knife he'd given me earlier and waving it, "but I have this."

"Can't you do anything the easy way?" he asked, but he was already shoving the car door open the rest of the way.

I gave him the best smile I could manage under the circumstances. "Just because it isn't your way doesn't mean it's not the right way. Remember that down the road."

Then I shoved the door open and climbed out.

Devon groaned but got out of the car without saying anything else.

The first thing I did once I'd shut my door was take a deep breath through my nose. It smelled like the outdoors. No rot. It was a good sign, but since we were in a pretty open area, I decided not to let my guard down. The wind could be carrying the stench away from us.

The door clicked behind me, but I didn't look back before heading after Devon. He had his gun up and ready and was walking slowly, taking measured steps that barely made a sound even in the stark silence.

His first stop was the Humvee. The doors were shut, so he grabbed the sideview mirror and pulled himself up until he could peer through the window. I stayed behind him, keeping a lookout while he checked the interior, and one glance over my shoulder was enough to tell me Kiaya was doing the same. Hank had stayed in the car, which was good, since as far as I knew, he wasn't armed—although maybe he'd managed to find a weapon sometime during the three days he'd been on the run from the zombies—but she had her gun out and ready just like Devon. Seeing it made my knife feel insignificant and useless. Hopefully, we'd be able to find a gun for me.

After a couple minutes, Devon hopped down. "Nothing

moving inside."

He reached behind him and shoved his gun in the waistband of his pants before trying the door. When it opened, I almost smiled. Almost.

Devon climbed inside, and I moved so I was standing in front of the open door. He was searching the interior, and while the Humvee didn't have the usual glove compartments and other nooks and crannies civilians were used to, there were a few places where supplies had been stashed. On the floor in front of the back two seats, Devon found a canvas bag, and inside were a couple MREs, a canteen filled with old coffee, and three notebooks.

He handed me the MREs. "These will come in handy, I'm sure."

"Probably," I said as I took them.

He went back to searching the interior, and I craned my neck, trying to get a look inside. The vehicle was set up so you could see all the way through it, and I spotted a couple green metal cases in the back. I wasn't sure how—movies, maybe—but the second I laid eyes on them, I knew what they contained.

Devon grabbed them and pulled them forward, opening the top so he could peer inside. He nodded in approval, but still frowned and looked up, his gaze moving to the shelter. After a few seconds, he was focused on the cases again, shutting the lids before lugging them forward.

"Not much useful in there unless we can find the gun these go to," Devon said when he jumped down a few seconds later, a case in each hand. "Hopefully, we'll have better luck when we search the tent."

"Yeah."

Kiaya stood halfway between the car and the Humvee, keeping watch, and she eyed the metal boxes when we headed her way.

"Ammo cases," Devon said, waving one. "Let's just hope we can get our hands on a gun."

He set them on the ground next to the car, and I put the MREs beside them. It wasn't much, but it was more than we'd had when we got here, so even if we didn't find anything else, I

FAR from HOME

was satisfied. Although Devon was right. The bullets would be useless unless we found a gun we could use them in.

He headed back to the tent, but I paused beside Kiaya. "You okay?"

"Yeah," she said, nodding.

My gaze moved to the car. Hank sat in the back, watching us through the window. "What do you think of him?"

"Not much so far," she said, glancing his way. "I feel bad because I've barely spoken to him, but to be honest, I don't know what to say. How do you ask a person about their life when you know they've lost everything?"

"I don't know," I said. "I was thinking the same thing. I mean, he said he lost his whole family, not just his mom and dad, so that means he probably lost brothers and sisters, too."

Kiaya stiffened, and I felt like slapping myself.

"Sorry. I shouldn't have said that. I'm sure your sister is okay."

She sighed, but her shoulders didn't relax. "It's fine. It's not like I don't know this is a long shot."

"Yeah," I said, then hoping to distract her added, "I guess we're going to have to figure out how to talk to people now. Everyone we meet from here on will be in the same boat, so it's not like it's going to get any easier."

This time, her shoulders did relax, but only so they could slump in what looked like defeat. "True."

I clamped my mouth shut when I realized I'd upset her once again. There was seriously nothing you could say these days that wasn't horribly depressing.

"I'm going to see if Devon needs help," I told her. "Keep an eye out?"

"I've got it," Kiaya said.

I patted her on the arm before jogging to the tent.

Devon hadn't gone in it, which was the only reason I'd stopped to talk to Kiaya. He was digging through some boxes stacked beside the tent, putting things that might be useful aside. There were a couple lanterns and a handful of flares, as well as a few more MREs. I was happy to see the lanterns since electricity would probably be out everywhere we went.

"Everything okay?" he asked when I stopped next to him.

"Yeah, just checking on Kiaya and Hank."

He nodded but didn't look up. "It's lucky finding that kid. Now we know we don't have to be too worried about a bite."

"No kidding," I agreed even as something in me tightened when I thought about that bite. It just seemed too good to be true.

I looked around, shielding my eyes from the sun. It had gotten low as evening neared, and my stomach twisted when I thought about continuing our journey through the dark countryside. About possibly driving through a town and not being able to see the approaching dead, or even coming upon dangerous people and being caught by surprise.

"You think we should try to find a place to hole up before it gets too dark?"

Devon paused so he could look up at me, squinting. "I didn't think you'd want that."

"I don't, not really. I'd love to just get home, but I'm thinking about what's best. Things are different now, and traveling during the day is dangerous enough. Do we really want to push it by traveling at night?"

"No," he said, "but I wasn't going to bring it up. I didn't think you'd listen."

Dropping my hand to my side, I frowned down at him. "You have a really low opinion of me, don't you?"

"No, Rowan, I don't." His lips twitched, and he went back to digging through the box. "I just think you're used to getting your way, which means most of the time you're not willing to listen to anyone else."

"Yeah, well, I think you're a macho jock who's used to everyone doing his bidding without question, which is why it bothers you that I have a mind of my own."

He paused like he was mulling my words over, his mouth turning down. "You might be right."

My mouth fell open.

Devon glanced up and let out a little chuckle. "Don't look so shocked. I'm capable of admitting when I'm wrong."

"I guess so," I said, shaking my head. "It just surprises me, that's all."

Devon stood, huffing as he lifted the heavy box he'd stacked our spoils in. "How about from here on out I agree to listen to you, and you agree to listen to me?"

"I hate that you're being so reasonable," I said, having to contain my own smile. "It makes it impossible to contradict you."

"Good," he said, laughing outright this time, "because I'm too tired to argue. At least for the rest of the day." His eyes flashed. "Although, I'm not going to lie, you do look awfully cute when you get all feisty."

"Cute?" I said, pretending to be offended even as a surge of delight shot through me. "Kittens are cute."

Devon only smirked.

We dropped the box off and headed back to the tent, and Devon pulled his gun before pushing the flap open. The interior was dark, and since I only had a knife, I held the flashlight up and panned it around, illuminating as much of the inside as I could. At the far end, four cots had been set up. They were all empty, and one was on its side, the blankets and pillow strewn across the canvas floor. I kept my flashlight focused on them as Devon moved forward, and when the splatters of red came into view, my heart began to race.

"Do you see that?" I asked, keeping my voice low just in case.

"I see it," he said.

He held his gun in front of him, his arms steady as he headed deeper into the tent. Nothing moved, but we weren't ready to let our guard down just yet. Not until we'd looked every inch over.

I moved the flashlight slowly to illuminate more of the interior. Shadows elongated as I did it, stretching out and becoming distorted until finally blending into the darkness, but still everything was quiet. Even more telling was the smell. Or really, the lack of.

After a thorough inspection, Devon let out a deep breath and lowered his gun. "Whoever was stationed here is gone now." He jerked his head to the right. "This way."

I obeyed, shining the beam where he indicated, and he moved forward. I spotted what he was going for before he'd reached it, but when he picked it up, the sight still made my heart jump for joy.

"A machine gun," I said as he turned to face me.

"An M16," he said. "And exactly the kind of gun we need if we want to use that ammo."

"Thank God," I replied, letting out a sigh.

And I meant it. Whether or not God had brought this virus down on the human race to punish us, I was more than happy for any little help He threw our way. Or in this case, big help, because we had to face the fact that a machine gun was going to end up being a lifesaver at some point.

14

We loaded the new items we'd found into the car, but before climbing in, Devon pulled the handgun from his waistband and held it out to me. I took it almost hesitantly. Like when I'd picked it up so I could shoot myself, the weight of the thing surprised me, except this time it didn't feel so ominous. If anything, it made me feel powerful. Not in a crazy way, but in a way that made me confident I would be able to defend myself if I had to. Which was a relief.

"I'll have to find some time to really teach you how to use it, but for now, you just need to know two things. One, keep the safety on unless you're ready to fire." Devon pointed to a small button. "This is it."

"Okay." I pushed on it, and a click followed. "What's the other thing I need to know?"

"How to aim. You need to look down the barrel like this." He grabbed my hips the way he had in the motel room, moving me so I was in front of him, then positioned my arms so I was holding the gun in front of my face. "See the sights? You need to line your shot up that way. Make sure the front one is dead center between the back two, let out a deep breath, then squeeze the trigger. Got it?"

His face was right next to mine, our cheeks practically touching, and it made my insides sizzle. It was ridiculous, considering how easily he irritated me, but I couldn't push the feeling away.

"Rowan," he said when I didn't answer, "do you understand?"

I swallowed. "Yeah."

"Good." He released me and stepped back. "Now, put the safety on so you don't shoot yourself. When we stop for the night, I'll show you how to reload. We don't have a ton of ammo, but I did find a box of 9mm bullets and an extra magazine with the gun. That will have to do until we can find a gun store or something."

I did as I was told and clicked the safety so it was once again on, then headed to the car. He had the strap of the M16 slung over his shoulder as he moved to the driver's seat. When he reached it, he slipped the gun off and put it in first, the butt on the ground and the barrel pointing up toward the ceiling.

"Wow." Hank leaned forward, his eyes huge and his hand outstretched like he was going to pick the thing up.

"Whoa," Devon said when he'd climbed in. "It's not a toy, so don't get any ideas."

The kid's cheeks reddened, and he sat back. His gaze darted to Kiaya, but he didn't look directly at her. He was obviously too embarrassed.

"I was just looking."

"Doesn't matter." Devon pulled the car door shut. "I need to know you understand how dangerous guns are."

He had turned so he could pin Hank with a serious look, and once again I found myself picturing Devon in uniform. He didn't even need the badge. He had the cop vibe down pat.

"Yeah, I get it," Hank mumbled.

"Good," Devon said and turned back around.

I saw Kiaya pat Hank on the leg, which was probably the only thing that could make the kid perk up at this particular moment. He was still slumped a little, but that didn't stop him from looking her way out of the corner of his eye.

FAR from HOME

Devon started driving again, but for the first time in a while, the silence didn't sit well with me. I was traveling with strangers, but I didn't want them to stay that way.

"Tell us something about yourself," I said, focusing on Hank when I twisted in my seat.

"Me?" The kid looked from Kiaya to me before shaking his head. "I'm pretty boring. I went to school and played video games. That was about it."

"How old are you? What grade were you in?" I stopped myself from specifically asking about his family, but since I didn't want to ignore the fact that they'd existed and he lost them, said, "Anything you want to tell us, really."

"I'm fifteen." He straightened and looked right at Kiaya. "Almost sixteen."

She had to know what he was getting at, but she didn't let on that she did. Instead, she gave him a sweet smile that he could have chosen to interpret as encouragement if he really wanted to, but that no one else would ever be able to accuse her of actually leading him on with.

"So, you were a sophomore?" I prompted.

"Yeah," Hank said. "That's right."

"What was your favorite subject in school?"

Hank paused as he thought about it, once again darting looks Kiaya's way like he was trying to decide what would impress her more. Her expression never changed. It was sweet and interested, and not the least bit encouraging, but I could tell Hank was trying to change that.

"Art," he finally said. "I liked to draw. Thought maybe I'd do something with graphic design one day."

His face fell a little when he realized that would never happen.

"I always loved art, too," I said. "It was better than math, that's for sure."

"I was a math girl myself." Kiaya's smile widened. "Physics, remember?"

"Kiaya is a bit of a brainiac," I told Hank, trying to get him talking again instead of thinking about what he'd lost. "She figured out how to siphon gas."

"Really?" His face lit up. "That's pretty cool. I thought about trying it myself so I could get out of Amarillo, but it seemed too hard."

"It isn't, really," she said, shrugging.

"Just basic physics, right?" Devon said, glancing back at her.

She laughed. "That's right."

I twisted to face Devon. "What about you?"

"What about me?" he asked, his gaze darting my way.

"School, dummy." I gave him a playful punch because I wanted to keep things light. We were talking about stuff that had vanished and would probably never return, so it was a stretch, but possible.

Devon pressed his lips together, and when he looked away, the expression on his face reminded me of how Hank had acted. But that was dumb. Devon wasn't trying to decide what would impress me the most the way Hank had. Was he?

"Honestly," he said after a few seconds, "I wasn't really big into school."

"Let me guess," I said. "You played football, maybe even one or two other sports as well, and dated the cheerleaders on the weekends. Other than that, you only tolerated class because you knew you needed decent grades or you'd get kicked off the team."

I was channeling Doug.

"How'd you know?" he asked, and I was relieved to see him grinning because as soon as I'd said it, I felt bad. It had sounded more accusatory than I'd meant it to.

"You remind me of someone," I said. "Remember?"

"Someone you don't like," Devon said, nodding, still smiling. "I do remember. Let me guess, since we're trying to get to know one another. It's an ex-boyfriend?"

I snorted and rolled my eyes, but like Devon, I was smiling. "One point for you."

"So, we get points for this game?" he asked, his grin growing wider.

"I guess," I said, laughing.

FAR from HOME

I twisted to face Kiaya. "You want in on this?"

"I don't think so." She shook her head, and just like that, the emotionless mask she'd worn the first few days we were together was back.

Of course she didn't. Kiaya didn't want anyone to know anything about her.

I didn't want to push her if she wasn't ready, but I wished she'd get comfortable enough to open up a little.

"You can't divert the attention from yourself that easily," Devon said, partly because he liked teasing me, but the other part was to save Kiaya.

"Fine." I lifted my hands in surrender. "I was just trying to make sure no one felt left out, but it's okay. I can take it."

"We'll see about that," Devon said, then narrowed his eyes on me like he was thinking. "You're a pleaser and a rule follower, so I bet you had straight As in school."

"I got a B once," I said, grimacing. "Geometry. It was like a different language to me."

"I loved geometry," Kiaya said.

I looked back, focusing on Hank. "You take geometry?"

"Not yet," he said, shrugging.

"Well, I guess you won't have to now," I said, then added, "The zombies saved you from that torture, which makes me think they aren't all bad."

Kiaya let out a sarcastic laugh.

"That's another point for me, right?" Devon said, drawing my attention back to him.

"Yeah, yeah," I grumbled then focused on him. "I'm guessing you go to the gym a lot."

It was Hank's turn to snort. "Seems a little too obvious."

"Seriously. I thought you were supposed to be learning new things about each other?" Devon lifted his eyebrows and smirked. "To answer your question, though, yes. I went to the gym every day or ran. Even did a few marathons. I was big into camping and hiking and all that stuff. Although this trip was my first time rock climbing."

"I should get a point for that," I grumbled but paused to

think about everything I'd seen him do or heard him say over the last few days. "You've been on your own for a long time, so you're independent and self-sufficient."

His smile didn't fade, but it did turn a little sad. "Like I told you, my parents died when I was young and my grandma right after high school. Thankfully, she left me everything, so I was set on a place to live, but I was eighteen years old and living on my own already, not a single family member to help me out. It was rough at first, learning to pay bills and do everything for myself, but I didn't have a choice, so I did it."

"I can't imagine," I said, even though it wasn't true. I was trying not to imagine what it would be like if my mom and dad were gone. "My parents do everything for me. Probably to a fault. My dad even takes my car to get the oil changed so I don't have to worry about it."

Took, I mentally corrected myself, *he took my car to get the oil changed, because he will never do that again.*

"You seem to be doing okay," Devon said, trying to reassure me. "You and Kiaya took the initiative to head into town and raid the gas stations. That was something."

"It was Rowan's idea," Kiaya said.

"Wanting to get the hell out of that town was a hell of a motivation," I told her.

"True," she said, nodding.

The conversation helped ease the atmosphere a little, so that by the time we reached the town of Shamrock, I was almost able to convince myself I was on vacation. That illusion was shattered the second I spotted a group of zombies stumbling across a deserted parking lot, headed for us.

"Damn," I said, slumping lower in my seat. "I was hoping we'd imagined them."

Devon only snorted.

"We're going to hit up the pharmacy first," he said, looking back at Hank. "Get you some antibiotics. In the meantime, everyone keep an eye out for a good place to spend the night."

The kid gave him a grateful smile.

Devon glanced my way. "Tell me if you spot it?"

FAR from HOME

I appreciated that he made it a question instead of his usual order. What was more, I took it as a sign that he was really trying to ease some of the conflict between us, which was something I appreciated even more.

"Sure," I said.

I wasn't sure if we'd be able to find it easily, but I scanned the distant signs anyway. Odds were good that it would be near other businesses, so my plan was to find those and go from there.

It ended up not being as easy as I anticipated, though, and we had to drive around in circles for a little bit. It was frustrating and stupid, and after getting a little tour of the town, I started to think we were chasing something that didn't exist. The place was small. Maybe they didn't even have a pharmacy, and we were wasting time and gas for nothing.

Daylight was fading, but even worse was the fact that we'd drawn a lot of attention. More than once we'd passed a street we'd already been down to find a group of zombies where before there had been none. They were searching for us, following the sound of the engine, and if we kept going around and around like this we were going to be in trouble.

I was just about to say as much when the word market jumped out at me from a sign.

"There," I said, pointing to it. "Most grocery stores have pharmacies, right?"

Devon hit the brakes just as he was about to pass the road, then turned into the parking lot.

The sign had made me hopeful, but upon closer look, I wasn't so sure. It seemed to be a combination grocery store and Ace Hardware, which was just strange.

"Maybe not," I said, frowning.

"It's weird, but if they crammed hardware and groceries in one building, maybe they put drugs in there too?" Kiaya suggested, looking between us hopefully.

"Maybe," I said, but I sounded as uncertain as I felt.

"There's only one way to know for sure." Devon yanked the keys from the ignition. "I'll go in first. I want everyone to stay close and stay quiet. We move as a group. Got it?" He looked between us before focusing on Hank. "Are you armed?"

The kid frowned. "No."

Devon swore and shook his head but shifted so he could pull out one of the two knives he'd found. He passed it to Hank, who took it in with wide eyes as his fingers closed around it. He looked like he'd never seen anything like it before, which didn't give me a lot of confidence in his ability to defend himself. Kiaya seemed steadier carrying the gun than Hank did with the knife.

"Stick to the middle." Devon threw the door open, mumbling to himself, "We need to find some more guns."

"We're in Texas," I said. "Doesn't everyone here have a gun? Maybe if we just raid a couple houses?"

Devon looked toward the small, nearby houses, his frown deepening. "I don't like the idea of going into a building that might hold several zombies when we're so unprepared. I'm the only one who has any kind of real training with a gun, and the last thing we need is for these things to get a jump on us."

"It's a risk, I know, but one bite isn't the end of the world," I argued. "If we wait until we get to a bigger town and run into a group of them, we're going to be in trouble whether or not we have an M16."

"You're right. I know you are. I'm just nervous about the idea of taking too many risks when we still don't know a whole lot. Maybe if we could find a police station." Devon blew out a long breath. "We'll talk it over after we get some medicine."

He got out before I could respond, but it was okay. He'd listened, which was all I wanted. He was as right as I was, which I could admit, so it made sense to talk it through before making a rash decision. Who knew? This was Texas, so it was possible we'd find a shotgun under the counter at checkout. I'd seen enough movies where people did that to believe it might be real somewhere. Even if it was a long shot.

We headed toward the building in a group, guns out and ready and Hank in the middle with the knife. Devon was right about one thing. We needed more weapons.

In the distance, I could see figures stumbling between houses, but it didn't seem like they were headed anywhere in particular.

FAR from HOME

My guess was they were waiting for something that sounded like dinner, which meant we needed to be as quiet as possible. This might not have been a huge town, but even so, a thousand residents translated to over eight hundred zombies, which was more than I ever wanted to run into.

Devon paused at the front doors, which I was relieved to see weren't automatic, and took a moment to peer in through the glass. Like everywhere else, the power was out, but a faint glow at the back of the store told me they had some kind of emergency lighting. It wasn't a lot, but it was enough that we'd be able to spot anything lurking through the store.

"Stay close," Devon reminded us before pulling the door open.

We filed in one by one, me behind Devon and Hank next, with Kiaya taking up the rear. The scent of rot hung heavy in the air. It made my insides convulse, but I forced myself to inhale through my nose. There was a very distinct difference between the smell of rotten food and the stink of death, and I wanted to figure out which one I was smelling.

I sniffed a few more times and swallowed when my mouth filled with saliva. My stomach was threatening to release the snacks I'd eaten during the drive, and I did everything I could to keep them down as I sorted through the various smells hanging in the air. The scent of rotten food was heavy, making it hard to distinguish anything else at first, but by the time I'd taken three steps inside, I was positive it wasn't alone.

I grabbed Devon's arm, and he paused to look back at me.

"Do you smell it?" I said, my voice low. "Death."

He swallowed, and his gaze darted around. "Are you sure that's what it is? I can only smell rotten meat."

"I'm sure," I said.

He raised the M16 and nodded, and I was suddenly very grateful we'd talked this whole bickering thing through. It was a hell of a lot easier facing the unknown when he wasn't hellbent on contradicting everything I suggested. And vice versa.

"Stay close," he said again and kept moving.

I could see the pharmacy sign at the back of the store, but I didn't focus on it as we walked. I was too busy looking around, searching for the source of the smell. It was here. I knew it.

We moved down the center aisle in a straight line, headed for the pharmacy, but only made it halfway before something scraped against the floor to our right. Heart in my throat, I turned, but the shelves were high, making it impossible to see into the next aisle. Devon waved for me to follow as he kept moving. I wanted to stay still and wait until I had a better idea of what to expect, but I followed anyway.

Each step I took had my heart beating harder, but I kept going, putting one foot in front of the other and telling myself to stay prepared. My hands were shaking when I clicked the safety off on my gun, and even though I wanted to move my finger to the trigger, I told myself not to. I was trembling too much to trust myself, and the last thing I wanted to do was shoot Devon. Or myself.

Footsteps scraped against the floor this time, the sound distinct and loud in the small store, and I brought my gun up, aiming it at the end of the aisle as I waited for whatever was lurking in the shadows to make itself known. Less than ten seconds later, a figure appeared, big and lumbering, and I made my move. I slipped my finger up, positioning it over the trigger, and lined up the sights the way Devon had told me to, and squeezed the trigger.

A boom echoed through the store, and Kiaya screamed, Hank let out a squeak, and Devon swore. He covered his ears and jerked away, and I realized I'd fired the gun literally right next to his head. The figure ducked and dove, and something about the movements struck me as wrong. They were too fluid and coordinated. Too human.

"Shit, Rowan." Devon grabbed the gun out of my hand. "You trying to give me a heart attack?"

"I was trying to shoot a zombie," I snapped, but my face was burning.

"If it had been a zombie, I would have understood. As it is, you're damn lucky you're a bad shot." He snapped the safety back into place and handed my gun back before lifting the M16.

FAR from HOME

"Come out with your hands up. I'm not going to shoot you, but I want to get a look at you before I decide what happens next."

"Promise," a deep voice replied.

"Yeah," Devon said, sighing, "I promise."

The figure reappeared, and even though I'd already accepted that it wasn't a zombie, I stiffened. He was large, tall and heavy, but when he stepped into the light and his face came into view, the terrified expression in his big, brown eyes made all my uncertainty disappear. He was in his thirties, I guessed, dark skin and hair that was cut short, and big, meaty hands raised above his head. Despite his size, he had a gentle air about him that was impossible to overlook. Even Devon must have seen it right away, because while he didn't lower his gun completely, his stance did relax.

"I don't want any trouble," the guy said.

His hands were up, and there was something clutched in the right one, making me stiffen until I got a good look at it. A Hershey bar.

"We don't either," Devon replied. "We're just passing through. Needed some antibiotics. After that, we'll be on our way."

We'd planned on staying the night, but I knew why he was omitting that part. No need to give this stranger any more information than necessary. Even if he seemed trustworthy.

"You sick?" the guy asked, concern in his voice as his gaze moved past Devon to the rest of us.

He looked from Devon to me, then back to Hank and Kiaya.

"He was bitten," Devon said, nodding to the teenager at his back.

The guy's expression changed in a blink, all his worry melting away and replaced by fear. He backed away, his hands still up, and shook his head. "Stay back. I can't get sick. They need me."

"It's okay," I assured him. "It was days ago. He's fine. We're just trying to prevent infection."

The guy froze, blinking in confusion. "Days ago?"

I turned to Hank. "Show him."

When the kid stepped forward, the guy took another step back.

"I'm not going to do anything," Hank assured him. "I don't even have a gun. Just this." He lifted the knife, then passed it to me when the guy's eyes grew wider.

Hank lifted his hands then, mimicking the guy, then waited a second before taking another step. When the guy didn't move, Hank took another, slowly lowering his arm and twisting it so the bite was visible.

The guy in front of us didn't lower his hands, but he did move forward. His gaze focused on the bite, and his expression changed, becoming thoughtful at first, and then relieved.

"Is this real?" He looked up at Hank. "You got bit, and nothing happened?"

Hank shrugged. "Real enough that it hurt like a bitch."

The guy let out a laugh and finally dropped his arms. "Wow. Wait 'til everyone hears! They'll be so happy."

"Well, I don't know about happy," Devon said, "But it does take away one big worry, that's for sure."

He had his gun down, and now that the guy had relaxed, he started walking again, heading for the pharmacy, which luckily wasn't locked up.

I followed, smiling at the guy. "You with a lot of people?"

"Yeah." He nodded enthusiastically. "We're at the Western Motel. Most of us aren't from here, though. We were passing through and had to stop." His smile disappeared like he just remembered why he was here.

"We were in the same boat," I told him. "Only in Vega, Texas."

He only nodded in response.

Devon had just reached the pharmacy when the guy seemed to recover and said, "There are no drugs."

Devon turned to face him. "None?"

"No." The guy shook his head. "We took them all to the motel. But I came back for this." He held up the candy bar, still gripped in his meaty hand.

"Shit," Devon muttered.

FAR from HOME

We were silent for a moment, then the guy perked up. "You could come back with me. Everybody will be so happy to find out you can't turn from a bite. I bet they share. It's only a little, after all."

Devon looked at me and frowned, thinking it through.

It was risky. This guy seemed okay, but it didn't sit well with me that he was out here alone. Why hadn't anyone come with him? Were they all cowards, selfish, or was he lying about everything he'd said?

"How many people are at the motel?" Kiaya asked, sounding like she was thinking the same thing.

The guy shrugged. "Twelve. Or more."

"That's a lot," I said.

"We're all on the second floor. We blocked the stairs so the zombies can't get us. It's safe there, and nice."

"And this group of yours," Devon said slowly, "what are they like? A lot of men? Women? Kids?"

"A little of everything." The guy acted like he didn't know what Devon was getting at. "They're just people."

"They're friendly?" Kiaya prompted.

He frowned. "Some are. Some aren't. Just like normal, I guess."

"We need to talk it over," I said, looking between the others.

Devon nodded. "Yeah. It's a risk no matter how you look at it."

The guy's frown deepened like he still didn't understand what our problem was. He seemed kind of slow on the uptake, but I wasn't sure if he had some kind of cognitive issue or he was just naïve. Or outright dumb.

"Give us a second," I said, shooting him a reassuring smile.

The stench of death still hung in the air, so I kept my eyes open as we headed to the side of the store. When we reached it, I discovered the source of the stench and cringed. A zombie was lying on the floor, its milky eyes open and staring at the ceiling. There was a hole right in the middle of its forehead.

"What do you think?" Devon asked, focusing on no one in particular.

"We need the drugs," Kiaya said, "but that doesn't mean we can't get them somewhere else."

"True," Devon agreed.

Like the guy, Hank acted as if he didn't understand our hesitation. "This guy seems okay."

"Yeah, but I don't know if I trust his judgment when it comes to other people." Devon glanced back at the guy, who hadn't moved and stood watching us. "He seems a little too trustworthy."

"I think he's just naïve," Kiaya said. "Didn't you notice that he acts a lot younger than he is? He's like a big kid. That doesn't necessarily mean the people he's with are bad, but it doesn't guarantee his judgment is good either."

So, she'd noticed the same thing I had.

"I agree with Kiaya," I said.

Devon blew out a long breath. "That doesn't tell me what you want to do."

Kiaya and I exchanged a look. She shrugged, and I mimicked her, and we both looked back at Devon, who was frowning even more.

"You're leaving it up to me?" he said, then focused on me. "I thought you didn't want me making all the decisions."

"I wanted you to be open to listening if I had an idea, but I honestly don't know what to do about this."

"Great," he said under his breath.

We stood in silence as Devon studied the guy, his mouth pressed into a line, his expression serious and filled with concern. Maybe it was shitty to leave it all up to him, but I trusted Devon's judgment better than my own. He'd been a cop before all this, so odds were good that he'd seen a lot more than I had. Hell, Hank had probably seen a lot more than I had. My cushy existence had made things easy for me, but it left me feeling pretty unprepared for this world. And as much as I hated not being in control, I had to trust Devon knew better when came to some things. Like this.

"We're here, and it's getting late," Devon finally said, "so we might as well give it a shot. If we get there and things look iffy, we can always change our minds. That okay with you?"

Kiaya nodded, as did Hank, and I mimicked them.

"Okay," Devon said, sighing.

We headed back over to where the guy stood waiting, and his face lit up like he knew what we were going to say before we did.

"You're coming?"

"We are," Devon said.

"Awesome!" He pumped his fist in the air like a little kid, and the gesture seemed to confirm what Kiaya and I had already picked up on.

"What's your name?" she asked him.

He beat his fist against his chest and smiled. "Randall."

"Nice to meet you," she said, returning his grin with a shy one of her own. "I'm Kiaya."

She introduced the rest of us, and as she did, Randall studied our faces, nodding as his lips formed our names like he was silently repeating them. He definitely had some cognitive issues, and it made me worry for him more than for us. He'd indicated that he had people depending on him, and thinking about the world we lived in now and the people out there who would take advantage of someone so trusting was frightening.

"You were traveling with family?" I asked Randall as we headed out of the store.

He nodded enthusiastically. "Yeah. My sister, Bethie, and her kids. We were going to California to see my aunt, but Bethie got sick." Again, his face fell like he'd just remembered why we were here and what was going on. "She died."

"What about her kids?" Kiaya asked in a soothing tone that reminded me of a mother talking to a scared child.

"Dee got sick too." His frown deepened but only for a moment, then his mouth turned up and he looked around excitedly. "But Lexi and Mikey are okay. They're back at the motel. You can meet them."

"That's good," I said, patting his arm.

Dear God, I hoped Lexi and Mikey weren't too young.

Kiaya and I exchanged a concerned look, but Devon seemed to be lost in thought as he led us out of the store.

"My sister died, too," Hank told Randall.

It was the first real detail we'd gotten about the family he'd lost, and I waited to see if he'd say more, but he didn't.

"From the virus?" Randall asked.

"Yeah. My parents, too." Hank frowned, focusing on the ground. "Regina was a year older than me, and we didn't really get along, but I didn't want her to die."

"Of course you didn't," Kiaya said in that same gentle tone.

For once, Hank didn't look hopeful when he glanced up at her, just grateful.

We stepped outside, and Devon stopped, looking around with a frown. "Where's your car?"

Randall shook his head violently. "I don't drive. Bethie drives me to work or I walk when it's nice. She doesn't like for me to walk, though. Sometimes I get distracted."

Devon's eyebrows shot up. "You walked here?"

"I walk everywhere, and I can be real quiet if I walk like this." Randall moved forward on his tiptoes, his hands lifted like a cartoon character sneaking into a room.

It actually would have been really adorable if the situation weren't so scary.

"Well, you don't have to walk back," Kiaya said, smiling. "You can ride with us."

Randall stopped walking and beamed down at her. "Really?"

"Of course," I said.

"Thanks." He threw his arms around me, smashing me in what could only be described as a bear hug.

He was a big guy, tall and soft, and if his grasp hadn't been so firm, I probably would have fallen over. The slightly salty scent of body odor clung to him, as well as the stench of death that was probably going to be nearly impossible to avoid going forward, but otherwise the gesture was as sweet as he was. The only problem? He'd wrapped one of his arms around my waist, making contact with my still tender cut, and biting back my cry of pain was impossible.

I cried out, and Randall released me and scurried back, his eyes wide. If Devon didn't rush to my side, I would have fallen over for sure.

"I'm sorry, I'm sorry, I'm sorry," Randall repeated as Devon

FAR from HOME

said, "Are you okay?"

I swallowed and forced out a smile, trying to comfort the gentle man in front of me. "I'm okay. I just have a little cut on my back. You didn't know."

Randall said nothing, but his eyes got bigger.

Devon lowered his voice. "Are you really okay?"

I nodded a couple times, but the truth was, I didn't know. I thought Randall might have pulled a few stitches free, which was going to suck big time.

"I want to look at it," Devon said, already reaching for my shirt.

I shrugged him off. "It's okay. You can check it out at the motel."

He frowned but didn't argue. Thankfully.

I turned to Randall, forcing out a bright smile despite my throbbing back. "You ready?"

He nodded, but it was hesitant.

Picking up the slack, Kiaya waved for him to follow as she headed for the car. "Come on."

Less hesitant than before, Randall followed.

Hank stood looking wide-eyed and confused but followed as well. I held back, though, waiting until they were in front of me so I could reach behind me. The cut throbbed when I touched it, and just like I'd thought, the bandage was damp. I pulled my hand way to find my fingers covered in blood.

"Rowan," Devon hissed when he saw it.

"Stop." I gave him a stern look. "I'm okay, and that man didn't mean to hurt me. We'll deal with it when we get to the hotel. For now, I just need something to press against my back so I can try to stop the bleeding."

Devon sighed but didn't hesitate before pulling his shirt over his head.

There was nothing like a firm chest and sculpted abs to distract a girl from the pain.

I swallowed as I took the shirt, trying not to stare—and failing.

"Thanks."

I pressed the shirt against my back but didn't move.

He grabbed my free arm and pulled me toward the car. "You can stare at me later. After we get to the motel."

I rolled my eyes.

Kiaya was squished between Hank and Randall, and with the two rotund men in the back, my Honda Civic looked suddenly tiny. A bigger car would have been nice right about now.

"What happened to your shirt?" Randall asked when Devon climbed in.

"A zombie ate it," he grumbled.

I elbowed him and glared.

He didn't react.

"Where is this hotel, Randall?" he asked as he started the car.

"That way." Randall pointed to the left.

Devon sighed. "Tell me where to turn."

15

We only made a couple wrong turns on the way to the motel, both of which Randall apologized profusely for.

"I usually walk," he said for the fifteenth time. "I didn't know. I'm sorry."

"It's okay, Randall," Kiaya said, patting him on the arm. "Isn't it, Devon?"

"Yeah," he mumbled.

I would have elbowed him again except Randall was paying attention, and I didn't want him to see it. Devon was being a jerk. Again.

And I was just starting to warm to him. Okay, so *warm* wasn't the right word, but still.

"That's it!" Randall shouted from the back.

It felt like the words had punched me in the eardrums, and I had to jerk away.

Devon grumbled something under his breath I couldn't hear, and I didn't resist the urge to glare his way. Seriously? He was being impossible. I couldn't wait until we were alone so I could lay into him.

He pulled into the parking lot of the Western Motel, and

I leaned forward to get a better look. It was painted orange, making it look very authentically western, and two stories. Like Randall had said, I could see items at the top and bottom of the two staircases, blocking them so it wasn't easy to get up. It didn't look very secure, though, so whoever was inside was fortunate there were no zombies nearby. We'd passed a few on the way here, but so far it looked as if most hadn't figured out how to leave their homes. Thankfully. It would be nice to discover the few who'd managed it back in Vega were in the minority. At least then we stood a fighting chance.

There were no people in sight either, which might have been the reason the few zombies wandering the town hadn't made their way here. But it only took one look at the place to realize it was a short-term solution, which had me thinking about what we'd do after we finally got home. I lived in a decent size neighborhood, surrounded by two-story houses and fields. There were hundreds of people just in that little area and pretty much no way to secure my home and make it safer than it already was. What then? Where did we go from there?

I had no clue. Even worse, I didn't even know if it mattered. My dad was probably gone, and Mom could be, too. I could get home to find her dead, to find her stumbling through the neighborhood. Probably wearing that stupid purple bathrobe she refused to get rid of, her feet bare since she said they got sweaty when she wore socks. Her long, brown hair would have been in a braid—she always braided it before she went to bed—but by now it would have come loose.

Would I even recognize her?

Did I want to?

"Hey," Devon said, jolting me back to reality.

We'd parked, and the others had climbed out. Devon had, too, and he must have grabbed a new shirt from his bag in the trunk because he wasn't shirtless anymore, and he was leaning through the open driver's door, staring at me.

"You okay?"

The concern on his face was stark and heartwarming, and exactly what I needed at the moment.

FAR from HOME

I swallowed down my sorrow and nodded. "Yeah. Just thinking."

His frown deepened, and sympathy flashed in his blue eyes, but he didn't ask. "Let's go inside."

There was something about the statement that seemed open-ended, but I didn't know what that meant.

I reached for my gun before climbing out, but Devon lifted his hand, showing me he had it. "I don't want to take the M16, both because it could be intimidating, and because I don't want to give our hand away. Just in case."

In case we needed to use it to get ourselves out of a sticky situation.

"Smart," I said. "It's in the trunk?"

"It is," Devon said.

"Okay."

I climbed out and followed the others. Randall was in the lead, practically skipping as he approached the stairs. When we got closer, I saw a dresser had been dragged from one of the rooms and set in front of the steps. An okay barricade assuming none of the zombies were more coordinated than the others. Since I'd seen one open a door and knew better, I couldn't help thinking it was half-assed. Done by someone who was too lazy to break a sweat by grabbing a couple more large items to pile on of top of it.

Devon seemed to think the same thing and stared at the dresser with a look of disdain.

"This way," Randall said, climbing over the dresser and jogging up the stairs.

Hank followed, barely reacting, but Kiaya shook her head as she scrambled over.

When I started to follow her, Devon moved to my side. "Let me help."

I was still pressing his shirt against my back with one hand, so I didn't resist. Not that I was prepared when he scooped me into his arms. I was so caught off guard that my arm went around his neck on instinct. He set me on top of the dresser but didn't release me, and I looked up to find his face inches from mine, his blue eyes intent as they studied me.

"What?" I asked.

"How old are you, Rowan?"

I shook my head. "What?"

"I know you were in college, but how old are you?"

"You're asking me how old I am? Now?" I looked around. "Seriously?"

He smiled. "Just tell me and stop being difficult."

"Twenty," I said, unable to hold in my own laugh. "How old are you?"

"Twenty-eight."

"I would have guessed younger," I said.

He chuckled. "If I hadn't seen you, I would have guessed you were fifty."

I smacked him on the chest, and he let out a real laugh.

"Rowan?" Kiaya's voice floated down to us. "Devon? Are you there?"

"Coming!" I called.

Devon finally released me, and I scooted forward. My heart was pounding from the encounter, and my head spinning. Devon had flirted with me since the first moment we saw one another, but this was different. He'd been different. More open, more sincere. More real. It was unsettling, but nice, too.

Kiaya and Hank were waiting at the top of the stairs where yet another dresser blocked the way, but Randall had already moved on. I could see him near the end of the catwalk, standing at an open door and talking animatedly. Whoever he was speaking to didn't step outside, though, and I wasn't sure if that was good or bad.

"What's going on?" Kiaya asked, looking between us. "What took you so long?"

"I was just checking Rowan's cut," Devon said.

Before I could even look back at him, he'd scooped me up again, this time depositing me on top of the dresser and releasing me immediately. I was still sitting there when he climbed up, and the way Kiaya was looking between us told me she wasn't buying it.

FAR from HOME

Not that I could tell her what was going on, because I had no idea.

Devon scooted off and automatically reached back to help me even though he didn't look my way. It was so strange.

I allowed him, still pressing his shirt against my back. Once we were all up, we headed to where Randall stood talking to someone.

"This is them!" he said, waving toward us.

"I can't believe you brought other people here," a man with a slight Texas twang grumbled.

A second later, a man stepped out, his eyes already narrowed like he expected to find a group of bandits preparing to steal all his supplies and burn the place over his head. He was in his sixties and round in the middle, although not anyone I would describe as overweight. His long, gray-white hair was pulled back and fastened into a ponytail at the base of his neck, and his beard was scraggly, although not long. He looked like someone's grandpa, really. Unassuming. Unthreatening at first glance. But the expression in his eyes said he wasn't happy to have new people here, which put me on alert.

"Hi!" Kiaya called, smiling wider than I'd ever seen.

It was a good call, the man immediately relaxed. Why wouldn't he? I had never met anyone more disarming than Kiaya.

Except maybe Kyle. Poor guy.

Slightly less wary, the man took a moment to look us over.

"Sorry for the less than cordial reception," he said, his gaze pausing briefly on Devon, but obviously deciding he wasn't a threat, because he moved on. "The past week has been...difficult."

His gray eyes clouded over, and he glanced around, but he wasn't focused on the ground, so I got the impression it wasn't zombies he was on the lookout for.

Beside him, Randall beamed but said nothing.

"Sorry for intruding," Devon began. "We're just passing through and needed a place to stay for the night. As well as some antibiotics if you can spare them."

He waved to Hank, who looked doe-eyed enough to possibly come across as less threatening than Kiaya, and definitely sympathetic. Nothing like he had in the car when he was drooling over Kiaya. This kid must have been able to play his teachers like a fiddle.

The man studied Hank for a moment, pulling at his beard as he did. "Randall said you were hurt?"

"That's right." The kid held his arm out so the bite was on full display.

"Whoa, now." The man took a step back just like Randall had in the grocery store and put his hands up as if to ward Hank off. "I think you should keep your distance."

"It happened a couple days ago," Kiaya explained, "and he's been fine. Only it's getting infected, which is why we were looking for antibiotics."

The man eyed Kiaya like he was trying to decide how trustworthy she was, then shifted his gaze to Hank again. "Tell me what happened."

The teen sighed but started talking, once again relaying what had happened in Amarillo. His family dying, hanging out with his friend, discovering the bodies had come back, and finally being attacked.

"I thought it was the end for sure, but nothing happened other than this." He waved to the swollen bite. "I should have thought to get antibiotics right away, but I was too focused on the fact that I was about to turn into a zombie." His lips turned down into a frown.

The man nodded slowly. "That's an interesting story, and it sure gives us something to think about."

"You don't believe him?" I asked.

"He's the only one who was there, right?" The man's gray eyes studied us as we nodded. "Then you can understand why I'm hesitant to accept it as fact."

"Of course," Devon said, taking charge once again. "It only makes sense to be hesitant, and you have my word that we'll keep a close eye on him. If something needs to be done, it will be taken care of before anyone else is hurt."

The man relaxed a miniscule amount. "I appreciate that."

FAR from HOME

Before anyone could say anything else, a door burst open, and a little girl, probably no more than six, rushed out. "Randall!"

She threw herself against Randall, hugging his leg since the top of her head barely reached his hip. Like him, she had dark skin and large, brown eyes, and a round face that resembled his a great deal.

"You left," she said, the words muffled with her face pressed against his leg. "You left."

Randall patted her head but said nothing. He was still smiling, but he looked uncertain. Like he didn't know how to comfort the girl, or maybe he thought he might have done something wrong.

The door opened again, and another kid walked out. Calmer than the girl and more serious. He was ten, maybe, and slight, but like the girl, he resembled Randall even if his face wasn't nearly as round.

"Lexi was worried," the kid said, looking up at Randall. "Where'd you go?"

"She was hungry and sad, and I know she likes chocolate." He pulled the smashed Hershey bar out of his pocket, smiling. "I got her some."

The boy's serious expression didn't ease. "You can't run off like that. You scared her."

"I'm sorry, Mikey." Randall hung his head, the hand still holding the chocolate bar dropping to his side and Lexi still clinging to his leg.

I didn't miss that Mikey only said her.

After a moment, the little boy relaxed. "It's okay, Uncle Randall."

His uncle's eyes lit up. "You can have some of the chocolate, too, Mikey."

"Thanks," the kid said, but when he took the candy bar from Randall, he knelt next to his sister and rubbed her back. "Look what Randall got you, Lexi."

The girl pulled her face away from her uncle's leg just enough that one eye was visible, but the second she saw the chocolate, she let him go and snatched it up. She was grinning as she tore into it, and Randall was next to her in a second.

Mikey stood, watching them as they shared the candy bar and talked. He was a serious kid, acting a lot older than his ten years, and I had a feeling he'd taken on more of the role of caring for his little sister than Randall had. Maybe he was even looking after his uncle a little.

The man with the ponytail shook his head, but he was smiling slightly he turned to face us. "I'm Buck, by the way."

Devon stuck his hand out, "Nice to meet you, Buck."

He introduced us while the three family members talked, then turned to face them. "And this must be Lexi and Mikey. Your uncle told us all about you."

Lexi beamed up at him, her mouth too full of chocolate to respond.

Her brother frowned. "Mike. Only Randall still calls me Mikey."

His uncle, who was smiling as wide as Lexi, didn't even blink.

"Nice to meet you." Devon said in his usual tone, not softening it or talking down to the kid at all, and he held his hand out like he was meeting a peer instead of a ten-year-old kid.

Mike took it without blinking, but I didn't miss the appreciation that flashed in his eyes. He probably didn't get a whole lot of respect because of his age, but I had a strong feeling he deserved it. From what Randall had indicated, his sister had been a single mom with three kids and a special needs brother to care for, and Mike had probably been the oldest, meaning he'd most likely grown up helping out.

"What do you say about those antibiotics?" Devon said, turning to Buck.

The older man sighed and ran his hand over his white hair. "Honestly, if it were up to me, I'd say yes. Unfortunately, it isn't. We're going to have to check with Corporal Miller about that."

"Corporal Miller?" I asked.

Buck pressed his lips together like he was trying to decide what to say. "He was a soldier working at one of the nearby checkpoints when his team got sick and died. He's kind of taken over running things. Having a military guy in charge has been a comfort to a lot of folks. I guess it makes them feel like the government isn't really gone and eventually things will get back to normal."

I could read between the lines. Buck wasn't a fan of Corporal Miller for some reason.

"You're also going to have to check with him about staying the night." Again, he paused to press his lips together. "He has the room keys."

"Well," Devon said, sighing, "I guess we should meet him."

Buck nodded but didn't say anything before he headed off, waving for us to follow.

We headed after him as a group, silent and tense, leaving Randall and the kids where they were. I looked back as we walked away, curious, and found Mike watching us, his expression thoughtful and still serious. Kiaya caught my eye, and we exchanged a look. She was as worried as I was. We hadn't voiced our concerns, but I knew it had to do with both the kids and the corporal we were about to meet. Buck's uncertainty was very telling.

There weren't a lot of rooms on the second level, making me doubt Randall's assertion that they had over a dozen people staying here. No one came out as we passed, but a couple times the curtains moved and faces appeared in the windows, wide eyes watching us. Old and young, white and brown, men and women. Every face I saw was different, a menagerie of survivors banded together in this little town in the middle of nowhere, and it hit me that this was the future. People from different areas and different backgrounds—different races and religions, probably—united by one common goal. Survival. It put a new perspective on things, making issues from the past suddenly obsolete and even making some seem silly in the light of our new world of worries.

Buck stopped when we reached the end of the catwalk, outside the last door. He didn't glance our way before knocking, and I looked down at the parking lot when the thud bounced off the motel. The area was clear, but figures were visible in the distance. Quite a few, actually. The sight of them sent a shiver down my spine, and my gaze shifted to the staircase closest to us, then the one at the other end of the catwalk. Those dressers weren't going to be enough to keep the dead out once they realized where the survivors had congregated. They needed something more secure.

The door clicked, and I turned as it opened. The guy who stepped out frowned when he saw Buck, and when his gaze landed on Devon, it deepened. He was young, probably only a year or two older than I was, and several inches taller than Devon. Although not as fit. He was in uniform, the two stripes on his arm announcing his rank and the nametag on his chest proclaiming his name. Miller.

"You find some stragglers?" he asked, his hazel eyes focusing on Buck without looking at the rest of us. He ran his hand over his brown hair, which wasn't long but was slightly shaggy, and he shook his head. "I thought we talked about this. We don't have the resources to take anyone else in."

"Randall found them," Buck said. "He went out again—"

"That fucking moron is going to get himself killed," Miller broke in. "Then where will we be? I'm not taking care of a couple kids because their idiot uncle got his face eaten off."

Buck frowned. "You won't have to."

I already didn't like this guy, but when Devon shifted and Miller's gaze snapped toward him, his eyes narrowing in a threatening way, my dislike grew.

"We're just passing through." Devon lifted his hands as if trying to surrender. "We'll be gone in the morning."

Miller's lips puckered as he studied Devon, looking down at him in a way that made it seem like he was trying to intimidate the other man. For the first time, I was grateful Devon was so sure of himself. This asshole wasn't going to make him feel small.

"I see," Miller said slowly.

He finally looked past Devon to the rest of us, studying Hank briefly before turning his gaze on Kiaya. At the sight of her, his eyes lit up, his expression only growing friendlier when he looked at me.

Great.

He forced out a smile. "Well, I guess we can afford to be hospitable for one night."

FAR from HOME

Devon's back stiffened, and Buck shook his head, but Miller was still focused on me, and he didn't see it.

The corporal stepped back, pushing the door open wide, and motioned for us to enter. "Come on in so I can get you set up with a room for the night."

We did as we were told, and when Buck followed, Miller frowned like he wasn't thrilled with the other man's presence. It was obvious the moment Buck mentioned the corporal that he didn't care for him, and I could tell the feeling was mutual. I didn't blame Buck one bit. Miller was a kid—as much as I hated to admit it since we were so close to the same age—but he was throwing his weight around and probably not listening to advice from anyone else just because he wore a uniform.

"Was there something else you needed?" Miller asked Buck.

"There was something we needed to discuss." The older man nodded to Hank. "Go on and tell him."

The teen stepped forward, his arm out and the bite visible, and repeated his story for Miller.

Unlike Buck, who had listened with a cautious light in his eyes, the corporal's expression got more and more excited with each passing second, so that by the time Hank had finished, he looked like a kid on Christmas morning.

"This is fantastic news," he said excitedly. "It's what we've been wondering, and now that we know, it's going to change everything. We don't have to be as worried."

Buck's eyebrows lifted. "You don't think we should be a little cautious?"

"Why?" Miller gave an exaggerated roll of his eyes. "Look at his arm. It's obviously a human bite and it's not very recent, yet the kid's still standing." He nodded a few times, his expression thoughtful. "You know, I've been going back and forth about staying here, but this decides it. Staying in an area where the population was so low is smarter. Safer."

The last little bit was said quietly, almost like he was talking to himself.

Devon cleared his throat, grabbing Miller's attention. "I hate to be a pessimist, but I agree with Buck. This is just one possible scenario."

"What do you mean?" Miller asked, sounding annoyed.

"I mean, we could all react differently to this thing. Hank survived, but that doesn't mean everyone will. Just like with the virus."

Miller waved him off. "We were all immune to that, which is the only reason we're standing here. So we must all be immune to this, too."

Devon ground his teeth when the corporal gave him a condescending look.

Kiaya elbowed me and leaned closer until her lips were practically touching my ears. "Antibiotics."

Right. Hank needed medicine, and there was no way in hell Devon was going to get anywhere by asking for them. If Kiaya or I did, however, Miller might be inclined to share. Just to get on our good sides.

Not that he had a chance in hell of that.

"I'm so sorry to interrupt," I said, stepping forward and flashing Miller a big smile, "but Buck said we needed to talk to you about getting antibiotics."

Miller's expression changed, tensing for just a moment as he thought about it. His gaze moved down, sweeping over me, then to Kiaya, and by the time he was once again focused on my face, he was relaxed.

"I think we can manage that."

I had to force the smile to stay on my face.

Buck nodded to Hank's arm. "We can get somebody to take a look at that, too."

"You have a doctor?" Devon asked.

"Just a nurse," Miller said, as if having a nurse was nothing.

"She's good," Buck assured us.

Kiaya was the first to respond. "I'm sure she is."

"We can have her look at your stitches, too." Devon was focused on me, his expression concerned. "I want to make sure I didn't screw something up."

"I'm sure you did a good job." I gave him a smile, and like on our way up, something sizzled between us that made it impossible to look away.

At least until Miller cleared his throat.

"We can have her come to your room after you get settled." He looked at me again, thoughtfully, then narrowed his eyes on Devon. "I'm assuming two rooms would probably be better."

"Whatever you have, we're grateful for," Devon replied.

Miller gave him a stiff and unfriendly nod.

16

The motel room was cleaner than the one in Vega, but plain and somewhat cold feeling despite the yellow and orange décor. It had all the typical furniture. Two beds, a small round table and two chairs that reminded me of something from the dorm, a mini fridge and microwave—that were now useless—a dresser, and a desk. All cheap, all cookie cutter, but nonetheless welcome because they didn't smell like death.

"This is it," Miller announced, waving around the room like he'd singlehandedly decorated it.

If he had, he shouldn't brag.

"Thank you so much," I said, forcing out a smile.

Kiaya dropped her bag to the floor, frowning at the corporal who was staring at me with a Cheshire smile on his face. "I'm going to check on Randall and the kids. See if they need anything."

I turned my back to Miller and shot her a look, my eyes wide as I silently pleaded for her not to leave me. Kiaya only shrugged before heading for the door.

Seriously? I thought she was supposed to be the considerate one.

"Alone at last," Miller pronounced the second the door had

clicked shut.

My entire body stiffened.

Before I could even turn around to face him, someone knocked on the adjoining door. Saved by the knock!

I rushed to get it without looking at the corporal, and when I pulled it open to find Devon standing there with Hank right behind him, I let out a sigh of relief.

"Kiaya said you're getting settled in," Devon said, shooting me a wink.

I took back every bad thing I'd ever thought about her. Kiaya was a saint.

"We're working on it," I said, giving him a relieved smile before turning to face Miller. "Thank you so much for letting us crash here."

"Of course," he said, trying to sound gallant but failing because he was glaring at Devon.

Another knock sounded, this one on the front door, and the corporal's smile faded even more.

"What now?" he grumbled as he headed toward it.

A woman in her mid-to-late thirties stood outside the door. When she saw Miller, she frowned as if confused, but it turned into a smile when she looked past him and saw us.

"One of my patients, I'm assuming," she said as she walked in, a red bag in her hand.

"I'm Rowan, and yes," I said then waved to where Hank stood at Devon's back. "And the other one is Hank."

Her smile widened and she stuck out her hand. "Lisa. It's so nice to meet you."

"You, too," I said, taking her hand.

So far, everyone we'd met seemed awesome with the exception of Miller. Maybe he needed to be on his way.

As if I had magic powers, he cleared his throat and said, "I guess I'll head out."

The smile I gave him was more sincere this time since I was so thankful to have him leaving. "Thanks again."

He nodded but said nothing else before slipping from the room.

FAR from HOME

Once he was gone, Lisa tossed her bag on the bed and nodded toward a chair. "Let me see what I have to work with."

I did as I was told, taking a seat and turning before reaching back to lift my shirt.

The cut was covered by gauze—which was saturated in blood by now—and at the sight of it, Hank let out a groan. "I'm out of here. Blood isn't my thing."

He rushed back into the other room, not shutting the door completely but leaving only a crack.

I got it. I wasn't totally immune to feeling a little lightheaded at the sight of blood, but I figured it was the perfect time to toughen up. Hank needed too as well, but that was obviously a conversation for another day.

Cold hands touched my back, and I winced when Lisa pulled the medical tape from my skin. It tugged at the hairs on my back and the cut throbbed, only making it worse. Despite how hard I tried to bite it back, I let out a hiss of pain.

"Sorry," Lisa said, looking up to give a sympathetic smile.

At first glance, I'd thought she was in her thirties, but now I wasn't so sure. She had fantastic skin, which told me she'd worked hard to take care of it, but the roots of her brown hair were about a quarter of an inch long and streaked in gray. She'd probably had an appointment to get a touchup that had been interrupted by the zombie apocalypse. I knew the feeling, since my last nail appointment was supposed to be next week.

Lisa's brown eyes moved back to my wound. "It was deep?"

"It was," Devon answered for me.

He was standing over us, watching as Lisa inspected his handiwork, a slightly worried expression on his face. I didn't know why, though. He'd done the best he could, and no one could fault him if the stitches were crooked or I ended up with a jagged scar. It wasn't like I would have been able to do the same if our situation were reversed.

"I wish I could irrigate the wound, but it's a little late for that." Lisa glanced at him, still smiling. "Not that I'm criticizing. You did more than most people could, and the stitches are good. It looks like one tore, but we should be okay without replacing it." She focused on me, her expression getting stern. "You just need to take it easy."

"So, no hand to hand combat with the dead?" I half-joked.

Lisa snorted and rolled her eyes. "Exactly, as crazy as that still sounds."

She wiped the cut down with alcohol before grabbing some clean gauze from the bag she'd brought, then taped it over the wound.

"That's it!" she said, standing.

I turned to face her, smiling. "Thank you."

"You are very welcome," she said, looking between me and Devon, "and thank you for bringing us such good news. I've been trying to decide what to do. If I should risk moving on or stay here, and knowing a bite doesn't mean certain doom makes it easier."

Devon frowned, only hesitating for a moment before saying, "I'm not sure we really know that for sure, despite Hank's good fortune."

"What do you mean?" Lisa paused in the middle of twisting her thick hair into a bun at the base of her neck.

"Well, you have medical training, you tell me. Does the same virus affect people differently? Is it possible for one person to be okay while others are still affected?"

Lisa didn't respond for a moment, her expression thoughtful as she turned his words over in her head. The more she thought about it, the more her mouth turned down, and the more I became convinced she was closer to her mid-forties. Damn, her skin looked great.

"I suppose it can affect people differently," she said thoughtfully. "Years ago, when my husband and I were first married, I woke up feeling horrible. Turned out I had strep. We thought for sure my husband would get it, too, since we were newlyweds and we'd kissed about a hundred times the day before." She let out a little laugh and shook her head. "He did come down with a fever, but he was over it in no time, and he never tested positive for strep. Meanwhile, I was sick for two weeks and miserable."

FAR from HOME

"That's what I'm saying," Devon told her. "I just think it's better to be cautious at this point. At least until we've seen a little more."

Lisa nodded slowly. "I see what you mean."

"So, I take it you're not from Shamrock," I said.

"No." She blew out a long breath. "I was in California at a medical conference for emergency room workers. The virus got bad, and travel was cut off, and I got stuck. I was trying to make my way home to Atlanta with two coworkers, but they got sick. They died, I didn't, and now here I am."

She waved to the room like she wasn't sure what else to say.

I liked this woman.

"I'm sorry," I said.

"Me, too." She let out a deep sigh. "The worst part is knowing there's nothing to go back to. Which is probably the real reason I haven't moved on."

"Your husband was sick?"

She gave me a tight smile that made the skin at the corner of her eyes crinkle just a little. "We divorced years ago, and I wasn't seeing anyone. No kids. My parents are dead, too. It's just me. With no job to return to, I just don't know what to do with myself."

"Staying here seems..." I hesitated, trying to choose my words, but couldn't come up with something nice to say.

"Awful?" Lisa laughed. "Believe me, I know. There are some good people, and then there's Randall and those kids. It just breaks your heart. And Buck is a gem. But it's not going to be long before the town runs out of resources, and Corporal Miller is challenging. To put it mildly."

"He seems like he's taken over pretty thoroughly," Devon said.

"You could say that." Lisa exhaled as she turned to clean up the medical supplies, signaling she was done talking about it. "I should check on my other patient, but let me know if you need anything else." She turned to face us once she was packed up, smiling again. "And be sure to say goodbye before you leave tomorrow."

215

"We will," I told her. "And thanks again."

Lisa gave us another smile before slipping into the other room, leaving the door open only a crack, and the whisper of a quiet conversation followed.

I was glad Miller had found it in his heart to give us two rooms, but more than that, I was grateful they were adjoining. We didn't know these people, and while almost everyone we'd met was friendly, I agreed with Lisa about Miller. That guy was a creep.

"We should see if she wants to go with us," I said to Devon, keeping my voice low in case she could hear us.

Devon frowned. "Lisa?"

"Yeah." I almost rolled my eyes. An old habit that might never go away.

"We don't exactly have the room," he pointed out.

I sighed. He was right, and while part of me thought it would be easier to find a new car, another part didn't want to give up my Civic. My parents had bought it for me, and the idea that I might never see them again made it that much more special. Even if we were crowded.

As if sensing the reason for my hesitation, Devon didn't mention trying to find another car or say anything else about it, and like when he'd set me on the dresser, his gaze held mine, making my scalp prickle. I shifted from foot to foot and couldn't look away even though I wasn't exactly comfortable. The expression on his face had me thinking about how he'd run his hand up my back at the other motel, as well as the way he'd held me when we arrived here.

What was he thinking? It was impossible to know. I was beginning to accept that my first impression of Devon hadn't been correct, but that didn't mean I understood him completely. And I definitely didn't understand why his touch made my body tingle when most of the time I found him irritating.

"Kiaya has been gone for a long time," I said, unable to stand the silence.

"It's Kiaya," he said, an appreciative smile pulling up his lips. "She's probably teaching Lexi to read or to tie her shoes."

FAR from HOME

His words stung, but at first I wasn't sure why. Then it hit me. He liked Kiaya. Not in a romantic way, but in a respectful way. He thought she was good to the core, which she was—she proved that back at McDonald's on our first day of travel—but he thought I was selfish and spoiled. Even worse, he wasn't totally wrong.

I looked away from him and headed for the bathroom. "Maybe we should start calling her Saint Kiaya."

I wasn't able to keep the hurt out of my voice, which only made me feel worse.

"Rowan," he said when I passed him.

I ignored him and continued walking, but didn't get far before he'd grabbed my arm, forcing me to stop.

He studied me for a moment before he said, "What's wrong?"

"Nothing." I didn't look at him.

"Rowan," he said again, this time his voice more firm. "Look at me."

I did, turning slowly. I lifted my gaze to his face only to find him six inches from me, his blue eyes piercing and serious as he waited for me to say something.

"What is it?" he asked when I still didn't talk.

Tears had sprung to my eyes for some stupid reason. Not that it was anything new. I was an emotional crier. It didn't matter what it was, I cried. Anger, sadness, happiness, a touching story on Facebook. It all made me cry. I literally had no control over the tears.

I blinked, trying to keep them back and barely succeeding. "You think I'm a worthless, spoiled brat."

He started, shaking his head in confusion. "What?"

"Don't deny it. You've implied how spoiled I am too many times, and you made me stay by the pool when you and Kiaya searched the cars because you thought I would get in the way."

"I did that because you were hurt," he said gently, "and I didn't want to have to worry about you."

The knowledge that he was concerned for me didn't erase the fact that he didn't even try to contradict my other statement.

I yanked my arm out of his grasp. "Well, if you're lucky,

we'll get back to Ohio tomorrow, and you can be on your way."

"Rowan," he said again, sounding more exasperated this time.

I ignored him, still blinking back the tears, and continued to the bathroom.

Once again, I didn't make it there.

He grabbed my arm, forcing me to spin around. A second later, my face was between his hands and his mouth was on mine. The kiss stole my breath. Shocked me. Took me so by surprise that I could barely react enough to kiss him back. Then his thumb caressed my right cheek, bringing me to the present and making me totally aware of how his lips moved over mine, and the way my head was spinning. I had to hold on to him when the kiss deepened, as his tongue brushed my lips, urging me to open my mouth. Which I did. When his tongue brushed mine, a jolt went through me. It was like lightning. Like an electrical shock. Like the hand of God.

Even when he finally broke the kiss, he didn't release me, but instead held my gaze with his. "I think you are smart and resilient. I think you're strong. Maybe you had an easy life and maybe I resented that a little when we first met, but know this. That says more about me than it does about you, because there is nothing worthless about you. Believe me."

I was breathing heavily, having a difficult time catching my breath and an even more difficult time trying to figure out how to respond. The kiss had caught me totally off guard even though Devon's actions had told me he was attracted to me, but even more shocking was how my body had reacted to him.

"Say something," he prompted when I didn't respond, irritation ringing in his voice but worry flickering in his eyes.

"You kissed me," was all I managed to get out.

His mouth turned up into a smile. "And I plan on kissing you more. I hope that's okay."

"It's okay," I mumbled.

"Good," he whispered before closing the distance between us again.

The kiss was softer this time, and after a second, he moved

FAR from HOME

his hands to my shoulders then slid them down my arms. Goose bumps popped up on my skin from the caress, and I shivered. It was the good kind of shiver, though. The kind that made you feel like you were home.

His lips were still on mine when a scream penetrated the closed door.

Devon pulled away but didn't let me go, his head snapping toward the door. My heart was already pounding, but it started beating harder, thumping against my ribcage like it was trying to break free.

"What was that?" I said even though he knew as much as I did.

He shook his head, but the door burst open before he could even venture a guess.

Kiaya rushed in, her eyes wide and her shoulders heaving as she gasped for breath. She blinked when she saw how we were standing but shook her head.

"Lexi ran off!"

"Lexi?" Devon released me and charged toward the door, sweeping the gun he'd given me up off the bed on his way by.

"Yes," Kiaya snapped.

Devon pushed past her and hurried outside, and she followed. I rushed after them.

Outside, the sun was setting, the horizon a bright orange that matched the color of the motel, and unlike before, the catwalk was crowded with people. The parking lot, too, was no longer empty, only the people down there weren't survivors. They were zombies.

They'd converged on the motel, either making their way from town or liberating themselves from rooms on the first floor. I wasn't sure, but it didn't matter because a little girl was out there and in trouble, and we had to find her.

"What happened?" Devon called as he charged down the catwalk.

I saw Buck and Corporal Miller, as well as a few other people I hadn't met, and beyond that, Randall and Mike. They stood at the top of the stairwell, behind the dresser that had been placed there as a barrier, staring down. Seeing the expression on the little boy's face made my heart jump to my throat. He looked so determined, so motivated.

"He's going to go after her," I said, talking to myself since no one was around to hear me.

Buck and Miller had turned to Devon.

"We don't know anything for sure," the corporal was saying. "She's missing, but she could be anywhere."

"Like hell," Buck growled. "You told everyone they could survive a bite, and she went out there looking for her mom."

He pointed to the parking lot.

"Her mom?" Kiaya asked, cutting in. "She's dead, though. Right?"

"She is, but we've spotted her a few times in the motel parking lot," the man beside Buck said. "It's like she's drawn here, if that makes sense. It's been rough on the kids."

"She couldn't possibly be stupid enough to think her mom would recognize her," Miller said, shaking his head.

"She's five," Buck snapped.

The man at his side spit, his lip curled up in disgust as he looked at Miller.

I pushed past them as they continued talking things through, rushing toward Randall and Mike. Like I'd thought, the little boy was already climbing on top of the dresser.

"Mike!" I called, moving faster.

He was crouched on top like he was ready to jump, but he turned to face me.

"Stop," I said, reaching for him despite the six feet still separating us. "Randall, stop him!"

His uncle looked at me with wide, uncertain eyes, but did nothing.

A cry rose behind me as other people realized what was happening, and before I could reach him, Mike jumped.

"No!" I shouted, running faster, ignoring the throbbing in my back and not caring if I ripped every one of the stitches.

I reached the dresser and leaned over, looking down just as Mike disappeared at the bend in the stairs.

"Shit," I said, hoisting myself on top of the dresser.

"That's a bad word," Randall said, his eyes still wide and full of uncertainty.

I had to bite back my reply, knowing it wasn't fair. Knowing this man wasn't equipped for the job he was facing. Knowing it wasn't his fault there were zombies.

"Rowan," Devon called after me, "stop, goddamnit!"

I slid over the dresser, landing on the top stair just as Devon reached the steps. He grabbed hold of my upper arm before I could move, refusing to release me even when I tried to shake him off.

"Let go!" I yelled. "He's ten!"

"You don't even have a gun," he said.

He was right. I'd seen Mike at the stairs and taken off running, not thinking about anything else. But I was unarmed. Unlike Devon.

"Give me that one." I held my hand out.

"No." He somehow managed to keep hold of me while also pulling himself up and sliding over to stand next to me. "I'll go. This isn't because I don't think you can do it or because you're worthless. This is because you're still healing, and we haven't had time to even teach you how to shoot. Do you understand?"

His words pierced my worry over the kids, and I managed to acknowledge he was right. I was unprepared and already hurt, and running out there would be stupid.

"Fine," I said, "but you get those kids and make sure all three of you get back here safely. Understand?"

His lips twitched. "Always so bossy."

"Go," I ordered, proving his point.

He released me and charged down the steps, and had just made it to the bend in the staircase when someone else jumped over the dresser. Corporal Miller was the last person I expected to drop down next to me, but the wink he shot my way told me what his motivation was. He wasn't the least bit interested in saving the kids.

"Don't worry. I'll get them back safe."

He charged after Devon, and I turned when something else

scraped against the dresser. The man I'd seen with Buck was dragging himself over as well. He was as old as Buck but less fit, and he huffed as he dragged himself over, swearing up a storm. Somehow, he managed to get over.

"Charlie, you old bastard," Buck shouted, practically throwing himself over the desk. "You ain't going without me."

Charlie only snorted before heading after the other two men, and Buck was right behind him.

It made me feel better. Buck cared about those kids, and between the four men, there was a good chance they'd make it back here okay.

"Rowan." I turned to find Kiaya holding her hand out. "Come back up here before you tear another stitch."

I took her outstretched hand and pulled myself back over the dresser, landing on the other side with a huff. Randall stood there, tugging on the hem of his shirt as he looked out over the railing toward the parking lot.

I followed his gaze.

The commotion had drawn even more of the dead, and at the moment, dozens of them were stumbling our way. They were heading down the street and from in between houses, and there were more in the distance. They were all headed in our direction.

Holding on to the railing, I leaned over so I could get a look at what was happening below me, ignoring my throbbing back. I spotted Devon, Buck, Charlie, and Miller kneeling behind a truck, and three vehicles over saw Mike's head sticking out from under a car. A zombie stumbled past him, and his eyes grew wide, but he didn't move, and the thing wandered off without realizing he was there.

Something bolted across the other side of the parking lot, grabbing my attention, and I saw Lexi just as she climbed under a truck.

"There," I hissed, pointing to her as she disappeared from sight.

Kiaya's eyes got wide. "We need to tell them where she is."

"Yeah."

I began waving my arms, knowing I couldn't yell and draw

FAR from HOME

more zombies this way. Kiaya mimicked me, the two of us jumping up and down and waving our arms like maniacs while Randall stood quietly at our sides. He looked shell-shocked, and not for the first time I realized he was not equipped for this world and these responsibilities.

It took a few seconds, but eventually Devon looked our way. His eyes grew huge when he saw us, and he lifted himself up on his knees as if that would give him a better view. I began pointing toward the truck Lexi was hiding under, mouthing the words, *over there*, while I silently prayed he'd get the point.

Devon leaned around the truck so he could see, after a second moving back to say something to the other men. Then he looked our way once again and gave a thumbs up before charging from his hiding place, the other men right behind him.

Kiaya grabbed my hand. "They're going to get her."

I could only give it a squeeze in reply.

The men stayed low, moving from car to car, pausing when they reached each one so they could look around. My heart was thudding like crazy as I watched, my gaze moving from them to the nearby zombies and back again, and my hand still in Kiaya's. She was as tense as I was, and all across the catwalk the other survivors were the same. I spotted Hank all the way at the other end, just outside our room. He looked like he was frozen in terror, and I couldn't help wondering if he was thinking about his friend, remembering how the zombies had torn him apart.

I shuddered.

"It will be okay." Kiaya released my hand and put her arm around me.

If the situation hadn't been so intense, I would have turned to look at her. This wasn't the closed-off girl I'd grown used to.

"Bethie," Randall said, grabbing my attention.

My head snapped his way. He was staring down at the parking lot, and I followed his gaze, searching the dead. It took a minute to find one that could have been his sister. They were all so decayed, and from this distance, it was tough to distinguish them from one another, but once I saw her, I knew.

Her brown skin was ashen and decaying, torn in places, and

she must have had a weave, because pieces had ripped off and the few strands of curls remaining were knotted and ratty. She was two cars away from Lexi but headed that way, and my insides convulsed when I thought about the little girl spotting her mother and possibly running to her. Maybe a bite didn't turn you—so far, that was how it seemed, anyway—but that little girl against a full-grown zombie wouldn't result in just one bite. It would be a bloodbath.

"Do you see her?" I whispered to Kiaya, afraid to raise my voice.

She only nodded before raising her arm.

Kiaya began waving again, trying to get the guys' attention, and I joined her. It was futile, though. They were too focused on what was happening in the parking lot to look our way.

The four men had reached the truck where Mike was hiding and were in the process of pulling him out. He fought them, struggling to stay under, and the scraping of his feet against the pavement was loud in the otherwise silent town.

My heart jumped to my throat, making me feel like I was on the verge of choking.

Once he'd managed to wrangle Mike free, Devon passed him to Miller, who threw the boy over his shoulder and took off for the motel.

Of course, he'd be the first to return.

By then, Bethie had gotten even closer to Lexi's hiding place and was seconds from reaching a point where the little girl would be able to see her. Buck, Charlie, and Devon were a row away, still, but on the move, and I found myself holding my breath as I waited to see what would happen. Without thinking, I reached out and took Kiaya's hand again. She didn't resist.

Footsteps pounded up the stairs behind me, and I knew Miller had made it to safety. I didn't look back, though, not even when Kiaya released my hand and rushed to the stairs. She and Lisa began fawning over the kid, and Randall's voice joined them, asking if he was okay. Miller was next to me a second later, huffing and sweaty and acting concerned as he looked out over the parking lot.

"That's her mom," he said, nodding to Bethie.

"I know," I said.

I didn't look at him.

Devon turned down the row of cars just as Bethie did from the other end, and only a second later, Lexi scrambled from her hiding place.

"Mommy!"

I had to clamp my hand over my mouth to stop from screaming when her little cry reached me. I wanted to shout, to yell to Devon to grab her, but it was no use. Not only would it draw more of the dead, it was pointless because he was right behind her, steps behind Lexi as she rushed toward her mom.

The dead woman let out a growl and moved faster when she saw the little girl. Her arms were out, reaching, and her mouth open and ready. It was a grotesque sight, but the child didn't seem to register that. All she could see was her mom, and like so many other things, it brought tears to my eyes. And not just because I was a consummate crier. My own mom was so far away and possibly dead, possibly even a zombie, and it felt like someone was tearing at my heart.

About six feet of space separated Lexi and the zombie when Devon finally reached the girl. He grabbed her around the waist, scooping her into his arms as he spun around and rushed in the opposite direction. Buck and Charlie were waiting for him at the end of the row, waving for him to move faster.

Devon reached the older men, and together they took off, heading back toward the stairs. The little girl screamed and fought, but Devon didn't slow, didn't ease his grip, didn't lose focus as he ran. The other two men had more than thirty years on him, and while Buck was in decent shape, Charlie wasn't. It wasn't long before he was struggling, and soon there was four feet of space between him and Buck. And even more between him and Devon.

As if realizing it, Devon slowed, but Buck waved him on.

"Go!" he shouted. "Go!"

He headed back to help his friend, and Devon only hesitated for a second before running faster. That was when I realized

225

exactly how his extreme sports had helped prepare him for this world. He was fit and didn't tire easily, and he knew how to push himself, which was what he was doing now.

"They're coming," I said when he neared the bottom of the stairs. "Go!" I shoved Miller in that direction. "Help him!"

The corporal didn't look happy about it, but he obeyed, jogging to the staircase a lot slower than I would have liked. He threw himself over the dresser and scrambled down, and I watched from the top as he disappeared. I couldn't see what was happening on the ground from where I was, and it made every inch of me tense in anticipation, but I also couldn't make myself move away from the stairs.

A minute passed before Miller reappeared, a still struggling Lexi slung his over his shoulder.

"Stop squirming," he grunted, holding her legs tighter as he ran.

I waited a few seconds longer, but when Devon didn't appear, rushed back to the railing.

He'd gone back to help Buck and Charlie. The latter must have twisted an ankle or something, because he was limping and leaning on Buck. The two men were using knives to hack at the dead that had converged on them, but more were coming. So many more I couldn't even register where they'd all come from.

Devon joined them, taking Charlie's other arm and draping it over his shoulder so he and Buck could work together. It made them vulnerable, less able to defend themselves, and I wanted to help, but I couldn't. I wasn't armed, but even worse was the knowledge that even if I had been, there was nothing I could do. I couldn't help them from up here because I'd never even shot a gun. I was more likely to hit Devon or Buck or Charlie than one of the dead.

Miller was huffing when he stopped next to me, and I turned on him. "Do something!"

"What do you want me to do?" he asked, sounding irritated.

I waved to the gun at his hip. "You're a soldier, you can shoot, so shoot!"

His expression twisted in doubt, but it was gone in a second and he had the gun out. Below us, Devon and Buck were dragging Charlie back while hacking at the dead, but the progress was slow. Much too slow for comfort.

Suddenly, a zombie stumbled from the shadows right behind them, and I reached out like it would help even though I knew I was useless, my mouth opened as I prepared to yell, but a bang broke through the air, drowning out my words. The zombie dropped.

Devon glanced up, and I turned as well, expecting the shot to have come from Miller. It hadn't, though. It had come from Lisa, who had a small handgun aimed at the dead.

She prepared to shoot again, and I refocused my attention on the dead. Devon, Charlie, and Buck were so close to the stairs now. So close to safety. I clenched my fists, saying a silent prayer and begging God to let them be okay. A zombie lunged, and Buck slashed at it with his knife, the blade sinking into its skull. Another grabbed for them, but Devon managed to kick the thing away. Lisa fired, taking the zombies out with expert precision, and even Miller had joined in, but more staggered toward the men, and a chorus of moans rose around us.

I was holding my breath, watching and praying and waiting, and when a zombie lurched from beneath the overhang right behind Devon, the air burst out of my lungs in a scream.

He turned, alerted to danger by my shout, but it was at the exact moment Buck stabbed at another zombie. He stumbled one way and Devon the other, and Charlie went down.

The zombie lunged.

He grabbed Devon, and they fell to the ground, and without thinking about it, I took off, running toward the stairs.

Kiaya called for me when I passed her, still kneeling in front of Lexi, but like before, I didn't care. Lisa was on her way, too, a foot in front of me, and she practically threw herself over the dresser when she reached it. I scrambled over a little less gracefully but made it, and rushed down the stairs behind her.

She was ahead of me, and before I even turned the corner, a shot rang out. A zombie's head exploded as I limped up beside her, barely registering the throbbing in my back but also knowing it was slowing me down. Devon was up, as was Buck, and they had Charlie and were dragging him toward us. Lisa fired again and again, taking out the dead that were hot on their trail, but no matter how many fell, more seemed to take their place.

Where had they all come from?

"Here," I yelled when the men reached us, reaching out to help Charlie over the dresser.

He tumbled over, falling to the stairs, but I didn't turn to help him again, too focused on Devon.

Buck was next, quickly followed by Devon, but there was no time to relax because something else had grabbed my attention. The dead. They were right behind him. Dozens of them. All of them lumbering toward the stairs where the pathetic excuse for a barricade would do nothing to keep them out.

"Up!" Devon shouted as he and Buck worked together to lug Charlie to his feet.

"Go. I'll cover you," Lisa said, her focus on the dead as she fired yet again.

Devon gave me a shove with his free hand. "Move. Now."

I did as I was told, pulling myself up the stairs one painful step after another. He and Buck were behind me, supporting Charlie between them, and as I turned the corner, I caught sight of Lisa only a few steps behind. She was walking backward, still shooting, but one woman—no matter how badass—was no match for the dozens of zombies in front of her, and already the dead had started climbing.

I forced myself to move faster, holding on to the railing to pull myself up as I climbed.

"They're coming!" I screamed as I ran.

Kiaya's face appeared above the dresser, her eyes like saucers. She waved for me to move, but I had reached my limit and couldn't push myself any harder. Still, it took only a few seconds to reach her, and once I did, she was grabbing my arm and pulling, lugging me up and over the dresser.

Miller was behind her, and he reached out to help me as I toppled onto the ground, but I shoved him away. "Help them, you asshole."

FAR from HOME

I pulled myself away from the stairs so I didn't trip anyone up then dragged myself to my feet. My back throbbed like I'd been stabbed by a huge piece of ceramic all over again, but I ignored it, watching as Kiaya and Miller helped Charlie over, aided from behind by Buck, who quickly followed. Devon didn't appear, but I hadn't expected him to. He'd go back for Lisa because it was what he did.

They appeared at the same time, both of them pulling themselves over the dresser so fast it was like they were competing in an Olympic event. They toppled to the ground but were up in seconds, and even when I reached for Devon, he didn't seem to register I was there. He was too busy shouting orders.

"We need more people firing! Anyone who can't shoot, work together to get another dresser. Now! There are too many of them, and this thing won't hold them off for long."

Kiaya rushed to the nearest room, which someone had already opened. I turned to head after her but was stopped short when Devon grabbed my arm.

He pulled me away, shoving me to the other side of the stairs, and barely looked at me when he said, "Not you. You're already bleeding, and I don't want you to pull another stitch."

It hurt, but I obeyed because the expression of panic on his face made it impossible to argue.

Gunshots rang through the air as people started shooting. Devon, Lisa, Buck, and Miller were four of them, and there were two others whose names I didn't know. Even with the six of them firing into the advancing dead, I couldn't imagine it would be enough. There were so many that it seemed never-ending.

It was, though. It didn't take long for the zombies to slow, and I realized their numbers were actually a disadvantage. The staircase wasn't very wide, and as bodies dropped, they began to pile up, making it difficult for the creatures behind them to continue climbing. A few tried pulling themselves over the other dead, but they were uncoordinated and slow, and before they could get far, a bullet to the brain took them out.

Soon, the firing stopped, and people began to collect themselves. A second dresser had been pulled out, and a few people worked together to lift it so it was on top of the first. Again, it was a temporary solution, but it was better than nothing and the only thing we could do at the moment.

With that done, I let out a deep sigh and turned to look for Devon, desperate to make sure he was whole. That was when I spotted Buck. He was on the ground beside Charlie, Lisa kneeling next to him. When she shifted, the bite came into view. It was on Charlie's neck, right below his ear, and the sight almost made my heart stop.

17

I took a step toward Charlie, my hand out like I wanted to help, but there was nothing I could do, and I couldn't utter a word. There was blood everywhere. On his neck, saturating his shirt, dotted on his face and arm. So much blood. So much damage from teeth. From human teeth. How could it be? It seemed insane.

It will be okay, I told myself.

Hank had been bitten, and he was fine, which meant Charlie would be okay, too. He had to be. He'd risked his life to save those kids, and it seemed unfair that he'd die because of it. Having grown up in a world where life was fair, where if I worked hard enough I got what I wanted, where all I had to do was ask and it was mine for the taking, that was the only possible outcome I could wrap my brain around. I didn't know Charlie, but based on what I'd seen, I had to assume he was a good man, which meant only good things should happen for him.

My gaze focused on Kiaya, who was still kneeling in front of Lexi, trying to comfort the little girl. My certainty wavered. Kiaya was good. So good. Better than almost anyone I'd ever met. But her life hadn't been sunshine and roses.

"Are you okay?" Devon asked, popping up at my side and

distracting me from thoughts of Kiaya.

Worry shimmered in his blue eyes as he looked me over, and his hand was half out as if he'd started to grab me but stopped himself. In the chaos, the kiss we'd shared had slipped my mind, but now it came crashing back. My face flushed despite the tension still surrounding us, and I found it difficult to meet his gaze for some reason.

"I'm okay," I said. "What about you?"

"I'm fine," he said, the words coming out like a sigh of relief.

My gaze snapped to where Lisa was cleaning Charlie's wound. Buck sat beside the injured man, concern written in every line of his body.

"What happened out there?" I asked.

Devon followed my gaze. "We got to the stairs and were climbing over that damn dresser when a zombie popped up out of nowhere. Buck and I didn't even see it until the thing had taken a bite out of Charlie. I couldn't stop it from happening. I don't even know where it came from."

The last two sentences were mumbled, his voice full of regret and self-doubt.

"It's not your fault," I said, and reached out to put my hand on his arm without thinking.

Devon's gaze moved down, staring at my hand on his arm for a moment, then he shook his head. "I know. It's that bastard Miller's fault. He's the one who rushed to tell everyone a bite wouldn't hurt them. That was all Lexi would say when I grabbed her. 'Mommy isn't going to hurt me. The soldier said Mommy won't hurt me.' If he hadn't told the others, she wouldn't have run off."

I didn't totally disagree with Devon on that point—Miller was taking all of this for granted—but he wasn't the only one to blame. Randall had been left alone to fend for two young kids, but in so many ways he was a child himself. Why hadn't any of the other survivors stepped in to help? Why in God's name had they left the care of a five-year-old to a special needs man and her ten-year-old brother?

FAR from HOME

Devon wasn't looking at me. He was glaring at Miller, who was busy talking with two other men. They were at the end of the catwalk, looking down to the bottom of the stairs like they were trying to decide if they needed to take any action. I couldn't see what they were looking at from here, but it didn't matter. They were eventually going to have to do something to make this place more secure. One staircase was now completely covered in bodies—the stench was already bad, and I couldn't imagine what it would be like after a couple hot days—but the other wasn't any better. There was still only one measly dresser at both the top and the bottom of the stairs. They needed a better barricade.

Things began to settle down, and people filed back to their rooms. I hadn't met most of the survivors, and while a few shot curious glances our way as they headed off, most avoided looking directly at us. As a whole, they seemed shell-shocked and out of it. Totally unprepared for what had happened and unwilling to do anything to change that. It was why, I realized, they were okay with Miller calling the shots and why his presence was a comfort. They wanted to believe they'd be safe if they stayed in the bubble they'd created at the motel. They wouldn't, and hopefully this little incident helped them realize that. This was not a safe place to stay, especially with the shitty barricades they'd created.

Kiaya came over to where Devon and I were standing. "I'm going to help Randall with the kids."

I wasn't the least bit surprised.

"How's Lexi doing?" I asked her.

"She's shaken up, and she still doesn't really understand why she couldn't see her mom. Randall and Mike have tried to explain that her mom is dead, but Lexi can see her walking around." Kiaya's frown deepened. "She just can't understand."

"I can only imagine," I said, looking past Kiaya to where Randall was talking to his niece. The poor guy looked as stricken as the little girl. "Do you think they'll be okay with Randall?"

"I think," Kiaya said, "that Mike has taken on most of the duties when it comes to his sister. Randall tries, but from what I understand, he lived with his mom, who did everything for him before she died, then he moved in with his sister. He was babied.

Treated like a little kid instead of being taught to be independent. He's never had to grow up and take on any real responsibilities. Being thrown into this…" She trailed off, shrugging.

"It's too much for him," I said.

Thinking about the three of them staying here and how vulnerable they would be, not to mention the many derogatory things Miller had said about Randall, filled me with dread. If only we could take them with us. I didn't have the first clue how to raise a kid, and I doubted Devon and Kiaya did either, but together we could make it work until we got home. Then Mom would know what to do.

If she was alive…

I shook the thought off.

"You'll come to the room when you're done?" I asked Kiaya.

"Yeah." She lifted her eyebrows a tad and shot a look toward Devon but didn't say anything else.

Again, I flushed.

Not wanting to address what she'd walked in on since he and I hadn't even discussed it yet, I said, "If I decide to go to bed before you get there, I'll keep a flashlight on in the bathroom so you can see."

"Okay," she replied but lifted her eyebrows higher.

I rolled my eyes before turning away.

Devon was with Buck and Charlie, who was patched up but hadn't stood.

Lisa was kneeling next to them. "He was responsive at first, but now he's acting a bit lethargic.

"Maybe it's shock?" Buck said, his focus on the other man.

"Maybe," Devon said a bit uncertainly, "although it seems unlikely. He was cussing up a storm when we first came up the stairs."

Buck's frown deepened, growing more exaggerated.

"How's our hero doing?" Miller asked, coming up behind Devon.

He was grinning, his chest puffed out as he looked down to where Charlie, Buck, Devon, and Lisa sat, and I couldn't quite reconcile the expression on his face with what had just happened.

FAR from HOME

The shitty barricade they'd made had proven to be worthless, the one staircase was now crowded with bodies, the parking lot was overrun, and Charlie had been bitten. It had been a disaster, as far as I was concerned, and I didn't even want to think about how we were going to get out of here tomorrow now that the dead had converged on the motel.

Devon grimaced, but didn't look up.

"He's being pretty unresponsive right now," Lisa, who did look up at Miller, said. "It's weird."

Seemingly unconcerned, Miller shrugged. "He's probably just hurting. The bastard got a pretty good chunk taken out of him."

"Yeah, maybe." Lisa didn't look convinced.

"You going to do something about that other staircase?" Devon asked, nodding to the steps that weren't covered in bodies. "We saw how easily the dead got over that dresser."

Miller scoffed. "Only because they were following you. They're mindless creatures. It isn't like they have any real problem-solving skills."

Devon's jaw clenched, and he didn't look away from the corporal, who had his arms crossed and an expression on his face that dared the other man to challenge him. He wasn't going to listen to anything Devon had to say. It was obvious.

Miller's mouth turned into a self-satisfied smile when Devon didn't say anything else. "It is getting late, though, and with the parking lot full, we should clear the area. We don't want to draw any unwanted attention our way."

I looked out over the parking lot to the dozens of zombies lumbering around. There were more in the distance, all headed this way. He was a little late if he was trying to avoid unwanted attention.

"We should get him inside," Lisa said, turning her gaze on Devon and Buck. "Do you think the two of you will be able to get him up and to his room?"

"Sure," Devon said, as Buck mumbled, "Not a problem."

They each took one of Charlie's arms and urged him to stand. He needed minimal assistance, but he acted more like he was

235

working on autopilot than actually participating, and he didn't seem to be very aware of what he was doing. It was strange, and the longer I watched, the more dread began to pool in my stomach. This just didn't feel right.

Lisa and I followed the men as they directed Charlie to his room, which he was apparently sharing with one of the other men who'd been helping Miller. The guy, who was probably in his late thirties, was silent as his roommate was brought in, watching with weary eyes as Buck urged him to sit down.

"He okay?" the man asked.

"Shit, Fred," Buck snapped. "Does he look okay?"

Lisa ignored his outburst and said, "I'm not sure."

Buck stayed at his friend's side, but Devon stepped back from the bed. "Something isn't right. He acts like he doesn't know what's going on."

Buck didn't look away from his friend. "I've known Charlie as long as I can remember, and I've never seen him act like this." He looked up, frowning. "It just don't make sense."

"Maybe it's the body fighting off the virus?" Lisa looked from him to Devon. "Maybe he'll snap out of it."

I had no clue, and Devon apparently didn't either, because he only shrugged.

"What if he don't?" Fred asked.

Devon's focus moved to Buck. "Maybe we should have someone stand watch. Just in case."

The older man's frown deepened, and he ran his hand down his face. "Yeah," he said, sounding older than he was, and exhausted.

"You mean in case he turns?" Lisa asked, even though the worst-case scenario was obvious.

Devon nodded in response, at first appearing like he wasn't going to say anything else, but then said, "I think it would be wise to have someone on watch outside as well. We all saw how easily those zombies crawled over the dresser. If they realize there's another way up here, we could be in trouble."

"Even if they managed to get up, it ain't like they're gonna get us in here," Charlie's roommate said, sounding slightly irritated.

Devon and I exchanged a look.

"What?" Lisa asked. "What do you know that we don't?"

"I've seen one open a door," I told her.

"Bullshit," Fred said, while Buck cursed under his breath.

"It's true." Devon was focused on Buck. "That barricade is shit, and we both know it."

"Good luck trying to convince Miller of that," the older man said.

"I don't need to convince him of anything," Devon replied. "We're here for the night, and that's it. Whatever happens after we leave is up to you guys to figure out. I'm sorry if that sounds cold or selfish, but I just can't fight with someone who won't listen to reason. Not when I have other things going on."

"I understand," Buck said, nodding.

"What I can do," Devon continued, "is stand watch outside while I'm here."

"Miller ain't gonna like that," Fred said. "He wants us staying in the rooms as much as possible."

Devon snorted but didn't look away from Buck. "Can you watch Charlie?"

"I'll keep an eye on him," Buck said.

"Then I'll stand guard outside."

"The whole night?" I shook my head. "Devon, you can't stay awake the whole night. You need sleep."

"We'll work it out," he said, his expression softening when he looked at me. "I promise I'll get some rest."

I exhaled but nodded. Once again, I found myself wishing I had some kind of skills that were useful in this world so I could help take some of the burden off his shoulders. Thinking about how ill-equipped I was made me feel pathetic.

Lisa stood, stretching a little. "I can take a shift. Just come and get me when it's time."

"So can I," Fred grumbled, clearly not happy about it.

The way he glanced toward Charlie, though, made it seem like he wasn't too thrilled with the idea of being stuck in the room with him either.

"Thanks," Devon said gratefully, looking at Lisa.

She nodded. "In the meantime, I'm going to get some sleep."

At the mention of sleep, my body seemed to register just how tired it was. The last few days of stress and worry had taken a toll, and I suddenly felt like I'd been awake for days.

"Sleep sounds amazing," I said, following Lisa to the door automatically.

"I'll be right back," I heard Devon say, and I paused to wait for him.

Outside, we said goodnight to Lisa before heading toward our rooms. The catwalk was deserted now, but the parking lot wasn't. It was full dark, and with no electricity the world beyond was as black as the pits of hell, but I didn't need any light to know the dead were there. The stench of rot was thick, the putrid aroma hanging in the air like a fog, and their moans filled the night the way the chirping of crickets once had.

I shuddered, and Devon slipped his arm around my shoulders.

"How are we going to get out of here?" I asked as we headed back to our room.

"I'm working on it," he replied.

I didn't ask for details because I had faith that Devon would be able to figure something out.

We reached my room to find the door to the adjoining one open, but only a crack. It was dark and silent, and I could only assume Hank was sleeping. I'd seen him outside during the fight, but not after. He must have come back here right away, possibly running from the sight of Charlie's blood. The kid had been on his own for days and had to be worn out, so I didn't blame him for wanting the rest. I was also glad for the semi-privacy.

Devon eased the door shut as I flipped the switch on the small lantern, and a soft light filled the room.

"You going to be okay?" he asked when I turned to face him.

"Are you worried I'm on the verge of falling apart?"

"I'm worried we're all on the verge of falling apart," he responded, "it just so happens I'm more concerned about you than anyone else."

FAR from HOME

Warmth spread through me, and I lowered my head, looking up at him through my lashes because it was all I could manage.

"Was it okay that I kissed you?" he asked.

"It was a surprise, but yes."

Devon's eyebrows lifted. "You were really surprised?"

"I thought you couldn't stand me," I said, "so, yeah."

Devon chuckled as he reached out to flick my braid. "I'll blame the blonde hair."

After that statement, I had no problem looking up to glare at him, but the irritation was pushed away when he swept me into his arms and covered my mouth with his. I melted, giving in to the kiss and allowing his strength to hold me up as his mouth moved over mine. It was deep, but slow, and I could feel it all the way in my toes. I concentrated on how soft his lips were, and how warm. How secure I felt in his arms.

It seemed to go on forever, but when he finally broke the kiss, he didn't ease his hold on me.

"I should go."

"Yeah," I said, staring up at him.

"If something goes south," he said, his voice quiet, "if you hear anything that makes you think there's trouble, lock the door and don't come out. Don't open the door for anyone but me."

"You want me to hide in the room even if I think you're in trouble? Do you seriously have a problem with a woman coming to your rescue?"

"Not at all. In fact, once we get to a place where we can safely do it, I'm going to teach you how to shoot. When that happens, you can come to my rescue whenever you want. Until then, you stay where you're safe. Understand?"

I sighed but nodded because—once again—he was right. "Fine."

"Good." Devon finally released me and stepped back. "Hopefully, we won't have to worry about it. Lisa might be right. Maybe Charlie's body is just fighting off the virus. Maybe Hank went through the same thing but doesn't remember it."

"True," I said.

He nodded a couple times like he was trying to convince himself, then shot me one final look before heading for the door. It clicked shut behind him, leaving me alone, and I stripped to my underwear and tank before moving the lantern to the bathroom. I kept the door slightly ajar so it blocked out most of the light, then slipped into bed. My mind was spinning so much I didn't think I had a chance of falling asleep despite the exhaustion weighing me down. In minutes, though, my body began to feel weightless, and I slipped into a dream world.

18

Through the haze of sleep, I became aware of the door clicking, but I didn't surface enough to register where I was. In my sleepy mind, the footsteps belonged to my college roommate, Riley. It was so like her to stagger into the room in the middle of the night after a party. I rolled over, pulling my pillow over my head to block out the sound of her high heels thumping against the floor when she pulled them off. In minutes, I was back to sleep.

The second time a click sounded through the room it was farther away, but for some reason woke me more. I opened my eyes and blinked as the haze of sleep melted away and focused on a sliver of light in the darkness. It took a moment to register that it was coming from the other room, but once I had, I pulled myself from bed and padded toward it.

The door was still only cracked, and I pushed it open a little so I could peer inside. Devon was on the other side of the room, the light from a small lantern illuminating him as he pulled his shirt over his head.

I pushed the door open the rest of the way and stepped in, my gaze darting to the bed where Hank slept. He didn't move.

"Devon," I whispered.

He turned, smiling when he saw me. "Did I wake you?"

"Yeah, but it's okay. How's Charlie?"

"He snapped out of it about two hours ago, thank God. I think it's going to be okay." Devon undid his pants and slipped them off so he was standing in only his boxer briefs. "I stood watch at the stairs after that, but Fred took over so I could get some sleep."

"I'm surprised."

Devon let out a low snort. "No kidding. I think Lisa bullied him into it. She seems to be one of the few people who isn't scared to contradict Miller, and since she's the only person with medical training, she has a little more pull than anyone else."

"Makes sense," I said. "Miller wouldn't want to risk her deciding to hit the road."

"Yeah," Devon said.

He turned his head and covered his mouth, trying to stifle a yawn, but it didn't work. As usual, it was catching, and a second later I mimicked the gesture, earning a smile from him.

"I'll let you get some sleep," I said, "I just wanted to check on Charlie."

"I'd protest, but I think I need it."

I nodded, smiling as I backed away. "See you in the morning?"

"See you in the morning," he said.

I turned and headed back to my room, aware that I was in nothing but a pair of bikini underwear and tank top and that he was probably checking out my ass despite his exhaustion. I walked slower than necessary.

It wasn't a creak that woke me next. It was a scream.

I bolted upright, instantly awake. Despite the stuffiness of the room, the covers were wrapped around me, and I had to kick to get them off, while in the bed next to me Kiaya rolled to her feet. Like me, she wasn't dressed, and seeing her in nothing but a small pair of shorts and a skimpy tank top hit me like a punch. How stupid of us to wear so little after the horrible events of the previous day. What if we had to run outside right now? What if we had no time to change or grab other clothes? We'd be screwed.

We needed to plan ahead better.

I was thinking this through as I grabbed my leggings off the floor and pulled them on, my eyes already searching the darkness for my shoes.

A light flipped on, and my corneas almost burst into flames. I had to squint even though it was dim, but despite the near blindness from the sudden light, I managed to spot my shoes. I'd just shoved my feet into them when the door adjoining our two rooms burst open and Devon, already dressed, rushed in. Hank was two steps behind him, his eyes wide and terrified.

"What's happening?" Kiaya asked.

"I don't know." His gaze moved from her to me. "But we should be ready to make a run for it."

"We're one step ahead of you," I said as I shoved the few things I'd dragged into the motel room into my bag.

Thank God I hadn't brought my hulking suitcase up.

He nodded, the gesture quick and clipped. "Okay. I'm going to check it out. I want the three of you to stay here."

"I'm not staying here," Kiaya hissed before I could respond. "There are children out there who could need my help. I may not be much use when it comes to killing zombies, but I can watch out for those kids."

"I'm going with her," I said, straightening my shoulders.

Hank took a step back like he was considering going into the other room and locking the door.

Devon blew out a long breath but nodded again. "Fine. But watch your backs and stay together. Once you get to the kids, find somewhere to hide and stay there. I'll come get you when it's safe to move."

Kiaya grabbed her bag, already packed, and slung it over her shoulder before swiping her gun up off the dresser. "Let's do this."

Since the M16 was in the car—it would have been nice to have it right about now—Devon had my gun, leaving me emptyhanded.

I spun to where Hank stood, visibly shaking.

How had this kid gotten up the courage to save us when he was so obviously terrified? Maybe it had seemed like his only way out.

"You can stay here, but I need the knife."

He nodded, and his dark, shaggy hair fell across his face, covering his eyes. He disappeared into the other room while Devon and Kiaya headed for the door where they waited for me. Only a few seconds later, Hank had reappeared. His hand was trembling when he held the knife out.

"Thanks," I said as I took it. "Lock the door after we leave. You'll be okay."

The kid swallowed. "Okay."

It seemed to be all he could get out.

I went to join Kiaya and Devon at the door, my own bag slung over my shoulder. He had his hand on the knob, waiting, and knowing he was looking for a signal that I was ready, I forced out a nod. It was a lie. I didn't think there was a scenario where I'd ever be ready to face zombies.

He pulled the door open and stepped out, and we followed.

The night was a tornado of chaos. Beams of light cut through the darkness, giving us glimpses of the horror and pandemonium. A body, bloodied and torn apart lying motionless on the catwalk, a woman screaming as she held her arm, which was covered in blood, another woman, lying on her back, terrified eyes staring at nothing as a puddle formed beneath her, flowing from a bite on her neck. Lisa was beside her, trying to staunch the blood even though it was obvious it wouldn't be stopped, while other people ran around, shouting orders and questions as they tried to figure out what had happened.

"Keep your eyes open," Devon ordered as he led us forward, gun in one hand and a knife in the other.

Kiaya was a step behind him, looking ready to bolt toward

FAR from HOME

Randall and the kids' room at the other end of the catwalk.

Devon paused when he reached Lisa. "What's happening?"

"I don't know." She shook her head, barely looking up as the woman beside her gasped for breath. "By the time I got out here, things were already crazy."

"You seen Fred?" Devon had his gun up and ready and was searching the chaos. "He was supposed to have taken over for me out here."

"No," Lisa replied. "But it's dark."

Through the shouting, the moans and growls of the dead seemed to grow, making the hair on my arms stand up. The darkness made it impossible to see much, but occasionally the beam of someone's flashlight shone into the parking lot, giving me a glimpse of how dense the horde had gotten. The stench was unbearable, thick and suffocating, but even worse were the scratches in the direction of the previously unclogged staircase.

Peering through the darkness, I squinted, trying to get a look at it. A beam of shaky light cut through blackness, briefly illuminating the stairs, and my stomach dropped.

"They're coming up," I said.

Devon and Lisa looked toward the stairs, but Kiaya grabbed my hand. "We have to go," she hissed.

"Shit," Devon said when he saw what I had.

Figures on the stairs, dozens of them climbing over one another as they tried to get up.

Lisa was on her feet in a second, her gun out and the injured woman—who was no longer moving—forgotten. "We have to do something."

"We will," Devon said then turned to us. "Go!"

I didn't try to stop Kiaya when she pulled me forward, past Lisa and Devon. I wanted to stay with him but remembered the promise I'd made the night before. Plus, Kiaya was right. Randall and the kids needed us.

Two rooms separated us from theirs, and just as we were approaching one, a person staggered out. He was looking the other way, his back to us, but I recognized the thinning, gray hair.

"Charlie! Do you know what's happen—"

He spun to face us, and my words died on my lips. His eyes were milky and his skin ghostly pale, and when he opened his mouth, he moaned. He reached for us, and Kiaya jumped back, letting out a scream as she lifted her gun. She pulled the trigger, and a bang echoed through the night, leaving a ringing behind in my ears. The shot was wide, though, missing him by a mile. He lunged again, not giving her a chance to shoot a second time, and she slammed the gun against his grasping hands, trying to hold him off.

"Rowan!" I heard Devon shout.

I didn't look back, but instead ducked under Charlie's arms so I could get behind him. My back throbbed, screaming in protest, but I ignored it. The man who had once been Charlie was determined to get at Kiaya, his focus so single minded he didn't notice me until I'd grabbed his shirt and pulled him back. That was when he growled and spun, and the sudden movement whipped me to the side. His shirt slipped from my grasp, and I slammed into the railing, crying out from the pain. There was no chance to nurse my injuries, though, because in no time zombie Charlie was lunging toward me. I was shorter than he was, but I decided to use it to my advantage and ducked down, evading his grasp. When he was right over me, I half stood, thrusting my knife up as I did. The blade sank in right beneath his chin, and I shoved it harder, forcing it up. The sickening squish of it cutting into flesh made my stomach lurch, but he hadn't stopped moving yet, so I pushed harder, crying out as I did. He was pulled away from me a second after he finally stopped moving, and the now motionless body crashed into Devon.

He stumbled back but released Charlie before they both fell, instantly spinning to face me. "Are you okay?"

I nodded, gasping. "Yeah."

The throbbing cut on my back said differently, but I kept that to myself.

Devon gave a tense nod, his head barely moving. "Get to the kids. Now! There are more climbing the stairs."

Kiaya moved, grabbing me, and we took off.

She banged her hand against the door the second we reached

FAR from HOME

it, and it was immediately pulled open. Mike stood in front of us, a small knife grasped in his hand, while behind him Lexi and Randall huddled in a corner, holding on to one another.

Kiaya rushed inside, urging Mike to move, and I followed, pulling the door shut behind me.

The boy's eyes were huge as he looked between us. "Are there more zombies?"

"We don't know yet," I lied.

Kiaya had already moved to the other side of the room, and seeing her, Lexi rushed forward. She threw herself against Kiaya, sobbing, but I couldn't understand a word the little girl said.

Mike looked at them, then to me. "She misses our mom."

"I know," I said. "You're doing a good job, though."

The kid only nodded.

The bang of gunshots penetrated the door, and I moved to the window, hoping to get an idea of what was happening, and Mike followed. The dark night was a blur of barely discernable movement, but a beam of light was just visible near the other end of the catwalk. From where we stood, we could see nothing, though. No people, and no zombies. We were totally in the dark about what was happening as gunshot after gunshot rang through the night.

After a few minutes, I looked toward Mike. The kid was standing beside me, his wide eyes focused on the ground just outside the window. I followed his gaze and found myself staring into the lifeless eyes of a woman whose name I didn't know.

I looked away.

Behind me, Kiaya was whispering to Lexi—telling her a story, it sounded like—and Randall was with them, listening in rapt attention. Mike and I stayed at the window, looking out in silence. The sun was struggling to make an appearance, lending more light to the scene. The gunshots became fewer and more spread apart, finally stopping altogether and telling me the chaos had finally settled. I stayed where I was, waiting, but Devon didn't come to the room. I couldn't see him from here, but I could see other bodies. Four of them, including Charlie and Fred, his roommate. Before I'd seen them, I'd pieced together what had happened. Fred had shirked his duties and returned to his room, where Charlie turned and attacked him. Then he'd somehow managed to either get out of his room or was let out by someone who went to check on them. Then he attacked more people.

Eventually, the sound of a very heated discussion penetrated the closed door. I pressed my face closer to the window, hoping to see what was going on, but whoever it was, they were too far away.

"I'm going out so I can see what's happening," I said, not looking away from the window.

"Devon said to stay here," Kiaya responded.

"It's safe." I turned to face her. "I'll be right back."

She nodded but said nothing, and I returned the gesture before heading out.

Thanks to the rising sun, the remnants of the carnage were clearly visible. Blood spatter on the wall and catwalk, as well as bodies that had been ripped apart. I looked toward the other staircase as I started walking, not the least bit surprised to see that it was now as crowded with bodies as the first one.

Miller was a fool, and the sooner we got out of here, the better.

I avoided looking directly at the bodies as I passed them, keeping my focus on the people gathered at the other end of the catwalk—right beside the now impassible steps. Now that I was outside, I could tell Devon was involved in the argument. The others were Miller and another man whose name I didn't know.

"You're blaming this on me?" Miller spit out. "Fuck you. I was keeping these people safe before you showed up. Don't act like you're some kind of savior."

"Safe?" Devon replied. "Bullshit. I saw the results of your so-called safety precautions. And where the hell were you tonight? After what happened earlier, you should have had people on watch. Hell, you should have been one! We're just damn lucky Charlie didn't do more damage and that we managed to stop the zombies before they got up here. Can you imagine how many people would have died if they had?"

"They're uncoordinated and slow." Miller rolled his eyes.

"We can take them. Or at least I can."

The corporal shot Devon a condescending look.

"Son of a bitch," Buck, who was standing beside Devon, muttered. "You're a cocky son of a bitch, which is why we're in this position in the first place. We tried telling you we needed to be cautious, but you just wouldn't listen. Now look what happened! Charlie was bitten and turned. You're a damn fool."

Obviously drawn out by the argument, a door opened behind them, and Hank stuck his head out, drawing everyone's attention. Miller's face was red by then, and at the sight of the kid, it got even redder.

"This is his fault." He pointed at Hank. "He obviously lied about being bitten."

"I can't believe this guy," Devon muttered, shaking his head.

Hank's eyes got wide, and he lifted his hands as if trying to ward off another verbal attack. "I didn't lie. It was a zombie."

"Right." Miller didn't look at him this time.

Devon's gaze flitted toward me when I walked up, and he let out a deep breath, shaking his head again in frustration.

For a moment, no one said anything. Most of the survivors staying here were missing—probably cowering in their rooms—but those gathered around looked like they didn't know what to do. The commotion, both from the attack and from the argument, had riled up the dead, and they were moaning and reaching up as if trying to grab one of us. I looked down, scanning the parking lot and counting. Over twenty still moving around, and those were just the ones I could see. We were drawing too many our way. It was already going to be difficult to get out of here, and with each zombie that stumbled into the parking lot, the risk grew.

I turned back to the group. "We need to take this inside. You're making too much noise."

"What's the point?" Devon grumbled. "It's not like he's going to listen. And it doesn't matter, either. We're out of here today."

"I want to come with you," Lisa said from out of nowhere.

All eyes turned on her.

"This place isn't safe. I've known it for a while, but leaving meant traveling alone, which was just too risky. Now that I have someone to watch my back, I want to get out of here."

Buck was nodding as she talked, his mouth turned down in the corners. There was genuine grief in his eyes, and not just over the loss of Charlie, because I knew what he was about to say and what it meant.

"Me, too." The older man sighed as he looked out over the parking lot, his gaze sweeping over Shamrock. "I've lived in this town my whole life, and I hate the thought of leaving, but Lisa is right. It isn't safe. Not anymore."

Devon nodded and patted him on the arm. "We'll have to find another car, but we're happy to have you." His gaze moved to Lisa. "Both of you."

"I have a car." Lisa pointed to the parking lot. "The white SUV. It will fit five people comfortably and still have room for supplies."

"Okay, then," Devon replied, then looked toward the others. "Anyone else?"

Miller snorted. "No, thanks. Traveling across a zombie-infested country is the dumbest thing I've ever heard."

Devon ignored him and looked over everyone else standing around, his gaze stopping on each person for a moment. No one spoke up, no one said they were going to join us, and while it made Devon shake his head in disgust, he didn't try and talk them into going. I didn't blame him. These people were anchors, which was the last thing we needed out on the road.

"All right, then," he said when no one else had responded. "We'll get a plan together and hit the road later today. The sooner the better."

"Where are you going?" a small voice asked.

We all turned to find Mike standing on the catwalk only four feet away from us.

Devon studied the kid for a moment before moving toward him. He crouched so they were eye level, but like before didn't talk down to him. "Ohio. It's where Rowan is from."

Mike nodded as he thought about it, his dark, serious eyes moving to the parking lot before refocusing on Devon. "I want to go. Me, Randall, and Lexi, I mean."

"You can't be serious," Miller snapped.

Devon lifted his hand but didn't look away from Mike. "This doesn't concern you." He paused, really studying Mike before saying, "It won't be easy, and it might be scary, and I don't know what we're going to find when we get there. Are you sure you want to go?"

Mike gave a firm nod. "Lexi likes Kiaya. Plus, this place isn't safe." His eyes flitted to the left, looking down at the zombies. "They're going to get up here eventually."

"Okay, then," Devon said, patting Mike on the shoulder, drawing the kid's attention back to him. "I'll talk to Randall about it."

"Thanks," Mike said.

Devon smiled before standing, turning to face the rest of us. "Now we just have to figure out how we're going to get out of here."

19

"You can't do this by yourself," I insisted.

"Well, you're not going." Devon didn't look up from where he stood, digging through his belongings. "It would be nice if I had some long sleeve stuff," he mumbled to himself.

He was wearing jeans, but his arms were terrifyingly exposed. Images from the night before flitted through my mind, filling me with dread. Charlie's milky eyes as he opened his mouth, ready to take a bite out of Kiaya. The woman sitting on the ground, holding her arm as she screamed. The other woman gasping for breath as she bled out.

The bite on Hank's arm.

Hank was okay, and he'd been bitten. I tried to cling to that knowledge as Devon zipped his bag. It wasn't easy after what had happened the night before because, thanks to Charlie, we now knew that wasn't always the case. Only we had no idea what the odds were.

Miller's sneer when he'd accused Hank of lying popped into my head, as well as the condescending look he'd given Devon. He was a self-important prick, which was the only reason he was still wearing that uniform. Because it gave him some kind of status in this new world that he never could have achieved before.

The uniform! Why hadn't I thought of it before? It had long sleeves and thick material. There was no way teeth could rip through it. At least I didn't think so. Either way, it would give Devon a better chance of getting out of this thing unscathed. Assuming I could get Miller to loan it to us. True, it would have been better if he went himself, but there was no way in hell that would happen. He was too much of a coward. If only he understood that what Devon was about to do would benefit whoever stayed at the motel as well as give us a chance to get away. But it was hopeless. The man was a selfish ass.

Still, that didn't mean I couldn't talk him into loaning Devon the shirt. I'd gotten him to give us antibiotics, hadn't I? A friendly smile and a bat of my eyelashes. It wasn't like I didn't know how to get what I wanted. Hell, I'd done it my whole life, and not just with my parents either. A pretty face could do wonders when it came to guys, which I knew from experience, and I could be very persuasive when I needed to be.

I dashed for the door, calling over my shoulder, "I'll be right back. Don't you dare leave before then."

"Where are you going?" Devon called after me.

I ignored him and ducked outside.

The early morning sun was bright and the day already warm, magnifying the stench of death. As usual, the catwalk was deserted. Not that it was a surprise. The people who'd been too shell-shocked to come out before the two altercations with the dead definitely wouldn't want to be out here now that the stairs were clogged with bodies and the parking lot teeming with zombies. With the sun beating down on them, baking their rotting flesh and filling the air with the putrid stench, it was tough to really blame them. Not impossible, though. They were scared; I got it. I was terrified as well. But hiding in the motel wasn't the answer. Even worse, sooner or later it would get them killed.

I hurried down the catwalk to Miller's room, trying unsuccessfully to avoid looking down as I did. The dead were impossible to ignore. Their stench and moans were a constant reminder of just how much things had changed over the last few days. Even worse, it was a reminder of what I might face when I finally did make it home.

I knocked when I reached Miller's door, and only a few seconds later it was pulled open. His eyebrows jumped in surprise when he saw me standing there, and a smile spread across his face that felt out of place, considering everything that had happened.

"Rowan," he said, pronouncing my name slowly, like he was trying to caress it.

I had to hold back a shudder of revulsion.

"Devon is going to head out soon. He wants to create a distraction on the other side of town that will lead the dead away from the motel."

"Smart," Miller said almost begrudgingly, crossing his arms, "assuming it works."

"There's only one way to know for sure," I replied, not trying to hide my annoyance even if I had come here intending to butter him up. "The problem is, he doesn't have any long sleeve shirts. It puts him at greater risk. I was wondering if he could borrow your uniform shirt."

Miller's mouth turned down. "He wants to borrow my shirt?"

"That, or you can go." I lifted my eyebrows in a silent challenge, knowing how much he'd love the idea of putting his own ass on the line.

Miller's body jerked, and he shook his head. "I think I should stay here. These people are depending on me."

"Fine." I had a hard time not rolling my eyes. "Let him use your shirt, then."

He pressed his lips together as he thought it through, not speaking. After a few seconds, he sighed but started unbuttoning his shirt.

"Thank you," I said as relief flooded through me.

Miller gave me a smile that didn't quite reach his hazel eyes. "Are you sure this isn't just your way of getting me to take my clothes off? If so, you could have just asked."

Again, I fought back a shudder.

"I think there's a little too much going on at the moment to even think about that," I said.

He frowned, but not because of the situation. He was upset that his baiting hadn't worked. He was an okay looking guy, I supposed, so he was probably used to getting what he wanted. If we'd met under other circumstances, I probably would have even thought he was attractive. But not now. Now I couldn't look at him without my stomach twisting almost as violently as it did when I inhaled the stink of decay from below.

"True." Miller slipped the shirt off, his gaze holding mine as he held it out. "Here you go."

"Thanks," I said, taking it.

"Tell Devon good luck."

I nodded and ground my teeth to stop from telling him what a coward he was.

I turned to head back to our rooms, but Miller's door didn't click, telling me he was still standing there. Watching me walk away. I could actually feel his gaze on my ass, but unlike the night before when Devon was behind me, I didn't slow. Instead I moved faster, practically running.

What a creeper.

In the room, Devon was sitting on the bed, waiting. He stood when I walked in, his gaze moving first over me and then to the uniform shirt in my hand. He visibly started.

"Miller's?" he asked when he was looking at my face again.

"Yeah. I wasn't sure if he'd give it up, but when I suggested he go instead of you, he seemed a little too eager to hand the thing over."

Devon gave a little snort and said, "I'm not crazy about the idea of you asking that guy for favors. He might take it to mean you owe him."

"Like it matters," I said. "We're leaving soon, remember?"

"True," Devon said thoughtfully.

When I held the shirt out, he took it, grimacing as he pulled it on. I didn't have to ask why. Miller was taller than he was, but not as fit, and Devon's muscled arms strained against the material.

"It's a little snug," he said.

"Nothing a big, strong man like you can't put up with," I

replied.

He gave me a half smile that was a little too stiff to be called relaxed, then grabbed me by the belt loop and pulled me toward him. "Come here."

I didn't resist, and when his arms went around me and his mouth covered mine, I leaned into the kiss. It was deep but quick, over before I'd gotten my fill of him. Then he released me, and I was forced to take a step back.

"I just wanted to do that before I left," he said in a husky tone.

"Don't say it like that." I swallowed to try to control my trembling voice. "It sounds like you're telling me goodbye."

"I could be," he reminded me. When I shook my head, he held his hand up. "Listen. I'm going to do my best to get back here, but if I don't make it, if I'm not back within an hour, you get the cars loaded and go. Understand? Don't wait for me."

The idea of him not coming back had my insides in knots, which was so strange. We'd just met, and I'd barely moved on from feeling irritated every time he opened his mouth. The attraction I felt toward him was new and confusing, but even that wasn't what made me ache. Devon had helped get us here. Not alone, because the three of us had worked together, but I wasn't sure if Kiaya and I could have done it without him. Maybe, or maybe not. Just like it was possible Devon wouldn't have made it this far without the two of us. We were a team, and I wasn't ready to lose a member even if we were gaining a few.

"I don't know if we can make it without you," I reminded him. "Kiaya and I don't know anything about survival, and we're useless with a gun. Devon, we need you."

"Lisa and Buck will be with you now. Lisa is a good shot and smart, and she has medical training. Buck's been a hunter his whole life. They can help you if I don't make it back."

He was right, as much as I hated to admit it. "I know."

"Good." Devon let out a deep sigh and ran his hand over his head. "The sooner I do this, the sooner we get out of here."

"I know," I said again.

I couldn't wait until it was over, and I was finally home.

Finally, safe.

Lisa and I stood at the top of the stairs, watching as Devon picked his way down. It wasn't just terrifying watching his progress. It was repulsive as well. He had to climb over the bodies, clinging to the railing as he slipped in black goo and stumbled over limbs. The thud of Mike and Randall banging on the railing at the other end of the catwalk echoed through the day, nearly drowning out the moans of the dead, but thankfully, it was working. Every zombie in the parking lot had headed to the other set of stairs or was currently on the way, leaving a clear path for Devon.

"Where's the kid who got bitten?" Lisa asked, not taking her eyes off Devon's progress.

"In the motel room with Kiaya and Lexi. When we first picked him up, I thought he was tough. He saved us literally at the last possible second." I had to pause and swallow down my terror at the memory. "I'm beginning to wonder, though. He seems to hide every time anything even a little risky happens."

"He's going to have to grow some thicker skin," she said, "and not just for his own benefit. He's going to be a liability out there if he freezes up in the face of danger."

She had a point.

I glanced toward Mike and Randall, momentarily taking my focus off Devon. Buck stood behind them, gun in hand just in case any of the dead happened to make it up. Like before, they were trying, but with as uncoordinated as they were, none of them were making much progress. It made the staircase of bodies a better barricade than the dressers had been, but it couldn't stay this way, and the people here had to know it. How long could they stand to be around rotting bodies? Even if it wasn't unsanitary, which it was, it was just repulsive.

FAR from HOME

Lisa grabbed my arm, drawing my attention back to Devon. He reached the turn in the stairs and disappeared from sight, so together we rushed to a different spot so we could see when he reappeared. A few tense moments of me clinging to Lisa until my knuckles ached passed before he was once again visible. Seconds later, he reached the bottom and scrambled over the dresser blocking the stairs, once again stumbling over the dead we'd taken out the night before. He caught himself, though, and was off in seconds, charging across the parking lot in the opposite direction from where the dead were gathered.

When he was out of sight, I turned to face Lisa and let out a sigh of relief. "Getting down isn't going to be easy even after he draws the dead away, so we're going to have to be ready. We need everything we're going to take with us out here as soon as possible."

"You think Lexi will be able to handle it?" Lisa looked toward the stairs. "I haven't seen Bethie in a while, but she could be there, and Lexi will be looking for her."

"Kiaya will know what to do." She was with the girl now, packing her things and talking her through what we were about to do. Kiaya was a natural with that kid.

"She's a tough one," Lisa said. "Have you two known one another long?"

"I'm not sure we even know each other now," I replied, "but no. We teamed up to get across the country. Before that, we'd never even laid eyes on each other."

"And Devon?" she asked.

"Met him at another motel after his friends all died from the virus."

"So, you've only known him for a couple days," Lisa said thoughtfully. "I never would have guessed based on the way you two look at each other."

I rolled my eyes when heat moved up my cheeks.

Lisa laughed at my reaction. "Let's get our stuff together."

Buck, Randall, and Hank had already headed into the room, and they were almost all packed up by the time Lisa and I joined them. I studied Hank as we finished gathering the few belongings in the room. His wild hair was a mess, covering a lot of his face and casting shadows across it, but even without being able to get a good look at him, I could tell he was terrified. Lisa was right. He needed to snap out of it, or we were going to be in trouble.

I moved across the room so I was kneeling in front of him. "How are you doing?"

"Fine." His trembling voice said otherwise.

"Hank," I began, keeping my voice gentle, "I need to know you're prepared for this. Like you were in Amarillo. You put yourself on the line to save us, but all that bravery seems to have vanished."

"I didn't do it to save you. I did it to save me," he said. "I needed to get out of the city. I thought once I did, things would be okay. But they aren't."

That explained a lot.

"I can't tell you when they're going to be okay again, Hank. I'm sorry. I wish I could. What I can tell you is that we're only going to get through this by working together. We need you, especially when things get rough. If we have to worry about whether you're cowering in the corner when things get bad, it will put us all at risk. Do you understand?"

He swallowed and nodded, but fear still shimmered in his eyes. "I don't know how to be brave."

"You did it in Amarillo," I reminded him. "Even if it was more to save yourself than us, you were still brave to set that alarm off and draw all the zombies away. Remember that."

"Okay," he said.

I gave him what I hoped was an encouraging smile before standing.

When I turned to face the others, I was met with a nod of approval from Lisa. Beside her, Buck had his hand on the gun at his waist, and Mike and Randall stood at his back while Kiaya had Lexi on her lap. Seeing all of us gathered like this, ready to face the dead and make a go of it, brought the foursome from the other motel to mind. Angus James and his band of misfit survivors. Where were they now? He'd said they were going west, but had they made it, or had the zombies taken them by surprise and killed some—or even all—of them? I'd most likely never know one way or the other.

I exhaled. "Are we ready?"

Nods followed the question.

"Okay. Let's grab the bags and head out, then," I said, sweeping the nearest bag up and heading for the door.

Devon's, Hank's, Kiaya's, and my bags were already stacked at the top of the stairs, and I tossed the one I'd taken from the room down next to them. My plan was to throw anything that wouldn't break over the railing so we didn't have to carry them down, which was pretty much all of it. We could grab them once we reached the ground. Now we just had to wait for whatever distraction Devon managed to create.

In the meantime, I studied the stairs, replaying Devon's descent in my mind. Getting down was going to suck, especially with Randall and the kids. Then again, I wasn't sure there was anything that wouldn't suck just a little anymore. We had no electricity and the world was overrun with zombies. The life I'd always known was gone for good. It was a depressing thought, but I wasn't ready to give up. It would take a lot to get me to that point.

Devon hadn't been gone long—less than twenty minutes—when a shrill wail broke through the air. It was the same rhythmic pattern I'd heard dozens of times throughout my life, and in Amarillo when Hank had come to our rescue.

"A car alarm," Lisa said, "he's a genius."

"I think we owe the idea to someone else," I said, smiling at Hank. "You know you gave him the idea, which means you probably just saved us a second time."

For the first time since we got to the motel, Hank squared his shoulders. I could tell he had to work hard to smile, but there was genuine pride in his eyes. Good. Hopefully, the kid would pull through.

The alarm was distant, but still loud enough to grab the attention of every zombie below us. One by one, they turned and began stumbling in the direction of the alarm, finally abandoning their attempts to get up the stairs. The parking lot began to thin out, but we stayed where we were. I wanted to be ready when Devon got back, but I also wanted to make sure the dead were a good distance away before we made our move.

Slowly, they disappeared between nearby houses until not a single zombie was still in sight. By then, I'd begun to search the distance for Devon, knowing he'd be making his way back to the motel. Time ticked by and nothing moved, and with each passing second dread began to build inside me. He hadn't been gone that long, but anything could happen.

"When do you want to make a run for it?" Kiaya asked, making me jump.

"Soon." I swallowed and sucked in a deep breath. Hank wasn't the only one who needed to toughen up. "We can get everything loaded and ready while we wait for Devon. I especially want to get Lexi down before any of the dead decide to come back this way. If she sees her mom again, we could have trouble."

"Yeah," Kiaya looked toward the little girl, who was currently in her uncle's arms.

"You're good with her," I said, nodding to Lexi. "Natural."

"I don't know about natural," she said, her mouth turning down. "If I had been, maybe Zara would still be talking to me."

"Zara?" I asked.

Kiaya's gaze snapped my way. "My sister."

A dozen questions popped into my head, but she wasn't a big sharer, so I didn't voice any of them. I did, however, raise my eyebrows, silently inquiring what she meant.

Kiaya hesitated, and I expected her typical brushoff, but to my surprise, she said, "I was the big sister. I was supposed to look out for her, but I didn't."

It wasn't a lot of information, but it explained a few things. Why Kiaya didn't want to talk about it, as well as why she hadn't tried to call her sister on the road. There was only one problem with her logic though. It was crazy.

"Kiaya, I'm not going to pretend to understand what you and your sister went through, but I do know one thing with complete certainty. There is no way anything that happened was your fault. You were a kid, too. Not just that, but you are one of the most

FAR from HOME

caring and kindest people I've ever met. If you couldn't save your sister from something, it's not because you didn't try. Sometimes, no matter how hard you try, things don't go your way."

She thought it through for a moment, then shook her head and turned away. "Let's get the bags down."

Kiaya was being too hard on herself. She had to be.

She'd already grabbed a bag and tossed it over by the time I joined her, and Lisa and Buck moved to help as well. The thuds of the bags hitting the ground echoed through the day, making me pause to look around each time, but the area was still clear of the dead. The distant alarm had been going for so long now that I'd almost gotten used to the sound, but it couldn't last forever. Those things usually had an automatic shut off to avoid running the battery down. Hopefully, by the time it cut out for good, the dead were long gone.

Once we'd gotten all the bags taken care of, Buck and I headed down while Kiaya and Lisa stayed with Hank, Randall, and the kids. Just like it had looked when Devon did it, getting over the bodies was tricky. I had to hold on to the railing to stop myself from falling every time I put my foot down. There was just nothing solid to step on, and the bodies shifted under my feet, making it feel like I was descending a slippery mountain.

Even worse was the way they squished or cracked. Thick black goo would ooze from cuts or orifices when I stepped on a body, or the snap of a bone would sound, making me cringe and my stomach lurch. It was grotesque, and I had to work hard to keep down my breakfast of prepackaged muffins.

Behind me, Buck swore every few seconds, telling me he wasn't loving it any more than I was.

I made it to the dresser without any real problems though and scrambled over the top with Buck right behind me. The second my feet were on solid ground, I pulled my knife and spun around to check on my surroundings and was grateful to see the parking lot was clear of anything moving.

Buck had his gun up as he, too, glanced around. "Looks clear."

"Devon's plan worked, thankfully," I said.

Buck grunted in agreement as we headed to the bags we'd tossed over.

We grabbed as many as we could before heading for my car. I pressed a button on my key fob, and the trunk popped open.

Buck let out a low whistle when he spotted the M16. "That's an awfully pretty sight."

"It would have been handy yesterday," I said, pulling it out, "but Devon was afraid to take it in."

"Can't say that I blame him. I have a feeling Miller would have tried to confiscate it."

I snorted. "Sounds about right."

We loaded as much into my trunk as we could before heading to the vehicle Lisa had pointed out. Just like she'd said, there was plenty of storage space in the back, and after another trip to grab more bags, Buck and I had everything loaded.

By then Hank, Kiaya, and Lisa were on their way down, Randall and the kids with them. Buck and I headed their way to see if they needed help, but my focus was only half on them. The other half was busy searching the distance. I was looking both for any sign that the dead had decided to come back this way, as well as for Devon. He'd been gone for too long and should have been back by now, and I was starting to worry.

"It's okay," Kiaya was saying to Lexi, holding on to the little girl with one hand and the railing with the other. "Just look at me. Don't look down."

The bodies covering the stairs moved less under the girl's weight than they had when Buck and I climbed down, but more for Randall. He seemed to slip a little more with each step, his eyes widening as the bodies shifted and his grip on the railing tightening. Good thing Hank and Lisa were at his side. Mike, on the other hand, traversed the dead with no problem, his serious expression twisted in concentration as he studied the bodies in front of him before taking another step. He was in front and reached me first. I doubted he needed it, but I held my hand out so I could help him over the dresser anyway.

Once he was on the other side, he turned to face the stairs. "You're almost there, Lexi."

FAR from HOME

His sister looked up, focusing on him instead of Kiaya as she continued down.

Randall slid forward, only staying upright thanks to Lisa, and beads of sweat broke out on his forehead.

Kiaya and Lexi reached the bottom and were over in no time, and less than a minute later, the others had made it as well. Once we were all in the parking lot, all we could do was sit and wait. It was too hot to hang out in the cars with them off—and we couldn't waste gas—so we settled for sitting around them. Randall, Hank, and the kids on the ground, sitting in the shade of the SUV, and Lisa and Kiaya on the hood of my Civic while Buck stood in front of the car, hand on his gun. I sat at first, but it wasn't long before I got up and started pacing. I could actually feel the minutes ticking by, and with each one, Devon's words echoed in my ears.

...if I'm not back within an hour, you get the cars loaded and go...Don't wait for me...

I couldn't drive away from him. I just couldn't.

But how long could we afford to wait?

The car alarm had been silent for close to ten minutes, and there was no reason to think the dead wouldn't eventually find their way back here. We had to get out of here before that happened, but I wasn't ready. Not yet.

I was pacing in front of the car when Kiaya cleared her throat, grabbing my attention. She nodded behind me, back toward the motel, and I turned. Miller was on his way down, picking his way over the bodies. For once, he wasn't dressed in his uniform, which was a strange sight. Even more odd was the bag slung over his shoulder.

"Son of a bitch," Buck muttered.

Lisa was staring at the corporal as well. "What the hell do you think that's all about?"

"One guess," Kiaya said. "Rowan."

My gaze snapped to her. "What?"

"He thinks Devon is out of the picture, and he's going to try and be the hero."

Lisa reached back to twist her long hair around her hands

and let out a snort. "Hero? Miller?"

I said nothing as I watched him reach the bottom of the stairs and climb over the dresser. He jogged our way, an expression of mock sympathy on his face and his eyes focused on me.

"It isn't looking good," he said when he'd stopped in front of us. "I'm sorry."

"We don't know anything yet," I said.

"I know," he replied, the corners of his mouth pulling down.

"What's with the bag?" Kiaya asked, nodding to the red backpack slung over his shoulder.

Was he planning on going with us? He'd made such a big deal about staying here, about how stupid we were to even try, and he hadn't even come out to see if we needed help or to say goodbye, and yet now he was planning on joining us?

He was more of an ass than I'd thought.

"I figured you could use some help, especially if Devon doesn't make it back." Miller grimaced like saying it hurt, but his eyes didn't match the expression. "I've been thinking about it and decided you're right. Sticking around here is a death sentence. I figured my military training might make me useful."

"I thought the people here needed you," I snapped. "That's what you said before."

"I tried to talk some sense into them." He shook his head. "They're all too afraid to leave. They think the motel is their best chance of survival. Those people are hopeless."

I couldn't disagree with him on that point. The people here weren't going to make it long because they weren't willing to change, and to survive this new reality we had to change. It was the only way.

Still, I couldn't stomach the idea of this guy coming with us, especially if Devon didn't make it back. Miller seemed to think his shooting skills and training were a good substitute for Devon, but they couldn't even compare.

I looked to Buck, then to Lisa and Kiaya, but no one said anything. They were just as unsure about what to do as I was. None of us liked him, but I'd long ago accepted that there was safety in numbers. Plus, Miller would be one extra gun, which would be helpful even if Devon did make it back—please, God, let him make it back.

I exhaled, shaking my head before I'd even managed to get the words out. "You can come, but I want to be clear about something. You have to help. No matter what."

"Of course," Miller said, grinning.

It looked totally out of place in this world.

20

We couldn't sit here long, but I wasn't willing to leave. Not yet. I had to give Devon more time to get back to us.

"What are you doing?" Miller said, twisting in the passenger seat to face me. "Go."

I had to tear my gaze from the road in front of us so I could look in the rearview mirror. Behind me in the back seat, Hank's eyes were huge, and next to him, Buck was quiet but just as tense as I was. My focus shifted again, this time to the SUV at our backs. Lisa sat behind the wheel with Kiaya in the passenger seat, and I could tell that, like Miller, they were wondering what was happening. Hell, even I was wondering, because I'd made a promise to Devon. Staying here was stupid. I was putting everyone at risk by waiting for him and making his sacrifice worthless on top of it. I couldn't even imagine how scared Randall and the kids were right now.

But how could I drive off without first taking a look around? What if Devon was trapped somewhere? What if I could save him?

"Rowan," Miller said, his voice tenser than before, "we have to go."

My gaze moved back to the road. Zombies had appeared in front of us, stumbling from between a few buildings. There were only three of them, but there would be more. For all we knew, the entire undead population of this town had been drawn outside by the sound of the car alarm. If they were all together now, moving as a horde and on their way here, we would find ourselves in a situation like what we'd faced in Amarillo. Then we'd be screwed because the odds weren't good that another terrified teenage boy would rally long enough to save our asses.

"I'm going," I said, mostly to myself.

I put the car in drive and pulled onto the road. On instinct, I turned left instead of right, not heading out of town, but in the direction we'd seen the dead stumbling when the alarm started going off. I would have to be careful, have to be ready to turn around and speed out of here at the first sign of trouble, but I had to do it. Had to take a quick look around. Just in case.

"Where are you going?" Hank asked from the back seat, his voice shaky the way it had been in the motel when we had our talk.

"I need to double check before we go." My gaze flicked up to the rearview mirror, but instead of focusing on Hank, I looked at Buck. "He risked his life for us. I can't go without trying to find him."

His gray eyes flashed with understanding, and they only held mine for a few seconds before he nodded. It was all I needed to feel more confident in my decision.

"I'm ready in case," he said, holding up the M16.

"I still can't believe you had that this whole time," Miller said as I pulled onto the road.

"We didn't know who was in the motel, and we didn't want to show our hand in case there was trouble." My hands wrung the steering wheel as I turned onto another street, and I didn't look at him. "Now, shut up and help me by keeping an eye out."

Miller crossed his arms and grumbled, "It's property of the United States Army, you know."

"There's no more United States Army," Buck barked, his

FAR from HOME

Texas twang thicker than usual. "Hell, there's no more United States of America. What we got here is the United States of fuckin' Zombies, and if you don't shut the hell up and help out, you're going to find out firsthand how scary that can be."

I tore my gaze from the street one more time so I could shoot Buck an appreciative look.

Miller only grumbled something under his breath.

We lapsed into silence as I drove up and down the nearby streets, my hands tight on the wheel and my gaze constantly moving. The SUV followed a few car lengths behind, staying close but not crowding me. I scanned the road in front of us, then the houses we passed and beyond them as far as I could see. Here and there a lone zombie would stumble, but for the most part there was no movement. And no sign of anything living.

Where was he?

"We're drawing some attention," Miller said, nodding out his window.

I looked past him and found a group of zombies headed our way. There were a lot of them, too many to count right now, but they were thirty feet away from us and slow. Not a threat, assuming we got out of here soon and didn't get cut off by a big horde. Which meant I had to make a decision.

"Five more minutes," I said, gripping the steering wheel tighter.

Miller's jaw clenched like he was holding back what he wanted to say. Not that I cared. He was tagging along, an afterthought, and not part of our group. He had no say in what I did.

I turned left, heading away from the dead Miller had pointed out. My knuckles ached from my grip on the steering wheel, and I was leaning forward like it would help me find Devon. My legs were trembling, and the tremors only got worse the farther down the street I drove. Five minutes, and I would have to throw in the towel. Five minutes, and I'd be forced to drive away if I wanted to keep all of us safe.

I wasn't sure if I could do it.

The seconds ticked by, slipping away like sand in an hourglass.

I drove, wringing the steering wheel. Miller said nothing, and Hank and Buck didn't talk either, but they were looking. I could hear them shifting around in the back seat, moving from side to side so they could get a look out the window. Nothing was around, though. Nothing but the dead.

"Five minutes," Miller said, and I knew he was telling me it was too late. Telling me to leave. Telling me Devon was gone.

I let out a long breath, trying to blow away the emotion clogging my throat. Tears sprang to my eyes when I turned left again, this time not so I could make another pass, but so I could drive away from Shamrock. Away from Devon.

I blinked the tears back so I could focus, and while they obeyed, my body wouldn't. I was as stiff as a board, as tense as a knot pulled tight. Leaving him felt so very wrong, but it was something I would have to do.

I'd driven another block when a streak of movement to my left caught my eye, making me slam on the brakes. Devon flew from between two houses, charging toward us at full speed, waving his arms like he was trying to get our attention.

Only a few seconds later, a group of the dead staggered into view, hot on his trail.

"Open the door!" I shouted.

Buck slid across the back seat, M16 in hand, and shoved the car door open. To my shock, he stepped out, and the bang of gunfire sounded only a second later. Devon was running across the front yard of the nearest house, panting and sweaty, and behind him the zombies began to go down. One hit in the head, another in the neck then the head, a third had its skull blown off in a burst of black goo and blood. Devon ducked and jerked with each gunshot like he thought he might be the next to get hit, but Buck's aim was good.

When Devon reached us, he dove into the open back door, gasping.

Buck slid in behind him and pulled the door shut. "Go!"

The tires squealed against the pavement when I slammed my foot on the gas. A grunt sounded from the back, but thanks to the pounding in my ears, I couldn't tell if it was Buck or Hank or Devon. I just knew we were on our way and all okay. We'd made it.

I would have shouted for joy if I thought I could get a word out.

As we sped down the street, I glanced in the rearview mirror to make certain the SUV was behind us, and once I was sure, my gaze focused on Devon.

"You're okay?"

He was still trying to catch his breath, so he only nodded in response.

I exhaled, and all the tension melted from me.

No one spoke until we'd made it out of Shamrock and were once again on Route 66. That was when Miller turned in his seat. "Took you long enough to get back."

"Shut up, Miller," Buck and I snapped at the same time.

In the back, Devon was grinding his teeth as he glared at the corporal. "What the hell are you doing here, anyway? I thought you said driving across the country was a suicide mission."

"I had a change of heart," Miller grumbled.

"Right." Devon snorted. "More like you thought I wasn't coming back and saw this as your chance."

"My chance for what, exactly?" Miller said, glaring back at Devon.

"You know exactly what I'm talking about."

Devon wasn't wrong, but I still didn't want to discuss it. Especially when we had another fifteen hours or more in front of us.

"Drop it," I said, glancing back at Devon.

He exhaled slowly, then sucked in a deep breath. He did it again, then two more times, and I was beginning to think he wasn't going to be able to get control of himself when he finally let out one final breath and said, "I want to stop soon. In the middle of nowhere."

"The middle of nowhere?" Miller shook his head. "Why?"

"We need to teach people how to shoot. I should have done it as soon as we found out about the dead, but late is better than never."

"What's the point?" Miller asked. "As long as we stay in the cars, we're okay. A couple zombies are no match for a car."

"We don't know what's going to happen," Devon said. "I want to be prepared for anything."

"I just don't—"

"Shut up, Miller," Buck said for the second time since leaving Shamrock.

"*You* joined *us*," I reminded him, "which means you aren't in charge anymore. We're stopping."

Miller sat back, his arms crossed and a scowl on his face. He reminded me of a pouting toddler. What an ass.

A rustling sound from the back drew my attention, and I glanced over my shoulder just as Devon managed to wiggle his way out of the uniform shirt Miller had loaned him.

"Here's your shirt." He tossed it at the corporal.

Miller grunted when it hit him in the face, then grimaced. "It smells like shit."

"No," Devon said, "just like the dead."

Miller's face scrunched up more, and a second later air whooshed through the car when he rolled down the window. He tossed it out, and I watched in the rearview mirror as it flapped then hit the ground, twisting a few times before being run over by the SUV and finally vanishing from sight.

It looked like Miller was separating from the military for good.

"Here," Devon said only about thirty minutes later. "This looks good."

I slowed the car and pulled to the side of the road, and behind me Lisa did the same. Fields surrounded us pretty much as far as the eye could see, and in front of us the road seemed to stretch on forever. There wasn't a car in sight and no buildings anywhere nearby. It was the perfect place to stop.

Devon had the door open before I'd even turned the car off and was climbing out. I left the keys in the ignition and jumped out as well, and he was already headed to the back of the car when I caught up with him.

"Hey," I said, grabbing his arm.

FAR from HOME

He turned with little prompting, and my throat tightened when our eyes met and I thought about what might have happened. We barely knew one another, and I had no idea what this thing between us was or where it would go, but I liked this guy. He was good and strong and an asset to our group. We needed him.

"I'm glad you're okay," I managed to get out.

"You were supposed to leave me," he replied even as he grabbed me by the belt loop and pulled me closer. "But I'm glad you didn't."

"I had to look for you. I couldn't drive away without knowing for sure."

"I know," he said, his voice low.

He reached up and ran his hand down the side of my face, tucking some hair behind my ear. Neither of us said anything as we stared at each other, but we didn't kiss. Part of me wanted to, but another part couldn't take that step. Kissing in the privacy of the motel room was one thing, but in front of everyone meant taking this to a whole new level, and there was too much going on right now to even think about it. Plus, the idea of a post-apocalyptic romance seemed absurd. Who jumped into something like that when the world was falling down around them?

The doors of the other car were thrown open, and a second later Lexi shouted, "Devon!"

I stepped back as the little girl came running, and something about the way she slammed into him, throwing her arms around his legs, made my heart constrict. Kiaya was only a few steps behind her, not running as fast but not moving slowly either.

She had a huge grin on her face when she hugged him. "I knew you were okay."

"It was a close call," he said as he gave her a one-armed hug. His other hand was resting on Lexi's head.

"Devon!" Randall joined the group by wrapping Lexi, Devon, and Kiaya in a huge hug.

Lisa stood behind him, smiling in relief, and even the normally serious little Mike had a grin on his face. It was good to see. He was so young but had taken on so much. I hoped we could take some of the responsibility from him.

Buck had the M16 slung over his shoulder when he stopped next to me, and on the other side of the car, even Hank had managed to smile. I was grinning as I watched it play out, thinking about how much had changed and how fast, and it suddenly hit me that not all the changes were bad. Like this one. Finding myself surrounded by a misfit group of people who'd been nothing but strangers a few days ago. It was a comfort, and it gave me hope that not all was lost. Even if we had to fight to get there, the future still had potential.

Eventually, Devon extracted himself from the hug. "I'm glad to be here, believe me. But we're not in the clear yet. We still have a long way to go, and we need to be prepared. Which means teaching people to shoot."

His gaze moved over the group, and he frowned like he wasn't sure how to proceed. I got it. Mike was ten, and Randall had the mentality of a child. Should we teach them? Before all this, I would have thought it was ridiculous, but now I wasn't sure. What if something happened to the rest of us, and they were left alone? They needed to know how to defend themselves.

"I think you should teach everyone," I said, looking from Buck to Devon to Lisa for confirmation.

They were the ones who knew about guns, so I would leave it up to them, but to me, it seemed irresponsible to ignore what could happen.

Devon looked at Buck. "What do you think?"

"I think it couldn't hurt to teach the basics." His mouth pressed together as he looked at Mike, then nodded as if agreeing with his own statement. When he focused on Randall, his expression wavered, but not a lot. "It could save us one day."

Miller had been leaning against the car, his arms crossed and a scowl on his face, but he stood up straight when Buck's meaning sank in. "You can't be serious."

"I think he's right," Lisa said. "I'm not saying we arm them—"

"Good," Devon interrupted, "because we don't have enough guns to do that."

Lisa frowned and nodded. "That's something else we need to

address. In the meantime, though, they should at least know how to use a gun if the time comes."

"Her, too?" Miller asked, pointing at Lexi.

"No. She's too young. But there's no reason Mike and Randall can't know the basics." Devon turned his back on the corporal and focused on me. "Pop the trunk for me, will you?"

I did as I was told, then stood back while Devon dug through the supplies.

When he pulled my pink hardcover suitcase from the trunk, he shot me a grin, and acting like he'd never seen it before said, "I'm assuming this is yours?"

"You know it's mine," I said, rolling my eyes.

"Even if I hadn't seen it before, I would have known."

"Because it's pink?"

"Because it's pink." He winked, but then grew serious. "I want to use it, but you should know it might end up with holes in it." His gaze flicked behind me to where the others stood talking. "Scratch that. It will end up with holes in it."

"I don't think there's much in there I'm going to need in the near future," I said.

The thought was depressing, but true. I had flip-flops and tiny tank tops, a couple dresses, even. I couldn't imagine wearing any of that stuff in this world. Talk about making me vulnerable to a zombie bite.

Devon gave me a sympathetic smile, almost like he could read my mind, then grabbed a couple cans and turned to the others. "Who wants a snack?"

At first, I didn't understand why he'd switched gears so fast, but I didn't question him as he began to hand out canned fruit. Lexi beamed when she saw the mandarin oranges, and Randall chatted away, telling Lisa all about how his mom used to give him a bowl of peaches with every meal. I got the fruit cocktail—with extra cherries—and tore it open, thankful that whoever had packed all this stuff we'd scavenged from the motel had bought the cans with pop tops.

"Too bad we don't have spoons," I said as I stared down at the syrup packed fruit.

"Do this." Lisa set her can down so she could bend the lid, then scooped up a peach and popped it into her mouth.

"Nice," I said, smiling.

I mimicked her while Kiaya helped Lexi bend her lid before doing the same with her own, and after that, we were all silent as we shoveled sugary fruit into our mouths. Devon was the first to finish, having simply dumped the contents of his can into his mouth instead of bothering to create a spoon, and I was still trying to dig the last few cherries out of mine when he dragged my suitcase down the street, his now empty can in one hand.

He stopped about twenty feet away and set his can on top, then turned to face us. "I need some more cans whenever you're ready."

Now I got what he was doing.

Buck, who hadn't put the M16 down for a second, headed Devon's way with his own can clutched in his hand.

I was a few steps behind, dumping the rest of the fruit into my mouth as I walked, and stopped beside the two men just as Buck slid the M16 from his shoulder.

"I recommend not letting this out of your sight," he said as he passed it to Devon. "Miller's already made a few comments about who he thinks it rightfully belongs to."

Devon took it, frowning. "Why the hell doesn't he have one? If he was working at one of the checkpoints, there would have been a few lying around after everyone else died."

"That's a good point." Buck's mouth turned down into an exaggerated frown as he looked back to where Miller stood, away from the group. Scowling. "I hadn't thought about it before."

"You think he's lying?" I asked, looking between them.

Devon's eyes clouded over. "I don't know why he would."

"Power," Buck replied, turning back to face him. "People bowed to his every wish the second he showed up simply because he was in uniform."

"Well, that's not happening in this group." Devon threw the M16 over his shoulder before slapping Buck on the back. "Thanks for saving my ass, by the way."

"I think you woulda been all right, regardless, but you're

welcome."

Devon just nodded, but his expression said he wasn't so sure.

Once we had several cans lined up on top of my suitcase, we headed back to the car. I scanned the distance as we walked to be sure nothing was moving. Since we were literally in the middle of nowhere, it was a long shot, but we needed to stay alert and ready. Just in case.

"Okay," Devon said, raising his voice so he could be heard over the quiet chatter. "We want to make this fast so we can get back on the road, but while we're here, I want everyone to learn to shoot." His gaze flicked to the kids. "Except Lexi."

Miller grumbled to himself again.

Devon ignored him and focused on me when he said, "Who's first?"

"I'll go." I raised my hand like I was in school, then felt stupid when his lips twitched.

The amused expression was gone in a second, though, and he was waving me forward, holding the 9mm out to me.

I took it, once again marveling at the weight, and moved forward.

"You know the basics," he said, "but remember the safety. On when you are carrying the gun, off the second you see trouble. Never put your finger near the trigger unless you're ready to shoot, and don't ever point the gun at anything you don't want dead. Got it?"

I nodded.

"Good," he said. "Now, step up and give it a shot. Line the sights up the way I told you to."

I did as he said, holding the gun steady and lining the sights up the way Devon had shown me before. A few seconds later, I pulled the trigger. The clap of the gunshot rang through the air, and the scent of gunpowder filled my nostrils, but I barely registered it. I was too focused on the hole in my suitcase. It was below the can I'd been aiming at and to the right, which totally sucked. If that had been a zombie's head, I would have gotten him in the cheek, maybe. Not the brain. We hadn't had a lot of opportunities to test the zombie killing theory out yet, but at this point, we were all assuming it had to be a headshot. Which meant the thing would still be stumbling toward me.

"Try again," Devon said.

I nodded as I lifted the gun once more, lining up the sights and taking a deep breath. I blew it out, trying to relax, and concentrated. This time when I pulled the trigger, the bullet hit the can. It flew from the top of the suitcase and clanged against the pavement.

I lowered the gun, smiling, and turned to Devon.

"Good," he said, but his own smile was small. "Try again. This time try to get three cans with three shots. One after the other."

I lifted the gun again, taking aim, and fired off a shot. The first bullet missed, so I fired again, and this time the can went flying. I moved to the second and fired, and it joined the other can on the ground. The next shot was wide, but I managed to get the final can with the next bullet.

"Good," Devon said again. "A zombie's head will be a bigger target, but it will also be moving. You're going to have to take your time and be ready to fire off a second shot if you miss. Don't hesitate, and don't let your guard down."

I nodded. "Okay."

Finally, he smiled, his eyes twinkling just a little. "You did a good job. How does it feel?"

"Weird because I never thought I'd fire a gun." I looked down at the weapon in my hand. "But good, too. I don't want to be useless."

When I lifted my gaze to his, he gave me a sympathetic smile. "You're not useless, Rowan. You're unprepared. The only way you'd be useless was if you refused to even try to change."

His gaze moved past me, and I didn't have to turn to know he was looking at Miller.

"I didn't know how to make him stay behind," I said.

"I get it." Devon exhaled. "Hopefully, he proves to be less of a pain in the ass than I think he's going to be, although that's a long shot."

"I know," I said, sighing.

FAR from HOME

Miller looked up and frowned when he saw us staring at him. "You two about done? We need to get on the road."

Devon shook his head and turned away, ignoring him. "Who's next?"

I passed the gun to Kiaya when she came over, and she took my place next to Devon. Like me, she already knew the basics since she'd been carrying a gun for a few days now, and before I'd even made it back to the others, the bang of a gunshot had made me jump.

I let out a little laugh when my gaze met Lisa's. "It shouldn't have surprised me, but it did."

"I think you're wrong," she said. "It should surprise you. Call me crazy, but I hope we never reach a point where the sound of a gunshot becomes a normal part of life."

"Good point." I leaned against the car next to her and scanned the area as I said, "How'd you learn to shoot?"

She didn't answer immediately, and I heard her swallow before saying, "I was sexually assaulted a few years ago."

My gaze snapped to her, but I said nothing. She was scanning the distance like I had been a second ago, but I knew she was only partly keeping a lookout.

"It was a few months after my divorce. I was in a parking garage late at night after a long shift, and this guy came out of nowhere. I never saw him. Never got a single detail about him that would have helped the police find him. After that, being alone scared the shit out of me." She shook her head. "I went to a support group, and someone suggested I get a gun. At first, I thought it sounded nuts, but then I went to a shooting range with her, and it actually made me feel better. More in control. It was an illusion, and I knew it, but I didn't care. I've been going to a shooting range nearly every weekend since then."

"Wow," I said, shaking my head. "And you took your gun with you to California?"

"Actually, no. The one time it would have really come in handy, and I didn't have it." Lisa laughed. "I went to a gun store after I got my papers. Had to pay four times the retail value."

"It's lucky you did that," I said.

She snorted. "No shit."

Kiaya finished and headed our way, and Hank had taken her place with Devon. Behind him, Randall and Mike stood listening to Buck as he explained how to use the gun. I'd agreed with it, but I still cringed inwardly when he passed the gun to Mike. Seeing it in the hands of a ten-year-old felt so wrong, but so did the idea of him not being able to defend himself.

"That retard is going to blow someone's head off," Miller said from behind me.

Lisa and I both spun to face him.

"What's wrong with you, Miller?" she snapped, while I just glared.

He snorted. "What's wrong with me? You guys are arming kids and retards."

My back stiffened as I curled my hand into a fist. I could punch him. I should punch him.

"We're preparing them in case something bad happens, not arming them," I said through clenched teeth.

Miller only rolled his eyes.

He walked off, leaving Lisa and me alone.

"We should have left him at the motel," I said.

"Yeah," Lisa replied, "maybe."

Kiaya stopped next to us. "Everything okay?"

"Miller," I said, knowing I wouldn't have to give any more of an explanation.

Her frown deepened. "Am I the only one who thinks it's strange that it never occurs to him to pull his gun? I mean, back at the motel when the zombies were climbing the stairs, he was the last to start firing."

"No," I said, "you're not alone. Everything about Miller is strange, but that especially."

"You can say that again," Lisa mumbled.

"We should be to Indy by morning," I said, switching gears. "Are you ready for this?"

Kiaya shrugged, her frown growing darker. "I don't know if that's possible. Are you ready to get home?"

"Yes," I said, then shook my head, "and no."

FAR from HOME

I had no idea what to expect when we got there, and since cell service seemed to be down for good—I hadn't had a signal since leaving Vega—it was impossible to guess. Although the state of the other towns we'd gone through was a big clue, as much as I hadn't wanted to admit it.

"No matter what," Lisa said firmly, "I'll be here. For both of you."

She took my hand in her right one and Kiaya's in the left, giving both a squeeze. It was a comfort even if we barely knew one another, because it reminded me that even if my mom was gone, I wasn't alone. I had people to lean on, and people who needed to lean on me.

"Thanks," I said, returning the squeeze even as I focused on Kiaya. She seemed just as comforted by Lisa's words as I was.

21

"You're in the back," Devon said when Miller opened the Civic's front door. "Rowan's up front."

The corporal frowned but didn't argue, although he looked on the verge of exploding when he slid in the back. He was behind me, and Hank was already situated in the middle. On the other side of the car, Devon passed the M16 to Buck, and the look they exchanged said they were both growing more concerned about Miller by the minute. I couldn't blame them.

Before getting into the passenger seat, I looked back at the SUV. Lisa was behind the wheel again and Kiaya was getting Lexi buckled in. She looked my way once she'd shut the back door, giving me a shaky smile. We still had a good thirteen hours or so of driving before we got to Indy, and we'd have to drive through the night, something none of us were looking forward to, but we'd be there in no time, and we both knew it. Soon we'd learn the fates of the people we'd traveled all the way from Phoenix to find. It couldn't come soon enough.

Devon already had the car running when I slid in, and he gave me a tense smile when I pulled the door shut. A second later, we were driving, and I watched in the side mirror as the SUV pulled onto the road behind us.

"Tell me if you need me to take a turn driving," I said, turning to Devon.

"I will." He smiled. "Although I doubt I'd be able to rest even if I wasn't behind the wheel."

"You're not the only one," I replied.

Buck made a sound that said he agreed, and I looked back to see both him and Hank nodding. Miller, however, didn't respond. He was pressed as close to the door as possible, staring out the window. The more time I spent around him, the more he seemed like a spoiled child, and I couldn't get Devon's observation about the M16 out of my head. It just didn't make any sense.

"Tell us about yourself, Miller," I said.

He jerked like I'd startled him and tore his gaze from the window, focusing on me. "What do you want to know?"

"Anything. I mean, I just realized we don't even know your name. It seems strange to keep calling you Miller."

He pressed his lips together, looking at me for a moment before glancing toward Hank and Buck. They were both watching him as well. The expression on the teen's face was simply curious, but Buck looked downright suspicious.

"Marcus," Miller finally said. "Marc."

"Nice to meet you, Marc," I lied, forcing out a smile. "So, where were you stationed before all this?"

He ground his teeth before saying, "A base in Texas."

"Aren't Army forts called posts?" Devon asked, glancing back.

"Yeah," Miller said a little too quickly. "But most civilians don't know that. It's easier to say base."

"Makes sense." I plastered the smile on my face. "Where are you from originally?"

"Delaware," he said, and something about his tone made it seem like it was the first true thing he'd said this entire time. "But it's been a long time since I was home. I joined the Army right out of high school and never looked back. I don't like to talk about it, but let's just say I didn't have the best childhood."

I lifted a hand as if stopping him. "Say no more. I get it."

FAR from HOME

He nodded, but it was tense, and his gaze darted around like he was trying to figure out how to escape a dangerous situation. "What about the rest of you? I know nothing about what you did before this or where you're from."

"Well, you kind of know about me since we're headed to my house in Ohio, but Kiaya and I were at the University of Phoenix. We met Devon on the road." I nodded to Hank. "We picked Hank up in Amarillo."

"And you can probably guess that I was a high school student." The teen shrugged like he wished he had something more interesting to add.

"You?" Miller asked, focusing on Buck.

"Lived in Shamrock my whole life," he said, "worked as a mechanic 'til three years ago when I retired."

We lapsed into silence, all of us focused on Miller except Devon—although he did glance back at the guy—but the corporal had his mouth clamped shut, telling me he wouldn't be saying anything else.

I sighed. "Well, it's nice to have everyone with us."

Buck gave me a strained smile before I turned back around.

It was midday and the sun was high, shining down on the landscape as it flew by. Here and there I spotted a figure, usually pretty far off, but for the most part, the world felt deserted. We never saw another car or living person, or even any signs that anyone had been by any time recently.

The small towns, diners, gas stations, and truck stops we passed were another story. They had an abandoned feel to them, but more often than not, they weren't totally deserted. Zombies could be seen moving through the parking lot or even trapped inside cars the way they had been at the motel in Vega, and those that were outside would turn and stumble toward us when they heard the car. There weren't enough to really put us in danger, though, and before they'd even reached the road, they had disappeared from sight. Still, seeing them had my insides tightening into an intricate web of knots. This was what the future held for us. I'd known it even before we left Vega, but seeing it mile after mile made it all too real.

We passed abandoned cars on the side of the road, some with doors or trunks open like they'd been searched, and empty checkpoints. Devon didn't even bother slowing at those, and by the time the sun had begun to set, I had stopped trying to search for a sign of life when they came into view.

In the back, Miller snored. His head was leaning against the window, while next to him Hank's was resting on Buck. The older man was awake but didn't seem to mind, and he acted like sleep was the farthest thing from his mind.

When I spotted St. Louis in the distance, the arch illuminated by the moonlight but the city as black as a cave, I couldn't help thinking about Kyle. Were his parents alive? His brothers and sisters? Kiaya had taken his phone, but as far as I knew, no one had ever returned her call. I wasn't sure if that was a comfort or not. At least if they were dead, they weren't wondering what had happened to him, but I hated thinking his whole family was gone even though I'd never met them.

It was nearing dawn by the time we passed the Welcome to Indiana sign. We still had nearly two hours of driving before we reached Indy, but my heart still leapt. Soon, we'd be there, and then we could be on our way to Troy. It wouldn't be long now.

Then, in what seemed like the blink of an eye, the city was looming in front of us. The sun was coming up by then, painting the horizon in bright colors that made the day in front of us seem promising and less scary.

We'd been driving in utter silence for so long that I jumped when Devon said, "I'm going to have Lisa lead."

He slowed to a stop as I rolled my window down, waving for Lisa to pull up beside us. Her window was already down when she did, and Kiaya was leaning over her so she could see out the driver's side window.

"Lead the way," I called to them. "We'll stay close."

Kiaya nodded in response, and the way her jaw was clenched made it look like she was too tense to talk.

The city was to the right, and the closer we got, the more ominous it looked, contrasting with the bright horizon. The utter stillness surrounding it raised the hair on the back of my neck.

FAR from HOME

It was so dark, so empty looking. No lights in the buildings or on the streets, and no headlights from cars, even. It was like the entire population of the world had disappeared. Of course, that would have been awful, but probably a lot less scary than what had actually happened. The people were gone, but in their place were monsters intent on killing anything still living. It was worse than a horror movie.

There were signs of the living as we drove, little things that told me we weren't the only ones alive, but we didn't see any people. Even the dead were a rare sight. It was odd, considering how close we were to the city and how many homes we drove past, but I was grateful for it just the same. The fewer zombies we saw, the better.

"How far to Troy from here?" Devon asked as he followed the SUV through the suburban neighborhood.

"About two hours," I said. "We'll grab Interstate 75 when we reach it and head north. It's a straight shot."

He nodded, his head barely moving, but said nothing.

Less than ten minutes later, Lisa pulled to a stop outside a house. It was two stories and white, with an overgrown front yard that had probably been well-maintained until recently. I leaned closer to my window, peering up at the house as I searched for any sign that someone inside might still be alive. We all knew it was a long shot. Even if Kiaya's sister had survived the virus, she might not have survived the aftermath. The dead coming back would take anyone by surprise, and I was sure a lot of people had been too unprepared to even have time to fight back.

The thought of Kiaya having to see that made me almost physically sick.

"You're going in?" Miller asked when I reached for the doorknob.

I shoved the door open without looking back at him. "I'm not making Kiaya face this alone."

Devon and Buck followed, and even Hank climbed out. Kiaya and Lisa had already exited the other car and stood waiting for us at the walkway leading to the front porch, and I was glad to see Randall and the kids had remained inside. Kiaya looked like she might be sick, and Lisa's expression was twisted with concern as she watched us approach.

A door slammed behind us, and I looked back to find Miller standing beside the car, his arms crossed and a frown on his face.

He was seriously getting on my nerves.

"I think we should go in first," Lisa said, focusing on Devon and Buck. "We don't know what we're going to find."

She'd read my mind.

"Yeah." Devon exhaled as he looked toward the house. "Good idea."

"I have to see her," Kiaya said.

"What if she isn't her?" Lisa asked. "Or worse, she's been ripped apart? Can you handle that?"

Kiaya looked suddenly ill. "I don't know."

"That's why I think we should go in first," Lisa said gently.

After a second, Kiaya nodded.

I moved to her side. "I'll stay with you."

"Okay," she said, her voice low and tremulous.

We walked with Devon, Buck, and Lisa to the front porch, and Hank followed but hung back when they moved to the door. Devon and Buck had their guns up and ready while Lisa tried the knob. I flinched when it turned and the door clicked open. I couldn't imagine it being unlocked if someone inside was still alive. It was simply too risky.

"Here goes," Lisa said before pushing on the door.

She pulled her gun as it swung open, then she, Buck, and Devon stepped in. I leaned forward, trying to get a look, but the interior was dark. It was silent, too. From out here, I couldn't smell anything that indicated whether there were bodies inside, but that didn't mean much. If they'd died upstairs, we might not be able to smell it all the way out here.

Devon, Buck, and Lisa disappeared, and at my side Kiaya shifted. I had my knife out, but she'd pulled her gun. Just in case. She was trembling, and the little light that had broken over the horizon shone off the blade of my knife as it shook, emphasizing that I wasn't doing much better. We were both so jumpy I doubted we'd be much use if a zombie did come charging, so I looked back to make sure Hank—and maybe even Miller—were ready to jump in if there was trouble. The teen had a knife out, fortunately, but the corporal was unarmed.

Why the hell didn't he pull a weapon?

No noise reached us from inside, but I wasn't sure what that meant. If the others were still quietly searching or if they'd finished and were now trying to decide what to do. Minutes passed, and Kiaya got more and more restless. I could tell she was running out of patience, and while I couldn't blame her, rushing in right now was a bad idea.

"They'll be back in a minute," I said, hoping to calm her.

She didn't respond, but it turned out it didn't matter because only a few seconds later footsteps became audible. They were headed our way, and even though they sounded even and not at all labored, I tensed and prepared for a fight. Just in case.

Devon stepped into view, followed by Lisa and Buck, but the shadows made it impossible to read their expressions. Then it didn't matter, because they were moving aside, and I caught sight of someone else behind them. Not just anyone else, either. A teenage girl who resembled Kiaya so much it was like she'd been cloned.

"Zara!" Kiaya dropped her gun, and it clanged against the cement, then she rushed forward, throwing her arms around her sister.

The younger girl hugged her back, sobbing. "I was so scared."

"I emailed you. I told you I'd get here," Kiaya said.

"But it took so long, and there were zombies." Zara let out a hiccupped sob. "Zombies, Kiaya."

"I know," her sister said soothingly. "It's okay. We're going to be okay."

Zara pulled back so she could focus her tear-filled eyes on Kiaya. "How?"

Kiaya looked back to where the rest of us stood. "I don't know, but we're going to figure it out."

"I DRAGGED MY FOSTER PARENTS OUT OF THE HOUSE AFTER THEY DIED," Zara was telling her sister.

The two of them were sitting on the couch in the living room holding hands, and I couldn't stop staring at them. They looked so similar, more like twins even though Kiaya had to be at least three years older.

"I felt bad. They were nice people, but I didn't know what else to do. The phones weren't working and there was no electricity, and I couldn't just leave them in the house to rot." She swallowed, and genuine terror shimmered in her brown eyes, which were a carbon copy of Kiaya's. "What if I had?"

Her sister gave her hand a squeeze. "Don't think about it. You're okay, and that's the important part."

"How did you find out about the zombies?" Lisa asked, drawing the younger girl's gaze to her.

"I saw some people walking down the street. I almost went out, but there was something so strange about them." Zara paused once again to swallow. It seemed to be the only thing that was holding back the tears shimmering in her eyes. "Someone else did go out, though. One of the neighbors, an elderly woman. The people on the street attacked her. They tore her up, and I could hear her screaming for help. I didn't know what to do or what was going on. I didn't—"

A hiccupped sob shook her body, and she covered her mouth as her tears finally broke free. Kiaya wrapped her arms around her sister, whispering soothing words, while the rest of us stood or sat in silence.

We'd come inside for multiple reasons, only two of which were to allow Zara the chance to pack some things and to see if there was anything useful in the house. So far, though, all we'd done was listen to Kiaya's sister tell her story. I was trying not

FAR from HOME

to be impatient, but it wasn't easy. I was ready to be on the road.

I wasn't the only one, either. While Lexi, Randall, Hank, and Mike sat in the kitchen eating chocolate pudding, Devon stood with his arms crossed, frowning. Like me, he was trying to hide it, but he was more than ready to address the next and most pressing issue, which was our need for another car and more gas. We'd made it this far thanks to what we'd siphoned along the way, but we had to be getting low now.

Lisa was more laidback, although that wasn't a surprise, as was Buck. Miller, however, looked ready to jump out of his skin as he paced the room, occasionally stopping to glare at the sisters. It was his irritating marching that helped keep me in check. It was obnoxious, and I had no desire to come across the same way.

Zara was still crying, and Kiaya still had her arms around her when she looked up, meeting my gaze. I could tell she knew we both needed to get on the road and that I was dying to move on, but there was a helplessness in her expression that also said she had no idea what to do. It seemed at odds with the Kiaya I'd gotten to know. The one who had answers for the most random things—like how to siphon gas out of a car—and had done such a good job with Lexi. Zara was family, though, and if there was one thing I'd learned about Kiaya, it was that her family and her past were her weakness.

Hoping to help, I cleared my throat.

Zara, still sniffling, lifted her head, and I gave her a sympathetic smile.

"I'm so sorry you went through that. I can't imagine being alone through all this."

She sniffed and nodded but said nothing.

"I don't want to rush you, but we're on our way to Ohio. To my house." I stopped short of telling her we were going to see my mom because the truth was, I had no idea what we were going to find. "We need another car, though."

"There are two cars in the garage," Zara managed to get out, her voice still shaky and her eyes wide. "But that's where *they* are."

"They?" Devon asked, dropping his arms to his sides.

"My foster parents," Zara whispered. "I've heard them banging around in there. They're zombies."

The last word hissed from her mouth, and Devon and I exchanged a look. Zara had dragged them to the garage, and they'd turned, and she'd probably thought she was safe since they were no longer living, but she'd been wrong. They could open doors; only she didn't know that. She was damn lucky they hadn't managed to get inside already.

Devon pulled his gun, and I turned to Kiaya, holding my hand out. "Give me your gun."

Kiaya finally released her sister, and Zara's eyes got huge when she saw her sister pull the weapon out from behind her back. She handed it to me, and I nodded to Devon. Buck and Lisa had their weapons out, too, but as usual, Miller was unprepared. He had stopped pacing, though.

"It's going to be dark in there," Devon said, looking us over, his gaze landing on me. "I want you and Lisa to stay at the door with flashlights. Buck and I will do the shooting since we have more experience."

I nodded, as did Lisa.

Zara already had several flashlights out, thankfully, so all Lisa had to do was swipe them up off the kitchen counter and hand me one.

Meanwhile, Devon had turned his attention on to Kiaya's sister. "Which door leads to the garage?"

Zara pointed a shaky finger toward the kitchen, and I turned. There was a door right next to the table where Randall, Hank, and the kids sat.

"Out here," Lisa called, waving for them to hurry. "Come on."

Mike was the first one up, and he grabbed Lexi and hauled her from her seat before taking off. Randall and Hank were right behind them, and the four of them rushed into the living room. When Lexi pulled from Mike's grasp and threw herself at Kiaya, Zara's eyes got huge.

I was already turning my focus to the kitchen.

Devon and Buck moved to the door, their guns up, and Lisa

and I followed. I tried to mimic what I'd seen other people do in movies, holding the flashlight in one hand and the gun in the other so they were both up and aimed forward. It wasn't as easy as it looked, and I doubted my aim would be any good, but it made me feel better anyway.

Devon paused at the door and looked back. "Everyone ready?"

Tense nods followed the question.

Once again focusing on the door, he sucked in a deep breath before turning the knob and ripping it open. Lisa and I lifted our flashlights, trying to aim into the dark garage, but the beams were cut off when Devon and Buck rushed in. It was only momentary, though, and then the room was lit up. Two cars sat in the garage, parked side by side, as well as other random items. A few bikes, a lawnmower, boxes stacked on top of one another. I barely had time to focus on them, because something to the left moved, grabbing my attention.

I shifted the flashlight, and the zombie came into view. It was Zara's foster mom, or had been, at least. Now she was dead and rotting, her gray skin looking doubly sickly in the dim light as she rushed forward. Her hands were up, her mouth open, and her milky eyes somehow focused on Devon. A moan ripped out of her, but it was cut off by the crack of a gunshot. The sound bounced off the walls and came back to slam into me before fading away, and her head jerked back. Behind me, Zara screamed as the zombie dropped to the ground.

A growl came from the other side of the garage only moments later, and I joined Lisa in panning my flashlight around, our two beams bouncing through the darkness as we searched for the other zombie. Something moved, scratching against the floor, but the thing didn't appear.

Devon and Buck stood at the ready, guns up, but still nothing happened. Other sounds, shuffling and moaning, echoed through the room, but that was it.

"Where is he?" Devon muttered.

We waited in silence for a few more minutes before Buck let out a sigh. "We're gonna to have to go in."

Devon nodded, his body so tense it seemed like his head barely bobbed. He took a step forward, and Buck followed. Lisa and I moved as well, holding the flashlights up as we went. I had to stay to the side so Devon didn't block the beam, but once we reached the car, I realized how impossible it would be. There was less than a foot of space between the garage door and the back of the car. The men would have to go first since they had guns, but they'd be going in blind. It was bad, too risky.

I looked around, trying to decide what to do, and my gaze landed on the car. It was the best chance we had.

"Wait," I hissed, and everyone froze. "Just hold on."

I headed back to the front of the car, but before I could do anything else, I had to put my gun away. I stuck it in the waistband of my pants, wincing when it brushed the still healing cut, then climbed up on the hood. The car groaned beneath me, and I slipped as I scrambled forward, but managed to make it on top in no time. Once there, I turned the flashlight to the other side of the garage.

"Okay!" I hissed.

A moan followed.

I could hear the others moving, but I didn't look their way. I was too busy searching the darkness for the zombie. The garage wasn't big, but it still took a moment to locate him. Only the top of his head was visible because he seemed to be on the ground on the other side of the car, close to the front bumper. I couldn't see what he was doing from here, but whatever it was, he seemed to be stuck.

"There," I said, pointing.

Devon had just rounded the back of the car, and he nodded as he headed that way, Buck right behind him and both their guns up. Lisa rushed to their side so she could give extra light, and more of the zombie came into view. Still, I couldn't figure out why he wasn't moving, because he was clearly trying to.

The men got closer, and I tensed. Part of me expected the thing to jump up once they were in front of him, like maybe he'd been playing a trick, but that didn't happen. He thrashed and clawed and tried to stand, but he couldn't.

FAR from HOME

When Devon reached the front of the car he paused. "Looks like his legs are tangled in something. Rope, maybe?"

"Seems to be," Buck said.

Devon snorted out a little laugh then lifted his gun, taking aim. The gunshot followed only a second later, echoing through the small room, and the zombie went still.

Devon turned back to face me, having to shield his eyes when the flashlight nearly blinded him.

"Sorry," I said, lowering it.

He dropped his hand, smiling up at me. "That was a good plan."

"I guess I'm good for something," I said.

His smile stretched wider. "I never said you weren't. Remember?"

22

We got lucky and discovered that both cars were almost full, meaning we'd have plenty of gas to go around once we drained one of the vehicles. Armed with the gas cans we'd gotten in Vega, Kiaya got to work while Devon and Buck began loading the supplies we'd found. There wasn't a lot, and unfortunately these had not been gun people, but the little bit of nonperishable food we found and the extra flashlights would help.

Zara watched her sister siphon gas from the car we weren't taking with a look of awe on her face. "How do you know how to do that?"

"Physics," Kiaya said, using the same nonchalant tone she had with me a few days ago when she'd tried to explain it.

Zara glanced my way, and I shrugged. "Don't ask, because it still won't make sense."

Once she'd gotten everything she could out of the car, Devon dragged the gas cans outside so he could distribute the fuel between the two other cars. We'd be on our way soon, and I couldn't wait.

"Stick close to us," I told Kiaya.

Zara had already climbed into the passenger seat, and Hank was in back. I kind of wished Miller had decided to go with them as well, but he'd stubbornly insisted on sticking with us. Of course.

"I will," Kiaya assured me.

We stared at each other, not talking, then without warning, she put her arms around me. For a moment, I couldn't respond to the sudden and unexpected hug, but then I returned it, squeezing her harder than necessary. It wasn't a goodbye hug. I knew that even before she spoke. It was a thank you hug and a peace offering, a sign that things had shifted between us once again.

"Zara and I are only three years apart," she said, speaking quietly so no one else could hear, her breath brushing my ear. "I was the oldest, and I was supposed to look out for her. I knew that. I always did. Mom started doing drugs when we were young, and it was all we ever knew. Most nights, she didn't even come home.

"I was ten when I finally told someone at school about it. I didn't want to because I was afraid of what would happen, but Zara and I had gone the entire weekend without seeing our mom or eating, and I was watching her waste away right in front of my eyes. I had to do it.

"They came to the house and took us, and she was so scared. So little. I begged for them to keep us together, and I think they tried, but they couldn't find a home for both of us."

Her arms tightened around me, and I got the sense she was having trouble going on.

"So, you were ripped apart and Zara blamed you."

Kiaya nodded.

I squeezed her harder. "It's not your fault. I've seen who you are, Kiaya. You are a good person. You did what you had to, and if Zara doesn't realize that yet, she will soon. I promise."

She swallowed. "Thank you for believing in me, Rowan."

"Thank you for trusting me."

Footsteps scraped against the ground, and we pulled apart. Devon stood in the doorway, watching us curiously, but he didn't ask.

"Ready?" he said as he moved toward us.

FAR from HOME

"Ready," we said at the same time.

I gave Kiaya's hand one last squeeze before she headed off, and once she was behind the wheel, Devon and I moved to the garage door.

"What was that about?" he asked.

I shrugged. "Nothing."

He only lifted his eyebrows, letting me know he didn't believe me, before bending down and grabbing the bottom of the garage door. Since he'd already pulled the cord to detach it from the motor, all he had to do was lift the thing. It rolled up, and light flooded into the dark garage, reminding me of sunshine after the storm.

I WAS LITERALLY ON THE EDGE OF MY SEAT WHEN DEVON PULLED into my neighborhood. Like everything else we'd passed since arriving in Troy, it was so familiar and yet so different at the same time. There were no children playing in yards the way they usually would have been on a day like this, no people vacuuming out cars or mowing lawns, and no one walking dogs. The usual bustle had disappeared with the rest of society, and all that was left was a sad remnant of the neighborhood I'd grown up in.

"Turn left at the stop sign," I said, telling him where to go without even having to think about it.

We were two streets in when I saw the first zombie. There were dozens of houses and hundreds of people, so the odds that it was someone I had once known were small, and yet it seemed it didn't matter.

I covered my mouth, trying to hold in my sob, but it broke out of me anyway.

Devon glanced toward me. "You know her."

It wasn't a question, but I nodded anyway. I had to swallow before I could say, "Mrs. Carver."

It was all I could say, but I couldn't stop staring at her as she lumbered down the street—right in the middle of the road—and a whirlwind of memories came rushing back.

Mrs. Carver had lived at the end of my street for as long as I could remember. I'd sold her Girl Scout cookies when I was younger, had been one of the kids who'd taken turns shoveling her driveway during the winter after her husband died ten years ago, and she'd even come to my high school graduation party. I still remembered the little note she'd written on the twenty-five dollar check she'd given me.

You will do big things!!!

The three exclamation points had made me laugh, but the gift had touched me because she was on a fixed income.

"She was such a sweet lady," I whispered, blinking back my tears.

Devon put his hand on my knee, and the warmth sank into me, giving me strength I'd need. I wasn't sure if it would be enough, but at least I knew I wasn't alone.

He kept it there as I gave him directions, telling him when to turn and doing my best to avoid looking directly at any of the other zombies we passed. I wasn't always successful, though. Sometimes, movement would catch my eye, and I'd turn my head before I could talk myself out of it, but thankfully, none of the others looked familiar. I was sure I'd eventually see other people I knew, but at the moment I was grateful they were all strangers because I couldn't stomach it right now. Not when I needed all my strength for what I was about to face.

We turned onto my road, and my house came into view. It sat at the end of the street in the cul-de-sac, directly ahead of us. I pointed a shaky finger at it, and Devon gave my knee a squeeze to let me know he understood. He slowed but didn't pull into the driveway, instead parking the car on the street in front of the house. I knew why. It would be an easier and faster getaway than if we had to back out. I just prayed it wouldn't be necessary.

He shut the car off but didn't move right away. "What do you want to do?"

"You mean do I want to go inside?"

He frowned. "Yeah."

"I think," I said, having to force the words out, "we should do the same thing we did with Kiaya."

"Me too," he said, his gaze moving to the house.

The day was cooler than it had appeared when we climbed out, or maybe I had just gotten used to the heat of Texas. Whatever the reason, I shivered and hugged myself when a cool breeze blew. The others had climbed out of their cars as well and were waiting. Their expressions were somber, and I understood. The world was too silent to miss the roar of a car engine, but no one had come to the door. I wasn't stupid, and I knew what that most likely meant, but I couldn't let go of my hope just yet. Zara hadn't come to the door either, yet she was okay. Mom could still be alive.

"Buck," Devon said when we reached the rest of our group, "why don't you come in with me? Everyone else can stay here and keep an eye out." His gaze darted around. "We've seen a lot of zombies walking around, and chances are good that they're going to follow the sound of our cars. Stay alert."

"Will do," Lisa said, answering for the rest of us.

Devon nodded once, his focus on me. "We'll check it out and let you know what we find."

"Okay," I mumbled.

"No matter what," he said, "you're going to be okay."

I exhaled. "I know."

There was no confidence in the words.

Devon and Buck headed for the house, and I followed but stopped before stepping onto the front porch. Now that I was closer, I noticed something I hadn't before, and it made everything in me clench. The door was open. Not a lot, only a crack, but enough to tell me no one was inside. It told me something else, too, but it was something I didn't want to acknowledge just yet, so I pushed the thought down.

Devon looked back at me, frowning, before pushing the door open the rest of the way. It swung in, and I caught a glimpse of the all too familiar entryway. It was as dark and empty as the rest of the world. Not that I'd expected anything different.

Buck led the way, with Devon only a step behind him, and in seconds they'd disappeared from sight.

Kiaya stopped next to me. "You okay?"

I turned to look at her, and in her eyes I could see the same truth I was trying to deny.

"I don't know," I said honestly.

"Devon was right," she replied. "It will be okay even if it hurts."

I could only nod.

We stood side by side in silence, waiting for them to return. A dog barked somewhere in the distance and the wind blew, rustling tree branches and making the neighbor's flag flap, but otherwise the world was silent. So quiet that when the scraping of feet against the pavement broke through, it seemed loud even though it wasn't.

I turned, knowing what I'd see but still totally unprepared for the sight.

I'd pictured her in her bathrobe, it flapping behind her like a cape as she stumbled toward me, but that wasn't what I found. She was dressed in jeans and wearing Dad's Harvard Medical School sweatshirt. It was huge on her, even bigger than it used to be because she was wasting away. Still, I knew it was her the second I laid eyes on her. It didn't matter that all the life and color had drained from her face or that her hair was a knotted mess, or even that her blue irises weren't visible through the milky haze covering her eyes. I would have recognized my mother anywhere.

"No!" I wailed, my cry echoing through the air and bouncing off the walls. "No!"

I took one step before collapsing, dropping to my knees on the sidewalk, my body shaking as misery ripped its way out of me. It felt like someone had reached into my chest and grabbed my heart. They had it in a punishing grip, making it difficult for me to catch my breath. I gasped and shook, I clawed at the ground as panic and pain settled over me, weighing my body down.

Around me, people were talking, but I couldn't hear their words. Kiaya was at my side, that much I knew, and she was tugging on my arm, trying to get me to stand. I couldn't make myself, and not just because my legs were too wobbly. It felt like a bomb had dropped on me, and moving was now impossible. My mom was still a good distance away, but she wasn't alone. Devon had been right. The dead must have followed the sound of our cars, because there were dozens of them now, with more coming from between houses. They were all heading our way, and my brain told me to move, to listen to Kiaya and get to my feet, but I couldn't. Even if I did, I wasn't sure it mattered. I felt broken and half-dead.

Devon and Kiaya had been wrong. It wouldn't be okay after all.

"Inside!" I heard someone—Buck, I thought—yell.

A rumble I didn't recognize cut through the moans that had filled the silence, and I registered that the garage door was now open. Kiaya and Lisa were still with me, trying to get me to stand, but Devon was behind the wheel of my car, pulling into the garage. The SUV followed, parking beside him, and I registered Miller behind the wheel when he passed. A second later, a door slammed, and Devon was rushing toward me, alarm etched in every line of his face.

"Go," he said when he reached us, talking to Kiaya and Lisa. "Get the doors barricaded."

They were gone in an instant, and then it was just Devon and me. He scooped me into his arms, lifting me like I was a small child, and I clung to him as he ran toward the house. The garage door was still open, but Miller and Buck were waiting. Devon rushed inside, and the same rumble I'd heard before followed as the two men worked together to get the heavy door shut. It went down easier than it had gone up, slamming into the ground with a thud that seemed to vibrate through the garage.

Devon was still moving, and the next thing I knew, we were in my living room. He set me on the couch, his expression twisted in concern, but he didn't stay at my side. A whirlwind of activity surrounded me, but I was too shell-shocked to really focus on it. Numbly, I registered the presence of Lexi and Mike on the loveseat, and Randall standing not too far away, wringing his hands as the others rushed through the house. Everyone else was running around, and the house was filled with noises I couldn't place. Scraping sounds, things crashing down, even the shattering of glass. It seemed to take forever to settle, and even once it had, I felt like I couldn't focus. Voices surrounded me as I curled up on the couch, closing my eyes. I wanted to wipe the image of my zombified mother from my brain, but it was impossible. Her face danced across my vision even with my eyes shut, taunting me.

Mom was gone. Dad was gone. I was an orphan.

Maybe life wasn't worth fighting for after all.

SLOWLY, I EMERGED FROM A RESTLESS SLEEP, OPENING MY EYES TO darkness. There was something familiar and even slightly comforting about my surroundings, but it took a moment to register what it was. I inhaled, and the familiar scent of home filled my nostrils. My room. That was where I was. I was in my bed, in my room, back home in Troy, Ohio.

No comfort accompanied the realization because everything that had happened came rushing back. Immediately, I wished I could return to the comfort of unconsciousness. This world, this new reality, was just too painful.

Something shifted in the darkness, and I tensed but relaxed a second later when a dim light flicked on and Devon came into view.

"You're awake," he said.

I nodded, shifting so I could sit up, and he moved to the side of the bed. He lowered himself beside me, setting a small flashlight on my nightstand before taking my hand. For a moment, he said nothing. He just sat there holding my hand and staring at me.

"It will be okay," he finally said.

"Will it?" I managed to get out.

"It will. I know it doesn't feel that way right now, trust me, but I've been there, and I promise it will. I'm not the only one either. Keep that in mind. Lexi and Mike have lost their mom, and they're just kids. Hank, too. They need you to be strong, Rowan. We all do."

I thought about the things he'd told me, about losing his parents at such a young age and then his grandma right after high school. Then I thought about the kids and Randall and how alone they must feel, and Kiaya and Zara. They'd never even had parents, not really. At least I had twenty happy years to cling to.

"It just hurts so bad," I said

"That's normal, and it's okay. You're going to hurt, but it isn't something you can't get through. You're strong, and you can do this."

"How are you so sure? I'm not."

"Because I've seen you rush down the stairs to save a little kid you don't even know. Because I've seen you fight off zombies even though you have no training. Because I've sat next to you this entire trip and seen how resilient you've proven yourself to be at every turn. You can do this, Rowan."

I sucked in a deep breath, wincing at the pain in my chest, then blew it out.

I can do this.

Three times I repeated it, and with each exhale, I felt myself get a little stronger. Devon was right. This was horrible, painful and gutting, but I was stronger than this. I wouldn't let it get the better of me.

After a few minutes, I let out one final breath and said, "What now?"

"We figure out a way to survive in this world," Devon said. "It's all we can do."

I nodded, trying to embrace his words and the strength he'd brought out in me over the last few days. I was home, and I was glad, but we were far from safe, and Devon was right. We needed to find a way to survive. And we would. Together.

**To be continued in
FAR FROM SAFE**

ACKNOWLEDGEMENTS

January 3, 2020
Forty books. Wow.

There are a lot of people to thank for getting me to this point, but first and foremost, I need to thank YOU. The reader. I wrote *Broken World* in 2012, and it went against every recommendation I'd seen from editors and agents. There was no market for zombie books, or at least that was what every online post about getting published claimed. The story was in my head, though, so I wrote it. Then I wrote the second book in early 2013, and the third that summer. At the time, I didn't expect much from the series, and I had no clue how many more books I'd write even though I knew *Mad World* wasn't the end of the journey for Vivian, Axl, Angus, and friends. When I released *Broken World* in July of 2014, my only hope was that one or two people other than family and friends would read it. By the end of the month, I'd had over 700 ebooks sold or borrowed through Kindle Unlimited. Over 1200 the following month. Now, more than six years later, well over 10,000 ebooks of *Broken World* have been sold or downloaded, and millions of pages have been read through Kindle Unlimited. People are still asking for more—especially more of Angus James.

So, back to my thank yous. A huge thank you goes out to every person who has ever taken a chance on me. To everyone who saw a new author and thought *I'll give it a shot*, to every person who decided to try out a zombie book even though it wasn't normally their thing, to every reader who loved it and told a friend, and to every person who took the time to leave a review or send me a message telling me how much they enjoyed the series. Thank you, thank you, thank you. I cannot say it enough.

To the people who read *Broken World* first and gave me feedback. Erin, Sarah, and Tammy, the three people became my writing cheerleaders when I lived in California. My husband, Jeremy, who doesn't read that often but read and didn't hate *Broken World*. Russ James, our awesome friend from California, who shared my love of dystopian fiction. Lisa Terry, who was my first great critique partner and who helped my writing grow so much. Fellow authors like Jenn Naumann, Lori Whitwam, and Jenn Foor, who I met because they read my series and loved it. To the members of NAC who helped spread the word: Diana Gardin, Ara Grigorian, Meredith Tate, Annika Sharma, Marie Meyer, Sophia Henry, Marnee Blake, Missy Belote, Jamie Howard, Jessica Ruddick, Amanda Seger, and Laura Steven. To friends from Oklahoma who became readers: Laura Johnsen, Ginny Foss, Carey Monroe, Lindsey Read, and Mary Jones. To family members who have devoured my books and encouraged me: Rebekah Caillouet, Peggy Mary, Sue Hale, Cyndi Caillouet, Amy Mary, and Clint Caillouet. To readers who became collaborators by helping read and critique my books: Jan Strohecker, Julie Dewey, Courtnee McGrew, Karen Atkinson, and Tina Young. And to my children who always tell their friends and teachers about me, who leave me alone when I need to edit, and who are so proud of what I do. Thanks!

I know there are so many more people to thank, and if I've missed you, I'm sorry. Know I am so grateful for the part you played in helping me build my career and the slip wasn't at all intentional.

Now on to this book.

Thanks to Jan Strohecker, Courtnee Mcgrew, and Julie Dewey for those first few reads. To Lori Whitwam for your editing skills, to Amber Garcia for your PR help. Thanks to everyone who offered to make my 40th birthday special by sharing the release. Thank you, as always, to everyone involved with *The Walking Dead* who inspired me to write this series to begin with, to Dean Samed of Neostock for the great stock images as well as the video tutorials that have helped me improve my skills.

ABOUT THE AUTHOR

Kate L. Mary is an award-winning author of Adult, New Adult, and Young Adult fiction, ranging from Post-apocalyptic tales of the undead to Speculative Fiction and Contemporary Romance. Her YA book, *When We Were Human*, was a 2015 Children's Moonbeam Book Awards Silver Medal winner for Young Adult Fantasy/Sci-Fi Fiction, and a 2016 Readers' Favorite Gold Medal winner for Young Adult Science Fiction. Her book *Outliers* was a Top 10 Finalist in the 2018 Author Academy Awards for Sci-Fi/Fantasy Fiction, a Finalist in the 2018 Wishing Shelf Book Awards, and the First Place Winner in the 2018 Kindle Book Awards for Sci-Fi/Fantasy Fiction. Her post-apocalyptic novel, *Tribe of Daughters*, was an Honorable Mention in the 2018 SPR Book Awards, a Bronze Medal Winner in the 2019 Readers' Favorite Book Awards for Science Fiction, and a Semi-Finalist in the 2019 Kindle Book Awards for Sci-Fi/Fantasy Fiction.

Before starting her writing career, Kate was a stay-at-home-mom for over ten years to four amazing kids - two boys, two girls - and the wife of an Air Force pilot. Her family moved around quite a bit during their eleven years of active duty, and she's gotten to experience many different parts of the country, and it isn't uncommon to find some of the places she's lived as the setting for her books. She's lived in Georgia (*When We Were Human*), Mississippi, South Carolina (*The College of Charleston Series*), California (*Broken World*), and Oklahoma (*The Loudest Silence*), but has recently returned to the Dayton, Ohio area (*The Blood Will Dry, Collision*). Military life has had its up and downs, but Kate has made some pretty incredible friends along the way who have been amazingly supportive of her writing.

You can learn more about Kate L. Mary and her books at http://katelmary.com/.

Printed in Great Britain
by Amazon